Pilot's Dawn

Pilot's Dawn

A Novel

Thomas Kirkwood

Authors Choice Press
San Jose New York Lincoln Shanghai

Pilot's Dawn
A Novel

All Rights Reserved © 2001 by Thomas Kirkwood

No part of this book may be reproduced or transmitted in any form or by any means, graphic, electronic, or mechanical, including photocopying, recording, taping, or by any information storage or retrieval system, without the permission in writing from the publisher.

Authors Choice Press
an imprint of iUniverse.com, Inc.

For information address:
iUniverse.com, Inc.
5220 S 16th, Ste. 200
Lincoln, NE 68512
www.iuniverse.com

Where real places or corporate names are used in this novel, they appear in an exclusively fictional context. No reference to actual names or places is implied or intended.

ISBN: 0-595-19939-9

Printed in the United States of America

For my parents

Epigraph

My fingers (and toes) turn to ice, my stomach leaps upward into my rib cage, the temperature in the tip of my nose drops to the same level as the temperature in my fingers...and for one screaming minute my heart and the engines correspond as we attempt to prove again that the laws of aerodynamics are not the flimsy superstitions which, in my heart of hearts, I *know* they are.

Fear of Flying
—Erika Jong

Acknowledgements

I wish to thank the many aircraft industry employees and airline pilots without whose help this novel could not have been written.

Part I

Atlanta
May 1995

Chapter One

Liz Hallman hated to fly. Her mere presence in the boarding area for Flight 20 to Frankfurt constituted an act of love. She hoped Ken appreciated it.

Jennie, their nine-year-old daughter, returned from her vigil by the window and crawled into her mother's lap. She smelled good, the way little girls do.

"Mom, do you know what that elevator truck is for?"

"The food, I think"

"Right. What about the Delta pick up out there by the wing?"

"I couldn't say."

"Got you! See those big hoses. It's pumping gas from a tank under ground."

"How on earth did you get so interested in airplanes?"

Jennie brushed her hair from her eyes, looking for a moment the way Liz knew she would look as a young woman—blonde, poised and very pretty. "Oh, dad told me a lot of stuff when we flew to gramma's. I sort of forgot about it, then Jason brought this book to school when he heard I was flying to Germany. Jason is the boy who made those rad paper airplanes at my birthday party."

Liz hugged her. "I remember Jason and his airplanes. I also remember the crystal lamp he bombed."

"Anyway, mom, he wants to know all about this plane we're flying on. Like what kind it is, and are we going first class, things like that."

"Well, we're not going first class because we want to save our money for Germany. The plane's a Delta. See the big blue letters on the side?"

"It's not a Delta, mom! That's the airline company. I mean, what kind of *airplane* is it?"

Liz glanced at the enormous jet. "I think it's a 747."

"A 767," said a tanned, elderly man sitting beside them. "A 747 has four engines and a second story on top. This one only has two engines, but they're very powerful."

Liz said, "Thank you kindly, sir. It's a 767, Jennie."

"Made by the Boeing Company," the man added. "The same people who make the 747. It's a very good airplane. I flew it for a few years before I retired."

"You were a pilot?" Jennie exclaimed.

"Yes, ma'am."

"Wait till I tell Jason I met a pilot!"

Liz saw that Jennie was about to blanket the stranger with questions. She didn't feel like including a third party in this special time with her daughter, so she thanked the man again and stood up. "Come on, Jennie, let's walk over to the newsstand. I'll bet we can find postcards for Jason with pictures of airplanes like the one we'll be on."

"Good idea, mom."

When they returned to the gate, the boarding had begun. As they walked down the long jetway to the plane, Liz could hear the whine of engines and smell aviation fuel. This was when she always got queasy. Though an educated person, she still found it hard to believe something as big as the airplane they were boarding could lift itself off the ground

Her fears made her feel ridiculous. Doing what millions of people did every day couldn't require that much courage. She took a deep breath, cursed Porsche for extending Ken's consulting job and marched ahead, squeezing Jennie's soft little hand instead of answering her questions.

Jennie took the inside seat and pressed her face against the window. "Mom, look! There's a man standing on the wing! He has to stay on that stripe they've painted for him, see? What happens if he steps off it? Will he die?"

"Of course not."

Their seats were on the left side above the leading edge of the wing. When Liz finally looked out, she saw a huge jet engine partially blocking her view of the ground. It reminded her of a white cement mixer.

Jennie was watching the mechanic in rapt silence as he kneeled down on the vast aluminum surface of the wing to check something.

When the fueling and loading were completed, the armada of service vehicles scurried away. A ladder truck came for the man on the wing, leaving a glint of sunlight on the spot where he had worked. Liz tried to forget about all these technical people and their machines. She looked beyond them at the evening sky.

The sun was about to set. It lay in a rusty band of haze on the horizon, painting the thunderheads over the city dirty orange. It would be summer when they returned, she thought. Best of all, they would be together again as a family. The thunderheads would appear every evening. Ken would cook steaks on the grill. And long after dark, when Jennie was asleep, there would be some skinny dipping in the pool.

She felt the airplane being pushed back from the gate. The engines made a faint whine when they were started, sending tiny vibrations through her nervous system. A flight attendant appeared on the movie screen to talk about life rafts and emergency exits. Liz wondered if she really was a flight attendant or some gorgeous actress hired to take your mind off the unpleasant aspects of the message.

The whine of the engines rose steadily to a roar. When the jet began to roll, the roar settled back to a monotonous hum.

Liz could feel the immense weight of the airplane by the way it took the bumps. Her father had let her drive his old Plymouth coupe when she was in her teens, and it had felt about the same. She hoped these airline people were as thorough as they seemed.

They taxied for a while, then entered a traffic jam of planes and crept ahead, one position at a time. On the runway beside them, jets thundered past in the opposite direction. Exhaust hung heavy over the field and rose in long smudged fingers toward the luminous western sky. Liz wondered how many gin and tonics they would let her have when drink service started.

Jennie finally unglued herself from the window. "Mom, do you think we'll be able to see our house?"

"I don't think so, sweetie. There are a lot of houses down there. They probably all look the same from the air."

"That's not true! They don't all have red roofs and swimming pools. I love our house."

Liz sighed. "Me too, especially when daddy's home. Sweetheart, do you mind terribly if we don't talk for a few minutes?"

"All right, mom. If you'll watch for the house with me after we take off."

"Deal," Liz said, closing her eyes.

The dreaded announcement came: "Ladies and gentlemen, we're number two for departure. We'll be in the air shortly. At this time we'd like the flight attendants to prepare the cabin for take-off."

Liz dug her nails into the armrests, hoping Jennie wouldn't sense her fear.

The engines roared to full thrust. The plane bumped along slowly at first, then began to accelerate at a breathless pace.

Liz felt her daughter's hand on her arm. "Come on, mom, open your eyes and watch!"

"Okay," she whispered, "okay."

She squinted to the side. She should be grateful. This beast was taking her to her man.

Maintenance hangars flew past, and concourses, and the control tower. The nose tilted up, there was a clunk that made her heart leap as the landing gear retracted.

She waited for the smoothness of flight, but the plane vibrated more than it had on the ground. The wing seemed to be shaking violently. All around her were groaning and squeaking noises. She jumped against her seat belt when an overhead compartment flew open and a rain of carry-on luggage crashed into the aisle.

Someone screamed, and it gave Liz a perverse sense of relief to know there were others even more frightened than she.

God, it was awful, flying was indescribably awful. If she hadn't done it before and experienced those strange shakes and howls of doom, she would think something was very wrong. She closed her eyes again.

Jennie squealed with delight, like a kid on a roller coaster. How strange, thought Liz, that her daughter had to have the lights on all night in her bedroom, yet was not afraid of this. Strange and wonderful.

"Mom!" Jennie cried. "The motor just came off!"

"Shhh. Don't joke. You might frighten someone."

"I'm not joking. Mom, look!"

Liz sensed something was wrong. The flight, which had begun with such crazy vibrations and noises, had now become smooth and deathly quiet. But they weren't flying in a straight line, they were yawing about like a boat. She had never felt anything like this.

She made herself look out. They were low, much too low, she thought. The earth raced past at a weird angle, that strange Georgia earth, its tender springtime green scarred with slices of bare red soil. What was wrong with the damned airplane?

"Mommy, look. The gas is squirting out where the motor used to be."

Liz was rigid with fear. She held her little girl's hand and peered out the window. The wing rose steeply, and she saw that Jennie had not been joking. The engine, the great white cement mixer, was gone. The pylon that attached it to the wing jutted out like a twisted stump.

There was a hideous wound on the front edge of the wing, a jagged gaping hole. Severed wires and tubes danced wildly around the opening. A white mist she prayed was not jet fuel blew back across the wing.

Liz squeezed Jennie so tightly she thought she had hurt her, but the little girl, stunned by the drama outside her window, did not seem to notice.

Several more passengers screamed. The panic hit Liz now and snapped her out of her daze. This could not be happening! Not to her, not to her daughter.

"Mom, look, **look**! That wire is sparking! What if it lights the gas? Remember when dad squirted stuff on the barbecue and it blew up? Will it be like that?"

Liz saw the sparks. "It's just water, Jennie. It's from the bathrooms."

"It is not! They put gas in the wing, remember?"

"Hold on to me, darling."

"No! I'm not afraid. I want to watch."

The captain came on the PA system, speaking as though he were giving the weather report. "Ladies and gentlemen, as you may have noticed, the number one engine separated from the aircraft at take-off. There's no need for alarm. We're not in any danger. We're presently returning to the airport. We've been cleared for landing and will be on the ground in a few minutes. Please remain calm and follow the instructions of the flight attendants."

Liz wanted to believe, God how she wanted to believe.

A man in uniform who looked like a pilot came down the aisle. He stopped at the vacant seat beside her, leaned over her and looked out.

"That wire's making sparks," Jennie said. "Is gas coming out of the wing? Are we going to explode?"

Liz looked imploringly at the pilot. She took his hand while he stared out the window.

He was about to leave when the wire hit the wing and unleashed a shower of sparks.

"Shit!" the man said, jerking his hand away. He ran toward the cockpit.

Liz felt her heart take a sickening leap. When they didn't even try to keep up the facade, you knew it was bad.

"Wait till I tell Jason about this!" Jennie cried. "Will he believe me, mom? Will he?"

"Hug me, darling."

"I want to watch out the window."

Liz put her arms around her daughter and buried her head in her blonde hair.

"Mom, look! Fire!"

Liz heard fear in Jennie's voice for the first time. She glanced out and saw the torch-like blaze shooting across the wing. "God, no. Please, no."

The pilot or co-pilot or whoever he was appeared briefly and bolted back into the cockpit. The man who had announced the loss of an engine called for one of the flight attendants. His voice was still cool and confident when he spoke to the passengers.

"Ladies and gentlemen, we have a wing fire. We have alerted the airport, and emergency equipment will be standing by. We are going to be exiting from the right side of the aircraft as soon as we have landed and come to a complete stop. It is important that you remain calm and follow the instructions of your flight attendants. If you make an orderly exit and avoid panic, there will be time for us all to get out. Darlene, please begin your briefing."

They were banking steeply, wing looming above, coming around to land. The fire was growing, panels on the wing had started to buckle. When they leveled off, Liz could see the blue Delta maintenance hanger. A big red sign on top said, "Fly Delta Jets."

Not everyone obeyed the captain's announcement. Dozens of passengers were already on their feet, fighting to position themselves near exits on the right side. Liz unlatched her seat belt, told Jennie to come with her and started to stand up.

A flight attendant shoved her back into her seat.

"Sit down!" she barked. "All of you, return to your seats and sit down! There's time for everyone to get out *if you don't panic.*"

The captain came on again. "Ladies and gentlemen, let me be very clear. If you do not return to your seats and follow the instructions of your flight attendants, you could cause a disaster on the ground. If you follow their instructions and exit in an orderly fashion, you will have more than enough time to get out of the aircraft safely. I implore you to return to your seats. We will be on the ground shortly."

"We're going to die!" screamed a fat man across the aisle from Liz.

The woman beside him slapped him in the mouth. "Shut up, you fool."

People began clawing their way over seat backs, fighting each other and yelling at the top of their lungs. Liz saw one of the younger flight attendants look out at the fire and collapse. No one helped her. She was being trampled.

Through the rising chaos the head flight attendant's emergency briefing droned over the PA like surrealistic background music.

It was too much. Liz turned away from the madness and hugged her daughter. She wanted desperately to tell Jennie how much she loved her, and how sure she was they were going to be okay. But the inferno blazing outside her window mocked her good intentions and strangled her voice.

They were close, so close. Warehouses, factory buildings, and an eight-lane highway came toward them, the cars nearly full size.

Come on, come on, they still had a chance.

She squeezed her child with all her strength and tried to say a prayer. The wing went up again, slowly, as if they were banking. Then, suddenly, the wing disappeared. It had broken off and flown away.

Jennie understood. She screamed and hid in her mother's arms, clutching at Liz like a terrified little animal.

Now it was Liz who could not shut her eyes. She watched with morbid fascination as the plane rolled, giving her a fine view of the spring-green earth with its red scars, and the Ford plant God had chosen to be their grave.

Paris
May 1995

Chapter Two

Steven rolled over and grabbed the receiver, kicking free of the tangled sheets. His bed smelled of a perfume he didn't like.

"LeConte."

"Hello, Steven. This is Sophie."

"Sophie, I'm glad you called. All I need is to be late for work again. Are you still upstairs?"

"No, darling, I've been at my office since nine."

"What time is it?"

"Eleven."

"What?" He squinted at the clock. "Damn French piece of junk. It never goes off."

"It went off, Steven. I heard it through eighteen inches of concrete and parquet. I hear everything above a certain decibel in your flat. Now look outside, darling. It's raining cats and dogs. I called the club before I left to make sure your lessons had been cancelled."

Steven glanced meekly through the shutters. "You shouldn't look after me, Sophie. I'm hopeless."

"I have ulterior motives, darling. I'm planning to exploit you. If you'd care to come by my office, I think I can offer you an excellent reason to get out of bed in the morning. I'll look for you around twelve thirty, okay?"

✶   ✶   ✶

Pilot's Dawn

The traffic jam on Boulevard Saint Germain persuaded him to take his bike instead of a taxi. He zipped up his rain suit and guided the big Harley Davidson between lanes of stalled cars.

Paris, thought Steven, was a great place for a motorcycle. You could take one-ways the wrong way, use sidewalks when you needed them and respond to the city's incessant noise with a roar of your own. And if the *flics* pulled you over, you were just one more dumb foreigner.

He crossed the Seine on the Pont Neuf and headed for the Opera District. He could hardly wait to see Sophie. Just being with her made him feel better about himself.

He'd never asked her how old she was but he figured she must be at least 70. A few years ago she had retired from her job as the *New York Time*'s Paris bureau chief. She could have given in to temptation and moved to one of those villages on the coast of Italy she loved. But instead of kicking back, she set up her own office and started to freelance. He'd seen her pieces in the *Economist*, *Le Monde* and one of those German papers at the train station where the only thing he'd been able to read was her name.

He had met Sophie by chance when he moved into her apartment building a couple of years ago. She was a rabbi's daughter from Trenton, which made her all the more exotic to this son of Anti-Semitic Protestants. She had natural blonde hair to match his, and when they walked down the street together—which was often these last months—she said they stood out like a beacon in this dark-haired city.

By the time he pulled up in front of her office, the sun had broken through. He went upstairs. In the elegant foyer Monique, Sophie's irritable but efficient French assistant, told him it would be a while until Madame Marx could see him.

Sophie swept into the leaden silence a few minutes later, propelled by her usual energy. She was wearing a flowered silk blouse and dark slacks, and looked terrific. She gave him a big hug and sent Monique off to lunch.

Sophie was more than just a great friend, thought Steven. She was a true soul mate. She shared his rebelliousness and contempt for bourgeois convention. Why these noble traits had contributed in equal measure to her success and his failure, he didn't know.

"Hey, I'm starving," he said. "Why don't we debauch on the terrace at Petits Péres? My aunt Janine will pay."

"An enticing idea, darling, but first there are some things I want to talk to you about in private. You never know who'll be listening in a Paris restaurant. I confess to an occasional bout of eavesdropping myself. Come."

She opened the heavy carved door and led him into her inner sanctum, a large, airy room dedicated to one of the world's great messes.

The place looked like it had been ripped apart by French counterterrorist agents. The furniture lay beneath a gargantuan litter of newspapers, books, faxes, notes, half-eaten boxes of chocolates, unwashed coffee cups, gifts wrapped with extravagant bows Sophie hadn't had time to give, decrepit black typewriters, state-of-the art computers—just about everything, he thought, except domestic animals.

He didn't know how she functioned in such chaos. She had explained to him the first time he came and beheld with an open mouth that there was an underlying order here, invisible to the uninitiated, an order one could not achieve with filing cabinets and neatness.

Steven wasn't sure he believed her, but he could not deny that her flawlessly crafted articles appeared, month after month, in the world's best newspapers and magazines. This stood in painful contrast to the production record of his own orderly little studio on Rue Monge. He had sublet the place so he could isolate himself and write without distractions when he wasn't teaching tennis. But in the years he had been in Paris, his own inner sanctum had turned out only unfinished pieces with dazzling leads.

He reached down to brush aside a heap of papers so he could find a place to sit. Sophie caught his arm. "Not those, darling! Over here."

Pilot's Dawn

She guided him to a Louis Quinze armchair hidden between a book pile and a fax mountain. When he was comfortably ensconced, she opened a folding chair and sat in front of him. "Now," she said, "let's talk about your tennis."

"My tennis? I thought you had something interesting to propose."

"Who's to say I don't? I know you're good, but exactly *how* good?"

He looked at her suspiciously. "You don't give a damn about sports, Sophie. Why the sudden interest?"

"Just answer my question, please."

"Okay, I'm good and I could have been better if I'd worked at it. I was U.S. amateur champ my junior year in college. Everyone expected me to be the next Mac."

"You never told me this."

"You always changed the subject when tennis came up."

Sophie laughed. "I suppose that's true. Why didn't you turn pro?"

"Because it would have denied me the pleasure of sitting here at age twenty-seven unable to make a living. Seriously, Sophie, I just couldn't bring myself to commit to such a regimented life. I wanted to enjoy my youth, if you know what I mean."

"Of course. But you're saying you were good enough to play on the tour if you'd chosen to?"

"I could have started in the top twenty. I beat some of the big names in exhibition matches."

"I guess you were saving your talent for me."

"What? I don't get it."

"Patience, darling."

Sophie stood and took her habitual stroll around the office, always in a counter-clockwise direction, always punctuated by thoughtful pauses at landmarks he couldn't identify beneath the mess.

Trying to make sense of what she had said was impossible, so he gazed out the window at the strange obelisk in the center of Place Vendôme. He was going to have to leave Paris soon if his writing didn't produce some income. He'd spent most of his small inheritance from his aunt, and his paltry earnings from the tennis club would hardly pay the rent. His departure, if it came to that, would not be easy. He liked it here. Maybe it was those Huguenot genes he had inherited along with his French last name. Maybe it was his closeness with Sophie.

She finally ended her stroll and perched on the corner of her desk. "Steven, I want to offer you an assignment."

"An assignment? Me?"

"Don't celebrate yet. You might consider it beneath your dignity."

"I have no dignity. I'm broke. My answer is Yes, and that's final. Tell me what I'm supposed to do."

"*The New York Times* has asked me to write a series on contemporary France. They want, among other things, a meaty piece on that racist bastard, Michelet. No one paid him any mind until the conservative coalition brought him into the government. I think we've underestimated him, Steven. Twenty percent of the popular vote is nothing to sneeze at. I think he's dangerous."

"Come on, Sophie, that's the Holocaust speaking. The guy's no French Hitler. He's just another crackpot. Now that he's Minister of Industry, his supporters will see he can't do any better than anyone else. They'll learn the hard way that foreign workers and Americans aren't the cause of France's problems."

"I hope you're right, Steven. But just in case you're not, we're going to dig around until we come up with enough dirt to bury him. I want things known about him that will turn his presence in the government into an international embarrassment for his country. Seek and ye shall find, kid."

"You want *me* in on this historical vendetta of yours?"

"Very much, Steven. I plan to expand the Michelet research into a book on anti-Americanism in France. I'm too old to do the leg work. I need your help. I brought you here to ask for it. Want to hear more?"

"I guess. I've already accepted the job."

Pilot's Dawn

"Steven..."

"Yes?"

"I'm about to introduce you to my wicked side. I take off the gloves when it comes to racism and fascism."

"Your wicked side? Give me a break."

She smiled. "How I've conned you, poor lamb. Listen, Steven, I need a secret weapon. I've made my choice. You, darling, are it."

"Not me. You're shopping in the wrong arsenal. There's no way I can help."

"Oh, but you can. Michelet has a daughter. My sources tell me the two of them don't get along. The girl's mother died when she was seven or eight and her father never remarried. He stuck her in one of those horrible Catholic convent schools and left her there. She lived a very protected life until last year."

"What happened last year?"

"She turned eighteen. She started attending the university here in Paris. She lived at home with her father and housekeeper, but they couldn't shield her from everything. She's had a rough time adapting to the real world. Perhaps you can help her."

"What?"

"You know, meet her, enchant her, see what you can do for her."

"You're kidding? You want me to cozy up to the daughter of the most anti-American politician in France?"

"What better way to prove him wrong?"

"Jesus, Sophie, I don't know if I can fake it. What does she look like?"

"Better than the best you've schlepped home from the club."

"Even Irène?"

"Even Irène. I can't promise she'll be more interested in your balls than Mr. Wilson's, but if you put your heart into it, you should at least be able to make friends with her."

"How? Where would I meet her?"

"Simple, Steven. You'll be her tennis instructor. She's spending the summer at a villa near Nice. She belongs to a fancy club. I'm told she plays there every day. If you want the job, I'll arrange for you to be the visiting pro."

Steven felt slightly overwhelmed. "Come on, Sophie, how can you arrange something like that?"

"I've been in business a long time, darling. I have friends. Give me the nod and the pro down there will be offered a fabulous temporary job in Beverly Hills. Believe me, he's not the type to turn it down. The tentative exchange I've worked out calls for you to stand in for him while he's gone."

"Then?"

Sophie laughed. "Just follow that golden *schwanz* of yours."

"Hang on, hold on just a minute. You're actually going to send me down there to try to seduce Michelet's daughter?"

"With a large salary, a vacation home near the beach and a generous expense account. And to sweeten the pot, Steven, my job offer goes beyond the Michelet book. I'm asking you to become my assistant on all future projects. A few years apprenticing with me will make you a very employable journalist. That's what you want, isn't it?"

He shook his head in disbelief. He was happy, sure, but the whole thing sounded a little suspect. "Yes. And one thing's for sure. The usual methods of breaking into print haven't worked for me."

"How do you know, Steven? The 'usual methods' involve the submission of completed articles. From what you've told me, you've never completed anything. But enough on the negative side. If you stop procrastinating and learn the fine art of perseverance, you'll become a superb journalist. I hope you're not offended I'm asking you to begin your career by playing gigolo."

"Offended? I'm flattered you think I'm irresistible. But I'm not, Sophie. I get turned down all the time. Besides, I'm sure her father makes her wear a chastity belt. Even if I manage to grope my way to the winning combination, I'll get shot before I find out anything about the old man."

"But you'll have no trouble getting out of bed in the morning, will you?"

"Come on, Sophie. You're joking about all of this."

"No. And, Steven, I didn't say you had to seduce her. It would be preferable, of course, but if I must, I'll settle for a nice platonic friendship."

"It's not going to work. I'm a tennis playing bum who's quit enough jobs and graduate programs to give my father an ulcer. Why would the daughter of a cabinet minister be interested in someone like me?"

Sophie didn't answer immediately but made a silent counter-clockwise tour of her office. When she was ready to talk, she sat down and slid her folding chair forward until their knees touched.

"Steven, be a little gentler on yourself. You are a bright and extremely handsome young man who's had the guts to avoid the castration traps of career and marriage. You are not a bum, and even if you were it wouldn't matter. The French attach tremendous importance to the *family*. This is especially true of the social climbing bourgeois snobs you'll be associating with. You're from a rather prominent family, right? Didn't you tell me your father was CEO of New England Plastics?"

"I'm not my father."

"You're missing the point. To these people, if your family's all right, so are you. What about your mother? I'll take a guess. President of the local DAR."

"No. Chairman of the Connecticut Republican Party."

"That's marvelous. And your brothers?"

"Bob's an eye surgeon in Greenwich, John's a tax attorney in New Haven and Dean has become a big shot on Wall Street, don't ask me how."

"Perfect! And you, the most talented of this prestigious lot, have been saved for better things. I promise you'll be as socially acceptable as an

American in France can be. And trust my judgment, Steven. She's going to like you."

He felt restless—intrigued but restless. He had a powerful urge to fiddle with the books and papers lying all around but knew Sophie would be at his throat if he touched anything.

"Okay, here's where I stand. I don't mind befriending her or even sleeping with her if it works out that way, but I don't want to deceive her."

"What do you mean, Steven?"

"Well, let's say she goes for the whole enchilada. Do I have to make her believe I'm in love with her?"

"Let me ask you something, darling."

"What?"

"How much time do you spend telling your women friends here you *don't* love them? Relax. Be yourself. Once you get started, you'll forget your qualms."

"I'm not so sure."

"Hold my hands, Steven. I want you to feel my warmth. I want it to flow through your fingers and into your heart. You must not believe I'm a cold-blooded viper."

"Viper," he said, giving her his hands. She squeezed tightly, and he was surprised by how much warmth he felt.

She laughed. "You're going to do great. Even if you never meet Michelet, even if your information on him is hearsay, I'll still be ahead of the game."

"Sophie, just listen to me for a minute. I'm not saying I don't like the idea of getting close to the guy. I do. Even if he's not the danger to humanity you think he is, it'll make a good story. But there must be another way. We're supposed to be the decent one's. Aren't we stooping to Michelet's level if we set out to deceive his daughter?"

"Oh, my dear friend, lighten up! Can't you see you'll be doing the poor girl a favor?"

"A *favor*!"

"That's right. My sources tell me Michelet is determined to pick the husband. You know, there are circles in France where this is still done. It's a political thing. He wants her marriage to bolster his new image of respectability. Isn't that disgusting?"

"Sure, but—"

"Anyway, Steven, I'm told he has a list of men he considers acceptable, mostly aristocrats. Wouldn't you say you'd be doing her a favor if you gave her the chance to escape the old man's list of jerks and pick her own boyfriend?"

"You're just making this up so I won't feel guilty."

"No, it's the absolute truth."

"Jesus, Sophie, I don't—"

"I know, I know, you need some time to think about it. Fine. I'll give you until three o'clock. While I'm waiting, why don't we debauch at Petits Pères, as you suggested before your unseemly fit of Calvinism? We'll have a terrific lunch and an expensive bottle of Bordeaux, and I'll show you photographs of the girl I guarantee will dissolve any vestiges of piety still clouding your judgment."

Steven took a deep breath. Maybe Sophie was right. Maybe he needed to loosen up. If she was serious about the job, it was the opportunity of a lifetime for a guy who wanted to be a journalist.

She was halfway to the door. He caught up and took her arm. "By the way, Sophie, does this sweet young thing have a name?"

"Nicole."

"I like it," he said as they strolled out.

Washington, D.C.
May 1995

Chapter Three

Frank Warner had an ambivalent relationship to his telephone. On the negative side, he could never escape the bugger. It was set up to ring simultaneously in his Georgetown home and Washington office. If no one answered, the call went looking for him like a blood hound. He had a cellular phone in his government Caprice, a portable cellular for public places and a water-proof beeper for the beach. The previous summer a call had nailed him on the first day of his vacation while he was scuba diving in 20 feet of water off the Bahamas.

In the last quarter century, the wounds his personal life had sustained at the hands of his telephone were enormous. If he had been the type to discuss such things, he might have offered as an example the failure of his first marriage and his resultant childless state; or the failure of his second marriage and his present wifeless state. The calls had a way of coming at dinner parties his former spouses had planned for weeks, or during rare and wonderful moments of intimacy. And they could always be counted on to sniff out vacations 10,000 miles away.

Warner kept two packed bags by the front door of his home, one for warm climates, the other for the cold. An identical set of bags waited in his office. It was his policy to be en route five minutes after a call, day or night, and he required the same preparedness of his staff.

Apart from its frequent and sometimes inopportune intrusions, his emergency phone had another negative quality: it rang for the sole purpose of reporting an air disaster. Within hours of a call, Frank Warner, head of air crash investigations for the National Transportation Safety Board, would find himself at the site with his Go Team. It was a horrible experience no amount of repetition could soften, but if he missed those first grisly hours, he risked missing clues reconstructive work could never replace.

Those were the negatives, but the positives easily outweighed them. Warner had given up the two wives he loved and the children he wanted so that he could devote himself body and soul to the demands of his profession. He believed his work was more important than any pleasure he might derive from private life. He knew he had an incomparable talent for ferreting out the causes of an air crash and was convinced he had been placed on earth for one reason, to exercise that talent.

His close-cropped hair was mostly gray. When exhausted, which was often, the bags beneath his attentive brown eyes grew heavy and their whites became badly bloodshot.

The rest of him, however, showed few signs of aging. He was 6'2" and built like a tight end. Except for an occasional cigar he did not smoke, and he carefully monitored what he ate and drank. The stress of his work took care of any excess calories.

At age 53 Warner drove himself and his staff without regard for anyone's personal comfort. He demanded superior performance and got it, even when an investigation required 20-hour days and uninterrupted weeks on the road. In spite of this, he was a well-liked boss. It was clear to everyone he wasn't in the thing for self-aggrandizement, a refreshing quality in official Washington.

When the call came that warm May night, he received it with his usual ambivalence. He experienced irritation at being yanked away from a lovely evening with Claire, his new girlfriend; and a sadness that innocent people had once again died. But by the time Warner hung up the phone, his disparate emotions had crystallized into a fierce resolve to meet the challenge head-on, to get to the bottom of this latest crash so that it would never repeat itself.

When he returned to the terrace, Claire was already clearing away the half-eaten plates of Lobster Newburg.

"I have to go," he said. "Simmons is in the area. He's coming by for me."

She put a hand on his arm. "How bad is it, Frank?"

"Bad. They won't know the exact dimensions for a while."

"Can you talk about it?"

"No, I'm sorry."

It was almost summer on the Potomac, and he was going further south. He kissed her and went for his warm weather bag by the door, the same tattered leather valise he had carried to Brazil the trip his second wife had left him. Claire accompanied him out front and waited with him at curbside. She was an M.D., specialty trauma. She knew what it was to be on call. She stood with him in silence until his ride came.

He drove with Simmons to National Airport. An hour later he and the 10 members of his Go Team were aboard an NTSB Gulfstream II, climbing through 20,000 feet en route to the Peach Tree-DeKalb Municipal Airport on the north side of Atlanta.

✶ ✶ ✶

Warner opened the briefing in the conference area at the back of the plane. "Simmons, please bring us up to date."

Tim Simmons, 35, an engineer with youthful good looks, had gone from being Warner's goat when he joined the NTSB fresh out of graduate school to his most trusted investigator.

Simmons said, "I roused Delta Operations during the drive to the airport. It was a Seven-Six, outbound for Frankfurt, two-hundred-eighteen on board. No information yet on survivors, though the prognosis is doubtful. The aircraft lost an engine shortly after take-off, visual confirmation from the tower. The engine landed on airport property, which will simplify our task."

Simmons lit a cigarette, and the non-smoking contingent let him get by with it this once. "All indications are that the pilot kept the aircraft under control. In other words, no violent maneuvers to regain control after the engine broke loose that would explain later events."

Simmons politely blew his smoke behind him. "The pilot radioed the tower for clearance to land on runway Two Six Right. Clearance was granted. No indication of further trouble until the captain reported a wing fire. The entire flight was visible from the tower."

Warner took over, his voice several octaves deeper. "Thank you, Simmons. Please put out the cigarette. The visual reports indicate that the fire, which was burning near the point at which engine number one left the wing, grew rapidly. Roughly one mile from the end of runway Two Six Right, the burning wing separated from the aircraft. It is lying in a field several hundred yards from the main body of the wreck.

"The aircraft, I'm sorry to say, slammed into the Ford plant just off Two Six Right. We're told a late shift was working. You're going to need a strong stomach for this one. Estimated casualties on the ground will easily make this the worst crash in history."

"It had to happen sooner or later," Jack Kendall said. He was the newest, youngest, and most idealistic member of the Go Team, bright and unseasoned. "I told you, chief, we should have pushed harder for Congress to set national standards on what can be built along approaches."

"Maybe this will get their attention," Warner said. "Words unfortunately don't have much impact. Returning to the business at hand, the people from Boeing won't be here until early morning. The Pratt & Whitney guys have a shorter flight. They should get in soon after us. We'll convene for a quick briefing, then hit the field.

"Clifton and Ward, take the Pratt & Whitney people, a man from Delta and someone from the Airport Authority out to the engine. I want to know which way it was facing when it hit, if it was rotating, the usual. If it's positioned in such a way that you have access to the mounting structures, I would like a preliminary report. The mounting bolts? The mounts themselves? Any attached remnant of pylon that might indicate a crack, such as we found on the DC-10 at O'Hare?"

"Right, sir. We'll get it done."

"Connors, McCauley and Johnson, the wing is yours."

"Frank," Johnson said. "You've indicated it's out in a field somewhere. Are the authorities making certain it's not disturbed or are they too involved with the main wreckage and the fire?"

"Good question. Allen, call the Atlanta P. D. and confirm that the cops are protecting the wing. If they tell you their men are all needed at the Ford plant, explain to them what happens to our investigation if the wing is tampered with."

"Yes, sir. I'll try to make them understand."

"Roth, I want you to coordinate the salvage operations. Find someone in the city government who can give you a listing of reliable local operators."

"Right, Frank. Where are we going with the wreckage? Have you lined up anything yet?"

"No, but the old Eastern hangar at the airport is vacant. If we can get it, it would be the most convenient place to reconstruct the aircraft."

"Do you want me to check into that, too?"

"Please. Downey, you book the hotel. We'll need a place for meetings and eleven rooms—unless some of you are volunteering for double occupancy."

Jack Kendall said, "How long do you think we'll be here, Frank? I promised my wife I'd give her a 'best estimate.'"

"Don't get into the habit of doing that, Kendall. Families need to understand that you have no control over the length of an investigation. Clear?"

"Yes, sir."

"Good. I want the rest of you to come with me to the Ford plant. It won't be a pretty sight, so prepare yourselves. I don't know if this thought helps you at such times, but it helps me: for each body you see tonight, others who would have ended up the same way will live—if we control our guts and do our job."

Simmons said, "By the way, Frank, I've chartered us a few helicopters from Peach-Tree DeKalb over to the main airport. A look at the accident site from the air seemed like a good idea."

✶ ✶ ✶

Warner stared in silence out a window of the Bell Jet Ranger. If someone had the inclination to loot a shopping mall across town, he thought, there would be no obstacle. Every police car, fire truck and rescue vehicle in the Atlanta metro area seemed to be jammed into the parking lots around the Ford plant.

It had been a direct hit, precisely the sort of thing they had all been dreading since the big jets took to the air. Perhaps the young idealist, Kendall, was right. Perhaps he should have pushed the NTSB to put more pressure on Congress, though he doubted it would have done any good.

They flew closer.

The center section of the Taurus assembly line building was a mass of blazing rubble. The fire was still spreading to wings of the plant that had not been hit directly by the plane. A hundred thousand pounds of aviation fuel, thought Warner, could make stone and metal burn.

"Jesus, there's the tail!" Simmons exclaimed. "Look at that, Frank."

"Yes, I see it." The inverted tail section of the 767, with one rudder still attached, loomed like a great wounded beast above the shadows of an outlying lot. The blaze a couple hundred yards away lit up the Delta markings on its aluminum skin. They looked as fresh and reassuring as they did in the TV commercials.

Warner remembered the days when the first people on the site of a crash were the airline paint crews, working in fire and wind to white out the company name. This was a terrible accident, one that would not sit well with the flying public. He imagined the more mercenary corporate souls down in the bowels of Operations scrambling around for paint. They would be too late. He could see at least three separate news crews filming the tail. In 1995, the media, as flush as the drug lords, beat them all to the punch.

Warner frowned. He had just noticed something that made his blood boil. "Do either one of you see any cops around the tail or the first-impact debris?"

"Looks to me like media and souvenir hunters," Kendall said. "They remind me of vultures."

"This is unconscionable. The cockpit voice recorder and black box are in the tail. Doesn't anyone understand we can't solve a crash without the parts?"

*   *   *

They entered the terminal building at 11:30 p.m., three hours after the crash. Television news crews roamed the A Concourse like jackals, latching on to anyone who would talk to them. When they recognized Warner and his team, they attacked in a hungry swarm, blocking his progress.

"Ladies and gentlemen," he said in his flat but authoritative voice, "show the good judgment you ask of your government officials and move out of the way. The first hours of an investigation can be critical. You are impeding our progress, and hence the safety of future air travel. I can't imagine that will help your ratings. Step aside, please."

Miraculously they obeyed. Warner had that effect on people, even reporters.

Pilot's Dawn

The throng outside the Crown Room, which Delta officials were using as their crisis center, resembled an angry, grieving mob. Relatives and spouses of workers at the Ford plant had joined those who had lost loved-ones in the crash. Rabble rousers shouted down the Delta spokesman, who fielded all questions but refused to give substantive answers. Warner grabbed a cop, showed his I.D. and asked for an escort to the door.

Inside the quiet, elegantly appointed room, Delta executives, attorneys, crash investigators and media consultants had organized into groups to deal with the many-headed monster the crisis had spawned. There were decisions that had to be made quickly. How, for example, were they going to keep Delta reservations from plummeting in the days ahead? How could they best show an empathetic corporate face to those who had suffered loss in the crash without appearing to admit guilt—guilt which, if established, could cost the company hundreds of millions of dollars? How could they speed up their own internal investigation so that, if the crash had been a result of some inadequate or negligent service procedure on the part of the airline, safeguards against a repeat could be put into effect at once? What type of initial posture should they assume toward the Ford Motor Company, whose Taurus assembly plant one of their planes had reduced to rubble, and whose skilled work force it had decimated? A careless decision here could mean bankruptcy.

Into this solemn corporate war council marched Frank Warner and his Go Team. Every airline executive who cared to be honest with himself knew that, without the NTSB, airline travel would be a lot more dangerous than it was. But this didn't stop them from having a big problem with Warner. He was too harsh; he did not understand the needs of the corporate world; he saw the causes of a crash in black and white when gray would be more appropriate; he was a perfectionist in an imperfect world; and worst of all, he did not understand how to distribute the responsibility for a mishap.

A realist would have known how to pass the guilt around, 10% here, 20% there, so that one corporation didn't have to answer for the collective failure of the system. But if Warner thought you could have prevented the crash with some superhuman or impractical effort, he pointed his unwavering finger of guilt right between your eyes—or at least that's the way the conclusions he drew in his reports made you feel.

So he was a leper in the community of airline executives, an asshole with a salary not a tenth of theirs, an abusive eccentric they would have preferred to shun. But this was the Age of Images, and airline executives were realists. They pretended to like him because they feared if they let him know how they really felt, his roulette wheel finger might bypass Boeing or Pratt & Whitney and come to a stop at the bridge of their nose.

In spite of all this cozying up to him, Warner knew how they really felt. He was not offended. On the contrary, he considered their dislike the highest compliment they could have paid him. For in his view, coziness between the regulators and the regulated was a disease that had weakened the American system, and he wanted no part of it.

Reid Allworth, the brilliant, dashing chairman of Delta, came over and warmly shook Warner's hand. "Hello, Frank. I'm glad you and your men are here. Renaker and the boys from Pratt & Whitney are on their initial approach, so give them another twenty minutes or so. There's time for us to go over the aircraft's maintenance records and the pilot bios while we're waiting."

Warner stood stiff as a rod. "The records can wait, Reid. The engine boys can join us when they arrive. I need to get my people in the field while there's still something to examine. Are you aware that the tail section of your aircraft is sitting in the Ford parking lot totally unguarded?"

"What? Why, that's—"

"Reid, the CVR and black box are in the tail. If they're gone, so are our chances of solving this crash conclusively. What about the wing? Do you know for a fact that it's being protected?"

"Of course. I instructed the police—"

"I realize you've got a company to run. I know this is a very trying time for you. Nevertheless, Reid, your first responsibility as a public carrier is to the safety of your passengers. It's very difficult for me to conduct an investigation on a wreckage you have allowed the curiosity seekers to contaminate."

"Frank, what are you talking about? My first priority was to secure the wreckage. It's impossible that either the tail or the wing is unguarded. I gave the police instructions that could not have been more explicit."

"It's unguarded, Reid, at least the tail is. We had a good look at it from the air."

"I've got the local FBI," said Simmons, who had wrenched a phone away from one of the airline's media people.

"Thank you," Warner said, still seething. "While I'm talking, get me the Atlanta police."

The atmosphere in the conference room remained icy as Warner dispatched his teams to examine the engine, the wing and the tail, letting Allworth decide which airline people would work with each group. He would make his peace with the Delta chairman later, when he wasn't so angry. Right now he had his mind on the black box and the cockpit voice recorder, the CVR, which he hoped were still in the tail.

Eastern Germany
June 1995

Chapter Four

Paul Delors had driven all night to arrive in the village of Altenhagen, 160 kilometers north of Berlin, before dawn. When he pulled up in front of Claussen's farmhouse, a few stars still blinked overhead but morning was not far off. A band of steel gray light shone to the east, and he could make out the silhouette of pine forests and banks of fog that lay around like great sleeping beasts.

   He got out of his Citroën and stretched. A single dim bulb burned above the farmhouse door, illuminating a patch of faded stucco wall with chinks blown away by gunfire half a century old. Prussia, the Third Reich, East Germany, the Federal Republic. It didn't matter what you called the place, thought Delors, it never changed.

   He took his travel bag from the trunk. When he glanced up, Claussen was standing on the porch in his bathrobe, smoking a cigarette.

   Delors raised his hand in greeting, and Claussen responded with an almost imperceptible nod. "Good morning, Paul. You'd best come in before my fellows have their revenge on the French." He laughed, softly and without malice.

   Delors had been vaguely aware of a living presence in the darkness beyond his car, but had not wanted to appear jumpy. Now he looked around. A gaggle of large, silent geese loomed behind him, closing ranks as if they were about to attack. He quickly climbed the steps and went inside.

Pilot's Dawn

Claussen had prepared for his visit, which they had previously set for 30 days after the Atlanta crash. In the kitchen, the table was laid out for breakfast. A coffee pot gurgled on the counter and water for the eggs boiled on a black hooded stove. Claussen put in the eggs and set out bread, butter, cheeses and wurst. He took a bottle of clear schnapps from the refrigerator.

"Please have a seat, Paul. I know you're not accustomed to this level of modesty but I prefer to keep things simple."

"You don't have to apologize, Walter. I quite enjoy life in the country."

When everything was ready, Claussen sat. Delors watched him decapitate a soft boiled egg with a precise whack of his knife. He had steady hands that would have suited a surgeon, with long, delicate fingers. Though almost 60 years old, he looked to be in very good physical condition and was even more handsome than Delors remembered him being when they had last seen each other. Perhaps his face had a few more wrinkles now and his keen blue eyes a few more crow's feet at the corners. But his light brown hair had not thinned or gone gray, his teeth were still good and his strong chin had not been eroded by the wattles common to men his age. Claussen still had what it took.

*   *   *

After breakfast Delors offered him a Gauloise cigarette, as he had done when they met for the first time more than a decade ago.

That had been in a hotel room in Toulouse. Claussen, a total stranger, had appeared one gray winter afternoon and introduced himself as a man in a position to help Delors' country and career. He could, he said, further the interests of France by procuring technical and military secrets from the United States—secrets the Americans shouldn't have withheld from their ally in the first place.

For a modest fee, payable only upon satisfactory performance, he promised to provide Delors with information the French defense establishment needed. It wasn't until later that Delors learned that Claussen, an East German, was a spy for the Soviet Union, and that the same valuable information he was receiving was also going to Moscow. But this did nothing to discourage what had become an excellent working relationship.

Claussen's material lifted the French Ariane missile program out of the doldrums, gave the little Exocet its deadly guidance system and provided the Mirage fighter-bomber with a new lease on life. It also elevated Delors, who kept his source to himself, from mid-level agent to deputy director of French Intelligence, the SDECE.

Their relationship remained warm and mutually beneficial up to the collapse of the Soviet Union. Delors lost contact with Claussen in early 1991 and did not see him again until the previous March, when Claussen once more appeared out of nowhere and matter-of-factly outlined his proposal to make Airbus the world's largest manufacturer of commercial aircraft...

Claussen again accepted the cigarette. The two men smoked in silence, drank a shot of schnapps and watched the sun come up.

Delors finally spoke. "Walter, there are a few things you and I need to discuss."

"Of course." Claussen got up, opened the window and threw his geese some table scraps.

"Cannibalistic buggers," he said. "If you'll notice, they go first for the rye spread with *Gänseschmalz*." He stared out at the courtyard and the pines beyond.

Delors went to the hallway for his travel bag and placed it on the kitchen table. He took out a bottle of Château LaFite, a kilo of *foie gras*, a jar of black truffles.

"For you, Walter. I remember how you developed a fondness for some things French when you visited us."

Claussen looked the items over. "Thank you. Most thoughtful, Paul."

Delors said, "You're a full-fledged capitalist now, Walter, though you didn't do so badly in the old days. I hope it hasn't gone to your head."

"Why don't you be more specific, Paul?"

"Because I'd first like to shave, shower and have a rest. I'm tired, and this is not the proper setting for a discussion. Do you understand me?"

"I understand, Paul, that you're worried about being recorded. May I remind you that a tape of our conversations would implicate me as deeply as you. If you are uncomfortable, however, we'll find another place to talk. Your room is at the top of the stairs on the left. I'll wait for you in the library."

*   *   *

When Delors awoke, birds were singing and sunlight filtered through the fir trees outside his window. He grabbed his watch from the night stand, fearing he had overslept. Ten thirty, it could have been worse. He dressed and wandered through the cool, sparsely furnished house in search of the library.

The only decor on the white walls was an occasional watercolor, a nature scene without people or animals. The pieces were unsigned, but Delors had little doubt who the artist was. They were born of the same lonely, understated elegance as the man he had come to visit.

He found Claussen writing at a roll top desk. When he tapped on the open door, Claussen stood, limber as a young man.

"Shall we talk now?" Delors asked.

"Yes. I usually have a swim before lunch. I have packed an extra pair of trunks in case you wish to join me."

"Of course I'll join you."

They arrived at the Augraben River after a pleasant stroll through pine groves and meadows swarming with butterflies. The two men undressed and left their clothes draped over a carved marble bench, a relic, Claussen said, of the Junker estate that had been here before the communists collectivized agriculture.

Delors, into his trunks first, dived into the gentle green current, feeling strong and rested. He was an excellent swimmer and worked out in the indoor pool across from the "Piscine," the SDECE headquarters in Paris, several times a week.

He crossed to the other bank with a strong crawl, returning to meet Claussen in the center of the stream. "Which way?"

Claussen did not speak but swam with the current, his backstroke splashless and relaxed. Delors swam beside him, keeping the pace easily. They rounded a bend and the river flowed into a large lake with an island near the center.

"I usually swim to the island and back," Claussen said. "If I tire, I rest on the island for a while. It's about a kilometer and a half, round trip. Are you up to it?"

"Yes."

Claussen rolled over and breaststroked. He said, "Bismarck came to this old estate in the fall of 1869 to plan his attack on France. The place inspires good ideas, Paul."

"Let's swim," Delors said.

Claussen spit out a stream of water and picked up the pace. Delors stayed with him, but it wasn't easy. When they reached the island, Claussen lifted himself effortlessly onto the sagging boat dock. Delors was tired and accepted the German's hand.

Claussen stretched out on the dry wood, his lean, suntanned body even younger in appearance than his face.

Delors sat on the edge of the dock and waited for his breathing to slow down. He casually surveyed the island. It looked abandoned. He felt confident he could talk freely here without risk of being recorded or photographed. This was good. Though he basically trusted Claussen, extra precautions were in order. When you were dealing with something as enormous as the action he had decided to undertake, the possibility of blackmail could not be ruled out.

He said, "Before we discuss fees, Walter, there are certain conditions I am going to pose. If you cannot accept them, further negotiation will be pointless."

"Spell them out, Paul. Don't be timid. I'm not going to walk away from my own plan unless I feel you are trying to take unfair advantage of me."

"I assure you, Walter, after all you've done for me, that such a thing will never happen."

Claussen sat up. "Then let's hear the conditions."

"The mishaps must be similar to your Atlanta demonstration. Specifically they must involve newer model Boeing planes and be blamed on manufacturing or design defects traceable to Boeing or a major supplier."

"Such as Pratt & Whitney?"

"Yes."

"That's well and good, Paul. But what happens in the case of an over water crash where the wreckage cannot be fully recovered?"

"You must inform me of the identifying characteristics of the crash in advance, as you did with Atlanta. I'm obviously not going to apprise others in the government of our undertaking. I'm doing this for my country—but I'm also doing it on my own. What this means is that the funds I can siphon from other SDECE operations without an accounting are limited. In other words, Walter, I can't afford to pay you for coincidental mishaps that you did not cause."

"Fair enough, Paul. What else?"

"All crashes and all defects must appear to be random. They should raise suspicions about the quality of American workmanship."

Claussen showed no emotion, neither irritation nor excitement. He said, "That won't be a problem. Go on, please."

Claussen was being very cooperative, more so than Delors had anticipated. The biggest potential stumbling block was yet to come, but there seemed to be reason for optimism. Delors flared his nostrils and breathed deeply of the fragrant air. It smelled of water and pines and resin vapors from the sun-stoked dock. Even Prussia, he thought, could be pleasant on a warm summer day.

"The final condition, Walter, is that you accept the fee I am going to offer you. It is a reasonable fee, it will make you rich. Perhaps it is less than you expected. But I cannot involve others and I will not expose myself to the risk of an agency or government investigation. This puts limits on what I can pay."

"I'm not interested in your reasons, Paul. I'm interested in the amount. How much is it?"

"I am able to divert around five million francs a month from budgets that cover top-secret initiatives, and from certain other sources. In the past, you were paid from such diversions. If we take as our measure twelve crashes over the course of a year, this translates into one million dollars per crash. Can you live with it, Walter?"

Claussen laughed, a strange laugh that made the hair on the back of Delors' neck stand on end. "Well, Paul, I had in mind a more objective method of calculating my fee. Since this is an entirely Western affair, I think it would be nice if you showed a modicum of respect for the value of private property. This you can accomplish simply by paying me the replacement cost of each aircraft you hire me to destroy."

"Come on, Walter, don't be absurd. You're talking fifty million dollars a mishap, maybe more. That's completely out of line."

"Oh? I've done some calculations, based on unrealistically conservative estimates. A worldwide shift in aircraft orders of just twenty percent away from Boeing and to Airbus will result in twelve billion dollars in additional revenues the first year, six billion of which will go to France. It will further result in at least two hundred thousand additional jobs, half of which will go to France. Add up your savings in unemployment benefits, your additional tax revenues, and the economic stimulus this high-tech hiring bonanza will have on other sectors, and you will harvest an additional ten billion to twenty billion.

"In other words, Paul, if you pay me fifty million a crash for twelve crashes, you will be receiving a return on your investment of at least two thousand six hundred sixty seven percent—and that's only in the first year. France hasn't done this well since Napoleon looted Italy."

"Look," Delors snapped, "there's no way in hell I can get hold of six hundred million dollars. I'm not France, you know."

"I believe you said you were doing this for your country."

"Yes, that's right. But the demand for absolute secrecy puts strict limits on my fund raising ability."

Claussen laughed again. "I think you can find enough money, Paul. I think you cannot afford *not* to find it. But if you can't, very well. I agreed to fund the Atlanta demonstration myself, and I honor my agreements. You will owe me nothing.

"But you should know, Paul, that I am leaving for the States next month. The purpose of my trip is to dispose of the remaining assets of Operation Twenty-Six. The time when I will be able to perform this service for your country is rapidly coming to an end."

Delors wanted to say something that would get the bargaining back on track. Claussen was right. He could not afford to let this golden opportunity slip away. But before he could speak, Claussen dove into the lake and swam toward the distant shoreline.

Chapter Five

Looking at it from the NTSB work area in the abandoned Eastern hangar, the mock-up of the 767 made Warner think of the dinosaur skeleton in the main hall of the Natural History Museum. He had first seen that impressive behemoth when he was on a science trip in the sixth grade, and had been instantly fascinated by stories of the men and women who had found the bones and put them together.

Later that year Warner built a dinosaur skeleton of his own, making the bones of baked clay and fitting them together with an ingenious system of holes and wires. His parents persuaded him to enter the model along with his accompanying sketches in a contest. He remembered the moment fondly. It had set in motion a chain of events that made him the first, and perhaps the only, elementary school student from Winnemucca, Nevada, to win a national science competition.

Warner's prize had been another trip to Washington. Now he lived in D.C. and spent a lot of time assembling skeletons of dead aircraft.

Most of the skeletons Warner worked on these days eventually managed to look pretty realistic, thanks to the expertise and total devotion of his staff. They carted thousands of chunks of wreckage from swamps and forests and parking lots, and painstakingly pieced them together in rented hangars and warehouses. When the mock-ups were completed, you could see that the skeletons had once been airplanes healthy and graceful enough to fly. With any luck you could also see what had killed them.

Most of the pieces available for the present reconstruction, which had taken the team over a month to complete, were charred and

Pilot's Dawn

deformed beyond recognition. But not everything had gone badly. The engine that separated at take-off had landed in soft earth and had not burned. The wing that ripped off on the final approach had come down flat, remaining in large pieces. And the unburned hunk of tail section, when joined with the shards and scraps found along a swath of torn-up parking lot, looked almost as if it could fly again.

By chance, evidence of a serious flaw had survived intact on the number one engine. The team had put a rolling scaffold beside the engine from which one could view the aft mount. A piece of a broken pin was clearly visible.

Beside the suspect part, Warner had taped a typewritten note on 3"x5" card. It read, "Preliminary finding: Defective aft engine mount. As engine broke away from aft mount due to failure of horizontal pin, it took an upward trajectory, ripping off front engine mount and a segment of pylon. Departing mass or associated debris struck the leading edge of wing, where it punctured a fuel tank and severed the electrical lines to the left main fuel tank forward boost pump, as confirmed by CVR tapes."

Tomorrow the mock-up was scheduled to come down so that the analyzable parts, such as the broken pin in the mount, could be sent to laboratories all over the country. Over 60 experts had worked under Warner's guidance in this initial phase of the crash investigation. There were professional investigators from Delta, Boeing, Pratt & Whitney and Warner's own Go Team; agents of the FBI, FAA, and a dozen other government entities; representatives of the pilots' association; and specialists in everything from metal fatigue to autopsy analysis whom the chief had hustled in from the private sector.

From what Warner could tell they were all here tonight, going over the wreckage a final time in search of that one elusive clue that might change everybody's thinking about what had gone wrong. These investigations, he thought, had become as complicated as the machines whose failure they sought to understand. It was a miracle they ever managed to isolate the cause of a crash; and yet they did so with a remarkably high rate of success.

Of course, not everything was technical. Amid all of this space age wizardry, it was easy to forget that the human factor played a role in each air disaster, be it in the manufacturing process or in maintenance, in the control tower or in the cockpit. Even the most high-tech parts were conceived and tested by humans. When machines broke, it meant that someone, somewhere, at some point in time, had not done his job. One of Warner's priorities was to make sure his people, and the hundreds of thousands of men and women whose work affected the safety of air travel, remembered this fundamental and easily overlooked fact.

As he prepared to gather up his team for a final closed NTSB briefing before the flight back to Washington, Warner noticed that Hal Larsen, Boeing's 62-year-old CEO, had returned to the hangar. Larsen stood at the top of the scaffold examining the broken engine mount that his company had manufactured, a faulty part suspected of killing 1,239 people. His face clouded over with sadness, then incomprehension and, finally, anger. It was as if he had just been told that a stranger had murdered his family.

Of all the big shots Warner worked with in the line of duty, Larsen was his favorite. The others, good men though they were, had the same instinctive reaction to a disaster: how to avoid the blame. Larsen's attitude was refreshingly different. If there was something Boeing had done wrong, he wanted to "hear about it, face it and fix it."

He was facing it now. Confronted with condemning evidence, he was personally shouldering the responsibility for the worst air disaster in history. When that man got over his grief, thought Warner, someone at Boeing would have hell to pay.

∗ ∗ ∗

Pilot's Dawn

At five after eleven in the evening, Warner walked into the generic conference room of the Atlanta Airport Sheraton. Could have been anywhere, he thought, New York, L.A., Toronto. If they ever got around to requiring a similar level of standardization in airport layout and operations, he would get a lot fewer telephone calls in the middle of the night.

Remaining on his feet at the head of the table with both hands gripping the edge, he stared off in space. "Good work, all of you. It's been a long month, properly capped off by a small victory most of you don't know about yet. Yesterday afternoon, while taking a run in those fields out around the Ford plant, Simmons had the good fortune to stumble onto the missing cockpit voice recorder. Hence my comment on the note card beside the engine mount that may have confused some of you."

Simmons received a round of applause. "Do you want me to talk about what's on the tape, chief?"

Warner said, "Thank you, Simmons, I'll do it. The captain was everything his records indicated. When he stabilized the aircraft after the loss of the engine, he immediately sent the relief pilot back to check for damage to the wing. We learned an important thing from the tape. When the relief pilot returned to the flight deck, he knew there was a fuel leak and a hot wire whipping around near it.

"However, *there was no fire at this point.* The instant he reported his findings, the captain shut down all electrical power from engine number two generator, and did so with exemplary speed. But we know his actions were too late. So what does this mean? That the fire ignited while the relief pilot was delivering his message. There you have it. That's how close the crew came to bringing this one home safely."

"When did the captain find out about the fire?" Johnson asked.

"A few seconds later from the head flight attendant."

"How did he react then?" Downey asked.

"With healthy frustration," Simmons said. "To quote the transcript, 'Shit, anything else gonna go wrong tonight?' But he remained cool and proceeded to make the proper choices. From this point on, Flight Twenty appears to have been doomed."

"What strikes me, though," Warner said, "is that there was a window of opportunity, a few seconds, perhaps a minute or more, in which a severed electrical lead remained live. If the electricity had been shut down in that period, we would be researching an incident here rather than an accident. Please understand that I'm not suggesting pilot error. The pilot behaved swiftly and reasonably. However, if there had been some sort of warning of a live wire in conjunction with a fuel leak, the electricity could have been shut down in time to prevent the crash.

"One of my conclusions as we return to Washington is this: we need to study closely the critical period of the flight when fuel was leaking out and a hot wire flapping around but the fire had not yet ignited. I want us to come up with some solid recommendations in both warning system coverage and pilot training procedures to prevent a repeat of what happened here in Atlanta.

"Now, I'd like to turn to summations of your findings in the specific areas to which you were assigned. Clifton, would you or Ward begin with engine number one—"

* * *

The briefing didn't end until one in the morning. On his way through the hotel lobby to his room, Warner saw Hal Larsen in the dim light of the piano bar, hunched over a drink. The pianist had taken a break. Except for a somnambulant bartender and a few sorry drunks, the room was empty.

Warner, the regulator, sat down beside the CEO of the world's largest aircraft manufacturer. "Evening, Hal. Mind if I join you for a nightcap?"

"In fact I was hoping to ambush you. I know this could be considered improper, Frank, but I wanted to talk to you privately."

"I don't give a hoot about propriety, Hal. What's on your mind?"

"Do you think you'd feel more comfortable somewhere else?"
"This is fine."
"Would you like a drink?"
"As a matter of fact. Scotch, nothing fancy."

Larsen signaled the bartender, who obviously didn't know he was dealing with the head of a hundred billion dollar corporation. That was the mark of America, Warner thought: equality through ignorance. It had its bad and its good sides.

"Shoot, Hal."

Larsen toyed with his napkin, eyes averted. "You know me, Frank, and you know my attitude toward any shortcomings that might be traced to my company. When we have been guilty, I have always admitted this and done everything in my power to get to the bottom of the problem."

Warner sipped his scotch. "I don't disagree."

"Something with this engine mount doesn't add up. I've had my people back in Seattle pull the records on the part in question. No irregularities, it underwent all of the usual tests. You know how exhaustive our procedures are. The X-rays are on file and you will receive them. The part that failed was new, installed after the aircraft's last engine removal and overhaul. That's correct, is it not?"

"Yes."

"Frank, for this to happen, the pin must have been not only a little defective but grossly defective. Otherwise, in the event of abnormal stresses, the engine mounting bolts would have sheered off first and released the engine. But as I said, we have the test records and X-rays that indicate the contrary. The pin in the mount with the serial number matching that of the mount implicated in this crash was not defective."

The pianist returned and started a medley that began with *La vie en rose*. Warner wanted to strangle him. "Don't beat around the bush, Hal. This can remain between the two of us if you don't feel comfortable having your opinions voiced elsewhere. What are you trying to say?"

"Simply that the defect could not have originated with us."

Warner felt bad for the Boeing CEO. Larsen wasn't aware of it, but his unconscious mind had apparently gotten caught up in a strong process of denial. After all, that was the first stage of grieving, and Larsen was definitely grieving. "Hal, it's much too early to say that. The metallurgical tests haven't been completed yet. It's possible the engine mount that broke was not defective but that another defective Boeing component we haven't identified yet put it under abnormal stress."

Larsen snapped his fingers at the bartender for another round of drinks. "Which component? Could you be a more specific?"

"Look, the investigation still has a long way to go. It's pointless to speculate any further. We'll authenticate serial numbers and do everything in our power to determine if that mount could have slipped in through the counterfeit parts market. If we find any evidence to indicate that it was, we'll involve the proper authorities. Until then, my actions must be guided by the findings of my team. That's my job, Hal. You have to understand that I'm a crash investigator, not a cop."

"So you think Boeing's at fault? Is that it, Frank?"

"I don't know and I don't guess. I'll keep you abreast of our findings. That's the best I can do."

Larsen stood and extended his hand. "Thanks for listening." He tossed a twenty on the table and walked out.

Warner stayed for a while, drank another scotch and listened to a few old Billy Holliday songs. He hoped Larsen would be all right.

Chapter Six

Loyal as dogs, Michelet had said, deaf as stones. Perhaps. But the words Paul Delors was going to speak tonight had the power to turn dogs against masters and give stones ears.

He had waited through five courses of heavy Breton cooking to make his pitch, and now he would wait some more. He would wait until these two decrepit old servants at Michelet's country manor cleaned up the kitchen; wait until he could no longer hear sounds of running water and ringing china; wait until he was certain that Henri and Isabelle had left the house for the night.

His hour struck a short time later. He and Michelet had moved to the library, where they sat sipping cognac and discussing recent political events beneath the gaze of somber family portraits.

It thundered. Delors glanced outside at the chiaro-scuro of rain clouds skirting past the moon. In that moment he saw lights in the servant cottage across the way. Isabelle appeared in the window, a stooped silhouette tugging at the wind-blown shutters. Henri reached around her to help. The coast was clear; he could speak at last.

"Georges," he said, abruptly changing the subject, "I took the liberty of bugging Gaullist headquarters. I was shocked by what our conservative allies are saying about you. If you're not aware of it, you should be."

Michelet, a large, heavy-set man in his fifties with black hair and bushy eyebrows, put his snifter down hard. "I hope this isn't what you came here to discuss, Paul. Whether my so-called allies like me or not is irrelevant. My mandate comes from the people."

"But they do like you, Georges. They love you. They adore you. They can't believe their good fortune. They are convinced you made a fatal error in accepting the Ministry of Industry. The way they see it, they offered you a piece of tainted meat. They didn't expect you to bite."

Michelet took a thick Cuban cigar from the humidor and turned it over in his fingers. Delors expected him to launch into one of his venomous tirades, but he smiled instead.

"They still aren't listening to the people, are they, Paul? They don't understand how deep the hatred of foreign workers goes. They can't believe anyone would sacrifice economically in order to stand up to the Americans. But they're dead wrong, Paul. This is why I accepted the post. This is why I'm not worried about losing support."

He stood and walked to the window. The moon had disappeared, rain battered the glass. He looked out for a while, lit his cigar and strolled over to the dormant stone hearth. He bore a striking resemblance to the man in the portrait above him—his father, if Delors wasn't mistaken. They had the same prominent jowls, fierce eyes and imperious presence.

Michelet said, "We French want France back. Isn't that what this is all about, Paul? We don't want foreign workers taking our jobs and our women, and leaving their garbage in our streets. We don't want the goddamn Americans telling us what we can and can't do. My message is sweeping the country because it expresses what the people already feel. If the economy continues to worsen while I'm at Industry, the movement will not suffer. The supporters of Nouvelle France realize there can be no heroism without sacrifice."

"I don't think you can assume that, Georges. When one is at the center of something this intense, it's hard to know how loyal the marginal supporters are. But if the economy were to rebound under your leadership, you wouldn't have to make assumptions. You could count on an exponential increase in popularity."

"That's not going to happen any time soon, Paul. There's no point fantasizing about the impossible."

"But, Georges, what if circumstances unknown to you caused a brisk recovery? What would happen to your political opposition? What would happen to those voices saying Michelet can agitate but can't govern? It's clear, isn't it? Nouvelle France would cease being a single-issue movement on the fringe and become the largest political party of the right. As leader of that party, you would be a candidate for president of the republic, with a good chance of winning the next election.

"We have been blessed, Georges. Fate is smiling on us again at last. This is what I have come here to talk to you about. An instrument of destiny has been offered to us that will shock our economy out of its slump, a weapon that will change the course of French history by placing you at the helm."

Michelet left his post beneath his oil-and-canvass likeness and returned to his chair. "Your snooping on my behalf, Paul, has obviously not taken you into the realm of economic statistics. The recession is worse than anyone realizes, you included. You paint a very appealing scenario, but it depends on imaginary events which have no chance of occurring. Your metaphorical weapon, I'm sorry to say, does not exist."

Delors resisted the desire to preach the emotions stirring in his gut. One fanatic in a small smoky room—two if you counted the father—was enough. He needed to make his proposal in cool, rational terms and let Michelet come to his own conclusions about its inherent magic.

"Georges, will you grant me a half hour? Will you allow me to go back and document the origins of this potential bonanza for our cause?"

Michelet remained silent. He looked irritable. Delors cursed himself for having waited to broach the subject until the servants left the house. Michelet was departing on an extended foreign trip in the morning. Claussen's deadline was approaching. If he didn't plant the seed tonight, the opportunity of a lifetime would be lost forever.

"Georges," he went on, "the weapon you say does not exist is real. It comes from the same source that saved our Ariane missile program, the same source that solved our intractable problems with the Mirage Five's ground-hugging radar. You must listen."

"Don't get excited, Paul. I'm having a bout of indigestion. After what you've done for the movement and your country, I'm not going to cut you off. Continue, please."

Delors nodded, marveling at Michelet's ability to turn on you and then relent, making you feel grateful though he had given you nothing. He was a born leader, the sort of man whose energy and single-mindedness transformed adversity into triumph. He was the only Frenchman alive today who could take charge of the country in the spirit of Charles de Gaulle. He alone could give France back her dignity, belief in herself and her vitality. With Michelet as president, the leadership of Europe would fall to France, the only Western country that still had the guts to fight American cultural and economic imperialism. This was the real Holy War, and it could not be waged without Michelet. There was a lot riding on tonight's presentation.

Delors composed himself. "Georges," he said, "do you recall the first time I asked you for a contribution?"

"Yes, of course. It was to help defray the costs of bugging Mitterrand's office."

"That's right. Did you think I kept the money?"

"I didn't think about it, Paul. If you kept it, so what? I needed privileged information to build my movement. You were able to get that information for me, at great risk to yourself. A man has a right to compensate himself in such cases."

"That money, Georges, and all of your generous contributions since, went to finance the source of whom I spoke. I wasn't yet deputy director of the intelligence services; I didn't have access to discretionary funds. I was afraid that if I revealed my source, someone higher up would take credit; or terminate our involvement for ethical reasons. You see,

Georges, the information crucial to our military programs came from the United States. It was stolen from them by a Soviet spy experimenting with private enterprise on the side. Your contributions helped to pay him. In a sense, you have worked with this man before."

Michelet ground out his cigar and laughed a rare laugh. "You don't say? Incredible that it took a Russian to get the Americans to share with their allies. They really are hypocritical and self-righteous bastards, aren't they?"

"Yes, they are. But it wasn't a Russian, Georges, it was an East German named Walter Claussen."

"Stasi?"

"No, KGB. He was personally recruited by General Volkov while he was finishing his post-graduate work in aeronautical engineering in Moscow. Hand-picked, as it were, to set up the most ambitious fifth column operation of the postwar era.

"Georges, the operation was meticulously disguised on both sides of the Atlantic, so much so that not even Claussen's KGB colleagues knew of it. This was Volkov's wish. He evidently feared betrayal.

"Claussen moved to the States, where his papers showed him to be an emigrant from West Germany. He took on American citizenship, even married an American woman. He built a successful consulting practice in aerospace related metallurgy.

"His front never cracked. He recruited all of his spies from the ranks of his host country—Americans who had no idea for whom they were working. For specialty jobs, he relied on several high-ranking Stasi agents, all of whom have since died or been disposed of. Volkov passed away in March.

"Because of these extraordinary measures, Georges, there is no one alive today who knows of the existence of Operation Twenty-Six. No one, that is, other than myself, Claussen, you and a minor player scheduled for termination."

Michelet lit another cigar and grunted. "It sounds like this man has been trying to sell you a bill of goods. I'd like to know what this supposed magic economic weapon is?"

Delors didn't flinch at Michelet's initial skepticism. How else could an intelligent man respond before he knew all of the facts?

He said, "The weapon is a scheme to benefit the fortunes of Airbus. By 'benefit' I mean an increase in our market share from the current thirty percent to over fifty percent.

"I'm sure you have a general feeling for what this upswing would accomplish, but let me give you some specifics I've had the time to research. It will translate into a quarter of a million new jobs in the European Community, a hundred and twenty thousand of these in the high-tech sectors in France alone. It will translate into an enormous increase in government revenues from new aircraft sales and from the expanded domestic tax base. More importantly, Georges, it will jump start the economy—and the Americans will be paying the bill."

Michelet ground out his cigar. "It is true that such an improvement in the fortunes of Airbus would be a strong stimulus for the entire economy. But, Paul, in order to garner our present share of the market, we've practically had to give away airplanes. The confidential government estimates I've seen put the final sale prices ten million dollars below production costs. The Americans are already at our throats for subsidies that violate GATT, and that's going to get worse. I've seen confidential test results on Boeing's new plane, the Triple Seven. It's a better long-term investment for the airlines than our A-330s and A-340s. If you want to know my opinion, Paul, we'll be lucky to hold our thirty percent."

"Such pessimism, Georges," Delors said. He poured himself a cognac. "I'm going to tell you about Operation Twenty-Six. When I am finished, you will understand why all of your doom and gloom predictions are incorrect. You will understand why France is at the threshold of a new era of pride and independence; and why you are about to become the most significant European politician of the postwar era. May I?"

"Go on, but make it brief. I haven't packed for my trip yet."

"I shall try, George. After Russia's collapse in the Cuban Missile Crisis, General Volkov felt the sting of failure. The experience made him doubly determined to avoid another defeat and humiliation by the United States. It also changed his view of the way in which the superpowers were likely to react in the event of another showdown. Their reluctance to use nuclear weapons in Cuba convinced him that a conventional war in Europe was a possibility. This belief was the catalyst for what followed."

"Yes?"

"Operation Twenty-Six was designed to sabotage American civil aviation in the event of a land war with the Soviet Union. You saw in Vietnam and again in Iraq how the Americans use their commercial airline fleet to ferry soldiers to and from the front."

"I'm familiar with the practice. However, Paul, it would not be a realistic goal to think you could cripple an entire American war effort with civil aviation sabotage."

"You don't think so, George? I'm sure the Americans didn't either, because they left themselves wide open. If hostilities had broken out, they would have lost ten thousand soldiers in the first week of war. Who knows how they would have reacted."

"With nuclear weapons, I would think."

"And risk self-destruction? I'm not sure. They might have preferred to grant the Soviets some concessions in Europe—at our expense, of course."

"After having been sabotaged? I doubt it."

"They would not have been able to demonstrate that there had, in fact, been sabotage. One of the primary elements of Operation Twenty-Six was to make the crashes look like the result of shoddy or rushed American workmanship. In any case, George, whether or not Volkov assessed his adversary correctly is of no importance to us. What I can tell you with certainty is that part of the venture has outlived the Cold

War. The capacity thus exists to bring down Boeing jetliners in dramatic fashion."

"How do you know this, Paul? It seems rather farfetched."

Delors smiled inwardly. Proof was a lovely thing. "I know because last May's disaster in Atlanta was staged on our behalf to demonstrate precisely this capability. If you have any doubts, Georges, wait for the investigation results. A pin in the left aft engine mount failed. I was given the place of the crash, the type of aircraft and the cause two months before it happened."

"You mean to tell me," Michelet growled, "you mean to tell me, Paul, that you are proposing air crashes as the way to improve the fortunes of Airbus."

"Yes. One, the action could not be traced to us—or anyone else. Two, we must have the courage to fight for what we believe in. This is war, Georges. Just because the weapons are economic rather than military does not mean the stakes are smaller. If we let the Americans roll over us here, where will we stop them? It's time we quit talking and took our destiny in our own hands. May I fill you in on the details?"

Michelet did not say no, so Delors continued. When he wrapped up his presentation many hours later, a streak of dawn shone above the wet forests to the east and lights burned again in the servant cottage across the way. Michelet, he thought, was coming around. Slowly, yes, but that was to be expected. Delors himself had been a difficult convert.

Isabelle brought them coffee and croissants. She did not seem to notice that the two men had been up all night.

When she left the room, Michelet stretched and stood. "Well, Paul, before we go any further, I suppose I should inquire after Monsieur Claussen's fee."

"Fifty million dollars per accident—in the currencies of his choosing, and in cash."

Michelet looked almost as stunned as he had been by the original proposal. "That's ludicrous. That solves my dilemma. Our war chest is big, but not that big."

"Georges, you're leaving someone out of your calculations. I've researched the distribution of Albert's holdings. He would earn his investment back, and then some. He would do it for you. He would do it for France. May I bring him here when you return from Brussels?"

Michelet was moving toward the library door, a dark restless mass of energy. Before he went out, he stopped and stared harshly at his guest. "I don't know. I'll have to think about it. Good day, Paul."

Chapter Seven

Steven headed south the week after Bastille Day. The traffic was horrendous, and the heat brought back unpleasant memories of the summer he'd worked in the oil fields of Oklahoma. It was that humid heat you couldn't keep out of your socks and shorts, and it didn't help to have the Harley burning like a furnace between his legs.

Both lanes had slowed to a crawl. He was sick and tired of having to fight the cars, trucks and campers. No way back roads could be any worse than this, he thought. On impulse he took the Beaune exit and left the *autoroute*.

He had only stopped for gas since leaving Paris nearly seven hours ago. When he drove past a sidewalk café in the center of a provincial town where a few old men were drinking beer, he decided it would be wise to refuel his body. He ordered a *croque monsieur*, the closest thing to a sandwich he'd found in France, and a cold mug of Kronenbourg. While he was unwinding, he became fascinated with the cathedral directly across the square. The entire facade was painted with frescoes. Though their colors had been dulled by centuries of weather and pollution, the intricate figures were still beautiful. What painstaking work! Most impressive of all, someone had actually *finished* the goddamned thing.

Perseverance. That had been Item Number One on "LeConte's List of Lacking Virtues," a page of fake parchment on which Sophie had listed in a fine calligraphic hand the traits he would do well to acquire.

He couldn't remember what the other items on the list were. Promptness, maybe. He was a big procrastinator, which was why the parchment still lay unframed and unstudied on his desk. But one thing was certain: Sophie was right about his lack of perseverance. Unlike his brothers, parents, and the fresco painter across the square, he never seemed to finish anything.

He ordered another beer and ate his sandwich and wondered what kind of mistakes his parents had made raising him. "Where did we go wrong with this young man, Ashley? Where in the name of God did we go wrong?" That was his father's familiar refrain each time he dropped out of school or quit a promising job.

Christ, he didn't know where they had gone wrong either, but they must have really screwed up. Because the mere thought of becoming an eye surgeon in Greenwich or a tax attorney in New Haven or a nervous little stock market weasel on Wall Street made him existentially ill.

He felt a sudden unanticipated joy welling up from deep inside him, displacing the fatigue of too many hours on the road. What he *really* wanted to be was a guy on his way south to seduce some big shot politician's daughter. Yes, it was hard to believe, but he wanted to be the guy sitting right here in this café, in a town whose name he didn't know, drinking a beer and looking at a cathedral with a facade of beautiful frescoes some dogged bastard had worked for half a century to finish. He hadn't felt good about being just plain old Steven for years. This was a welcome change.

Beyond the outskirts of town, he accelerated the powerful bike into a curve. When the road straightened out, he could see the snow-capped peaks of the Alps far off to the east, rising above the summer haze.

The fields stretched to either side of the tree-lined road, soft green fields with streaks of lilac. Patches of bright red poppies grew here and there. He watched old stone farmhouses with tile roofs fly by. He took in the roll and geometry of the patchwork farming country, all chopped up by ancient stone walls and skewed hedges.

He was high on life. For this fine experience he had Sophie Marx to thank. Maybe her feeling toward him wasn't only maternal, he thought;

maybe she really needed him, really thought he could help her with her work. Who was he to say? Maybe he could.

* * *

He had only intended to locate the Michelet villa that evening, but when he saw a navy-blue Mercedes with a young woman in the passenger seat driving out the front gate, he couldn't resist following. The car climbed a steep winding road toward a hilltop village whose turreted silhouette was etched against the darkening sky. He stayed well back, merging with a few kids on mopeds sputtering along like mechanical fish.

The medieval stone wall around the village seemed to grow out of the cliffs. The entrance was a vaulted passage so narrow the Mercedes had a tight squeeze getting through.

Looking up at it as he approached, Steven found the place almost spooky. But once inside the wall, he saw that it was warm and hospitable, a quaint little town where people came to eat or stroll on a warm summer night.

Antique gas streetlights burned along the cobblestone alleys and light shone in the windows of shops and restaurants. This evening the strollers were out in force, and groups of teenagers hung around the outdoor cafés.

The Mercedes stopped at curbside near an elegant restaurant, dwarfing most of the other cars. Steven was glad he had showered and gotten into a fresh shirt and pair of jeans, but he doubted they'd let him in the restaurant if that's where fate was trying to take him. He parked his bike, sat on the back of a bench and watched.

The young woman got out of the Mercedes, not waiting for the driver to come around. Steven recognized her from the pictures Sophie had shown him. She was even more enticing in the flesh. She wore low heels, a tasteful smattering of gold jewelry, and a pale linen summer dress. She was slim, lithe and voluptuous, one of those young women who exude sexuality without trying. Her jet black hair shone brilliantly under the streetlights. Sophie was right: he liked what he saw.

His spine stiffened when the door on the driver's side swung open. A big man roughly his father's age got out. Michelet looked a lot less friendly in person than he did on TV. He had the aura of a powerful man about him, made you know he was the kind of guy who could take care of himself—and of you if he felt like it. Sophie, he thought, had given him one hell of a challenge.

When Michelet took his daughter's arm, she didn't look overjoyed. Steven felt like cheering. They started to walk toward the elegant restaurant.

He was trying to decide if he should follow them and take his chances on a dress code when a clean-cut young man came out of the restaurant and motioned to Michelet. Steven noticed that two other men had materialized just behind the walking couple. They seemed very alert, eyes scouring pedestrians, parked cars, doorways and overhead windows. Plainclothes security agents, he realized. Not exactly his kind of people.

In a little anteroom just inside the restaurant, he received a thorough going over. The maitre d' gave him another rigorous exam but finally, if not enthusiastically, decided to let him in. He shelled out a large tip and managed to get a table by the window, separated from the Minister and his daughter by nothing more than a party of three security agents.

The view from the window was breathtaking. The ground on which the restaurant had been built was higher than the village wall, so you could see over it and down the mountainside. At the bottom of the precipice lights snaked gracefully along the jagged coastline. Out beyond the lights, the Mediterranean stretched to the horizon, vast and calm beneath a low crescent moon.

Inside the restaurant Steven had less to look at, as the backs of the agents, and then the even broader back of Michelet, blocked his view of Nicole, who sat facing him. At least it wasn't a total eclipse, he thought.

He could see a tanned, slender arm when she reached for something on the table, a sheath of lustrous black hair when she tilted her head to the side, an occasional bare shoulder when she moved one way and her father the other.

After many courses, consumed, from what he could tell, in near silence, Michelet excused himself to make a pit stop. Two agents accompanied him, the third stood and stretched. Steven at last had an unobstructed view of the girl.

Nicole stared out the window, toying with her necklace. Then, as if the view weren't enough to hold her attention, she brought her eyes around to him.

He was quick, decisive and confident. He spoke to her across the vacant table as if they were guests at the same party. He made innocuous small talk about the lovely village and the cuisine and how glad he was to have come to the south of France. He did it in a way that spared her having to respond.

She smiled at something he said, a dazzling smile he hadn't seen before.

Michelet returned, paid the bill and hustled Nicole out. She smiled at Steven again as she passed his table.

He sat back, stretched and ordered a five-star cognac. This was an expense he didn't think Sophie would mind.

Chapter Eight

Claussen got off the train at the Friedrichsstrasse station, once the heart of East Berlin's rail system. He joined the stream of workers heading for the huge ailing factories along the Spree.

Glancing at his watch, he ducked into a sidewalk bar for a roll, coffee and schnapps. He stood at a round table while he ate and read the three newspapers he had bought at the station kiosk: *France-Soir*, *Le Monde* and the *Daily Telegraph*.

He was disappointed. Like the rest of the subject matter he had covered since he had received the go-ahead from Delors—some privileged, some not—today's news shed no light on the mystery of who, in addition to Delors, was paying his fee.

It was high time he solved that mystery, he thought. If he left Europe in the dark as to the identity of Delors' backers, it would not auger well for his life expectancy. With a secret as ugly as theirs on their conscience, and the blood of thousands of innocent travelers on their hands, these men would want him gone forever the moment he completed his mission. In fact, it wouldn't surprise him if they were already planning his elimination.

Claussen did not despise his backers for behaving the way he hypothesized: he would have done the same in their position. But he had to take care of himself. He was a realist. He knew he must have a device for offsetting their present advantage, a checkmate he could rely on.

He drained his schnapps. His concerns were still a little premature. Today was the day Maria was supposed to come to the island. She had been there when he and Delors had spoken, hidden in the overgrown boathouse, deadly as usual with her Leica. She had also monitored the receiver for the tiny bug he had installed under the dock. As a result of his preparations and Maria's help, he had a taped record of Delors' visit to complement the photos.

This was a good start, but it was only a start. Delors had no family. He would prefer death to revealing his backers. He was the real thing, a zealot who put the interests of his country ahead of his own well-being. He was blackmail-proof. To checkmate the others, whoever they were, Claussen had no choice but to uncloak them on his own.

Which was why he'd sent Maria to France the week after Delors had come to see him. She went armed with her knowledge of what Delors looked like and not much more. Claussen instructed her to try to spot him outside the Piscine, the Paris headquarters of the SDECE, and, if she did, to follow him wherever he went.

Claussen was guessing that the Deputy Director of the SDECE would embark on a fund raising drive when he returned to France. The task of finding that much money outside of official channels wouldn't be easy. If Delors was able to rouse sufficient interest in the Airbus agenda, Claussen knew there would be several meetings before any agreement was reached. Hence his instructions to Maria to look for a series of meetings involving the same people, and to monitor the participants' comings and goings for up to a month if she found something.

Claussen knew it was a long shot and did not give her a great chance of success. But as a tracker and recorder, she was a pro. He had learned a few years ago not to count her out. He had also learned that in his business long shots were not to be despised.

Claussen had come to Berlin to forge the documents he would need for his trip to the States. After availing himself of the KGB facilities he had set up in a rented warehouse after the Collapse, he caught the train to Neubrandenburg. He traveled second-class through the sandy pine forests of his youth, feeling reinvigorated. A tough mission always had that effect on him.

Pilot's Dawn

He got off the train at noon. From the station vendor he bought a bockwurst and roll, washed them down with a half liter of pilsner and mounted his old bicycle for the 20 kilometer trip home.

In a village along the way, he picked up a fresh round black bread, a kilo of butter and a sack of brown farm eggs. When he arrived at his farmhouse in the early afternoon, his geese were hungry and cantankerous. He fed them ten kilos of the meat-laced dog food pellets that seemed to keep them more aggressive. Then he went inside to fetch his swimming bag.

He walked at a brisk pace down the familiar path to the river, enjoying the warmth of the July sun. When he reached the water's edge he took the row boat instead of swimming to the island. He would have his swim when he got there, he decided, and return home warm and dry. He was respectful of the weather. The pale blue sky strewn with patches of dimpled white clouds told him rain was near.

Maria wasn't there when he arrived. Claussen tied off the boat, stepped agilely on to the dock and traded his street clothes for swim trunks. He made seven brisk laps around the island, then climbed back up on the dock and stretched out in the last of the afternoon warmth to dry. He had dozed off when he felt Maria's strong hands kneading the backs of his thighs.

"Walter," she said, "your body only improves with age. Do you know how often I dreamt of finding you here like this. The entire time I was in France shooting your pictures, my fantasies obsessed me. Nothing I did to myself could sate my hunger for you."

"That's very flattering, Maria, but I'm much too old for you. If I'm what you want, you'll have to live with deprivation. Were you able to bring me something useful?"

"Yes, Walter. Everything you asked for and more."

"I'm pleased."

Claussen lifted himself to a sitting position. He saw that Maria was wearing a string bikini. "My God, child, go for a swim."

She stood, pretended to pout and dove in. Soon she was back beside the dock, holding her wet hair up with both hands while she treaded water with her feet. Claussen could not help admire her full breasts, thin muscular arms and high Slavic cheekbones. She was a beautiful woman, she was available. But in his long career he had never mixed work with pleasure. He did not intend to start now.

"The photos are in the boathouse, Walter," she said. "Go on and have a peek if you want. I'd like to swim a few more minutes before it gets too chilly."

The boathouse was completely overgrown with tangled vines. From the dock it looked like nothing more than a clump of foliage. Claussen picked up his bag with his street clothes in it, ducked through a tunnel of vines and rushes and stepped inside. On the rough-hewn table lay Maria's backpack and a fat manila folder. An unopened bottle of Armagnac stood beside them.

The first photos Claussen looked at were of an old country manor on the edge of a densely wooded hillside. The second set included five perfectly focussed shots of Paul Delors. He was in front of the house, speaking with the driver of an unmarked van. Two workmen seemed to be preparing to conduct a security check of the premisses.

The third set of photographs had been shot at night with an infrared lens. Delors again. He stood in front of the entrance with a big slightly overweight man roughly his own age. The man had thick black hair and an irritable look on his face. They were greeting another man, who was short, stout and bald, and carried a slender attaché case.

The final set of photos was shot as the bald man prepared to leave. The quality was excellent. Dawn had come, making the use of the infrared lens unnecessary.

Delors stood near the doorway again. The large dark-haired man stood beside him, the same irritable expression on his face. The photographs left no doubt as to the men's identities.

Claussen smiled to himself. If they had been planning to kill him when the job was done, they were going to have to revise their plans.

Maria came in shivering. He looked away while she stepped out of her bikini, dried off and dressed in slacks and a long-sleeved shirt. "Prussian summer," she said.

Claussen smiled. "These are very good. Excellent. You've done another piece of fine work, Maria, up to the high standards we maintained in the old days."

"Thank you, Walter. I brought a bottle of Armagnac back from France to celebrate."

"I noticed."

"Want a taste?"

"Go ahead. I'll wait until later."

"Are we going to your house, Walter?"

"Perhaps."

Maria smiled with her broad, seductive mouth. "And you still plan to resist me?"

Claussen did not answer.

Maria took two glasses from the travel bag she'd brought along in her rowboat, set them on the table and filled one of them. "To us," she said, drinking.

Claussen ignored her. He was leafing through the first set of photographs, lost in thought. "What's the date on these, Maria?"

"The fifth of July, several days after I arrived. I suppose I got lucky. I was camped out across the street from the Piscine with the scope, pretending to photograph pigeons. Delors showed up for work in his own car around eight thirty. Ten minutes later he left the compound in an agency car with that truck you see in the photograph following him.

The traffic was heavy in Paris, and also on the *autoroute*. It was a simple matter to join the convoy along with a few thousand other cars.

"When they turned off, they ended up on a hilly, curvy country road. I hung back out of view, but I could see them ahead whenever they crested a hill. At the top of one of the hills, they turned into a long gravel drive. I went on past, parked my car and hiked in. There was an old barn about three hundred meters from the spot where they had parked. From the upper hayloft I had a perfect bead on the manor."

"I believe the photographs show the forest of Fontainebleau."

"Yes, Walter, a lovely place."

"What about the other photos? When were they shot?"

"Well, Walter, I lived in that smelly barn for many days. I wouldn't have done it for anyone else. There's always a lot lying around to eat in France. The peasants who work there are ancient, which helped my requisitioning. Nothing happened until the last night of my stay. I was about to pack up and leave for Germany."

"Yes."

She took a sip of her drink. "Delors arrived shortly after dark. The third man came after midnight. They stayed in the house until dawn, and that allowed me to photograph them clearly, without the infra-red, when they came out."

"The photographs are very good, Maria," he repeated.

"Thank you."

"Do you know who these people are?"

She giggled and put a hand on his arm. "Yes, Walter. I was curious. Do you blame me?"

"How did you learn their identities, Maria?"

"I asked. In a bar. At a newsstand. Very discretely, mind you. People recognized them. What about you? Do you know who they are?"

He warmed up, even managed a thin smile. "Of course I do. Now, Maria, why don't you come home with me? We'll have a bite to eat. I was in Berlin today and had the opportunity to convert your compensation into Swiss francs, as you requested. If you wish, you may stay the night."

"I wish, Walter. You know that."

＊   ＊   ＊

At dusk, they crossed the lake in their two separate boats and paddled vigorously upriver. Claussen, a few meters ahead, waved her over to the flat grassy bank with the ancient stone bench where he always began his swim. She was out of breath. He caught her backpack and helped her to shore with a steady hand, then tied both boats to the bench for the night. Maria thanked him and put her arm through his. This time he did not pull away.

The woods were still as they began the half hour walk to the farmhouse. Low clouds had rolled in, dark and fragrant with the promise of rain.

Maria found the night enchanting. She wondered out loud if Claussen would ever break down and make love to her. He implied with his silence that he would, and she hugged him tightly.

A cool persistent rain off the Baltic began to fall. When they arrived at the farmhouse, they were both soaked. The geese, stirred up by the presence of a female, attacked Maria so aggressively she had to beat them back with a stick.

"They're nice and plump, Walter," she said, laughing. "They sense that I grew up on a farm and am their enemy. You should let me fix you one for Christmas dinner."

"Perhaps, if I'm here," he said, leading her inside. "Would you like a hot shower, Maria?"

She nodded happily, her teeth chattering and goose bumps on her bare arms. "More than anything. Almost anything. Where is it?"

"In the second-floor bedroom to your left."

"Will you join me, Walter? Two get warm faster than one."

"Yes," he said. "And I'll bring the Armagnac."

"Wonderful." She ran up the stairs, her hard shapely calves glistening with rainwater. "I was beginning to think you could resist me forever," she called over her shoulder, her voice like a schoolgirl's. "I'm glad I was wrong."

When he heard the bedroom door close, he reached quietly into the second drawer for his stiletto. It weighed only three ounces, but was deadliest close-range weapon he had ever used. He taped it to the back of his right thigh, undressed in the kitchen and climbed the stairs naked. Her clothes were in a pile on the bed. He could hear water running. When he opened the shower door, she was standing with her back to him, washing her hair, her face turned upward toward the nozzle.

He plunged the stiletto between her shoulder blades, a precise thrust.

When she turned toward him, soap and water streamed down her beautiful face. He could see the stiletto's tip where it had run her through. It was protruding from the left center of her chest. A moment of silence ensued as she gaped at him, her large, dark eyes filled with incomprehension. She finally said, "Why, Walter? Why?"

He stepped back from the shower. She sat hard and shuddered. The blood, sparse in front, spurted from her back and formed a pool beneath her. "Why, Walter?" she repeated, her voice already weak.

"You knew too much," he said curtly. "You knew of my past, you knew of my mission, you were foolish enough to inquire about the identity of my employers. When I offered you the assignment, you should have refused."

She stretched her arms out toward him, fingers splayed and trembling. "Walter, please help me."

He kicked her further back in the shower and turned up the water. "Good bye, Maria. You should have been a paparazza." He closed the shower door and scooted a heavy armoire in front of it.

Pilot's Dawn

In the kitchen, Claussen put water on to boil, laid out two potatoes and a thick cutlet of veal. He put a glob of goose fat in the skillet and opened a bottle of Stierenblut wine.

While he surveyed the beginnings of his meal, he couldn't help laughing. Old Bauernsachs, the peasant down the road, was coming at five a.m. with a wagon of swine guts and two wagons of grain.

Bauernsachs used the machinery in Claussen's barn, which had once been part of a small state-owned dog food plant. Claussen charged him a share of the finished product adequate to feed his geese. This time there would be something other than pig guts in those pellets. His geese would have their go at Maria after all.

He ate heartily, putting ample butter on his black bread and potatoes and not bothering to trim the fat from his cutlet. He had learned long ago your system needed a little something extra when you demanded superhuman things of it. A few more trivial items of business and he would be ready to leave for the States. Upstairs, he turned off the shower, pleased to see no sign of Maria's blood in the stall. He left her and his stiletto to spend the night together in peace.

Chapter Nine

Soon after his arrival in the south of France, Steven reported to the Roches Fleuries Tennis Club for his scheduled meeting with the outgoing pro and the director. He already had the job, some sort of international exchange Sophie had worked out with friends in Beverly Hills and Paris. But the director of this exclusive club wanted to have a formal chat with him before he started.

Steven assumed there would be a lot of emphasis on dress codes, tennis etiquette and other things he didn't give a damn about. It was his image of Nicole in a short skirt responding to his hands-on demonstration of a proper serve that convinced him he could keep his mouth shut.

He was a few minutes early so he throttled back his bike and took a coasting tour of the facility. It was impressive. Twelve finely groomed red clay courts were set among Roman ruins high above the Mediterranean. The courts on the steepest incline were built on platforms that jutted out over the mountainside. Palm trees and pines ringed the courts, providing a windbreak and a measure of privacy, and gnarled old olive trees grew among the ruins. Flower beds with all sorts of brightly colored southern plants bordered the asphalt paths connecting the courts. Best of all, if you looked down at the coastline, you could see medieval fishing villages nestled into craggy coves, and sailboats plying the aquamarine water.

The clubhouse was a sprawling white stucco and glass villa. There was a stone patio with wrought-iron tables facing Court Number One, a first-class tournament court with a grandstand on the far side. A waiter in a white jacket held vigil over a dozen or so middle-aged women who were wearing too much jewelry and getting too much sun. He hoped they didn't like Americans.

He parked his bike among the fancy cars, introduced himself to the waiter and went inside. The girl at the reservation desk looked coldly at his T-shirt and cut-off jeans.

"May I help you?"

"I have an appointment with Philippe. My name's LeConte. I'm going to be your pro while he's in Beverly Hills."

She looked him over again as if to say, You're dressed like that and you think your going to be the pro here?

"This way, please, Monsieur LeConte."

He followed silently up two broad flights of stairs. She ushered him into a waiting room that reminded him of the waiting room of the shrink he had once gone to see as a condition of his father's continued financial support.

"I'll tell them you have arrived," the girl said.

"Hey, before you lock me in here, why don't you have that waiter down below bring me up a kir? It's hot out there."

"Are you sure you want to drink alcohol, Monsieur LeConte?"

"Of course I'm sure."

She consulted her watch. "But your match begins in three hours."

"Match? What match?"

"With Philippe. It's a big event. We are expecting most of the club members to attend."

"I don't know anything about a match. I didn't even bring my racket."

The director's door opened and a stern-looking middle-age man motioned with a condescending flick of his wrist for the girl to leave. He looked Steven over with cool gray eyes. "Monsieur LeConte?"

Steven extended his hand. "That's me. And you're Monsieur Denis du Pèage?"

"Yes. I trust you had a pleasant trip?"

"It's a long way from Paris."

"For an American? I thought you were used to distances."

"I've been in France for quite a while."

"I see. Well, Philippe will be here shortly." The director went back into his office, leaving a chill in the room.

Soon, a man in his mid twenties came in. He was lean and tall, 6'3" Steven guessed, with razor cut black hair and a gold chain around his neck. Dressed in the latest silver and mauve Sergio Tacchini warm-up suit, he looked like an ad in a tennis magazine.

"Philippe Denis du Pèage," he said coolly. He extended his hand but did not squeeze when Steven shook it.

"Denis du Pèage?" Steven said. "You're the director's son?"

"Yes."

"So what's this I hear about a match between the two of us tonight? No one mentioned it to me."

"It's tradition at the Roches Fleuries. The outgoing pro always plays the new man. The outgoing pro chooses the time of the match and the number of sets."

"Outgoing pro? You're only going to be 'out' for six weeks. I'm not after your job here, if that's what you're worried about. Let's skip the match. You don't have to piss on the corners of your territory because of me."

"My job is not at issue. I said it was tradition."

"Am I supposed to lose? Is that tradition, too?"

"Don't insult me or you will not be working at this club."

"Sorry, I was just asking. What time's the match?"

"Eight o'clock. Best of three. I hope you're not nervous playing in front of crowds."

"Look, Philippe, I'm very nervous. I didn't know we were playing so I didn't even bring my tennis things with me. It's an hour to my place in this summer traffic, and an hour to get back here. I haven't played a serious match in quite a while. I'd like to hit a few serves, maybe find someone to rally with. So how about being a good sport and rounding me up some shoes, clothes and a racquet?"

"There's a pro shop downstairs. If you don't have enough money, you can charge against your salary."

"Thanks, mate. I'll make the trip."

*   *   *

Nicole hadn't been planning to watch the match, but a tiff with their housekeeper, Francoise, had given her all the incentive she needed to get out of the villa. Now she was glad she had come.

It had been hot that day, but the evening was splendid. A light, shifting breeze carried the smells of the sea when it blew up from the south, and of wild sage and thyme when it came down across the dry mountain slopes. It was a pleasant change from the diesel fumes of Paris. The lights above the tournament court seemed to attract cigarette smoke and insects, but where she sat in the center of the grandstand, Nicole was bothered by neither. She was actually enjoying being alone when Jules and Luc, her two cousins from Grenoble, spotted her and came charging up the bleacher slats.

Jules had just turned sixteen and Luc was twelve. They could drive anyone to despair, including Nicole's unflappable aunt. The boys always wanted to be with her, though she had no idea why.

They squeezed themselves in beside her, kissing her politely on both cheeks. "Hey, guess what?" Luc, the younger, said. "That new guy hasn't even shown up yet. He's probably afraid to play Philippe."

"Afraid of Philippe?" Jules said. "Philippe's not worth a bag of monkey turds. Sorry, Nicole. I hear you're dating him."

"I am not dating him," Nicole said. "It was father's idea. And watch your language, *please*. If you two can't behave like gentlemen, I'm going to send you down there with Father Raoul."

"Send Jules," Luc said. "I didn't say anything bad."

"I didn't either. I just repeated what father said. Philippe couldn't beat his grandmother."

"Oh, yeah? Luc said indignantly. "When did you ever see him lose?"
"He never plays anyone decent."
"No? What about that slugger from Italy? What do you think, *cousine*?"
"I think Philippe is a solid player with exceptionally good form."
"You think so?" said Jules. "I think he's a phony."

The debate was cut short by the roar of a motorcycle on the pedestrian path. The boys and the entire murmuring crowd of two hundred spectators fell silent.

The new arrival, who was wearing a black helmet, a wildly colored shirt that violated all of the club's dress codes and tennis shorts, parked his bike beside the court entrance and got off. He exchanged his helmet for a New York Yankees baseball cap and grabbed two rackets without covers from his saddle bag, then walked casually over to the group of club directors, linesmen and ball boys who were waiting impatiently around the referee's chair.

"Hey," Jules said, "that's the guy we saw up at Sospel, the guy who promised us a ride. When the newcomer took off his baseball cap, Nicole recognized the good-looking foreigner who had spoken to her in the restaurant. She hadn't heard that Philippe's replacement wasn't French. It would be interesting, she thought, to see how he got along with these snotty southern haut-bourgeois.

One of the officials introduced the new pro to the crowd. There wasn't much clapping, people were still trying to make up their minds about him. He seemed to sense this, leaning over to speak into the official's microphone.

"Sorry I'm late," he apologized. "I didn't know the traffic downtown was so heavy. But I'm glad to be here, now that I'm finally here. This is a beautiful club."

That's all he said, though he spoke nearly perfect French. He bowed his head, ran his fingers through his blond hair and put the cap back on.

Philippe entered the court to subdued applause, wearing a beautiful designer warm-up suit. He carried an enormous Sergio Tacchini racket bag from which at least a dozen racket handles protruded. Nicole saw him look condescendingly at the new pro's shirt, which she rather liked, and walk around him so he wouldn't have to shake hands. He conferred with the officials and took off his warm-ups. He removed the rackets from his bag, tapped the strings to check tensions and appeared to make a careful, informed choice. Then he nodded.

The referee climbed the chair, the linesmen and ball boys took their positions, Monsieur Denis du Pèage strode to the mike and addressed the crowd.

"Messieurs, mesdames, I apologize for any inconvenience caused you by the delay. Monsieur LeConte assures me he will not be tardy to any other club functions during his stay with us. I know this match is being played late for many of you. Because of Monsieur LeConte's tardiness, I am requesting that the players forego their warm-up. Philippe, do you have any objections?"

"Of course not."

"You've been warming up all afternoon!" Jules shouted. "Let the other guy warm up."

"Jules!" said Nicole. "It's quite nasty what they're doing, but you must be quiet."

"Any objections, Monsieur LeConte?"

"No. I had a match last spring."

Subdued laughter rose from the stands.

"Then let us begin." Monsieur Denis du Pèage passed the mike to the referee.

"Quiet please," the referee said. "Monsieur LeConte, please serve from the south court."

Steven walked up to the chair and spoke near enough to the mike that his words were amplified. "You ask me to forego a warm-up and then you ask me to serve first without even a toss of the coin? What ever happened to sportsmanship? I'd like to ask my opponent, who has had the entire afternoon to warm up, to consent to a reversal of this order.

Philippe?"

"I can't consent to that. The incoming pro serves first. It is tradition. Perhaps you have no tradition in America."

"He's an American?" said Jules.

Nicole felt vindicated for liking the shirt. People might make fun of it now, but they were short-sighted. All of these California styles sooner or later became the rage in France.

Steven LeConte stretched and took a few practice swings behind the baseline.

Luc said, "Hey, Nicole, it's a good thing your dad went back to Paris. I heard him say some things about Americans on TV. I don't think he would like this guy."

"Quiet," said Jules. "The cowboy's about to serve."

"Look, he's right-handed," Luc said. "I thought Yanks were all lefties."

Steven hit a slice into Philippe's forehand corner.

"Out!" called the linesman.

"It was ten centimeters in!" yelled Jules. "Are you blind?"

Nicole put a finger to his lips. "Shhh! It looked good to me, too, but we're not supposed to yell."

He served the second ball harder. The "out" call came as Philippe dubbed the return. There was a murmur from the crowd.

"Love-fifteen. Quiet please."

Steven hit a grandmother serve square in the middle of the backhand court. Philippe teed off, trying to hit a winner. His ball carried a good foot behind the baseline. There was no "out" call.

"See," cried Luc. "Philippe's killing him. I told you."

"Quiet please. Love-thirty."

Steven hit another granny serve, obviously worried about the call. Philippe teed off again. The ball would have carried six feet long, but Steven took it in the air. He smiled, the crowd laughed.

Philippe hit his first good shot of the match, a cross-court forehand deep, and came to the net behind it. Steven tapped a dink up the center that landed at his feet. Philippe scooped it up and kept coming in behind his short approach shot, leaving himself open for a lob. Steven hit a topspin beauty. The ball just cleared Philippe's racket and came down too far inside the baseline to be called "out."

A few subdued cheers rippled through the crowd.

"Fifteen-thirty. Quiet please."

Steven scorched a serve up the middle. Philippe got off a weak return that looked like a wounded duck.

"Foot fault!" shouted the linesman.

"I told you," Luc repeated. "Philippe is killing him."

"Dammit," said Jules, "don't you see what's going on? They're calling balls 'out' that are in and 'in' that are out—and foot faults if the Yank hits a good serve. If this was a fair fight, he'd blow that *pédé* off the court."

Nicole said, "Jules, your language!"

"He would not, would he, Nicole?" Luc asked.

"Sorry, Luc, I have to agree with your brother. Now be quiet. Let's watch."

    *   *   *

The first set was close, with Philippe winning 6-4 on a late flurry of outrageous calls.

Philippe led the second set 5-2. Steven was playing well but had been penalized an average of two points a game for his antics. Jules particularly liked it when the Yank marked where Philippe's ball landed in the alley about a foot and a half outside the line with a mound of chalk from the line machine.

Even Luc had recognized by now that the match was rigged, and he stopped taunting his brother. The serious players in the crowd had grown bold with their comments about the officiating.

Nicole felt so sorry for the American, and so ashamed of the way he was being treated by these jerks, she felt like going onto the court after the match and apologizing to him. She was trying to decide if it would be appropriate for her to take her cousins and do just that when things got even more out of hand. Philippe was serving for the match. His first service was six inches wide *and* hit the net but neither a fault nor a let was called.

At that point Steven walked to the net. Nicole thought he was going to blast the referee, and she wouldn't have blamed him if he had. But it was Philippe he wanted to talk to, and talk he did. He spoke in a booming voice she could easily hear above the warnings the ref shouted into the mike.

"Okay, Philippe," he said, "I was going to let you win this match as your going away present. I'll still let you win if you have a chat with your buddies and get the remainder of the game officiated properly. Otherwise you'll force me to play you left handed and embarrass you in front of all these people."

"This is an abomination," Philippe complained to the chair. "This man has no tennis etiquette."

"Monsieur LeConte, you are penalized one point. The score is forty-love, which brings us to triple match point. Monsieur Denis du Pèage, serve please."

"Look at that!" shouted Jules. "He's switched hands. He *is* a lefty!"

Impossible, thought Nicole. He was going to loose anyway so he was poking fun at these people who had rigged the match. Maybe he was carrying things a little too far.

Philippe threw the ball high, arched his back in picture perfect form and hit his best serve of the match. He took two steps toward the net and watched open-mouthed as the left-handed return went whistling by him, sank with ferocious top-spin, hit near the service line and ricocheted like a bullet toward the backdrop.

Pilot's Dawn

Nicole ended up on her feet, jumping up and down with Jules and cheering so loudly she was embarrassed when she caught herself.

"Quiet, please. Forty-fifteen. Double match point."

Philippe smiled, arched his back and hammered his service into the corner. Steven's return, a sinker, came sizzling right at his body.

Philippe spun to get out of the way, slapping at the ball with his racket and popping it up toward the stands.

Nicole couldn't believe what happened next. The American was taking no more chances on calls! He went after the ball though it was a good 20 feet out of play, climbing the bleacher steps and smashing a winner dead into the center of the court while he stood between two elderly women. The shower of chalk that went up from the service T dusted Philippe's razor-cut hair.

The American stopped at the chair on his way back to the court. "If you don't call 'em out, I play 'em. Those are the international rules of tennis, aren't they?"

Steven had the crowd behind him now, and Philippe seemed to sense that if he didn't win his third match point he would be in trouble. He took too big a swing and connected poorly.

Nicole could see that Philippe expected a passing shot. He knew he had to gamble and lunged left. But the American must have known he would lunge to one side or the other, so he dinked a short soft return up the middle. The ball landed between the service courts. While Philippe watched helplessly, it made a leisurely bouncing journey across 15 feet of clay before it crossed the baseline.

"How are they going to call that one out?" shouted Jules.

"They can't!" cried Luc, having come full circle in his change of allegiances.

Now the left-handed slaughter began in earnest. It took Steven seventeen minutes to finish out the second set and a mere nineteen minutes to conclude the third and final set, during which he treated the crowd to a breathtaking display of smashes, topspin lobs, sinking backhands and scorching aces. By the end of the match, Jules, Luc and Nicole were hoarse.

Nicole was glad to see what looked like grudging admiration for the American's game from the linesmen and ref, and even from Monsieur Denis du Pèage. When he presented the trophy he had no doubt planned to give his son, he patted the newcomer on the back, a rare display of humanity from the club director.

"Are you taking lessons with this guy?" Jules croaked.

"Tomorrow," Nicole whispered, feeling a tremor of anxiety. She had found the stranger attractive when he spoke to her in the restaurant the other night, and she had smiled at him very openly, not once but twice. She hoped she hadn't given him the wrong idea. She certainly wouldn't have smiled at him that way if she had known she would be seeing him again so soon, and at such close quarters.

Chapter Ten

Wayne Jenkins polished the wine glasses with a paper napkin and, satisfied there were no more water spots, returned them to the table. He conducted one last survey of his work, making sure he had remembered all the little essentials he didn't want to be jumping up for during a romantic dinner—salt, the corkscrew, matches for the candles, Lori's wooden salad spoons. Everything was ready.

When she came home from taking Sean to the sleepover, he'd put the salmon on the grill and open the wine. From then on it would be clear sailing. He wasn't much of a cook, but how could you go wrong with hors d'oeuvres from the gourmet shop around the corner, two bottles of expensive Chardonnay and a salmon that had been alive a few hours ago?

He knew Lori would appreciate the effort. His promotion last year to Manager at the Spares Distribution Center had meant a lot of time on the job. She definitely got the short end of the stick when it came to work around the house. It shouldn't be that way, he thought. She worked full-time, was the mother of a spirited eight-year-old, and her job at the brokerage house, while it didn't pull in the $75,000 a year of his Boeing gold mine, was probably more demanding.

Now, finally, he had gotten smart and made the only ethical choice: he was coming to the rescue. Starting with this meal, he was going to share in the cooking and cleaning. And because his track record in that area was less than brilliant, he had signed them up for an *au pair* girl, a secret he would break to Lori over her favorite dessert, Haägen Dasz chocolate ice cream.

The way he saw it, tonight marked a real milestone in their relationship. They had been through hard times together, toughed it out and endured. He was giving up the siege mentality that had served its purpose but was no longer needed. He was going to start relaxing and enjoying family life. There would be some quality time with Lori in the bedroom, too, reminiscent of those peaceful afternoons before Sean was born and his troubles at Boeing began.

On the balcony he lit the grill and lingered at the railing to appreciate the fine view of Seattle. The clouds had broken to the west. It was incredible, he thought. After weeks of rain and sagging gray overcasts, there would be a proper sunset tonight at dinner. It was almost as if God were rewarding him for his efforts at self-improvement.

The telephone rang. He went inside to answer it, hoping Lori had not been talked into staying at the Overlie's for dinner.

"Hello."

"Wayne Jenkins?" inquired a slightly accented voice.

His heart sank. It was a voice from his past he had never wanted to hear again. "You know who I am, don't you?" the voice continued.

"I...Mr. Hecht?"

"That is correct, Wayne. I would like you to come to the downtown Hilton at once. Your old room, 2715, is booked in your name. We can chat comfortably there."

Wayne took a deep breath and tried to muster some courage. "Look, Mr. Hecht, this is a little awkward. It has nothing to do with you. It's just that I'm in the middle of cooking for a dinner party. Can't we do this some other time? Any other time at your convenience?"

"I'll be here another hour, Wayne. Whether you wish to come or not is entirely up to you."

"It's not up to me, Mr. Hecht."

"Then I'll look forward to seeing you shortly. Good evening."

Pilot's Dawn

Wayne stared at the receiver for a while, then scribbled a note to Lori about the late dinner he was planning for the two of them. He hurried with a pounding heart down to the garage.

As he drove toward the center of Seattle, he had to struggle keep his BMW in its lane. He thought about causing a bad accident, smashing head-on into a truck and killing himself, but he had thought the same thought so often it was too stale to motivate him.

It had been the year of his first big promotion when he fell into the pit, the year he got a little too full of himself. Lori was pregnant with Sean, and not having an easy time of it. Wayne started to cruise at night. At first he only drove, saying he was tense and needed to get out. But he soon got into the habit of stopping for a drink in one of the bars near the university.

He was 38 years old and somewhat thick around the middle, not trim and in shape like now. His face had become jowly and he was convinced the college girls saw him as a washed-up old man. Then she came out of nowhere and sat down beside him. Her name was Ingrid. She was a Danish exchange student, and talked freely about her problems getting used to life in the States. She said she had expected more of the university, the culture and above all, the Americans.

He told her she wasn't doing the right things or seeing the right people, and that he'd make sure she did if she'd let him. She was gorgeous, she was vulnerable, he had gotten lucky. He asked if they could get together next week so he could show her a more exhilarating side of America, one he promised she would like. She said she couldn't imagine anything nicer.

For their second meeting he took her on a drive along the coast and asked her if she wanted to sample the national drug, cocaine. The effect on her was swift and dramatic. She was up for everything. She wanted to make love to him, not out here in the wild but in a big bed in a fancy hotel downtown.

He took her to the Hilton, and for the next three months they continued, on her insistence, to use the same room—2715.

She was so needy, so beautiful, so hungry for him. He fell in love with her, took her on short secret trips he could not afford and went deeply into debt keeping her supplied with coke. When she complained about not having a car, he bought her a used MG. She was so happy it warmed his heart. He began to think about leaving his wife and yet unborn child.

One night that winter he came to the hotel and found a very different Ingrid sitting on the sofa where she always waited for him. Her long blond hair was up in a bun, she wore a black evening dress and diamond earrings. She looked stunning, sophisticated and ten years older.

"Ingrid, what's up? You look terrific. Have you got plans for us I don't know about?"

"Yes, Wayne. Were you able to buy the package?"

He dug in his raincoat pocket, feeling proud of the forceful manner in which he had conducted the transaction. "For you," he said, passing her the wrapped parcel and kissing her. She set it aside without bothering to look at it.

"Ingrid, is something wrong?"

"No." She got up and walked to the phone, dialed a number and hung up. It rang a few seconds later. "Wayne, would you get that please. It's for you. Talk to him politely. It will make things much easier."

"How do you know it's for me?"

Her appearance, her behavior, the package of cocaine she had sent him to buy…Could she have set him up? No, it was unimaginable. She was in love with him, no way she could have done the things she'd done if she wasn't. There would be some momentary complication, he thought, like an unannounced visit from her dad. He picked up the receiver.

"Yes?"

"Good evening, Wayne."

"Who is this?"

"My name is Mr. Hecht. Would you ask Ingrid to play back the videos for you now. I'll call again shortly."

"What the—" The line went dead.

"Did he have instructions for you, Wayne?" Ingrid asked.

"What's this about videos?"

She pressed the remote button. He noticed a VCR on top of the TV that didn't belong to the hotel's movie selection box. He was about to object when he saw himself on the screen, naked with her, doing things he had never done with another woman.

More shots from different evenings, his rage and panic not entirely able to dull their eroticism. At last he thought he had figured it out. She was going to create problems for him at home to make sure his marriage didn't stand between them.

"You don't need these, Ingrid," he said. "This is nonsense. I was going to leave my wife after the birth, you know that. Why would you do a thing like this?"

"You'll understand shortly, Wayne. It has nothing to do with your wife or the two of us."

"Ingrid…all I understand is that you have no business doing whatever you're doing. I'm going to take a walk. I'll call you tomorrow."

"If you leave, Wayne, the consequences will be needlessly cruel for Lori and, ultimately, for yourself."

"What the hell are you talking about?" he shouted. "I love you. Don't you love me? Why are you doing this?"

"Watch the television, Wayne. Mr. Hecht will be calling back soon to explain your options."

He glanced at the screen and winced. There he was, buying tonight's cocaine. Was she a narc or something? Jesus, what was going on?

He thought of his job at Boeing and shuddered. One picture like that sent to his boss, especially in light of his performance these past weeks, and he would be on the street.

The telephone rang.

"Go on," Ingrid said. "Talk to him. Your situation will be made very clear to you. It is not so bad, Wayne, once you get over the shock. The others have not had a problem with it, not a single one of them."

He picked up on the fifth ring. "Yes, what do you want?"

"Have you seen the tapes, Wayne? They are rather explicit."

The man's voice was pleasant and formally polite. He spoke English well though it was not his mother tongue.

"Look, if I ever get my hands on you, I'll—"

"You won't, Wayne, so let's not deal in hypotheticals. We want you to come to work for us. The work is neither dangerous nor demanding, and the compensation is excellent. If you look over on the table where Ingrid has placed your package, you'll see $50,000 in unmarked bills."

He glanced at the stack of banknotes and recoiled. This would not look good if it was being filmed. He surveyed the room for cameras but saw nothing. "Look, I don't know who you are or what you want, but I'm not interested. If you keep this up, I'll go to the police."

"I can understand your impulse, Wayne, but that would be most foolish of you. We hold all of the cards, as I think you'll agree if you take the time to reflect intelligently. The police in this city are rather a joke, certainly no match for us. Let me finish presenting our offer. Then you will have ten minutes to make your decision, Yes or No. May I?"

"I don't know. Okay, Jesus, go ahead."

"Thank you, Wayne. In addition to the $50,000 in this room, we have opened a numbered account accessible only to you in Liechtenstein. As soon as we have your Yes, we will deposit a quarter of a million dollars in that account. Or, if you prefer, you can have the rest of the money in cash."

"Look, whoever you are, I'm not interested in drug deals or federal prison. I—"

"It's a little late to think of that, Wayne. You've already done the drug deals, as several people are prepared to testify the moment I turn my material over to the D.A. In any case, my field is not drugs, as yours would seem to be, but information."

"What are you talking about?"

"In exchange for monetary compensation and our pledge to you of silence regarding your transgressions, you will agree to supply us from time to time with diskettes of Boeing's current commercial aircraft parts inventory. That's it, Wayne. No traps, no hidden agendas. If it's any consolation, you now have forty colleagues at Boeing who are helping us in one way or another. Not a single one of them was foolish enough to turn down our money or face the ugly personal consequences of not cooperating.

"Of course, Wayne, we do not pick our candidates at random. We research them well. We don't consider irrational types or wild-eyed patriots. We make our selections from healthy, balanced men and women who have a lot to lose and who are likely to make decisions in their own self interest. I would like you to talk with Ingrid, please. I'll call for your decision in ten minutes."

Wayne slammed the phone down and walked over to her, shaking with rage. "You mean it was all faked?"

"Of course not, Wayne. I enjoyed every second of it, as I'm sure you did. We are both winners. A win-win situation, as you Americans call it. And it will only improve. I hope we can make love tonight after your decision. I think you'll find you enjoy it even more now that you know I am not going to upset your life. You can have your wife and child, you can have me, and you can have the money. You can have it all."

"Yeah, right. Things don't usually work that way. Who the hell are you? Who do you work for?"

"I work for Mr. Hecht, Wayne, just as you will."

* * *

He turned off Sixth Avenue into the Hilton underground garage, still sick with fear, still overwhelmed by memories. He had gone to work for them, hadn't seen a way out. He had taken their money and lived in unrelenting terror that he would be caught.

Then a miracle happened: after several years of hell, Ingrid disappeared and Hecht's demands for information ceased. That was when he believed his interminable descent into hell was over. He straightened out his life, got promoted, rescued his marriage and grew to love his son. He was still making progress.

Now, five years later, the man he knew only as a voice on the telephone was back. Wayne wondered if Ingrid would be in the room, and whether he could resist her if she was. He felt aroused, which made him furious.

When he entered Room 2715, he was relieved but also a little disappointed to find it empty. He took two airline-size bottles of scotch from the bar, emptied them into a glass and drank. He could feel the ring of the telephone in his bone marrow seconds before it came. "Yes, hello."

"We'll make this quick, Wayne, so you can get back to your dinner party. Thanks for coming."

He had never heard Hecht sound so understanding. He tried not to feel relief but he did.

"Thanks, Mr. Hecht. It's an important night for me. What do you want me to do?"

"Nothing original. I need the inventory again. Bring the diskettes home with you Monday night. I'll send someone over to pick them up. Don't do anything stupid. It's the last request I shall make. It's almost over, Wayne. I realize it has been nerve-wracking for you."

"Well, not that bad, not really. There's no security on the inventory records. Sometimes I take them home myself to look them over. By the way, where is—"

"I'm sorry, Wayne, she's dead."

Pilot's Dawn

"Yes…well, I'll do as you say on Monday. Can I go now, Mr. Hecht?"
"Of course, Wayne."

*   *   *

Claussen gave a kid on his way home from little league ten bucks to go up to the Jenkins' door, ask for the package for Mr. Hecht, put it in his pocket and walk with it to the corner of 26th and West Fulton. He had his observation points carefully staked out, and knew long before the kid arrived that he was not being followed.

"Baseball cards," Claussen said, as he took the small package from his courier. "Very valuable. Thank you." He rolled up the window of his rental car and drove to the mixed neighborhood around the Wallinford waterfront.

In the gathering dusk he bumped up the back ally to the delivery entrance of Stein's Tool and Die. Karl Stein must have been watching for him. The gray metal bay door with matching spray-painted windows went up, and Claussen drove inside.

Stein came out of the office wearing a shop apron. His face was taut, as if the skin covering his bony features had shrunk. His hand felt like a leathery vice when they shook.

"Hello, Karl," Claussen said.

"Back again already, Walter? You're not joking about this resurgence?"

"I have been authorized by Volkov to advance you two hundred thousand dollars, with another three hundred thousand to follow when you have completed your tasks. Does that sound like a joke?"

"I'm sick of talk. The world has changed, Walter. It's cash, or I don't work."

Good, thought Claussen. Stein did not know of Volkov's death. Stein was afraid of Volkov, always had been. This piece of luck would make dealing with him easier. "Cash or you don't work? Is that a fact?"

"You heard me. Take the cement job here. Volkov promised me he'd pay for it. I go out, get the bids, arrange the job and what happens? The bastard sends me nothing. So here I am living on a dynamite keg I can't leave. You know the truth, Walter? He thinks if I sit on it long enough, I'll get scared and use my own money. I'd rather have my ass blown into orbit."

"You're wrong about Volkov, Karl. He has authorized the fifty thousand for the cement job and paid for it up front. One of your assignments is to get it done while I'm here."

"The son of a bitch doesn't trust me? He could have sent me the money."

"Let's concentrate on the present," Claussen said. He opened the trunk of his car, took out a brown paper bag and passed it to Stein. "Your advance. There will be more later. This will cover your first payment and the cement job."

Stein dug into the bundles of banknotes, visibly astounded. "Okay," he said, holding one of the bundles up to the light. "I apologize for being an *Arschloch*. We'll have some dinner. The refrigerator's full of cold cuts. There's a Polish bakery across the street. He's a lousy Jew but he makes good rye. When do I get the rest?"

"We should be finished in a couple of days."

Stein permitted himself a stunted smile.

*   *   *

After dinner they removed the hidden vault panels and entered the second basement, a level below the regular shop basement. The cement bunker was as clean as Stein's apron.

The lighting was good, the air pleasantly dry. Claussen could hear the dehumidification system humming as smoothly as it had when they had installed it over 30 years ago. Along the walls were labeled bins on stout metal shelves. In appearance, it was a parts inventory like any other.

Looking at it, Claussen shook his head. One could not imagine the amount of work this room represented, productive work, smart work, his work. Good that it would be used in some small degree before the cement trucks arrived. He was human. When that first plane went down, he had felt the satisfaction of a man whose labor has not been in vain.

On the workbench, he booted his portable computer and inserted Wayne's inventory diskette. He placed the diskette containing the current inventory of Pratt & Whitney jet engine parts to the side. He had received it by express mail that morning from a collaborator inside the engine manufacturer's Hartford plant. He would not need it for a couple of hours.

While his software searched the Boeing parts inventory for the item he had specified—a set of 767-300 ER engine mounting bolts—he instructed Stein to get the counterfeiter ready.

The somber gray press was a hybrid industrial stamper with multiple dials and settings, a masterpiece of German precision tool making from the pre-computer days. It could flawlessly reproduce the manufacturer's serial number on any of the 322 modified parts his operation had assembled over its 30-year life span.

The counterfeiter had been built in the early 1960s, but it was designed to accommodate new print faces, characters and number-letter combinations so that it would not become obsolete with the introduction of new aircraft models.

Volkov had sent Dr. Stahlwetter, the man who conceived the device, to Seattle every year until 1990. Working with Stein, he had checked and serviced the machine, then used the tool and die shop to make any new plates needed to keep up with changes in the industry.

Since Stahlwetter's last vist, there had been no changes in Boeing's numbering practices. The counterfeiter was thus able to deal with parts for all of the company's commercial aircraft now in service. Volkov had never activated the sabotage capabilities of Operation 26, so the stamper, while maintained in perfect condition, had not been used until the Atlanta demonstration. Nor would it ever be used again after tonight. What they were doing right now had historical significance. For Claussen, this made it an experience worth savoring.

"Ready," Stein said. "Give me the serial number, then the date code, in that order. We'll triple check before we imprint."

Claussen read from the computer screen, jotting down the long numbers as he spoke. He passed the paper to Stein and stood up briskly. "I'll find the corresponding part."

The bolts were on the shelf where they had sat undisturbed for the past five years, packaged in groups of four. Claussen carried one package to the workbench. He watched Stein finish up with the settings, check the numbers against those he had jotted down on his sheet of paper and place the first bolt onto the stamping platform. The muscles in his forearms rippled with effort, his veins stood out, the skin over his cheeks drew taut as drum leather.

He aligned the bolt, clamped it in position, then ran a trial by inking the plate and applying feather light pressure to the arm. He rechecked the accuracy of his numbers yet another time against those on the paper and on the computer screen, then pulled down the long handle of the press for the permanent imprint.

Stein removed the bolt, blew on it and examined his handiwork. He inhaled deeply and let out a long breath. "Well, Walter?"

Claussen bent over and studied the serial number. "I would say, Karl, that it is flawless."

Stein chuckled. "The investigators will be on a wild goose chase for years trying to find out who fucked the metallurgy. If you come across the reports I'd like to see them."

"Of course, Karl."

"By the way, you haven't told me Volkov's reasoning. Why is he doing this now? Operation Twenty-Six is obviously dead. What's in it for him?"

"I didn't come to here to chat, Karl. Briefly, it has to do with the disruption of East-West relations. He and his followers see such disruption as their only chance to seize power from the reformers."

"You mean the Americans will know who did it?"

"Never. But there will be suspicions. And suspicions, as you know, can be more corrosive to good will than facts. If you're interested, we can talk about these things later. We've got work to do now, Karl. A lot of it."

Stein said, "I guess I'm not interested, Walter. When the DDR was involved, that was one thing. I don't give a damn about Russia. That's Volkov's domain. What about you? Do you really care what happens to those bastards?"

"I work for myself now, just as you do. Get going, please."

Stein stamped the remaining bolts, then began work on the more sophisticated electrical and hydraulic components. Last came the modified GE, Pratt & Whitney and Bendix parts Claussen planned to slip into the parts stream on his drive east.

By two o'clock in the morning they were finished. Upstairs, Stein poured them each a double shot of clear schnapps and downed his as he always did, without holding it in his mouth.

* * *

Stein asked about the agenda for tomorrow. Claussen spelled out Stein's tasks: the stencils he would make for the lettering on the van, the disguises he would put together, the driving he would do and the arrangements he would make for the cementing job the morning after.

It was going to be a busy day, Claussen said, and Stein could expect him to be in and out. There were three former collaborators at Boeing he still had to interview. There were security systems to research, and documents he had not been able to complete in Berlin to forge. And there was the apartment of an Iraqi student, Hassan Aziz, to visit.

A busy day, Claussen repeated, and he hadn't told Stein the half of it.

Chapter Eleven

Nicole awoke before dawn, put on her running clothes and went downstairs to make coffee. She was heating milk when Francoise, the housekeeper, stomped into the kitchen. "Here, let me do that," she said, pushing Nicole aside. "Why, young lady, are you up so early?"

Nicole shrugged her shoulders and sat down.

Francoise, a severe, humorless woman in her sixties, had come to the Michelet household a year before Nicole's birth. Like her boss, she was a stickler for tradition and a firm believer in the value of a strict religious upbringing. She equated laughter with frivolity, and joy with sin.

Nicole's mother had died of a sudden illness when Nicole was seven. Michelet shipped Nicole off to the convent school at Sainte Geneviève shortly after the funeral. Each night the nuns made her pray herself to sleep; each night she wept and asked God why He had allowed her gentle mother to die, why He had not come for her cruel housekeeper instead.

When Nicole was 15, she reached the conclusion that nobody, not even God, wanted to deal with Francoise. That was when she decided that God was a coward and she'd better start learning how to live for herself. She wasn't sure she had made much progress in the last four years, but she was trying.

Francoise put a *café au lait* bowl down hard in front of her, poured it half full of strong black coffee and added the hot milk. She put the silver sugar bowl down even harder. Francoise and her father shared the irritating habit of putting things down hard when they were displeased.

"I asked you a question, young lady. When I ask a question, I expect a courteous answer. Why are you up so early?"

Nicole sipped her coffee, wishing she had gone directly to the beach. "I haven't been sleeping well lately, all right? What about you? There's nothing for you to do around here. You should sleep till noon. Why are *you* up so early?"

Francoise glared at her.

Nicole stretched her legs and wiggled the tips of her running shoes. "Well, Francoise, I asked you a question. I didn't hear *your* courteous answer. I guess your manners are as bad as mine."

"Don't get smart with me, mademoiselle. I don't like the way you've been acting lately. I've got a good mind to telephone your father in Paris."

Nicole got up and started for the door. "Go right ahead. You both seem to forget I'm nineteen years old."

"I'm going to inform him of your doubles games with the new tennis instructor. I don't think your father realizes he is an American."

"What difference does it make where he was born? He's a human being, isn't he? Or does God's love for his children stop at the borders of France? Besides, Francoise, I haven't been playing with him. It's been me and Jules *against* him and Luc."

"Madame Hersault called yesterday to report that you've been laughing yourself to tears right out there in public."

"She called to gossip and start rumors, and you know it. So what if I've been laughing? I'm having fun for a change. Steven is a breath of fresh air after the sour reign of King Philippe."

"Philippe Denis du Pèage is an upstanding man of noble birth. I would not be surprised if he is on your father's list of eligible candidates for your hand."

"He's a *crétin* with political connections. I'd drown myself before I'd marry him."

"Do you know something, young lady? You've taken a wrong turn since you graduated from Sainte Geneviève."

"Those godless unwashed radicals at the Sorbonne must have led me astray. Sorry. I'm beyond redemption."

"Do you *want* me to telephone your father?"

"No, Francoise. I just want you to leave me alone. I'll be at the beach. Good-bye."

* * *

Nicole parked her little Renault above the harbor at St. Jean-Cap-Ferrat. In summers past, Uncle Robert and Aunt Jeanne, her mother's sister, docked their sailboat here, the space having been provided by a pier owner who treated all relatives of Michelet like visiting royalty. This would have been a perfect morning to take the *Soleil de Nice* out. Too bad the older brother of Jules and Luc, her cousin Gérard, had sailed it to England this summer.

For a few minutes, she watched the fishing boats leaving the craggy harbor, their lanterns burning dimly against the gray summer dawn. These people who lived by the sea had a tough life, but she admired them. They were proud and free. And when you encountered them in town or at the market, you sensed how spontaneous they were with their joy and anger, how in tune with the gritty emotions of life. They were her brothers and sisters in spirit, she thought, just as her new American friend was. Among people like these, life in all its untidiness was God. If you brought Francoise down here to lecture the people on right and wrong, they'd throw her and her laxatives off the dock.

The walls of Nicole's prison were collapsing; she could feel them coming down a little more each day. Her father and Francoise had lost her—to life.

She took a steep path down to the beach and walked east toward Monte Carlo. The gray water lapped hungrily at the pebble shore-line. Gulls began to swoop. The horizon where the sun would rise glowed with streaks of orange and gold.

She picked up the pace, jogged a little until the sun was all the way up, then sat on a rock, hugged her knees and watched the sky and sea to the south slowly turn blue. The waves began to roll up on the beach, the morning's first breeze felt cool and moist on her skin.

It was the second week of August. Summer would be over soon, she thought, and they would be returning to their home in Paris. Father would be immersed in politics, Francoise would be condemning her with every breath she took. At the university, she would be pursued by men who wanted something from her: sex, notoriety, a chance to take a slap at her right-wing father by debasing his daughter. And now that the press had discovered how photogenic she was, the paparazzi would be hiding in toilets and bushes. If she mentioned any hint of trouble, her father would add a coterie of secret service agents to her entourage. And Steven, she assumed, would be going back to States. Not that she was disheartened. She had a mission, which was to break the stranglehold of her father and housekeeper on her life. She was looking forward to getting on with it. Once she succeeded, she would find her own way to come to terms with her problems. Still, it wouldn't be easy. She had better enjoy these last two weeks in the south.

The tide was rising. She took off her shoes and kicked her feet in the water. She was nineteen years old, had kissed only a cousin and had slept with no one. She found herself wondering at the oddest moments what it would be like.

If only she had the courage, she thought, she would give in to her curiosity. Steven would be the perfect "first man." He treated her like a human being rather than an object, he didn't make a lot of rude advances like her compatriots, and he made her laugh. It wouldn't have to be some heavy, apocalyptic, *Sturm und Drang* type of thing where lives were destroyed and souls lacerated by guilt. She could just say, "Why don't we do it?" They could laugh about it later, whether it worked out or not.

Pilot's Dawn

She kicked the water again. The tide had come in while she was fantasizing. She would have to swim back to shore. No use rushing; she was going to get her running clothes soaked whatever she did. She sat a little longer and wondered if her upbringing would prevent her in some odd unconscious way from experiencing physical ecstasy. Her body seemed to tell her it would not.

Why was she assuming she did not have the courage? Was it just an old worn-out reflex from her years of mental enslavement? Perhaps.

She imagined herself naked in his arms, laughing. She began to feel breathless. This was crazy. Francoise was right. She had changed. Something new and exciting was happening to her, and it was happening even faster than Nicole had realized.

* * *

"I hate Arabs," Stein said. He kept squeezing and releasing the steering wheel like he was doing isometric exercises. "How did you stand the smell in there?"

Claussen was beside him in the passenger seat of their Chevy cargo van, reviewing security codes he had been given by Lou Quinn, a Boeing collaborator of 23 years. He glanced at the speedometer. "Please slow down. You're four miles an hour over the limit. I don't want us stopped. We're behind as it is."

"Because you had to wait for that *stinkender* Arab to go out. What was so important about getting into his place? I don't get it. He was just some dumb student."

Claussen waited until the speedometer dropped to 55. "There was a document I wanted him to have, Karl."

"Is that all you're going to say? What kind of a document? I don't like it when you just sit there."

It was two o'clock in the morning, the traffic was sparse. The freeway dipped beneath an overpass. Claussen saw a police car prowling the shadows above. He glanced at Stein to see if he had noticed it. Light from road signs flickered across his bony face, making it hard to read his expression.

"Okay, okay," Stein said. "You don't have to stare at me. You were right about the speed. It doesn't make you God. Are you going to tell me about the document or not?"

"What's happening to your nerves, Karl?"

"Fuck you. My nerves are fine. If you don't want to talk, don't talk."

"I had planned to fill you in. I believe we're on the same team."

"We'd better be. For both our sakes."

"Precisely."

"So let's hear about the goddamned document."

"After the Gulf War, Karl, the Iraqis came up with a plan to heist parts from Boeing. The embargo was crippling their fleet of jumbos, and Hussein didn't want to take it sitting down. It was a decent plan, considering the limitations of their intelligence network. The Americans, as usual, were in the dark. Unfortunately for the Iraqis, they chose to consult Volkov."

Stein switched on the radio, and Claussen switched it off.

"Try to relax, Karl. It will be over soon."

"It's not me who's up tight. Go on. I was listening."

"Obviously, any attempted theft of aircraft parts by foreign agents would have led to tighter security at Boeing and elsewhere. This would not have served the interests of Operation Twenty-Six. Volkov asked me to make certain the Iraqi plan never got off the ground."

Stein started to reach for the radio dial, then jerked his hand back as if he had touched hot metal. "Go on, will you? You don't have to stop talking every time I move."

"There were two Iraqi agents involved. When I entered their hotel room in San Diego I found a faxed list of maintenance parts for Iraqi Airways' 747s. I filed that list away as I would have any intelligence-related document."

Pilot's Dawn

"Did it stink in the hotel room?"

"No, Karl, it smelled of expensive cologne."

"So what did you do to those guys?"

"That's unimportant."

"I hope you castrated them."

"You're up to fifty-eight."

"Okay, all right. Fill in the blanks, would you?"

"Of course, Karl. Tonight, in addition to our primary job, we are going to be selecting and loading 747 parts from my copy of that list. The document I planted this evening was the original list. When the FBI finds it buried among Hassan Aziz'es notes on political economy, this case will move to the trial stage. In the minds of the authorities it will be solved, irrespective of whether a conviction is won. I hope this explains the importance of the break-in."

Stein gave a hoarse, truncated laugh. "Smart, Walter. I'm glad to know you've been thinking about my future."

Claussen craned his neck and looked at the speedometer again. Stein was driving exactly 55. "Our future, Karl."

"What about the van? Feel like telling me?"

"If you're interested. It belonged to Operation Twenty-Six. I loaned it to one of our insider friends when I moved to Germany. He put the title in his name for licensing and insurance purposes. He of course had no objection to my using it for a couple of days."

"Wait till he gets it back with COLE DEHUMIDIFICATION SYSTEMS stenciled on the sides." Stein slapped his thigh and laughed like a Bavarian.

Claussen watched him, silently, sternly.

Stein said, "Knock it off, Walter. I'm not an idiot. It was just a thought. A funny thought. Sort of like the one I had when I heard about your car wreck."

They were ten minutes from the facility. Stein was growing more nervous by the second. Claussen wanted to keep him talking until they arrived. "Well?"

"Well, I thought of this man who loses control of his Mercedes on a stormy night and runs head-on into a concrete bridge abutment. His wife is killed. She's the passenger, and she's always refused to wear her seat belt."

Stein's hoarse laughter vibrated over the noise of the road. He sounded half insane.

Let him talk, thought Claussen, *let him talk*.

"Anyway, Walter, I'm sure you want to know about the driver. He gets out and walks away, not even scratched. This is because his Mercedes has a driver's side air bag. That's the best one I've heard yet. A driver's side air bag! You even fooled Volkov. He told me he was worried you might crack up after she died."

Stein chuckled to himself. "He thought you loved her, Walter. Did you ever tell him what really happened? Did you ever tell him you were just tidying up before you went home?"

Claussen checked the side-view mirror and smiled thinly. He had guessed right: Stein suspected he might try to tidy up again.

He said, "I don't believe I would have risked it in a Chevy van. Please drive safely, Karl. We're almost there."

✶ ✶ ✶

At 2:08 a.m. they stopped at the checkpoint to Boeing's huge commercial parts depot north of the Sea-Tac airport. A persistent drizzle misted their windshield and glistened on the barbed-wire fence. Wind rippled puddles in the deserted parking lot.

Two guards were in the ultra-modern security hut, alert and robust young men. One of them stepped outside. Stein rolled down his window.

"Thanks for coming," the guard said. "The super thinks we've got a freon leak. Sent the third shift boys packing almost before they clocked in."

"He probably did the right thing," Claussen said. "We'll have it fixed in a couple of hours."

"You'd better. The morning shift's coming to work at eight, leak or no leak. Sign in while I have a look in back." The guard passed his clipboard to Stein, and walked to the rear of the van.

While Stein signed the name of one of the two Cole Dehumidification Systems employees they had researched, Claussen kept his eye on the guard in the booth. The man was watching them with more than casual interest.

"Hey, nighthawks!" shouted the guard at the back of the van, "it's locked."

"I'm coming," Claussen said. "Just a minute." He signed the clipboard, took the keys from the ignition and jumped down.

The man in the guard booth stiffened when Claussen came toward him. Claussen held up the clipboard. "Want it?"

The guard looked around suspiciously, then opened. Claussen handed him the clipboard and slipped the stiletto into his sternum in the same motion.

The guard looked down, wide-eyed, then slumped silently to the floor.

Stein climbed down from the other side of the van and patted his breast pockets. "Jesus Christ," he grumbled loudly. "Did you bring the work order, Mack?"

The other guard looked around from behind the van. "Hey, get your butt back here and open the door. It's raining."

"Take it easy," Claussen said, strolling up to him. "This isn't New York." He put his key in the lock and pulled the door open.

The guard shined his flashlight into the luggage compartment, presenting his back while he stared, perplexed, at a small load of aircraft parts.

Claussen struck quickly, burying the stiletto between his shoulder blades and giving it a precise upward twist to cut the aorta. When he shoved the guard inside, the man writhed forward on his stomach.

Claussen closed the door and tossed the keys back to Stein. "Pull forward across the white line and wait."

While the van idled at the entrance gate, Claussen ducked into the booth. He stepped over the swelling pool of blood, pulled the first guard inside and relieved him of his massive key ring.

He took a moment to get his bearings, then sat at the security control panel and typed the codes he had reviewed during the drive: dock alarms off, internal alarms off, bay doors unlocked.

Minutes later they were inside the massive facility. It took them less than half an hour to exchange the bogus parts for their same-numbered twins. The rest of their allotted time, until 3:15 a.m., they spent loading 747 parts, the decoy, from the old Iraqi list.

From the parts depot, they drove on dark, rain-slick secondary roads to the university district. When they arrived in front of Hassan Aziz'es apartment, Claussen moved his rental Buick and Stein parked the van in the space.

Working in the blustery night like stevedores accustomed to each other's rhythms, they loaded the Boeing parts that they had replaced with counterfeits into the trunk of the Buick. The much larger quantity of 747 parts—the diversion—they left in the van.

At 4:22 a.m., eight minutes ahead of schedule, they drove into the loading bay of Stein's Tool and Die and carried the untainted Boeing parts meant to disappear forever to the second basement. When they were finished, Claussen opened the Buick door and started to get in.

"Hey, just a minute," Stein barked. "Just a minute. When are you coming back here with the rest of my money?"

"I told you, Karl, I've got four people to pay off ahead of you. It won't be later than seven thirty."

Pilot's Dawn

"Yeah, well don't get tied up. The cement trucks'll be here at eight, and the wops want payment in advance. Let's be clear on one thing. You're not going to pull Volkov's trick on me. If you aren't here, we don't pour."

"I'll be here." Claussen got in the car and gently closed the door.

Stein banged on the window. "Goddammit, Walter, give me back my garage door opener. You don't need it anymore."

"On the contrary, Karl. If you fall asleep, I don't intend to be stranded in the alley. I'll see you shortly."

Claussen pressed the button on the opener while Stein glared at him. The gray metal door with the spray-painted windows clanked open, and he drove into the wet night.

Chapter Twelve

Squinting over his sleeping wife, Wayne Jenkins tried to read the dial of their alarm clock. It was 4:53 a.m. and he hadn't slept a wink all night. He felt miserable. His mind had trapped him in a maze of useless mental activity he could only escape by getting out of bed. Easier said than done. He was exhausted. He dreaded the thought of a day on the job with too little sleep.

Maybe he should give up the fight and take a couple of Lori's Halcion sleeping pills. He had struggled for months to get off the stuff after Ingrid and Mr. Hecht had disappeared. His doctor told him that if he started again he would get hooked immediately, and the withdrawal would be even more painful the second time around. But what was he supposed to do?

Decided, then. He would take two Halcions and leave Lori a note asking her to call his secretary at Boeing when she got up. If he went to work at eleven, rested, he would accomplish more than he would in his present state in a month.

Lori was breathing deeply, evenly. He slipped quietly out of bed and walked to the bathroom, trying to convince himself he was being reasonable rather than weak. He knew where the pills were: he had scouted the medicine cabinet the night before. He took two, plus a sliver his wife had shaved off a third.

When he turned on the light in the kitchen, there was a crash in the living room. It sounded as if someone had tripped over the coffee table. He froze. Was Sean up already? No, he wouldn't be sitting out there in the dark.

Pilot's Dawn

He heard the floor squeak.

His heart started to beat more rapidly. How long till the Halcion worked? A half hour, an hour? He wished it would hurry. There were always harmless little noises at night. They sounded ominous, and you always felt a jolt of adrenaline when you heard them, but they were never anything to worry about.

Yet there was always that doubt until you knew for sure.

He felt a chill go down his spine. He wanted to return to the bedroom, crawl under the covers and hide his head.

The leather sofa emitted a tiny groan, a sound he knew well. Someone—or something—was in the living room. But who? What? The doors and windows were locked, he'd been careful to make sure of that ever since he had been summoned to the Hilton. The chances of a burglar were minimal. Maybe an animal had crawled down the chimney, or Sean was sleep-walking.

Just find out what it is and you can go to bed.

He started toward the hallway.

He smelled tobacco. A rush of horror took his breath away. There *was* an intruder in his house. He wished he had a gun. He wanted to flee out the back door but how could he? His wife and son were asleep in the house.

He grabbed the fire extinguisher they kept wedged in the space beside the fridge and tiptoed down the hallway to the living room. He flicked on the light switch and his blood froze. A stranger was sitting on the sofa, casually smoking a cigarette.

He wasn't armed, thank God for that. Wayne jerked the safety ring from the extinguisher. "What the hell are you doing in my house?"

"Good morning, Wayne. Have a seat, please. I would like to do this quietly. No need disturbing the others."

Wayne put a hand on the book case to steady himself. It was the voice from his endless nightmare.

"Mr. Hecht," he stammered. "What are you doing here? Do you need more information?"

The man smiled pleasantly. He had thin lips and hair combed straight back. He looked very cosmopolitan, very poised. "No, Wayne. You have met your last obligation."

"Then *why* are you here?"

"You must be quiet, Wayne, very quiet. If you make a sound, you will leave me no choice. Do the right thing, Wayne. Put the extinguisher down. Save your wife and son."

"What the hell are you talking about? Tell me what you want. Just tell me. You know me. You know I'll do it."

"I told you, Wayne. Put the extinguisher down."

"Listen, Mr. Hecht. Be reasonable. I gave you everything you wanted. I'll never talk."

Hecht laughed softly. "Are you begging for your life, Wayne?"

He was shaking violently now, he couldn't hide it. If he was going to fight, he'd better do it before he passed out. He readied the extinguisher. "I'm begging you to get out of here."

"Shhh! The others."

Wayne gaped, paralyzed, as Hecht slid a long slender switch blade from his pocket. He snapped it open, then picked up a sofa cushion with his free hand.

"Drop the extinguisher, Wayne," he whispered.

Wayne gritted his teeth and squeezed the trigger. A stream of foam shot out of the nozzle. Hecht backed up in slow motion, protecting his face with the cushion.

The stream soon fizzled, and Hecht threw his shield into the heap of foam on the floor. He was angry, his face contorted with silent rage.

"Wayne?" Lori called from the bedroom. "Wayne, are you all right?"

"Get out of the house!" he shouted. "Run for help."

"Wayne! What's wrong?"

Pilot's Dawn

She was coming, he could hear her bare footsteps on the parquet floor. He could also see Hecht, a foam man with a clean face and a malevolent smile circling like a panther to the point where the hallway opened into the living room.

"Lori, watch out! Stop!"

"Wayne!" She ignored him, came toward him, sleepy-eyed and confused.

Hecht pounced on her from behind. It all happened so quickly Wayne wasn't sure he had hurt her. Then she fell and he saw the blood spurt from her back.

Sean burst into the room, looked around and started screaming at the top of his lungs.

Wayne no longer knew what he was doing. He hurled the heavy metal extinguisher at Hecht's head. Hecht ducked out of the way. Wayne picked up an end table.

"Run, Sean!" he cried. "Run!"

Before the boy could flee, Hecht caught him by the hair, yanked his head back and slit his throat. Sean made a gurgling sound as Hecht shoved him away.

"You've made a mess of it, Wayne. It was not very courageous of you. But you're a nice fellow, even Ingrid thought so. I hope you'll forgive me if I shower in your home and borrow some of your clothes. Now, take your shot. Let's get it over with. I'm on a tight schedule."

Hecht was moving slowly, deliberately toward him, stiletto drawn.

Wayne hurled the end table. Hecht stepped out of its path and kept on coming. Wayne bolted for the terrace door. He hadn't gone two steps when he felt a slight thump between his shoulder blades. A burning sensation shot through his back and chest, not acute, not horribly painful. His vision blurred. He knew he was falling but it felt more like floating on air. When he hit the parquet floor he heard the crack of his head, a distant muffled sound. He could see his hands in front of him. They were clawing at the corner of an area rug, though he had not told them to claw. Then he watched them stop clawing, though he had not told them to stop, and darkness engulfed him.

*   *   *

After Claussen had driven off with the garage door opener, Stein went to the kitchen and took his bottle of clear schnapps from the refrigerator. He placed it on the formica table but did not open it. He would have a drink after he went over his pro-versus-con list one more time.

His doubts about Claussen had started when the son of a bitch said he was working for himself. If that was true, thought Stein, pacing the length of the room, why would Claussen bother to pay him another $300,000 for a job he had already done? Because they were both from the eastern part of Germany? Because they had served the same cause for 30 years?

Give me a break.

Claussen was going to come back to the shop, but it wouldn't be to pay him. It would be to kill him. Stein wasn't an idiot. He could see the handwriting on the wall.

They were pouring the second basement full of concrete because Operation 26 was over. They wouldn't be needing the aircraft parts any longer—which meant they wouldn't be needing Stein. He would be a liability, a useless leftover who might rat if he got caught.

Who could say, maybe he would. Old allegiances went to hell when everyone was out for himself. The idiots were the ones who kept on believing in loyalty. Loyalty to what?

He had played dumb until now, but he had not *been* dumb. The proof of this was in the pudding. When Claussen pulled into the loading bay, Stein would greet the arrogant bastard with a stream of .38 bullets. The way he saw it, someone was going down to his concrete grave

Pilot's Dawn

this morning. The only question was *who*, and Stein intended to make sure it wasn't him.

A lot of pros, but what were the cons to eliminating Claussen? The rental car? Not really. He'd drive it back where it came from during the after-hours drop.

Claussen was traveling in the States with multiple identities, all of them bogus. He had shown Stein a few of his passports and matching driver's licenses, and they were as good as in the old days. This meant Claussen still had access to the KGB or Stasi forging apparatus. The man who had flown to the United States on Lufthansa was not the man who had rented the Buick; and the man who had rented the Buick was not the man who had booked the hotel room wherever Claussen was staying. And none of the men were Claussen. If someone who did not exist disappeared, the authorities would not miss him—at least not the American authorities.

Who would?

Only those who knew Claussen was here.

Stein stopped pacing, took a glass from the cupboard and tapped it on the table. This meant Volkov, which *was* a problem. He would send someone over, or come himself, to find out what had happened to his ace. It would be a monumental pain the ass. He didn't relish the thought of lying to that prick.

But how bad could it be? Most of the modified aircraft parts that they had given serial numbers to would soon be in circulation. Several huge air disasters in quick succession would create enough havoc in the U.S. to make Operation 26 a success.

The key was this: Volkov didn't personally give a damn about his agents anymore than Claussen did. As long as the mission came off, any credible story Stein concocted to explain Claussen's disappearance would be accepted.

He uncorked the schnapps, corked it back up and started pacing again. Let's come at it from the other side, he thought. What if he was wrong? What if Claussen planned to pay him off and go back to Germany? What were the disadvantages of killing him under these circumstances?

Same as before: the bother of having to answer to Volkov, the return of the rental car. Avoiding these minor hassles was hardly worth the risk of waiting around to find out if his suspicions were justified. Claussen was a cunning son of a bitch you didn't want to underestimate. He could turn the tables on you at the eleventh hour. Stein had seen it happen to others. The way to deal with him was exactly as Stein had planned. He would hide in the bay and let Claussen have it the instant he got out of his car.

When would Claussen be back? He'd said seven thirty, so it wouldn't be then. Perhaps six, perhaps nine. The best thing for Stein to do was to be ready for anything. He would go to the bay now and wait. If he fell asleep, it wouldn't matter. The noisy metal door going up would wake him in plenty of time.

He felt better. He had his direction. Claussen had finally run up against a man with the brains and courage to challenge him. It would, he thought, be satisfying to see the expression on that arrogant bastard's face when he realized he had been outmaneuvred for the first—and last—time in his life.

Stein heard a car in the alley. A dog barked. He started for his revolver but the car went on past.

Five thirty, and already he was jumpy.

He poured himself his usual double shot and belted it down as he always did, not holding it in his mouth.

He knew the instant he swallowed.

He tried to spit it out. Nothing came up, not even saliva. He jammed two fingers down his throat to induce vomiting. All he produced was a searing belch that reeked of bitter almonds.

A fire like a river of molten iron followed the course of the cyanide down into his stomach, consuming him from inside out. He clutched his neck with both hands, a fiery rage boiling within his pain, and dropped to his knees.

His lungs stopped working. He could do nothing, absolutely nothing, he was suffocating and burning to death at the same time. For a man who considered helplessness life's greatest indignity, it was a hell of a way to go.

✶ ✶ ✶

"So Angie gets me up from lunch," Joey DiStefano shouted over the growl of the diesel. "When Angie gets me up from lunch, I know it's important. She's not stupid enough to bother me if it ain't." The ride of the fully laden McNeilus mixer was loud and bumpy.

"Why'd she do that?" asked his nephew, Chuckie Stafford. He had been trying his best all summer to learn the business.

"Because there's this foreign guy on the phone, won't get off and won't call back. He says he's willing to pay cash if we can move quickly. He's got the insurance money in hand, someone at State Farm has recommended us, and he wants the job done **now**."

"What's his rush, Uncle?"

"The way I understood it, he's got this second-level basement under his shop that should never have been built. Too close to the water table. The lower foundation started to sink and crack, and now the whole shop's about to be condemned. The guy had the city engineers from Building Inspections out and they said, Forget the steel beams, you gotta use concrete. You gotta give up on that space and fill it in."

"No shit?"

"No shit. So he's nervous now, thinking if he doesn't fill it in today his shop's gonna sink to where all he's got's a roof. Let's pretend I'm on vacation and you're running the business and you're booked solid for the next week. How do you deal with this guy, Chuckie?"

"I tell him I'll do it tomorrow and get a deposit, then I do it when I get time."

Joey grabbed his nephew's cheek and pinched him until he let out a howl. "You got your payroll to meet and a family to feed, Chuckie. You got three car payments, a two-grand-a-month mortgage and a daughter in private school who changes wardrobes more often than you change underwear. Who eats up most of your money?"

"I don't know. The house, the cars."

"Wrong. Uncle Sam. You got a guy willing to pay cash for a seven hundred yard job, you put everyone else off. You give him a little break, try to talk him out of a receipt. You save maybe ten grand on a job like this by not having the IRS vulturing in on the proceeds. Cash and no receipt, Chuckie. The opportunity don't come along often, but when it does, you jump on it."

"I'll jump, Uncle. But how do you know this guy'll settle for no receipt?"

"I don't, Chuckie, not for sure. But think about it. He's got his insurance money, he won't be deducting the job from his taxes. We cut him a two grand break, he puts it in *his* pocket."

"I get it. Good thinking, Uncle."

"You might learn this business yet, kid. I hope I'm not too old to take a vacation when you do."

Joey eased the cement mixer over a stretch of rough road. He stuck his arm out the window and motioned for the convoy of mixers following him to slow down. "Goddamn city," he said. "They ought to be ordering some of this stuff themselves."

* * *

Claussen, feeling fresh and renewed, dropped his rental Buick off at the airport and walked with his travel bag to the cab stand. He took a twenty minute ride to Will's Diner, a block from Stein's shop, and forced himself to eat an American breakfast of steak and eggs. He waited in the alley behind the shop until a scavenging bum moved on to the next row of garbage cans, then used the garage door opener. Once inside the shop, he closed and locked the bay door.

Stein, he thought, was the only person he had ever seen who looked the same dead as alive. Claussen fished out his keys and wallet, then dragged, carried, rolled and bounced the corpse into the second basement. He brought up the two dozen Bendix, Pratt & Whitney and GE parts they had stamped serial numbers on but not yet put into the parts stream, carried them to the adjoining garage and placed them carefully in the trunk of Stein's Audi.

The car's registration was current. Claussen compared it to his bogus Washington State driver's license, which he had made for himself before leaving Germany. The forgery was in Stein's name but bore Claussen's photograph. The data match was perfect.

He lifted the hood to check the oil and water. The engine was spotless, the oil on the dipstick clean as honey.

In Stein's apartment above the shop, he found the dead man's passport, identical except for the photograph to the one Claussen now carried. He would get rid of it. He didn't want two passports with the same I.D. number in circulation any more than two aircraft parts with the same serial number.

Little precautions made big differences.

He turned off all the appliances, prepared a neat "Closed for Remodeling" sign and taped it to the inside of the front window glass. None too soon. He could hear the cement mixers rumbling toward the shop like an armored column.

He glanced at his watch: 8:00 a.m. Nothing to do before he left but unlock the old coal chute cover and pay the men.

Joey stopped the cement truck in the alley as Stein had told him to do. "Get out, Chuckie," he shouted over the growl of the mixer. "Wipe the mortar off your ass and observe. Collecting is the hardest part of the job. How am I gonna leave you in charge of the business if you don't know how to collect?"

The two men, one in his late forties with graying sideburns and a pot belly, and the other a handsome young thin-hipped hotshot of twenty, climbed down from the idling truck and walked up to the bay door. Chuckie looked around for a bell, then beat on the sheet metal with his fist.

"Hey, cut it out," Joey said, grabbing his arm. "What's wrong with you? You wanna piss off a guy who's about to hand you money?"

"He said he'd be waiting for us, didn't he, Uncle? Cash in hand? If you ask me, this is a bad sign."

"Yeah, well no one asked you. Look over there."

A gray Audi pulled out of a garage one door down and stopped in front of the line of cement trucks. A trim, serious-looking man got out and came toward them. He was carrying an expensive looking attaché case.

"Mr. DiStefano?" he asked.

Joey put out his hand. "You got that right. You're Mr. Stein?"

"Yes." They shook. Chuckie extended his hand but Stein ignored him.

"Come with me, please," Stein said. He pointed to a rusty, large-diameter iron cover near the shop wall. The weeds and vines had recently been torn back. You could see fresh, loose dirt.

"What's that?" Chuckie asked.

Stein addressed Joey. "A coal-fired boiler used to be in the space you'll be filling. I would like you to pour through the coal chute. If you keep the mixture wet, as I recommended on the phone, you'll get even distribution. Take the cover off and have a look. I'd like to get your opinion on this before we start."

Joey and Chuckie struggled with the metal plate for a while, trying to get under it for a grip.

"It's locked," Chuckie said, tapping with a knuckle on the key hole.

Pilot's Dawn

"Christ," grumbled Stein. He added his hands to theirs and yanked. The cover came up far enough for Joey to get hold of it and roll it to the side. He and his nephew stood staring down a deep hole with slick metal sides.

"Well, Mr. DiStefano?"

"I don't see any problem. Like you say, if the mixture's wet, it'll spread out. It's gonna take a long time to dry, though."

"That's all right. How long until it's poured?"

"We'll have it for you before lunch."

"Very good. Did you make up a bill?"

"I was gonna talk to you about that, Mr. Stein. If you're paying cash anyway and aren't deducting, then maybe—"

"I understand," Stein said. "There's no use giving Uncle Sam more than you have to."

"A man after my own heart. It comes to thirty nine but we can take it down to—"

"Just do the job right, Mr. DiStefano. That's more important to me than a discount." Stein counted several bundles of hundreds from his attaché case and handed them to Joey. "And please put the cover back on when you've finished. Good day, gentlemen."

Joey and his nephew watched Stein drive off. When he was out of sight, Joey counted the money. "Forty grand, that was nice of him."

Chuckie whistled. "I sure would like to look down that hole before we get started, Uncle. I got this feeling someone's down there."

"You know something, Chuckie? You make another remark like that, you're gonna be right. Only trouble is, it's gonna be you."

Joey pinched his nephew's cheek and and stuffed a $100 bill into his T-shirt pocket. "Let's get to work. We don't wanna be late for lunch. Angie's making *gnocchi*."

✷   ✷   ✷

Claussen drove east, enjoying the mountain scenery and the Mozart concerto on the classical station. It irritated him when the announcer interrupted the music to bring word of the murders and theft at Boeing.

But he forgave her when she informed him that the police were looking for a Cole Dehumidification Systems van seen before dawn in the area of the crime.

Hassan Aziz was going to have a very bad day, which translated into a very good day for Hans-Walter Claussen.

Chapter Thireteen

"We'll work on your serve and volley next week," Steven said as they gathered up their gear. "I want you to start coming to the net in singles too, not just doubles. If you don't get in the habit soon, you'll be stuck on the baseline for the rest of your life."

"That's just how I feel," Nicole said. "Stuck on the *sacré* baseline."

"Hey, don't worry about it. You're curable."

He tossed her a towel and watched her wipe the perspiration from her face and neck. His lust, as Sophie called it, had not subsided. But something else was happening, and he was powerless to stop it: they were becoming friends, God forbid. After just one short month, he was prepared to confer on her the impossible rank of "soul mate," a rank held until now by Sophie Marx alone. The implications for his assignment were grave. What the hell was he supposed to do when one of his soul mates was bribing him to screw the other one? It was a nasty dilemma—but one he had plenty of incentive to solve.

"It hasn't worked in the past," Nicole said.

"What?"

"Steven, you're daydreaming again."

"I was thinking about how good a beer would taste."

"You're worse than my cousins at communion. You were telling me I should come to the net. I said, 'It hasn't worked in the past,' to which your thoughtful professional response was, 'What?'"

"It's been a long hot week. The reason it hasn't worked in the past is that you've been taught to worry more about your form than winning the point. I'm trying to teach you a more visceral style of tennis. If you master it, you'll be invincible."

"I'd like to learn to play better. I know I'm too timid. It was fun watching you trash Philippe."

"You'll be playing like you're on the woman's tour by the time Philippe gets back. He'll be a basket case when I insist on a departing pro match for myself and designate you as my second. I think you'll beat him."

"Right, Steven. And you'll be the next President of France."

"Sure, why not? I'm good at delegating. Listen, I've got a proposition. Why don't we follow the wisdom of my daydreams and have a drink on the terrace?"

"I'd love to, Steven, but—"

"But what?"

"A lot of people have been watching us."

"They should. We're more interesting than anyone else around here. If they want to watch us drink a beer, what's the big deal?"

She snapped her towel at him and laughed. "For someone who wants to be President of France, monsieur, there's a lot you don't know about this country. If you and I sat on the terrace of this establishment and had a drink, I'd be the talk of the club for months. 'My God, did you see them?' 'Scandalous, the way she's hanging out with that American.' 'You don't suppose she's seeing him without her father knowing?' 'She could make that poor man the laughing stock of France.' Steven, I tell you, these people are incurable gossips. Malicious, too."

"Laughing stock of France for having a beer with an American? I guess I don't get it. Maybe I'm not ready for the presidency. Anyway, how's this for a solution? What if we meet far from here where the gossips don't congregate. Is there such a place within a radius of, say, one thousand kilometers?"

She handed him back his towel and smiled. "Would it surprise you if I said, Yes, there is such a place and yes, I'll meet you there."

"Mainly it would delight me. I don't have a lot of friends here."

Nicole reflected for a moment. "Have you ever been to the harbor at St. Jean-Cap-Ferrat?"

"No, but I'm sure I can find it."

"Good. There's a café where the fishermen go. We won't have to worry about gossips."

"You're on. What time?"

She glanced at her watch. "Tonight, before dinner. Six o'clock."

*   *   *

This August, as every August, the city of Nice swarmed with gorgeous women. Whiling away the sweet fragrant evenings in town, Steven had studied the passing female droves with the critical eye of a connoisseur, and he had been very impressed. But the instant Nicole stepped into the café, the beauty of the city's women paled by comparison.

She wore a white cotton sun dress, gold hoop ear rings and leather sandals whose straps climbed her ankles in a provocative criss-cross pattern.

She pushed her sunglasses up on her jet-black hair and glanced around for him. He was about to stand and wave but thought better of it. He sipped his beer and looked off in another direction.

When she approached, he could feel her nearness like a charge of static electricity. She smelled good, too, some new fragrance he didn't recognize. "Nicole. You made it."

"Hello, Steven. Of course I made it." She sat before he could pull out a chair.

"Something to drink?"

"Sure. A kir."

"A kir? I doubt they know what it is."

"You're right. I didn't mean to be a snob. I haven't spent a lot of time around working people."

"You could join the plebeians like myself for a beer, you could have an apéritive or I could get us a bottle of the white wine some of these guys here are drinking."

She laughed. She didn't seem nervous in the least. That was a bad sign, he thought; it probably meant she wasn't planning to let their evening go past drinks. She said, "The local white will be fine, Steven. I've had it on sailing trips before. I rather like it."

He flagged the waiter and ordered. "Sailing trips?" he asked.

"Yes, my Aunt Jeanne and Uncle Robert...you know, Jules and Luc's parents...used to dock their boat around the other side. We sometimes went on day trips to Italy. This café would supply the provisions.

"Sounds very pleasant."

"It was—when my father didn't come."

"You don't seem to have a lot of good things to say about the man. Why is that, Nicole? Did he really treat you badly, or was it just the normal thing between kids and parents?"

The wine came and they drank a toast.

"Steven..."

"Yes, Nicole?"

"I know you saw him that night in the restaurant. But you didn't recognize him, did you?"

"What?"

"I mean, you don't know who he is?"

"I know he's your father."

"He's also the French Minister of Industry."

"You mean that right-winger the conservative parties had to take into their coalition?"

"Yes, that's exactly who I mean."

"You're kidding?"

"I am not kidding. If he knew I was in a café drinking wine with you, he'd have a stroke. He's based his entire political program on hating foreigners, especially Americans."

"Maybe he's right. There are Americans I hate, too. But why are his politics your concern? You're not a child. Isn't it your own business who you sip wine with?"

"My father's a very controlling man."

"Does he know you voted socialist?" Steven whispered.

Nicole turned ashen. "How did you know that?"

"Hey, relax. It was a joke."

He broke out laughing. It took her a while, but once she got going, she laughed loudly enough to attract a few smiles. Steven looked at her adoringly. It was hard to believe he was getting paid for this.

"Would you have voted against him as a little girl if you had had the vote?" he asked when she finally stopped laughing.

"Yes. He hasn't been a father to me. All he cares about is politics. When my mother died—that was a long time ago when I was in second grade—he sent me to a convent school. I didn't get out until last year. Time spent at home was miserable because of this nasty housekeeper my father relied on to raise me. She's still with us. In fact she's here in Nice."

"We'll pay her a masked visit some dark night. She sounds like she could profit from a good practical joke."

Nicole turned serious. "We can't, Steven. She'd know who was behind it. She'd wring my neck. Worse, she'd tell my father about you. She knows we're friends. The town grape vine links the club directly to Francoise."

"I learn something every day," Steven said. "Today I have learned that friendship in modern France can be dangerous. Well, let's be sensible. You are the only pleasant thing to happen to me this summer. I don't want to ruin it."

"Thank you, Steven. Anyway, that's my life in a nutshell. The only fond memories of my youth are of the summers spent in Fontainebleau with the caretakers of my father's country home and vacations with Uncle Robert's family. Otherwise it was the convent school or home in

Paris with my father, which was worse. I'm still living at home now even though I attend the Sorbonne. Father won't have it any other way."

"This is awful, Nicole. Why don't you run away? What's stopping you?"

"I don't know. I think I'm just beginning to realize that my life is mine and I have the choice—no, the obligation—to do with it as I want, not as he wants. You must think something's wrong with me for having taken so long to arrive at the obvious."

Steven refilled their wine glasses and snapped his fingers for another bottle. He mouthed the word "oysters." The waiter nodded and smiled.

"I don't think anything's wrong with you. You were basically in prison for eighteen years. It takes a little time to figure out how to handle freedom. You're going to do great."

"Do you really believe that?"

"Yes. And I'm glad I met you before you were any further along. You wouldn't have given me the time of day."

"That's not true, Steven. I was immediately drawn to you the night I saw you in the restaurant. It would have been the same no matter when or where it happened."

"Really?"

She shook her head, laughed and put a hand on his arm. "It's the truth. Steven, I can't believe I'm actually meeting you like this. It's no big thing for you, but it is for me. I envy you for being so…so uninhibited. Your family must have been wonderful."

Steven glanced at the second bottle of wine and smiled with approval at the plate of oysters. "Go ahead, help yourself," he said. "You may lose your appetite when I tell you about my own ordeals growing up. They can't rival yours for sheer horror, but they were pretty bad."

She took an oyster and let it slide down her throat. Steven had to look away. He hoped talking about his family would throw cold water on his desire.

He sampled the oysters, which were fresh and delicious. He tried to keep his mind on his words. "You should have heard the things my parents said about other human beings. Not in public, mind you. They put a lot of stock in being socially correct. But when they talked about Jews or blacks or homosexuals in private, they sounded like a band of ignorant skinheads.

"And that was only the tip of the iceberg. They were prejudiced as hell against everyone who was different from them. It seemed like the people I admired, like certain writers and athletes, were at the bottom of their human trash heap. They went out of their way to remind me.

"They had a plan for my life and couldn't have cared less whether it was what I wanted or not. **They** wanted me to practice medicine in Connecticut, or at least go into law or, at *very* least, into my father's business. So what am I doing at the tender age of twenty-seven? Playing tennis—and drinking wine with a beautiful young woman in the south of France. I'm not complaining. Don't get me wrong. If all those unpleasant years are responsible for my being here with you, they were worth it."

She seemed amused and genuinely surprised, and even blushed a little. "Thank you, Steven. That was a nice thing to say. I would never have guessed you rebelled against your family."

"I *really* rebelled. Look at me. If I were a loyal son of the American bourgeoisie, I would be drinking coke."

They laughed together. He would have loved to take her in his arms and tell her the world was crazy, and that nothing but friendship made any sense. Above all he would have loved to forget his assignment for Sophie. This girl was something special. When his secret got out and she rejected him, he was going to feel like a horse had kicked him in the stomach. Was there any way he could live up to his bargain with Sophie without deceiving Nicole?

What if he did something drastic and told her the truth? No, he couldn't do that. She would be gone. How could he blame her? If the price of honesty was no more Nicole, he couldn't pay it.

Trying to get his mind off the half dozen things that were tormenting him, he raised his glass. "To our rebellion against the mental tyranny of our parents," he said.

Suddenly she was crying, and he wasn't sure why. She looked around warily, then took his hand under the table.

"Steven, I don't know what I'm doing," she whispered.

"Hey, you're not alone. Whatever it is, it's all right."

She didn't seem to hear him. "I don't mean my coming here. I mean, what I'm doing with the rest of my life. I never rebelled like you did. I've waited too long to become an adult. Steven…I'm a virgin."

"Excuse me?"

"Yes, a virgin. Isn't that ridiculous at my age?"

Steven ran his fingers lightly across her beautiful, tear-streaked face. "I would say it's a cardinal sin."

She sniffled and took a deep breath. "When you said all that about your parents, how they had great plans for your life that you didn't give a damn about, it struck a chord. I lacked the courage to rebel. I guess I'm stuck on the baseline. Forgive me, Steven, but this is ridiculous. I don't know why I'm bothering you with my personal problems. I hardly know you."

He squeezed her hand. "Maybe that's why. I'm an outsider. You're in this closed society where everyone thinks the same way. They tell you you have it all, and if you don't happen to agree, they make you feel like a leper."

She withdrew her hand and wiped her eyes. "Look, I should go. I wanted to ask you a favor but I'm losing my nerve."

"For Christ's sake, Nicole, you can talk to me. If you leave now, I'll feel as horrible as you do."

Pilot's Dawn

"Why are we so distant, Steven?" she sobbed. "Why can't we just go somewhere and sleep together?"

He thought he would swallow his tongue. "It's the oysters speaking, Nicole. You don't really want to do this."

She giggled and moved closer to him so she could whisper in his ear. "It's not the oysters, *américain*, it's you. It started that night I was having dinner with my father and you came into the restaurant in your jeans. You did everything you weren't supposed to do. You even started talking to me across the tables. I really couldn't believe it. It would make you very conceited if I told you all the things that went through my mind. It's gotten a lot worse since. Steven…I don't care whether you love me or not as long as you're nice to me. I want you to make love to me."

He took a deep breath. This was incredible. He was supposed to be the seducer and here he was getting himself propositioned. That made dealing with his conscience a lot easier—didn't it?

"Nicole," he whispered, "I've been crazy for you, too, ever since I saw you for the first time. I want to make love to you, don't get me wrong. But I also like you. I care about you. Are you sure this is the right thing for you? Are you sure it won't complicate your life even more."

She dug her nails into his thigh. "I don't care. Let's just do it. All right, Steven? All right?"

"Yeah, sure," he said, motioning for the check. "We can go over to my place right now. We'll be completely alone. It's a secluded little summer house down the coastal road toward Cannes. Belongs to a friend of a friend. You wear my helmet. People will think you're Darth Vader."

*   *   *

On the back of his motorcycle at dusk, hiding behind the dark glass of his helmet, Nicole felt she was experiencing the fears and exhilaration of her entire missed adolescence. But when she stepped into Steven's summer cottage and fell into his arms, she knew it had been a lot more than just her adolescence that she had missed.

When he left her briefly to close the shutters, they had not shed one article of clothing. Yet she had already reached a state of sexual arousal she had never dreamed possible. He came back and carried her to the bedroom. He seemed to know exactly where to touch her, how to kiss her, what to say to her—which was very little and very nice.

Her knees grew weak and she sat on the bed. He unlaced her sandals and kissed her calves and thighs, then came and sat beside her. He unbuttoned her sun dress and lifted it over her head. She tried to take off her bra and panties but he wouldn't let her. He kissed her in the most exquisite way, gently stroked her body and whispered her name until she lost all track of time.

It grew dark outside. Wind rattled the shutters. The minutes stretched into hours, her pleasure reached heights she knew could never be surpassed. Then he would do something else to her and her pleasure would grow even more intense.

Slowly he undressed her, admiring, kissing and loving each newly exposed patch of flesh. When he at last entered her, she cried out so loudly she thought she must have awakened her father in Paris.

It was supposed to hurt the first time. If this was pain she wanted more of it. She was aware of something wild and urgent in her movements now, though she didn't know how she was moving or what she was doing. He kept slowing her down as she approached some burning mystery her body seemed ravenous to uncover. When he finally let her go, and helped her with a robust hunger of his own, the waves of pleasure kept coming and coming until she thought she would die if he didn't stop.

But he didn't stop. He would hold her and talk to her while she halfway recovered and make her drink a few sips of champagne. Then his hands would be stroking her again in the same magical way in the same forbidden places. His lips and tongue would find her breasts, and soon her body would be pulsing with desire.

Pilot's Dawn

She didn't remember when it all ended, but she would never forget waking up the next morning. Light was pouring in through the shutters, church bells were ringing in a nearby village and the angry honking of car horns rose from the coastal road. She looked at Steven. He was asleep, his blond hair a tousled mess. He was, she thought, the most spectacular man she had ever seen.

She sat up naked and stretched. Her breasts felt different, larger, more sensuous. Her belly tingled with sensations that were strange and wonderful.

And then it hit her. It was morning! She had not gone home, she had not even bothered to call. Francoise was probably at the police station reporting her absence right now.

What had Steven done to her? God, it was incredible.

She rushed through a shower, dressed and decided to go down to the beach. She would buy some running clothes and put them to the test. When she got home, her absence would look like a repeat of her previous early-morning excursion. She would claim she had spent the night in the villa, that she had slept on the porch or in another room, and that Francoise had assumed the worse. As long as she stuck to her story, she was safe! Only she and Steven knew what had happened. It was a good plan.

She went back to the bed to kiss him but the phone rang first. He answered sleepily. She could hear the irate voice of Monsieur Denis du Pèage the elder coming through the receiver, and she had to suppress a laugh. He held the phone out so she could better follow the old man's tirade, looking very blasé about the scolding, and kissed her playfully while they listened.

"I've got to go," she said. "I'll have some explaining to do when I get home. Steven…it was…wonderful. Thank you."

"You sound like it was the last time. I hope it's only the beginning. It was good for me too, Nicole. Very good."

"We have two weeks. Francoise will be watching me like a hawk, but I don't care."

"Two weeks? You mean you're throwing me over when we get back to Paris?"

"Paris?"

"That's where I live. Didn't you know?"

"You live in Paris? Oh my God, Steven. I thought you were on exchange from that tennis club in the States that took Philippe. You really live in Paris?"

"Yes. Is that bad? Did you only want me for my body?"

She broke down, laughing and crying. "I'm so happy. I mean, I guess I'm happy. It's going to be complicated, Steven. You have no idea. There'll be secret service agents and paparazzi all over the place, not to mention Francoise and my father. You'll be sick of me in one day."

He took her in his arms. "Don't kid yourself, Nicole. If you want to see me, the entire French Army couldn't keep me away. Come here."

She pulled herself away and stood up. "No, not now. You've got to get to the tennis club and I've…got to decide where I've been."

"Don't make me wait forever."

"I won't. I couldn't if I wanted to." She gave him another quick kiss and stepped out the front door, only to realize that her car was in St. Jean-Cap-Ferrat.

* * *

Claussen parked Stein's Audi in a section of the Bronx where he knew it would not survive the night and took a cab to his hotel at Kennedy Airport. He stretched out on the bed, feeling tired for the first time since his arrival in the States.

His work was over. The Feds were blaming the Seattle break-in on a clumsy Iraqi attempt to circumvent the embargo on aircraft parts, and

Pilot's Dawn

Hassan Aziz had induced them to take another giant step in the wrong direction by committing suicide on the third day of his incarceration.

* * *

The deaths of Wayne Jenkins and four other Boeing employees, murdered in their homes the night of the break-in, were likewise attributed to the Iraqis. When Boeing's security procedures came under harsh attack at a press conference, a Boeing spokesman tried to defend the company by implying that the dead men might have been collaborators. This possibility was obvious to everyone, but the image of a young boy with his throat slit from ear-to-ear seemed the greater crime by far and kept public outrage focused on Iraq.

In the aftermath of the break-in Boeing had conducted a painstaking search of its inventory. Other than the missing 747 parts found in the van in front of Hassan Aziz'es apartment, the search revealed no irregularities. The case seemed too cut-and-dried to warrant further investigation. Attention shifted to Washington, where diplomatic initiatives were in full swing and a resumption of the bombing against Iraq had not been ruled out.

As for Stein, he was a notorious loner who often put his sign in his window and left Seattle for his cabin in the northwest woods for months. He had not been missed and probably wouldn't be until late autumn. His concrete grave in the second basement of the shop had been drying for a week now, and Claussen doubted it would ever be disturbed.

All quiet on the western front.

He had visited Bendix and GE on his drive east. Last night Claussen had wrapped up the Pratt & Whitney stage of his mission, which was far and away the easiest.

Claussen's oldest collaborator at the jet engine facility, David Melchior, was the chief quality control engineer. Since his job required him to select items from the parts inventory for random testing,

Melchior was able to substitute Claussen's counterfeits for originals without appearing to do anything abnormal.

Melchior was delighted with the $300,000 Claussen had offered him as payment for the trifling assignment. He was a bon vivant, American style. Claussen believed he would have enjoyed the money, had he not succumbed to an apparent coronary 12 hours ago…

He glanced at his watch. Time to shower and dress for his evening flight. He was anxious to get home now, where he could announce his checkmate to Michelet and company, return to the composition of his memoirs and wait for the fireworks to begin.

Part II

Chapter Fourteen

Jim Hutchinson knew the statistics. He smoked, drank, ate what he wanted and limited his physical exercise to an occasional round of lay-over adultery. He was at the high risk end of a high risk group. Retirement age at United Airlines was 60; life expectancy for the company's international pilots was 62. If you believed the charts, this 757 pilot already had one foot in the grave.

He glanced over at Bob Gaines, the co-pilot they'd given him for the San Francisco-Honolulu run. He'd flown with Gaines before. The man did odd things, like going out for a run when they landed even if it was the middle of the night. And if he joined you at the table, you could tell he was more interested in counting fat grams than enjoying the food.

Not that there was anything wrong with him. He had a sense of humor if you skipped the ethnic jokes, and could hit the golf ball a country mile. But what he couldn't do—what none of the younger pilots could do—was get the statistical monkey of that death chart off their backs.

Jesus, it drove Hutchinson crazy. Here they were caught up in a profession that required you to abide by the most nitpicking regimens. The days of flying by the seat of your pants were over. Now all you did was read checklists, follow meticulous routines and let the computers do your calculations.

Fine. The complexity of aviation had made this necessary. But the younger guys took their checklists with them out of the cockpit and into life. That's what Hutchinson would never get used to. William, please run the fish dinner checklist. Is it fried? Is it salted? Is it fresh?

Jeremy, run the exercise checklist. Stretches? Warm up? Total miles? Minutes with pulse above 140? Warm down? Stretches?

Christ, they probably had bedroom checklists, too. If their life expectancy statistics looked better than his when they reached retirement age, big deal. He had done everything wrong and enjoyed the hell out of it. These guys had done everything right and been miserable most of the time. No wonder the company had to give them courses on smiling at passengers.

"Jim," Gaines said after a long silence, "I'm getting an irregular indication here."

"Yeah? What's that?"

"We're showing a loss of oil on engine number two."

Hutchinson snapped out of his reverie. Whatever his foibles on the ground, he was no slouch in the cockpit. "How much loss?"

"It's come down about three quarts in the last ten minutes. I'm thinking we might have a leak out on that engine."

"More likely a defective sending unit. Why don't you go back and see if you can see anything?"

Gaines took a stroll through the cabin. When he returned, he said, "Nothing visible, but you don't really have a good view of the engine."

"Well, we're still showing the loss. Two more quarts while you were gone."

Gaines sat down and studied the readings. "I don't think it's the sender, Jim. The pressure's down ten p.s.i and the temperature is climbing."

Hutchinson shook his head. "I'll be a son of a bitch. Looks like we're gonna find out if it was a good idea to send the Seven Fives out on the Hawaii track. Start the auxiliary power unit and run the engine shutdown checklist for number two."

The captain and first officer went through the standardized operations for shutting down engine number two, Gaines running the checklist while Hutchinson flew the aircraft. They made the transition to one-engine flight so smoothly only a fellow pilot would have noticed.

"All right," Hutchinson said. "Punch up the single engine data in the Flight Management System. Call Oakland Center and declare an emergency. Tell them we can't maintain this altitude without number two. When you get done with that, let's notify the company of the problem. Since we passed the equal time point seven or eight minutes ago, we'll continue on to Honolulu."

"Okay, Jim, we're cleared to descend to thirty-two thousand. Traffic Control wants to know if you can hold that altitude."

"According to the FMS, we can hold it at an airspeed of two hundred ninety knots." Hutchinson increased the throttle to max cruise thrust and started his descent. "You got the company yet?"

"I'm calling now."

"Why don't you give them an ETA based on our present speed? I hope you didn't have a golf game planned."

"A run on the beach," Gaines said. "I played golf yesterday. An hour this way or that won't bother me. How about you?"

"My post-flight entertainment, the blonde you were ogling when we got on board, is in the cabin. I guess she and I are on the same schedule. Think of me during your run."

Hutchinson glanced over at his co-pilot, hoping to get some sort of a rise out of him. At first, he thought Gaines might be pretending not to hear him, but when he saw the expression on the man's face, he knew something was wrong.

Gaines spoke before Hutchinson could ask him what the problem was. "Jim, what the hell is going on? Look at your indications. Now we're showing an oil loss on engine number one."

"Goddammit, that can't be. These new engines don't fail once in a million miles. What are the chances of losing *two* on the same flight?"

"I don't know what the chances are, but it's happening. We're down four quarts since we ran the checklist."

Pilot's Dawn

"Holy Christ. We're still almost two and a half hours out of Honolulu, two out of Hilo. Shut down the generator. Let's see if we can keep her from heating up."

"Roger, but I don't think it'll do much good. We're down to eleven quarts."

"Shit. Get me the company maintenance coordinator on the H F radio."

While Gaines established the communications link, Hutchinson picked up his hand set and called the head flight attendant to the cockpit.

Two knocks. He let her in and motioned for her to sit in the empty jump seat. He said, "They send two-engine planes over three thousand miles of water with nowhere to land. I'd say, Julie, that we're about to prove them foolhardy."

"You lost number two, didn't you?"

"Yes, and we're about to lose number one. There's not much chance we can keep this thing going to Honolulu. We're going to have to brief the passengers and prepare to ditch."

"But—"

"You'd better get it done. When that last engine conks out, we won't have long."

Julie Harper got up, stunned, and left the cockpit. He had his doubts she was up to the coming ordeal, but when he heard her masterful announcement to the passengers, he knew the cabin was in competent hands. One less thing to worry about.

"Jim, I've got company maintenance."

"Thanks. I'll take over. This is United One-Eight-One. Who am I talking to?"

"This is Evans, Seven Five maintenance coordinator in Denver. What seems to be the problem?"

"The plural, problems," Hutchinson said. "We shut down engine number two on account of substantial oil loss, a drop in pressure and a rise in temperature. Now we're getting indications the exact same thing is happening on engine number one. I've got no idea what's wrong. All I know is, we're over water a couple of hours from the nearest landing site. Do you guys have any idea what's going on and what we should do about it?"

"Well, I've never heard of anything like this before. Stand by for a moment, sir. I'm going to do a maintenance search on your aircraft and get the Pratt and Whitney tech rep on the line."

"Thanks, Evans."

He glanced over at Gaines, who was accustomed to being in control of situations. His co-pilot was pale and looked uneasy. Hutchinson felt like making a crack about the long-term health consequences of having to exchange a five mile run for a 1000 mile swim, but thought better of it. Now if ever was the time to foster a spirit of camaraderie in the cockpit.

"Hello, United One-Eighty-One. Captain?"

"Speaking."

"This is Holmes from P and W. Our twenty forty engine has no history at all of indication problems. If I've understood your people at United correctly, you don't think it's an indication problem anyway."

"It's not a goddamn indication problem, that's correct. We're losing oil, lots of it."

"All right, I'll stay on the line, but it sounds to me like a maintenance oversight. I don't have the maintenance history of your aircraft so—"

"Excuse me, this is Evans again in Denver. The aircraft just went through a C-check in San Francisco. This is its first time back on the line."

"Were the senders pulled?"

"Yes, sir, when the oil was changed."

"This is irritating to say the least," Hutchinson growled. "It sounds like some yo-yo forgot the O-rings. If I get out of this alive, I'm going to personally go looking for him."

Pilot's Dawn

"I understand your frustration, sir, but new O-rings appear to have been used. That was the first thing I checked. We've got a record of the requisition order for the correct items. They're looking for the mechanics to confirm that the parts were actually installed. In any case, sir, if the O-rings had been left off, you would have experienced an immediate oil loss similar to what you're experiencing out there now. If O-rings are the culprit, it would appear that they were installed but that something caused them to dissolve in flight."

"Jesus, you guys have gotta do better than this. I'm out here over the ocean about to lose my second engine. You know what the chances are for setting this thing down in water without killing everyone on board. About zero."

"This is Holmes, Pratt and Whitney, again. Captain, I think I might be able to help you. When we certify these engines, we run them without oil until they fail. We've had instances of engines running as long as fifty hours. My suggestion is this. Start up engine number two so you don't overstress the engine that's now carrying the load and run them both at a constant power setting. Remember, the tests are based on *constant* power settings. Ignore temperatures in the red, they can handle it. The engines should get you where you're going, provided you avoid any power fluctuations. That will take some good flying, but it seems to me your best bet."

"Thank you, sir, we'll try it." Hutchinson signed off the radio shaking his head. "I still think someone in San Francisco fucked up. Go ahead, Bob. Run the air start checklist for number two."

"There's no oil in it, Jim, and spooling up represents a power fluctuation. I don't think it's a good idea regardless of what P and W says."

"If we hit the water, what difference does it make if we've destroyed an engine?"

"Jim, think about it. If the thing seizes, it could torque off the pylon and damage the aircraft—or explode. The Pratt and Whitney guy isn't up here. It's easy for him to theorize with two feet on dry ground. I think it's too risky."

"Thanks for your thoughts, Bob. Now please run the air start checklist."

The engine spooled up. They had shut her down in time, there was no damage. Slowly, steadily, Hutchinson pushed the power up. He was about to relax when a huge vibration shook the aircraft and the engine seized.

Hutchinson shrugged his shoulders. "All right, we lost her. We had to try. Enough screwing around. We're gonna ditch before we lose number one. We're not going in as a glider."

"Jim, listen to me. I was right about number two seizing, so would you please just listen?"

"You were also wrong about number two. It did not torque off the pylon and it did not explode. Go on, what's your point?"

"I don't think ditching now is our best option. I think we're better off hoping number one will keep turning and get us in—if not all the way, at least close enough so we can get some ships out here to help with the rescue. We're nine hundred miles from land. Even if we survive the impact, most of us will be dead before anyone gets to us."

"It's still better than trying to land a swept-wing aircraft with no power. We'd have too steep a descent angle and too much speed. Not to mention that we've got to come in on the back side of a swell. Without power, I won't have enough control over our flight path to position the aircraft. The water will hit us like the side of a mountain. So our choice is either try to make it to Hilo or ditch now. We're going to ditch now, Bob."

"It's your call, Captain."

"That's right. Give Oakland Center our position, heading, indicated air speed, altitude and intent. Then run the ditching checklist."

"Got it." While Gains worked, Hutchinson summoned the head flight attendant back to the cockpit. This time he did not offer her a seat. "We're going in, Julie. You've been through the passenger briefing so go ahead and get the life rafts out of the bins and secure them in the galleys. Make sure everyone is wearing a life vest. How's the mood out there?"

"Bad, and I assure you it will get worse. We're even having trouble with one of the flight attendants. We're holding her in the aft toilet as discreetly as possible."

"Do your best. We've got our hands full up here."

"I will, Captain. What are our chances?"

"Keep your thoughts on the evacuation. Anything I tell you is speculation."

She left and he went back to work. Minutes later, the number one engine seized with a violent shudder.

"Goddammit," Hutchinson growled, "this is what I call a bad day."

"How do you want to do this, Jim?"

Hutchinson tilted the nose down to avoid a stall. "Finish up the checklist. When we descend through five thousand feet, I want you to start calling out our altitude in increments of one thousand feet. At one thousand feet, we'll configure the airplane. Then start giving me readings in increments of one hundred feet. In the meantime get on the radio and let them know what's going on. With any luck there'll be a ship or two in the area."

"Roger."

They glided in eerie silence toward the low clouds covering the Pacific, a silence interrupted from time to time by a muffled scream from the cabin.

They were at 18,000 feet now, airspeed 250 knots. Hutchinson made a crisp cool announcement to the cabin to help the flight crew with its impossible task of calming the passengers, then glanced at his co-pilot. He could see Gaines was taking the prospect of imminent death less well. No wonder. The poor bastard had tried to put life in a savings account, renouncing all of the things a man in his prime enjoyed so that he could have a secure and healthy old age. Bad choice.

"Any ships in the area?" Hutchinson asked.

"The carrier Enterprise is about two hundred miles away. They've got us on radar and have already dispatched search planes and rescue helicopters. Maybe our luck is changing."

"Maybe. We're passing through fifty-three hundred feet. I'm going to concentrate on bringing us in. Get ready to start with the increments."

"Roger…We're coming to five thousand feet and I'm completing the checklist."

The seconds ticked by, the descent continued. The aircraft bumped through a band of turbulence.

"Four thousand…"

Hutchinson took a deep breath. He still outperformed most of the younger guys in the simulator, so his instincts and hand-eye were good. On top of that, he had learned to fly in the old days when improvisation was the rule. If anyone could set this crate down, he could.

"Three thousand. Aren't you coming in a little fast?"

"No, I'm gonna hold it at two fifty to a thousand feet, then start to bleed the airspeed off as we configure."

"All right…Two thousand feet."

Hutchinson noticed his grip on the controls had tightened. He made a conscious effort to relax.

"One thousand feet."

The big jet responded well to the captain's input. As they entered the low overcast stretching across the water, the airspeed indicator dropped below 200 knots.

"Go to increments of a hundred. We just might be able to ease this baby in. Give me flaps one."

"Eight hundred…seven hundred…flaps five…six hundred…flaps fifteen."

"Complete the checklist. Lock your shoulder harness. Goddammit, I still don't see anything."

Pilot's Dawn

"Five hundred…four hundred…flaps twenty-five. I don't know what the altimeter setting is in this area. I've kept the altimeters on two-nine-nine-two."

"Let's hope we break through before we hit water."

They came out beneath the clouds. They were plunging toward an angry gray sea. Gaines breathed a sigh of relief.

"Shit," Hutchinson shouted, pulling up the nose still further. "We're heading right into the goddamn waves."

"Three hundred…"

"I've gotta bank twenty degrees or we're shark bait."

"Two hundred…one hundred fifty…spray on the windshield… watch your wing tip!"

"We've gotta come around, no choice."

"One hundred…"

Almost parallel to the swells, Hutchinson thought. A little luck and he might pull it off. Just gotta come around another ten degrees, just another eight or ten.

Nose up, slow the descent, keep that goddamn wing out of the water.

There, there it is, what I was looking for, the backside of a big swell. Soft, smooth and almost parallel. Straighten her out now, Jimbo, straighten her out.

"Fifty feet. Get the wing up!"

Hutchinson waited until the last possible moment, then moved the controls to level her out. No good. He had waited an instant too long. He felt the tip of the banking wing catch the water with a ferocious jerk. The 757 cartwheeled wildly. He knew it would all be over before he took another breath.

* * *

When Hutchinson awoke, he believed he was in the water about to drown. He tried to move his arms and legs. Pain shot through his body.

He screamed and gasped. A young nurse tried to calm him down while she rang for the doctor.

As his vision cleared, he saw that he was not in the ocean but in a hospital room. When he stopped trying to flail, the throbbing pain subsided enough that he could tolerate it. He took a quick inventory of his wounds: right leg up in traction, right arm in a cast, bandages everywhere.

He felt a sudden rush of exhilaration. He was alive! To hell with the goddamned chart. If hurtling into the Pacific from 38,000 feet hadn't killed him, he would live to be a hundred.

He was drugged, he didn't know with what. He drifted back to sleep but awoke when the young doctor came in.

"Captain Hutchinson, I'm Doctor Gray. How are you feeling?"

"Like I got run over by a bulldozer. Where am I?"

"Honolulu General Hospital. You're a very lucky man. Banged up but lucky. My prognosis is for a complete recovery."

"Doctor—"

"Yes?"

"How long have I been here?"

"You came in last night. Do you remember anything?"

Hutchinson shook his head. "Nothing from the time we hit the water. How did they rescue me?"

"Military helicopter. You were fortunate enough to have an aircraft carrier in the vicinity. They stabilized you on board, then sent you on to Hawaii by plane."

Hutchinson latched onto the doctor's arm as his mind cleared. "The others, did they make it?"

The doctor patted his hand. "Not all of them. It was a bad crash."

"How bad? How many survivors?"

"In addition to yourself, two children."

"Two!" Hutchinson felt frantic. His excitement about being alive gave way to an overwhelming dread. He tried to say something but his chin quivered so badly he gave up with a strangled curse.

Pilot's Dawn

The doctor said, "There's a psychiatrist on the hospital staff who deals with situations like yours. I'll arrange for him to come by and talk to you. You must not blame yourself for what happened. I was told about the engine failure."

"I could have done better…I…the wing tip, you see, we were just about there when it caught a wave. Don't bring your goddamned shrink in here. I fucked up. A lot of people died because I fucked up. I don't want some weirdo telling me it's okay. It's not okay, doctor. **It is not okay.**"

"Captain, you must remain still. You've got multiple fractures and over three hundred stitches. I'm going to have to give you something that will calm you down."

The syringe came out of nowhere, a big syringe filled with yellow liquid. Hutchinson was too weak to resist; and glad he hadn't when the sedative began taking the knots out of his gut.

Chapter Fifteen

Steven hadn't thought of anything but Nicole during his motorcycle trip back to Paris—the first night, the last night, the nights in between. He thought of the days, too, of her laughter and playfulness, and the sense of doom that came over her when they spoke too freely about the future. His love was great and growing; so was his dilemma. But he was having no trouble getting out of bed in the morning.

As he climbed the worn marble staircase of his old apartment building, he shook the water from the roses he had bought from a vendor on the outskirts of Paris. He had always hated homecomings, but this one promised to be different. There would be no parental judgment, no fraternal scorn, just the warmth and laughter of Soul Mate Number One.

Sophie opened the door, pulled him inside and gave him a warm hug. "Steven, darling! I've missed you. And roses! It's been years."

"They got a little roughed up sticking out of my saddle bags, but they're still pretty, aren't they? Jesus, Sophie, what did you get me into? That woman has turned me into a lovesick fool."

"You? My hero? Never. But what about our dear Nicole? Has she become your panting slave?"

"I don't know. I think it's the other way around."

Sophie hugged him again and laughed her husky laugh. He had never seen her look more delighted. She said, "I knew it! You're the real thing, darling. I'm pretty impressed with myself, too. In the game of human chess, I moved you leap by brilliant leap so close to our subject you'll soon be ready to whisper father in his ear."

"I don't think so, Sophie. In fact, I think it might be over. Nicole has big fears about seeing me in Paris. She didn't know I lived here until…after."

"She'll be back."

"But what if I don't hear from her? What do I do?"

"Not to worry, darling, you'll hear from her. Trust a woman's judgment. Now come, relax, have a drink and tell me everything."

He settled into her big comfortable sofa, vowing to say as little as possible about the more intimate details of his relationship with Nicole. After all, there were some things you didn't share, even with a soul mate.

His vow dissolved with the first swallow of pastis. Once he started talking, it was like spending money: he couldn't stop. He poured his heart out, marveling at how good it felt to have someone he cared about listening to him.

While he finished his drink, he told her about the incredible first-night encounter with Nicole in the fancy restaurant. When lunch was ready, he and Sophie moved to the dining room. Fueled by the best *Coquilles St. Jacques* he had ever tasted, and helped along by a terrific bottle of Bâtard Montrachet, he told her about the tennis lessons, the mischievous cousins, the doubles games and the constant laughter. He told how surprised he was that a genuine friendship had sprung up in the unexpectedly fertile soil of a planned deception.

When she had to interrupt him to serve the leg of lamb and pour from the bottle of Château Neuf du Pape, he felt as if she had stuffed a plug in his mouth to torture him.

But Sophie soon returned to her listening, wonderful Sophie. He ate lustily and described in excruciating detail their first night of love together, the explosions of passion, her virginity notwithstanding, the laughter, the tears—and how blown away he was that he, a guy with a past that seemed to stretch back to Eve, could feel so utterly in love with a nineteen-year-old girl.

They returned to the living room for cognac and coffee. He kept on talking, spilling his fears that she would be stolen away from him by tight-assed arguments from her bitchy housekeeper, who suspected something was up, her father, who was intent on selecting her mate, or the clerics who were being summoned in droves to "purify" her thoughts.

At last he sat back in his chair, feeling depleted. He smiled sheepishly. "I can't believe it, Sophie. I have actually silenced you."

"It was worth it, Steven. What a journey you've taken me on."

"What about you? I really hogged the conversation. How's the research on Michelet coming?"

"Slowly, but it's coming. I've been all over town collecting information." She glanced at her watch. "In fact, you and I must leave for an interview in half an hour."

"What?"

"Relax, darling. We'll be back in plenty of time for dinner. You don't think you'll ever be hungry again, but this is France and you will. I've reserved a table at Dusquenoy, my treat."

"No, Sophie, it's Aunt Janine's turn. My stay in Nice must have cost you a fortune."

"You're not the cheapest to keep in the field. The best never are. But great things are going to come of your work, I can feel it in these old bones. Therefore, my treat."

"Well…thanks. So, who are we interviewing?"

"An old priest who taught French history at Michelet's high-school—St. Claude, the French Exeter. Father Roget was quite the cultural historian in his day. He wrote an excellent book on renaissance theater."

"This is great. I'm really curious about the guy now, really curious. To hell with his politics. What I want to know is how a monumental prick like Michelet could produce someone as perfect as Nicole."

"It happens, Steven. This world of ours is a strange place."

"No kidding. Sophie, listen, I haven't been doing my part in this whole thing. I want to apologize. I've gotten so caught up with Nicole I haven't pushed to get to her father, or even to get stories about him out of her."

"And I say to that, release yourself from the unbecoming grasp of Puritan self-flagellation. Your job was to seduce Nicole so you would be in position to help me. You've performed brilliantly, so brilliantly, in fact, that I'm going to give you a raise. Now, shall we go?"

*　　　　　*　　　　　*

Father Roget lived with his 98-year-old mother in an apartment building in the industrial suburb of Billancourt. He wasn't more than a few years older than Sophie, but he looked like the product of a different century. The few remaining hairs on his head were wiry and white, as if they had grown on a corpse. His complexion was gray, and he was so stooped his mother could have passed for his wife.

Sophie knew something about resuscitation, Steven thought, watching her greet the cadaver. He would have treated the old priest like a fragile antique vase. Not Sophie. She shook his hand vigorously and thanked him in her fabulous deep voice for the opportunity to chat. When he told her he had read and admired her pieces in *Le Monde*, and had even been looking forward to meeting her in spite of his hatred of interviews, she threw back her blonde head and filled the drab room with laughter.

Father Roget's eyes came alive. His color seemed to improve. Steven could almost feel Sophie's boundless energy flowing into him. The old man responded with a laugh of his own, a charming, urbane laugh, and the ice that had seemed so thick was broken. He introduced himself to Steven with a firm, friendly grip, whisked his mother into the conversation and went to the kitchen to pour drinks.

"Monseigneur, I expect you to hold me to my promise," Sophie said when he returned and passed the glasses around.

"Please sit down, won't you? I don't recall any promises, Madame Marx."

Steven watched Sophie sit, cross her legs and push her hair back. It was incredible. She was charming the robes off this priest. If they had met 40 years ago, the guy's vow of celibacy wouldn't have lasted as long as Steven's vow of silence at lunch.

She said, "I promised, Monseigneur, that I would not press you to answer questions you did not wish to answer. You just have to let me know."

Father Roget made a gesture with his hand. His mother looked up from her knitting. He said, "Michelet is in a position to help the Church. He might be in an even better position by the end of the decade. The Church helps millions of people, my people. Now, it so happens that Michelet remembers me fondly as his teacher. It would be unthinkable for me to jeopardize this fine relationship with too much candor."

"I quite understand."

"Boys will be boys, Madame Marx. There were, of course, some of the usual incidents. However, you have assured me that you are looking for insight rather than vilification, and judging from the high professional standards of your essays, I have no reason whatsoever to doubt you."

"Tell me, then. How long did you have classroom contact with Georges Michelet?"

"Four years, Madame Marx. From the time he entered St. Claude until his graduation in nineteen fifty-three."

"He was a good student?"

"Yes, above average. More importantly, I think, he was a very committed patriot even then. French history—military, cultural, all of it—was his true love. It was amazing to witness how much our national defeats pained him, and how much our triumphs elevated him. One had the impression he was living these events himself."

"Did this vicarious participation in his country's history make him a social misfit? I mean, what about girls? What about friends?"

Father Roget chuckled to himself and patted his mother on the arm. She ignored the missed stroke he had caused her knitting and smiled at him, a mother who loved her son.

"He was a born leader, Madame Marx. There is a difference. As for girls, when he came to St. Claude, he was already planning to marry the woman he eventually married then tragically lost to illness, Beatrice Bacault. I remember his talking about her to me, her family, their values."

"An arranged marriage?"

"Semi-arranged in the French bourgeois tradition. The parents knew and approved of each other."

"You say he was a leader. Who were the followers? Do you recall?"

"How could I forget? The two most gifted boys in his class, boys of exceptional intelligence. Though they had higher scores and grades, they treated him with great deference, as if he were already head of government. It's a very specific quality Georges Michelet has, Madame Marx, an aura of strength and boldness. He is someone others perceive as being able to get the job done, no matter what."

"That's interesting."

"Yes. I remember thinking his tenacity would take him a long way in life, even though his grades in many subjects were unremarkable. Leadership, Madame Marx. It's a strange quality, easy to identify but hard to define. Your Mr. Reagan, who appeared to us here in Europe more like a comic strip character than a serious statesman, had it in his own country; and Georges Michelet has it here."

"You say the two most gifted boys in the class looked up to him, deferred to him. Did anything ever become of those two? Did you manage to keep up with them?"

"Oh, my. Oh, my." He gave his mother a double pat, and this time she growled at him to watch what he was doing. Father Roget seemed not to hear her. "Madame Marx, one of them was named Albert Haussmann. You see, it was a good year for us at St. Claude!"

"Well that's remarkable," she said. "The world-famous French financial genius passed through your school. He must have learned more than his three Rs. And who, Monseigneur, was the second boy you mentioned?"

Father Roget, responding to a persistent tug at the sleeve of his black shirt, apologized to his mother. "I don't remember his name, Madame Marx. He was not a student of mine, he was following the technical curriculum. But I knew from Albert and Georges that he had the highest scores in mathematics the school had ever seen."

"Very interesting," Sophie said. "Your class of fifty-three certainly was distinguished."

"Yes, yes, quite a distinguished class," Father Roget droned.

"Do you suppose you would recognize the second boy if I found a photograph of him?"

"I don't know, Madame Marx. It's been a long time and, as I said, he wasn't a student of mine. I'd certainly be glad to try."

"Thank you, Monseigneur. Well, what do you say? Shall we tackle the primary topic I came here to research, the origin of Michelet's keen interest in politics?"

"Of course, Madame Marx, and here I think I can make a real contribution to your understanding. We must go back to De Gaulle, the Second World War, the way the Allies treated the Free French. Of course, Vietnam and Algeria are important, too, very important."

Steven's mind started to wander. To his surprise, he felt hungry again—for dinner and for Nicole. France had some major defects as a country, he thought, but when it came to stimulating the appetites, She was without equal.

✶ ✶ ✶

Pilot's Dawn

Frank Warner arrived at Honolulu General Hospital two days after the crash. He was waiting in the corridor with Tim Simmons and Jeremy Little, an attorney for the Pilots' Association, to speak with Captain Hutchinson's physician.

Dr. Gray had brushed off their introductions when he came to examine his patient. He had disappeared into Hutchinson's room, muttering about schedules and interference. When he came out, Warner stood. "Well, Doctor, how's he doing?"

"Physically, he's doing fine," Gray said.

"What's that supposed to mean?"

"Mr. Warner, he's having a normal reaction to learning that one hundred sixty men, women and children with whose safe transport he was entrusted did not make it. He feels guilty for being alive. He holds himself personally responsible for the deaths. These are all quite normal reactions to the type of trauma he's been through. I'm confident he will get over them."

"Yes, I'm sure he will. Right now I need to talk to him."

"He's in my care, Mr. Warner, and you are *not* going to talk to him. I have consulted with the staff psychiatrist, whom your pilot refuses to see. Having a person of your authority judge Captain Hutchinson's performance at this fragile stage in his recovery could have severe long-term emotional consequences. You will have to wait until next week at the earliest."

Warner, all six feet two inches of him, blocked the doctor's passage, fixing him with the withering, red-eyed stare reserved for those who irritated him when he was exhausted.

"Look, Doc, you and I are going to get something straight. I don't know what business you're in, but I'm in the business of saving lives. We have no black box and no flight recorder from this crash. Other than the pilot, we have no adult survivors to tell us what happened. But that pilot is alive and healthy enough to talk, which is a miracle. We're going to interview him, not to judge him but to gain insight into what caused the crash. Waiting could endanger every person who steps aboard a Boeing aircraft in the next week. Is this what you want, Doctor?"

The doctor tried to look Warner in the eye but couldn't. "All right, if it's that critical you may talk to him for a few minutes. But I insist on being in the room. That's my condition."

"You can get in bed with him for all I care. Gentlemen, let's get this done."

Hutchinson was propped up on the elevated bed watching a college football game. In spite of the bandages, tubes, casts and traction devices, he looked pretty good.

"Who's playing?" Warner asked.

"Iowa and Purdue, not too interesting."

"May I turn it off?"

"Sure."

Warner squeezed the remote. The picture shrank to a bright dot and vanished. "Captain Hutchinson, I'm Frank Warner of the NTSB. This is Mr. Simmons, my colleague. The big guy is Jeremy Little, attorney for ALPA. Don't get the wrong idea. You're not being investigated. His presence is a formality. It's tough being up there in a jet with no power. I know. It happened to me in the Air Force."

"You probably handled it better than I did."

"Not exactly," Warner said, pulling up a chair. "I punched out. I would have done it differently if I'd had the wisdom of hindsight. My plane nearly crashed into a school." He sat down close to the bed. "When did you loose control?"

"At the very end. When the wing tip caught a wave. We had no information on surface winds or the direction of the sea. When we broke through the low clouds, we had to bank to get the aircraft parallel to the troughs. To tell you the truth, I thought I had it knocked. I was levelling off and preparing to set her down on the backside of a swell when it happened. I waited too long to come out of my turn. I guess I tried to be exactly parallel. I tried to make it too perfect a ditch—and you see the results. I'm prepared to take the blame."

"Blame for what?" said Warner. "The odds of ditching safely without power in a Seven Five are probably less than a hundred to one. The odds weren't with you that day or you wouldn't have lost both engines."

"Amen."

"So, Captain Hutchinson, stop blaming yourself. You are not to blame. We need to move on to more substantive matters."

"It just hurts to have come so close."

"I understand. Now, Captain, can you give us any idea why those engines started losing oil? Was there an irregularity you noticed at any stage of the flight that could provide a clue."

"Look, between you and me, it's gotta be those maintenance yo-yos at SFO. I'd bet what's left of my dick there's some kind of cover-up going on there. Have you checked it out?"

"We have. There's no cover-up. A supervisor and two line mechanics all saw the O-rings on the sender units when they were installed. We found the discarded parts I.D. numbers in the trash. They matched the computer record of the items requisitioned by the mechanics."

Hutchinson tried to reposition himself and groaned. Warner helped him turn on his side.

"Thanks," Hutchinson said. "I don't necessarily mean the O-rings themselves. I've been lying here for thirty hours trying to figure out the same thing you are. This morning I thought of an old incident I'd all but forgotten. I was flying the 727 back in the seventies. It happened on that red-eye from New York to San Francisco, remember it? Stopped in Chicago, Denver and Salt Lake, and could be pretty miserable in winter."

"I took it more than once," Warner said. "I was always glad someone else was flying. What happened?"

"We got diverted to Des Moines, snow in Chicago. It was past midnight and the maintenance crews were packing it in. Anyway, I needed the oil topped up in two of my engines. Maintenance got a couple guys out there who looked half asleep. They did the job, the passengers bound for Chicago got off and we continued on to the west. Everything remained uneventful until we reached cruising altitude coming out of Salt Lake City. All of a sudden the engines that had been topped up started pissing oil. Know what caused it?"

"Why don't you tell me?"

"Those dingbats in Des Moines had dumped in hydraulic fluid by mistake. The stuff ate through the O-rings after a few hours and caused the oil to hemorrhage. I was lucky they hadn't touched the third engine or we would have ended up in the Sierras."

"That's an interesting parallel, Captain. It seems to me I vaguely remember the report of that incident. Don't know why I didn't think of it myself. All the elements of the present crash were there, weren't they? A few hours of normal operation, then a sudden massive loss of oil."

"They're there all right. Can you look at the engines? How much of the wreck did you recover?"

"Floating debris only. The evidence is five thousand feet down. It's gone, Captain. Which means we'll have to concentrate on the other end, the maintenance fellows. You've certainly given me a fresh hypothesis to test. I appreciate it."

"You'll find something at SFO. I'm convinced of that."

Warner's cellular telephone, concealed in his briefcase, rang shrilly.

"Hey," the doctor said, "those things aren't allowed in this hospital. You could interfere with the operation of sophisticated medical equipment."

Warner ignored him and took the call. The doctor got to his feet but Warner's stare froze him on the spot.

Warner listened in disbelief. He rang off and shook his head, looking even more exhausted.

"What is it, chief?" Simmons asked.

Warner took his man aside. "Another Seven Six," he whispered. "Crashed on take-off at Pittsburgh, two hundred twenty on board.

Engine separation. Similar to the Atlanta mishap last spring, except that the aircraft exploded when the engine hit the wing."

"This is crazy," Simmons whispered back. "Look at the stats, Frank. From 1983 to Atlanta that's eleven years—you've got a total of one crash involving a 757 or 767. Since last May—that's what, five months?—you've got another three. It just doesn't add up. There's something strange going on here."

"Let's not speculate, Tim. Our job is to understand what caused each crash. I'm going back to San Francisco. I want you to assemble a Go Team for Pittsburgh."

Warner returned to Hutchinson's bedside. "I have to go now, Captain. Thanks again for your help. Give me a call when you get out and I'll let you know what we found."

"I'll do that, Mr. Warner. I'd like to get my hands on the bastard who fucked up."

"So would I." Warner turned the football game back on and walked out, his thoughts already on the most recent crash. If the aft engine mount had failed again, as it had in Atlanta, he might find a clue as to what was causing that particular part to break.

✶   ✶   ✶

Claussen, back from a brisk swim around the island, listened to the latest radio report of the Pittsburgh crash. Regrets were inevitable, he thought, pouring himself a shot of clear schnapps. The events of the last months proved beyond doubt that Volkov had underestimated the power of Operation 26. Judging from the ease with which he had caused the disasters in Atlanta, over the Pacific and in Pittsburgh, Claussen no longer had any doubt that the Soviet Union in its prime possessed the capacity to bring American civil aviation to its knees.

If just two dozen modified parts judiciously placed in the parts stream could provoke this degree of havoc, he thought, what would have been the destructive potential of his entire inventory? A hundred crashes the first day the Americans attempted to airlift troops to Europe? Three hundred? Not at all unthinkable, given the involvement of the line mechanics Claussen had recruited with such care.

Volkov had wanted 10,000 American soldiers eliminated before they reached the front; Claussen would have delivered; and rewarded him with an additional bonus of 40,000.

With the publication of his memoirs after he assumed his long-planned retirement identity in Bolivia, Claussen would have become the towering giant of wartime sabotage. His name would have become synonymous with brilliance, stealth, fearlessness, and the refusal to submit to the credo of the modern world—which was that important work was done by groups, that a single man could no longer make a difference.

Ah, well, he thought, gazing out at his cantankerous geese, it was not to be. He would have to content himself with a paltry dozen or so crashes of no long-term historical significance.

But not so fast, not so fast. These crashes were precisely the proof he needed to make the world believe that Operation 26 not only existed but could have effortlessly achieved what it was designed to do. Because of them, his memoirs would be credible. They would be received as the record of a genius at work rather than the rantings of a lunatic. That was a benefit he should not despise.

He threw his geese some scraps, slammed the window shut before they distracted his thinking and moved to his roll top desk. He was leaving for Liechtenstein tomorrow to take care of some minor financial matters. It would be a good time to post the letter that represented his checkmate in the power struggle with his employers. He would compose it now; he was in the mood.

Claussen could not help smiling as he drew his pen and wrote:

Pilot's Dawn

Dear Georges,

I know you wanted to remain anonymous—it's only human nature in situations such as these. But I never allow inequality to imbalance and ultimately threaten my working relationships.

Now that I know who you are, I would like to express my thanks to you, your colleague, Mr. Haussmann and, of course, to my old friend, Paul. I am pleased I could be of help to you in a matter which you consider vital to your country's economic and cultural independence. I am also pleased to report that everything is proceeding as planned and that you can look forward to a quick and successful conclusion of my assignment.

I want to stress that my knowing who you are in no way increases your risk of exposure. I have no interest in ever divulging a scheme that would take down all four of us. However, as a prudent man, I felt it wise to deliver you from the temptation to eliminate me after I fulfilled my part of the deal.

To this end, I have placed detailed records conclusively establishing your role in this operation with several of my attorneys. Some of the evidence contained in my "files," such as photographs of the three of you together at the Michelet country home and the visual and audio record of my initial meeting with Paul, will be delivered to you by special courier.

I stress again that my knowledge is harmless as long as your intentions toward me remain honorable. However, should I die or become incapacitated in the next five years *for any reason*, I have asked my attorneys to make your files public.

Take good care of me, gentlemen. It is in my best interest; and also in yours.

cc: Paul Delors
    Albert Haussmann

Claussen reread the letter, made two copies, and addressed three envelopes. After sealing the letters, he placed them in the zippered pocket of his briefcase. He stretched and returned to his desk. It was seven o'clock this fine September evening. He would work on his memoirs until ten, as he did most nights, then devote the hours till midnight to his watercolors. Life had never been more pleasant.

Chapter Sixteen

Frank Warner threw in the towel at nine o'clock in the evening. Calling his small contingent of investigators to his suite, he thanked them for their work in San Francisco and dismissed them. He was not accustomed to leaving the initial phase of an investigation so soon, and he was plagued by a persistent ugly doubt that he had missed something.

But he had no choice. He and his people had tested every conceivable hypothesis that might explain why the United Airlines 757 en route to Hawaii had lost oil and plunged into the Pacific. They had meticulously researched Captain Hutchinson's theory of hydraulic fluid in the oil, which sounded promising but had been soundly disproved. They had even located O-rings made from the same batch of compound as those installed on the ill-fated plane and had analyzed the compound for the slightest irregularities. There were none.

Given the point in the flight at which the leak had begun and the rate at which it had stabilized, Warner could not help clinging to the hunch that degradation of the O-rings was in some mysterious way to blame. But since he could find no supporting evidence, his own strict rules of investigation forced him to toss his hunch on the junk heap of dead-end suppositions accumulated by his staff. The investigation would have to be continued in labs and offices all over the country. His hands-on first assault had failed.

He telephoned Claire, whom he hadn't been able to reach for the last three days. It was after midnight on the East Coast and she still wasn't home. She had left him, he couldn't deceive himself any longer.

Probably inevitable, he thought, but he wished she had picked another time. This was shaping up as the worst week of his life.

No sooner had he hung up than Susan Waters from the New York office, who had been working with the team in San Francisco day and night, telephoned from the room down the hall.

"Yes, Susan, what is it?"

"A few of us have been talking, Frank. Why don't you let us take you out tonight for a leisurely dinner, some easy music. You know, get your mind off this whole frustrating affair for at least a few hours. You're looking very exhausted."

"That's kind of you, Susan. I appreciate it."

"Which means you won't join us?"

"I'm sorry, I'm just not up to it. Thank the others for me. It was a nice thought."

"Take care of yourself, Frank. Sometimes I worry you feel responsible for these crashes. You shouldn't."

"Good night, Susan. Enjoy your dinner."

Warner hung up and paced. Should he pore over the mountains of paperwork on the United crash again? No. He knew the material backwards and forwards.

Should he have dinner sent up and watch TV? He wasn't hungry and couldn't have cared less about anything on the tube.

Should he try to sleep? That brought a smile to his lips.

He picked up the phone and dialed United. Yes, he could still get to Pittsburgh by morning if he didn't mind changing planes in Chicago and airlines in Columbus.

He called Yellow Cab, already packing with one hand while he waited for an answer. It was a relief to be moving. Whatever he did tonight, he was going to be miserable and unproductive. He might as well use the down time to haul himself to the next crash site.

* * *

Pilot's Dawn

By the fourth day of the Pittsburgh investigation even the purists had given up eating cereal and grapefruit in the morning. The long white-clothed table in the Airport Sheraton conference room was strewn with half-eaten doughnuts, nibbled bear claws and dirty ashtrays. Used styrofoam and porcelain coffee cups stood around in clusters containing liquid of varying depths and hues. Tired men and women shuffled through the charts, transcripts, and computer printouts they had been studying half the night.

Tim Simmons came it at eight a.m. sharp, a light sweat from his morning workout still on his forehead. His tan suit fit to perfection, his shirt and tie looked new.

Simmons pushed the platter of doughnuts aside, poured a glass of orange juice and stepped to the podium. "Good morning. You're a gray looking bunch. Roth, Kendall, one of you please update the inventory of wreckage brought in yesterday."

There was grunting and more shuffling, a silent yawn and a noisy one. Simmons waited for someone to begin...

The biggest problem of the Pittsburgh investigation was the manner in which the 767 had come apart. The violent explosion at 900 feet had hurled debris a great distance in all directions and disfigured a lot of the wreckage. The crash had taken place over an unpopulated area, which was fortunate. But the forests and undergrowth were dense, the days rainy, and some of the fragments so small they were nearly impossible to spot.

After the second day Simmons had sent them all into the woods to help the hired hands—Ph.D.s in math, computer programmers, even Barb Lacey, who insisted on wearing high heels and stockings whenever she was on government time.

"Hey," Simmons said into the continuing silence, "we didn't come here to meditate. One of you get this show on the road."

Roth, Kendall and the others did not respond. They were all staring past Simmons at some spot on the wall.

"Come on, dammit," Simmons said. "Frank's gonna shit if he gets here and finds a bunch of hotshot specialists with nothing but muddy boots to show."

"This is true."

Simmons turned at the sound of that inimitable voice. Warner stood just inside the doorway, red-eyed, rumpled and unshaven. He looked as if he were trying to decide whose head to bite off first.

Simmons said, "Frank! Welcome. When did you arrive?"

"Seven-forty, U.S. Air out of Columbus."

"You've been flying all night?"

"And thinking."

"Well come on in. Have some breakfast. We'll bring you up to date and then you can get some sleep."

"I'll sleep when we figure out what happened here. In case you haven't heard, the pressure's on in Washington. You can count on it getting worse if we don't have some answers for this crash soon. I'm sorry to say we've gotten nowhere on the United crash. Finish your briefing and meet me at the work site, Tim. I'm going over there now."

*   *   *

In the brightly lit hangar Warner surveyed the reconstruction, which still had a ways to go. Enough of the main body of the aircraft had been found and assembled to reveal a gaping, charred hole in right side of the fuselage. An untrained eye might have taken the wound as evidence of a bomb blast inside the plane, but the inward bend of the surrounding metal made it obvious to Warner that the explosion had not originated in the fuselage.

An enormous patch of the right wing, from its point of contact with the body of the aircraft to well out past the attachment point of the engine pylon, was missing. Here the lacerated edges of the wing bordering the hole were bent outward, indicating an explosion of the wing tank.

Pilot's Dawn

Warner knew from the CVR that the pilot had experienced severe vibrations shortly after take-off, and several dozen spectators had seen the right engine develop a shake and wobble that quickly grew worse. The home video film of a man who had recorded the accident, a copy of which Warner had received in San Francisco, left little doubt as to what had caused the explosion. Examining the film one frame at a time, he could see the engine under full thrust tearing loose from its pylon, swinging on an upward trajectory and slamming into the leading edge of the wing.

Since this much was already known, the primary objective of the Pittsburgh investigation was to find out what had caused the engine to separate from the aircraft. The similar accident in Atlanta, also involving a 767 300 ER, made it tempting to assume that the aft engine mount had failed again. Warner hoped this was the case. If it was, it might reveal an inherent defect in the mounts that the Atlanta investigation had not turned up. But he knew he must heed the warning he never tired of giving his staff: assume nothing.

Tim Simmons came in a few minutes later. He gave instructions to several men sorting the wreckage that had arrived yesterday afternoon on a flatbed truck, then walked over to Warner and looked him in the eye. "Are you ready for the bad news?"

"No, but give it to me."

"It's easier to explain when you're staring the shit in the face. I kept the parts I knew you'd want to examine off to the side. They've only been here since noon yesterday. I didn't get to study them closely until after dinner. When I called you at your hotel, you'd already left. This way, Frank."

Warner walked with Simmons to a corner of the hangar where big pieces of wreckage were still being numbered, catalogued and photographed before making their journey to the reconstruction site. He passed a twisted piece of the main landing gear, its great tires reduced to a few pounds incinerated black gook; a fractured turbine blade bent like a scythe; a battered nacelle that must have been blown free of the engine when it hit the wing.

Arriving late had one advantage, he thought: you didn't see the bodies that had been shredded, pummeled, torn and burned by these same horrendous forces. You didn't see them, but you never forgot they had been there.

On a steel table beneath fluorescent lights, Simmons had laid out the front and aft engine mounts to the engine that had come off the plane, as well as two bent engine mounting bolts and remnants of two others that had sheered.

The mounts were both still attached to surviving chunks of badly burned engine pylon. It was immediately evident to Warner that the bends and nicks they exhibited were the result of impact with the ground. They had not failed; the cause of the Atlanta crash had not been duplicated here.

He experienced a sinking feeling. What the hell was going on? Why couldn't he figure it out? Boeing jets were beginning to drop like pheasants in hunting season, yet none of the crashes seemed to have anything in common. At what point did you conclude that this succession of disasters could not be coincidence? After three crashes? Five? Ten?

He examined the mounting bolts one at a time. He could feel Simmons watching him. "Well, Frank? Do you notice anything odd?"

"Yes. Two of these things evidently sheered off the way they're supposed to when there is severe engine vibration. You were lucky to find these, Simmons. Nice job. The other two bent but did not break—the front two, if I'm not mistaken."

"That's right, Frank, the front two didn't break."

"This apparently caused the engine to swing upward and strike the wing instead of dropping away harmlessly."

"You can see just that in the video."

"Yes. What do we know about the engine? Why did it produce such powerful vibrations in the first place?"

Simmons said, "This is where it gets bizarre. We've found all the moving components. The Pratt and Whitney people have been here, as well as two independent experts. They've examined the shafts, bearings, turbines, everything. They all agree nothing was wrong with the power plant. There was no catastrophic engine failure. The black box bears this out."

"Do you mean to tell me those two rear mounting bolts snapped under the normal stress of take-off?"

"Yes, Frank. We'll have them sent out and stress-tested properly in the next few days, but Johnson, the metallurgy guy, has already taken a look at them. He says evidence of metal fatigue is written all over them—pre-crash metal fatigue."

"This can't be, Tim. If you're right, it means that *all four* mounting bolts were defective, does it not?"

"Go on. Let's see if we're thinking along the same lines."

"Two sheered when they should not have, producing out of parameter vibrations from the engine. The other two, had their tensile strength been within specs, would have snapped at this point. But instead they resisted enormous forces. Look at them. Look at how they're bent. Have you ever seen this type of a bolt bend but not break?"

"Exactly, chief. I don't get it. In the thirteen years these Seven Fives and Seven Sixes have been flying, we've had absolutely zero trouble with any of the engine mounting components. On the 747, yes, but that's a different bird with a different mounting system."

"It's not right, I agree. We're going to have to look more closely into anything Boeing might have done to change the way these parts are manufactured."

"Where's that going to get us, Frank? You're forgetting that these things are examined with the most reliable equipment in the world before they join the parts stream. We know the equipment functions because it has and does uncover an occasional defect. Besides, your Hawaii crash involved engine components that are supplied by Pratt and Whitney, not Boeing."

"It could all be coincidence. In fact, it probably is."

"Maybe, Frank. But it seems to me we should at least consider another possibility.

"Which is?"

"Tampering. The possibility that something is going on between the time the parts are manufactured and the time they're installed. This 767 just had its engines removed and overhauled. It received new mounts and mounting bolts. In fact, of the three crashes we've had in the last five months, all three aircraft had just been in for maintenance. With the two Seven Six crashes, we know for a fact the parts that failed had been replaced. The same is probably true of the Seven Five crash. I'm sorry, Frank, but that just doesn't sound like coincidence to me."

Warner emitted a long frustrated groan. "It strikes me as highly irregular. But we've gone to great extremes to check and authenticate the serial numbers *and* the actual parts. I simply can't conceive of a scenario in which tampering could happen."

"Look, Frank, neither can I. But the circumstantial evidence is piling up. I don't see how we can ignore it."

"We can't ignore it. But we can't embrace it either—can't embrace it until we find some hard evidence. Go to work. I'll pay Larsen a visit. Maybe it's time we started listening to him. One more thing, Simmons—"

"Yes, sir?"

"I don't want the others to know about this. We're not cops. Conspiracy theories can be distracting. Go on and get distracted but don't corrupt the team. There are still plenty of unanswered questions that fall within the normal scope of an investigation."

"Got it, Frank. I think we're moving in the right direction."

"I hope so."

For a long time after Simmons left, Warner sat there with the mounting bolts, turning them over in his hands.

Chapter Seventeen

At O'Hare Airport, Ray Sels kissed his wife good-bye, shook hands with his boys, and told them how much he would miss them. Though they were only going to be in Los Angeles for five days, it already felt like an eternity. Chicago could be a lonely place.

He waited for them to disappear around the crook in the jetway, then went up to the new observation deck to watch their take-off and enjoy a few minutes of the fine autumn weather.

At 10:35, right on time, the jetway rolled back from the door and the tractor pushed the sleek silver plane with red and blue lettering out on to the taxiway. With its engines humming smooth and powerful, Flight 2217 turned and taxied to the far end of the field, joining a short queue of jets in waiting.

One by one, the aircraft roared down the runway and lifted off. It was an exhilarating sight when they were taking off in this direction. From the end of the field where they started to roll, they seemed to be coming almost directly at you. And when they thundered into the air, you could see the landing gear go up and the doors close over the wheels.

The American Airlines 757 taxied into position and waited for clearance. Ray imagined his family inside the cabin. Jimmy and Johnny would be watching out the window with delight while Sammy teased Kim about parachutes. He knew they were going to have a wonderful time. For a moment he regretted not being with them. Maybe he should have taken a few days off work, he thought. He wasn't really as busy at the office as he had let on.

Oh, well, next time.

The plane began to move, the sun glinting fiercely off its silver skin. Ray dropped his head for a moment of silent prayer. When he looked again, the jet was rolling fast, its nose wheel already in the air. It must be a light load, he thought. It had lifted off sooner than the other planes and climbed more steeply. He waved as the landing gear went up. Flight 2217 banked slightly to the right on its perfect departure for the heavens.

Suddenly, he heard a change in the pitch of the engines. The jet shuddered like a game bird hit by buckshot, yawed violently to the left and started to roll. Seconds later it slammed into the earth. There was a flash, followed by a deafening explosion. An orange fireball mushroomed before his eyes, pumping clouds of black smoke at the sun.

Ray took a step closer to the railing. He touched it timidly to make certain it was real. A perfect silence engulfed him as he watched the fireball swell. The smoke spread out in thick bulbous clouds and extinguished the sun. He heard the sirens now, and saw the rescue vehicles speeding across the airport grass. He held the railing more tightly. He felt nothing. It wasn't until the blaze was almost out that his heart began to scream.

*   *   *

Hal Larsen sat on deck, gazing across several miles of slate gray water at the crisp clean skyline of Seattle. There had been times these last few months when he felt like sailing the company yacht toward the South Seas and never coming back. But he knew he would never run away from disaster. He wasn't that kind of a man. You faced crises head-on. That's what life was about.

While he waited for Delta CEO Reid Allworth to come up on deck, his mind drifted back to his early years at Boeing. He had gone to work for the company in the fifties, his first job out of Stanford Graduate School. He was an idealistic young engineer with a fervent belief that the time for introducing commercial jets was now. The company had staked its survival on the same belief, which was why Larsen picked Boeing over Convair and Douglas, each of whom had offered him more money.

His vision, like that of his company, seemed for one fateful moment above Lake Washington in 1954 destined to suffer a terrible blow. It was the day that the prototype of the 707, Boeing's big gamble, was to be flown in full view of the public the first time.

For the occasion, over 300,000 spectators—among them media people, airline executives and legions of nervous Boeing employees—lined the banks of the lake, hoping to catch a glimpse of what Boeing touted as the future of air travel.

The plane, enormous by the day's standards, came roaring in just above the water at 450 miles an hour, climbed at an angle so steep it would have caused a prop-driven aircraft to stall, then spun into a 360 degree barrel roll.

Larsen felt his heart stop. It seemed certain that something had gone wrong with the jet and that its maiden voyage would end, like the Titanic's, as a tragic legend.

But nothing was wrong with the plane. It had not stalled or come apart in the air but had flown to the far end of the lake and returned like a fighter on a strafing mission. Incredibly, it had repeated the same steep climb and breathtaking barrel roll.

On that day the age of the passenger jet began in earnest and, with it, the rise of Boeing to the world's largest manufacturer of commercial aircraft.

Larsen believed his predecessor, Bill Allen, had ordered the daring show to demonstrate the structural integrity of the new aircraft. He did not learn until later that Allen had been furious about the maneuver, which had been done on impulse by the company's freewheeling test pilot, Tex Boullioun.

Structural integrity. That had been Boeing's reputation in the Second World War, when Flying Fortresses returned from raids over Germany missing great chunks of wing, tail and fuselage; and it was Boeing's well-earned reputation in the jet age. It hadn't been easy to bring down a B-17 with .50 calibre canon and 88 millimeter flak, and it wasn't easy to bring down a 767 today.

So why the hell were they crashing as if they were designed and built by drunken Russians? He would find out, the world would find out, but the important question was when. Right now he had his hands full just holding the company together. If he lost the support of increasingly skittish airline executives such as Allworth, he feared Boeing could go into a financial tailspin from which it would not recover—at least not in his lifetime. He had to be as strong as those wounded B-17s limping home from Stuttgart with two engines and half a wing blown off. He had to be. He hadn't led Boeing to the top to preside over its decline in his last year as chairman and chief executive officer.

Allworth had flown in from Atlanta today for the meeting. He had insisted that no attorneys or witnesses be present, just the two chairmen, face-to-face.

Larsen had agreed but had extracted a minor concession: that the meeting be held on the company yacht rather than at the Four Seasons Olympic Hotel, as Allworth had wanted. He did not divulge his reason for wanting to meet the Delta chief on the yacht because it was symbolic rather than substantive. It was on a similar boat that Delta and Boeing officials had broken the ice in the early seventies, a warming that led to billions of dollars of aircraft sales that would otherwise have gone to Lockheed and McDonnell Douglas.

Allworth had called from Atlanta to ask what kind of clothes he should bring. Larsen laughed to himself. Don't worry, Reid, he'd told him. You probably can't get a wool sweater in Atlanta. But you and I are the same size and I've got enough to fill a 747.

When Allworth joined him on deck, he was wearing his own wool sweater, not one of the two dozen Larsen had had sent to his hotel room. This was Larsen's first sign that his friend of two decades, and the man whose confidence he desperately needed to shore up the crumbling dikes, might have slipped beyond his grasp.

A server, a pretty girl with a British accent, brought out a superb bottle of champagne and a platter of Beluga caviar, standard fare for the airline executives being wined and dined on the yacht. Allworth, a bon vivant of some repute, ignored both.

This, thought Larsen, was the second bad sign.

"Are you feeling all right?" he asked.

"I'm all right, Hal. Thanks for meeting me alone. One does tire of all the lawyers and accountants."

"I should say so. Reid, before you get going with what you've come here to discuss, I hope you'll let me have a few words."

"Of course," said Allworth, the consummate southern gentleman when he wished to be.

"Thank you. First, I want to repeat what I've been saying from the beginning. This debacle with our planes is the work of an outside element. Our only failure, if you wish to view it as such, has been our inability to convince the authorities of this fact. I think they're coming around now. Warner called me this morning. I assure you we're going to get to the bottom of this thing very soon. When we do, and when the responsible parties are put out of commission, the stigma the flying public has started to attach to our aircraft will vanish.

"Second, Reid, we've had options for new aircraft cancelled to the tune of forty-seven billion dollars. We're suddenly finding ourselves in a position I thought impossible. The banks won't lend us money. We're on the verge of financial collapse.

"I need my friends to stand behind me, Reid. Specifically, I need the support of men like yourself, the CEOs of the big domestic carriers. Together we've made jet air travel a way of life. Together we can overcome this crisis and move toward a bright future. Don't cancel your options with us, Reid. Over the long haul, it would not be in Delta's best interest. And over the short haul it would deal me and my company a terrible blow."

Allworth had been looking out over the water during the entire monologue, unwilling to meet Larsen's eyes. Now he poured himself a glass of champagne and spread some Beluga on a cracker. Larsen waited, hoping.

Allworth said, "I hear you, Hal, but I'm afraid I can't help you. If we were talking about my personal resources, it would be different. But we're not. We're talking about my stockholders and employees. I'm their chairman. I have a fiduciary duty to them and owe them a special debt of gratitude for making Delta the fine organization it is. I cannot and will not let my airline sink because your aircraft have suddenly become unreliable."

"But, Reid, Boeing is not the cause of these crashes."

"I can't take a position on that. The planes are crashing. That's all that matters."

"For Christ's sake, this is ridiculous. You of all people know we go overboard to make our aircraft safe. You *know* we don't cut corners. You *know* we haven't become a bunch of careless slugs overnight. We've been building the safest jetliners in the world for forty years. We still are, Reid. They are being sabotaged. Listen, here's all I ask. Give me six months. I don't care if you ground your Boeing fleet until the mystery is solved. I don't care if you remain silent on your options for new planes as long as you don't cancel them publicly. Because if you do Reid, I'm not sure we can continue with the Triple Seven program."

"Hal, it pains me to say this, but you seem out of touch with the level of panic out there."

"I am not out of touch."

"You are, and I'm going to give you an example. You're upset I might cancel Delta's options. But, Hal, I've come to cancel our fifty-three firm orders. The options…how could you have thought we would *not* cancel these? The flying public doesn't give a hoot about anyone's loyalty to

Boeing. They don't care about the past. All they want is to get where they're going safely, and that means avoiding Boeing planes, period. So that's what I've come to tell you, Hal. We're pulling out of the Triple Seven deal."

"No you're not, Reid. A contract is a contract. We're going to hold you to it. That billion due Boeing next month is critical to us. You bought the planes. You can't pretend you didn't."

"Let me ask you something, Hal. What are you going to do to make us honor our contract?"

"What do you think?"

"Legal action?"

"You better believe it."

"Out of touch, Hal, you're simply out of touch. I sympathize with you, but American business doesn't run on sympathy. The rest of us in the industry are going to do what we must to protect our interests, just as you would in our shoes. Do you think a jury of people who fly, meaning any jury in the United States, is going to force us to buy planes they've come to perceive as murder weapons?"

"Now just a minute."

"No. You let me finish. We didn't enter into this deal to kill our customers and put ourselves out of business. I came here today as a friend, Hal. I came to give you the option of getting Boeing out of a lawsuit. Because, Hal, some members of my board actually *want* you to sue us. They want the cameras of the world's media on our attorneys when they stand up and say, we at Delta have a higher duty to our passengers than honoring a piece of paper, the duty of protecting their lives.

"What I'm going to tell you should not come as a shock to you, Hal. We have shifted all one hundred and six of our future orders and options from Boeing to Airbus, and we will be hitting this fact hard in our next advertising campaign. However, Hal, if you drag us into court, that advertising campaign might not be necessary. There's no way Delta could buy better publicity than to have you sue us for refusing to buy your aircraft."

Larsen was devastated. He got up, walked to the deck rail and stared into space for a long time. When he turned around to give it one last pitch, Reid Allworth had gone below.

Chapter Eighteen

Steven knew when he saw the flash that someone had taken one hell of a photograph of a kiss.

It was one of those September evenings in Paris when it's still hot as summer, but a drab murky twilight settles over the city long before nightfall. Maybe the photograph wouldn't capture the heat of that sweltering evening, he thought, but it sure would capture the heat of his passion for this terrific girl.

He wouldn't mind knowing what her expression was, either. He just hoped he wouldn't find out in some sleazy tabloid...

Nicole had telephoned him at his flat the night before, his first contact with her since they had left Nice two weeks ago. It had been tough upon his return to Paris not to go looking for her, but that's what she swore she wanted. Without Sophie's assurances that he had nothing to worry about, that Nicole would come around on her own accord if he just waited, he might have committed a big blunder by trying to find her.

But he hadn't, and Sophie was right, as usual. On this, their first evening together after their enchanting time in the south, he and Nicole were sitting in a tiny outdoor café having a lovers' quarrel about how they should carry on their relationship in Paris. When he had finally heard enough about her fears of being seen with him, he said the hell with it, reached across the table and took her in his arms.

She tried to push him away, she had been terrified of meeting him in public, let alone kissing him. Then she must have said the hell with it, too. Because all of sudden she stopped resisting and kissed him so passionately she knocked over his pastis. He heard the ice cubes hit the table and saw the flash in the same instant. They looked up in time to catch a glimpse of a teenager on a moped zooming off, his camera on a strap around his neck.

He expected nasty recriminations, even the stormy end of their relationship. Instead, she uttered a sedate *"merde"* and said she had been ridiculous. She was 19 years old, she loved him—God how she loved him. The two weeks without him had been time in purgatory. What difference did it make if her father disowned her? Steven had been right, he had convinced her: you either listened to your heart or shriveled up like an old prune.

He gave her directions to his flat, trying to hide his raging inner battle between horniness and conscience. What if he did ruin her life? It was beginning to seem like a real possibility.

Well, he couldn't worry about that when he was bursting with desire. He had to put his priorities in order, make sweet love to her, then wild love, then sort things out when the blood was again flowing to his brain.

Besides, it was possible the photograph was nothing, the work of some rank amateur who didn't even know who Nicole Michelet was. Or maybe the Japs had committed a first and manufactured a roll of bad film. You never knew, stranger things had happened. He hadn't burdened himself with excessive worry in the past. Why start now?

As he watched her hurry to her Renault, it struck him that he wanted more than anything for their relationship to continue.

He'd better force himself to think about what they were doing, he decided. If Nicole threw all caution to the wind, as she just appeared to have done, he was going to have to take charge and make sure they didn't self-destruct. He was going to have to come up with a reasonable plan for managing their affair—a plan with an eye to the future.

God forbid, he was thinking like his father and brothers.

He paid the bill, got on his motorcycle and hit the throttle, imagining her skirt, blouse and panties strewn all over his living room. No chance they would make it to the bedroom.

Pilot's Dawn

They didn't, not until the second time. While they sat up in bed listening to the city come alive after dark, he broached the dreaded subject of caution.

"I've been thinking, for a change," he said. "It wouldn't be right for you to have problems because of me. Things are so good. I don't want them tainted by any bad experiences. Know something, Nicole? You might not believe me, but I've never felt this way about anyone."

"I love you, I love you, I love you," she said. "What are you trying to tell me?"

"Well, I've decided you were right about being careful."

She pulled the sheet up over her breasts and snuggled close. "And I've decided I was wrong. I don't care anymore, Steven. Why should I give a damn what my father thinks? He's the bigot, not me. That makes it his problem, right? Anyway, it's only a matter of time until he finds out about us. Francoise knows, I'm sure she does. She's just waiting to catch us so she can go to father with more than suspicions."

"Maybe she sent that kid with the camera."

"No. She couldn't have known I was meeting you. I called from a friend's house."

"Okay, whatever. But my point is this. We're doing great as it is. Let them suspect, but why should we be stupid? No telling what your dad might do. He might have me deported. He might send you away. If I was a rich man it would be a different story. I'd say, come on, Nicole, let's go live in Montreal or Florence or some other great place where he can't touch us. But the way things are, I'm barely squeaking by on what I make at the club."

She laughed. "You're learning to be a good Frenchman. You play down what you have so the tax man doesn't come looking for you. You told me about your family. You had plenty of money in Nice. Why *don't* we go live somewhere else? It would be fun."

His heart skipped a beat. Everyday life had become a mine field. It was like being elected to Congress. All your lies had to jibe, which meant you had to remember what they were.

"Sure it would be fun," he said, "but we can't do it. What you saw me spending on the coast was a little nest egg from when my aunt died. But it's gone now, bad exchange rate, bad spending habits. Meaning you and I have to be practical. I have to keep my job here, and you have to make sure you don't get sent off to the salt mines. I'm broke, your dad isn't going to support us and I've got this feeling we'd both be lousy at living under bridges."

"Then we'll be practical," she said. "Whatever you think is best." She got up and walked naked to the kitchen. When she came back, she was carrying two glasses and a bottle of white Bordeaux he'd had chilling in his refrigerator—an expensive bottle Sophie had given him. Seeing Nicole like this, he was ready to tell her he was rich, postpone the discussion of practicality he had been postponing his entire adult life and take her in his arms again.

She slid under the sheets and kissed him.

God, everything about her was incredibly enticing. Most women looked a hell of a lot better dressed than undressed. Not so with Nicole. She was dazzling to start with, and the more she took off, the better she got. He was convinced he would still want to devour her on his deathbed.

Why, he wondered, did he have to find love now, when he was in the middle of an assignment based on the rankest deception? He could almost hear himself after he got caught trying to convince her that you could love and deceive the same person with equal intensity. That was even more ludicrous than the argument, "Okay, so I'm having an affair, it doesn't mean I love you any less than before." Never mind that *his* argument was true.

He had to tell her about Sophie and the scheme at some point. But when? And how? Jesus, you heard all the time about some poor bastard getting sucked deeper and deeper into something he thought he could get out of, sucked in until it wasted him. But until you experienced it yourself, you really didn't know what it was like.

He poured her a glass of wine, nothing for himself. He had to get some things handled, if not the big issue, then at least the small one of keeping things discreet. One sip of Montrachet and he knew he'd be rolling around with her again...

"Nice wine for a poor man," she said, laughing softly.

"A gift from the tennis club." He kissed her on the cheek. "Look, here's the way I see it. If it's true what you were saying, if everyone in France knows who you are now because of that *Paris-Match* spread, we either meet here or we meet somewhere they don't know you."

"Such as?"

"Switzerland, Italy."

"Steven! Francoise watches me like a hawk. I can't just go jetting around the world. Unless, of course, I plan on not coming back. And you tell me that won't work."

"Okay, what about this? You come here from time to time like I said. No problem with that, right?"

"Right."

"And when we want to do something else together, we do it at night. Say we want to go see a movie. You buy a ticket, I buy a ticket, we have this plan for meeting at a certain time and place inside. Or we go to the opera, I get us two seats side by side and we sit there like we each went alone and don't know each other. Then we come here separately afterwards, I cook a great meal and we pretend we're in a New York restaurant. Then comes the dessert, which takes us to morning—"

"Oh, Steven." She handed him the glass of wine he had refused and he drank it. Why not? He couldn't do any worse than he was doing.

"You don't like my plan?" he asked sheepishly.

"It's worse than the one I was going to present to you at the café."

She poured them both some more wine.

"Good, eh?" he said.

"Very good."

"So, what was your idea?"

"The same as yours, to start. I mean, the part about seeing each other here at your flat. Place Maubert is the perfect place. I've always come here to shop. Downstairs is a doctor's office, a florist and a travel agency. I could walk in here at ten in the morning and the gossip columnists from *France-Soir* wouldn't even take their noses out of their coffee."

She squirmed, snuggled closer. "But sitting together at the theater or the opera and pretending we don't know each other isn't going to work. They'd be whispering the first time, and the second time it would be like they'd caught us in bed. In this city we either come out of the closet or avoid all public contact. You saw what happened this evening with the photograph. That was just a kid, but it could have been a journalist or photographer for a big magazine. Since father got into the government, they follow me around sometimes. Anyway, you get the idea."

"Only a matter of time," mumbled Steven. "That's what you're saying, isn't it?"

"Yes." They finished the wine. "But there is a place we can meet that's conveniently located and private. Maybe if we saw each other there a couple times a week, we wouldn't feel so…you know, cloistered."

"Tell me about it."

Nicole took a deep breath. "My father inherited a great old manor out in the country near Fontainebleau. After mother died, he sent me there during school vacations. I spent the summers with Henri and Isabelle."

"Who the hell are they?"

"The two old people who live there. I think they were born on the property. Francoise used to have more family than now, so father would give her summers off. Those were the happiest times of my life—until I met you."

Steven kissed her for a long time. "Henri and whats-her-name are still there?"

"Yes, and they adore me. They couldn't have children, which was a big thing for them. They couldn't believe father dumped me off at convent school a month after mother died. Anyway, when I was with them, I could do no wrong. I was thinking we could meet out there. I could tell Henri and Isabelle you're my boyfriend, but that father's trying to marry me off to some jerk. I'm sure they would understand and keep things quiet. How does it sound?"

"Can they cook?"

"Like Bocuse, only with butter. They're angels, and they're deaf. That's another lucky break. They won't hear your accent. They won't have to know you're not French."

"I have an accent?"

"Slight but charming."

"What about your father? Did he just let the place go after he inherited it?"

"Not at all. He's poured a lot of money into it. You see, that's where *he* goes to do his planning. He's built up his whole political movement with his cronies out there. But they only meet Wednesday nights. Otherwise he's here, in town."

"Tonight's Wednesday," Steven said.

"Yes. He's there, I'm here and Francoise is out in Meaux with her sister. So we could meet Wednesday nights here and some of the other times there. For variety, Steven. It will be fun. We just have to make sure that Henri and Isabelle approve of you. I can't imagine they wouldn't."

"I can't imagine they would. Really, Nicole, it sounds to me like we're going into the lion's den."

"Scared?"

"For me, no. For you, maybe. I hope you know what you're doing."

"Steven, I promise you it will be all right."

"Good, if you say so. You name the day and I'll be there on my best behavior. If I'd known you had this hideaway, maybe I wouldn't have attacked you in the café."

"I'm glad you did," she said. "Now it's my turn."

* * *

Sergeant Stan Elliot, a 30-year veteran with the Seattle Police Department, took the ramp to the downtown freeway at ten miles an hour over the speed limit.

"You gonna tell me where we're going?" Officer Billy King asked. "Seems like you're in a hurry."

King was a rookie, so his partners either told him too much or too little, depending on who they were and what the situation demanded.

"I'm not in a hurry," Elliot said. "When I'm in a hurry, you hear rubber. It's no big deal, a gravy morning. Just a little bit of questioning about this guy who seems to have disappeared. If you get bored, you can look forward to lunch. I know a good diner in the neighborhood, cop friendly, nice waitresses, one in particular. It's Thursday. Means they've got peas and meatloaf like your mother used to make. Have another bear claw. It'll help you keep that hand off your gun."

King had already eaten two. He could have handled a third, no problem. For a change he selected a glazed doughnut, unsticking it carefully from the box.

He had lost 12 pounds in cop training, which he was very proud of. Trouble was, he had put on 15 since he'd been cruising around on active duty. His uniform, which had looked so smart six months ago, was starting to remind him of the skin on a sausage.

"Disappeared?" he said between bites. "That all you gonna tell me?"

Elliot changed lanes, ignoring the speed limit. King thought, at least he wasn't the kind of cop who got on a freeway where everything was flowing nicely and caused a traffic jam by going 53 m.p.h. That used to drive him crazy before he joined the force.

Elliot said, "Look, kid, someone in the department got a call a week or two ago about this carcass of a car that turned up in the Bronx. Back when I started out, they probably wouldn't even have bothered to trace it. But with all the computers they've got these days, it takes about two seconds to do a nation-wide search. Turns out the car belonged to this guy who seems to have disappeared."

King had another doughnut, the coconut-coated kind that made his uniform look like a dirty tablecloth. "So how'd they know the guy disappeared?"

"Coincidence. Someone sued him last month for an order he'd paid a deposit on and didn't get filled."

"An order for what?"

"Who gives a fuck? Dies, tools, shit like that. You gotta learn to focus on the important stuff. Anyway, the D.A.'s office sends someone out to serve this guy and there's a sign in his shop window saying he's on vacation. So everything gets more or less forgotten until we get this motor vehicle I.D. from New York. We do the computer search and find out this Stein guy, the guy being sued, the disappearee, is the owner of the car that showed up in pieces on the other coast. That's where we come in. Got it now?"

"Got it. Thanks for filling me in. Believe it or not, it can help to know what you're working on."

"Give it a few years, kid, and you won't give a shit. In case you haven't noticed, this world's falling apart. Sticking a finger in the dike here and there isn't going to help. You don't work to save the world. You work for a paycheck, benefits and the day you retire. Get that map out, would you? I think this is our exit coming up."

✶ ✶ ✶

The vacation sign was still in the window. No response to their knocks, and the grass on the tiny patch of lawn out front was badly overgrown. They questioned the neighbors, not real friendly people. A gun dealer, a pawn shop owner, the local Salvation Army drop-off mute. The only one left to question was the guy across the street who owned the Polish bakery.

Elliot had gone over to the diner at eleven for his peas and meatloaf, but King was so stuffed with doughnuts he couldn't handle the idea of lunch. He was alone at the bakery when he hit the bell on the counter.

Jaworski came out of the back wiping his hands on his apron. He was in his seventies, maybe eighties, old, bald, stout as a tree trunk. The smell of fresh rye came steaming in behind him, tinged with a whiff of his perspiration. He said, "So, what it will be, Mr. Police?"

King felt nervous. This was the first questioning he had done on his own. Hell, he didn't like rejection any more than the next guy. "Sir, we're looking for Gerhardt George Stein, the owner of the tool and die shop across the street. We wondered if you knew him."

"Stein? Yeah, I know Stein. From the old world. A Kraut. Hates Poles, hates Jews. I'm both. Give you an idea how he feels about me? But he says all the time, 'Can't get good bread in this fucking country. How you gonna live without good bread?' So he comes over here every day and buys his bread."

"Has he been in lately?"

"What?"

"Has he come in here to buy bread lately?"

"Stein? Hell no. You seen the sign in his window. I seen you over there snooping. He's been gone since a couple of months."

"Does he go away often, Mr. Jaworski?" King asked, feeling a little more like a cop, and enjoying it.

"Yeah, he go away often. Every year or two, he take a month or so, put a sign up and go away. You know how long since I take a vacation. Twenty-one goddamn years. And that was for the funeral of my wife."

Pilot's Dawn

"I'm sorry about that. Do you know where Mr. Stein goes for these vacations?"

"He got a cabin somewhere up in Canada. Goes up there to be alone, he tells me. Hates all these people. You can believe that? He is alone here all the time, so he goes all the way up there to be alone."

"Does he tell you when he's going?"

"Yeah, he tells me. Comes in and buys his bread for the whole time he goes. Says you can't get no fucking bread in Canada, just like the States. He takes it up there in those big freezers you put fish in. You know the things I mean?"

King felt his heart speed up. Here he was about to pop the question that would provide the clue. Not bad for his very first try at this sort of thing. He said, "Yes, Mr. Jaworski, I use those big freezers myself. For fish, not bread. Now, did Mr. Stein come in and buy bread for this trip that he left on a couple months ago?"

Jaworski scratched his bald head. "That son of a bitch," he said. "That son of bitch must have found some other baker. Can you believe that, Mr. Police? Thirty years he buys his bread from me, then he decides to go somewhere else. You know why that is, Mr. Police?"

"No," said King, trying not to smile. "Why is that?"

"Because he's a fucking Kraut and you can't trust the fucking Krauts. You better watch out, you Americans. You think the war is over. I tell you, you fuck up letting those people get their country back together. You think the last Hitler was bad, you wait till the next one."

"Thank you, Mr. Jaworski," King said. "We'll be more careful this time." He hurried to the diner just in time to catch Elliot scraping up the last of his lemon meringue pie.

∗ ∗ ∗

"Okay, okay, stop acting like Perry Mason," Elliot said. "You found out he didn't buy bread before he disappeared. That doesn't mean he was murdered."

"But—"

"Where was his car found, hotshot?"

"You said, New York."

"That's right, King, New York. You think they got any Pollack bakeries in New York."

"Sure but—"

"Just be quiet. He might have gone on vacation to New York, sold his car before it was stolen, decided to move back to Germany, what the hell do we know? You might have come up with a lead, you might have come up with rubbish. Speaking of rubbish, did you see that bum in the garbage bin?"

"The guy who took off when we walked into the alley?"

"Yeah, him. Go catch him and bring him back here. I'm gonna sit down for a few minutes and digest my lunch."

"But—"

"Get going, King. You're putting on weight."

The bum was a mean, defensive son of bitch who treated King like *he* was the garbage scrounger. King first had to threaten him with a vagrancy charge, then put an arm around his filthy shoulder, to convince him all they wanted was some information on the guy who owned the tool and die shop.

"What's your name?" Elliot said, when King returned with the bum. The veteran cop was sitting on Stein's back step.

"Charles the Third," the bum said.

"So tell me something, Charlie. You know the guy who owned this place?"

The bum's mouth froze. King said, "Let me talk to him, okay? We get along."

Elliot said, "Hey, anyone who wants to take a load off my back, be my guest."

King patted the bum on the shoulder again, encouraging him. "We're worried about Mr. Stein, Charles, that's all. Like I said, this has nothing to do with you. We got nothing on you and nothing against you. Stein put up a vacation sign quite a while ago. His car was found in New York, stolen. So we're asking questions of all the people around here to see if we can find out if anything has happened to him."

"I saw him leave," the bum muttered. "And don't patronize."

"What?" said Elliot, coming out of his post-lunch stupor.

"You saw him leave?"

King said, "What do you mean, you saw him leave, Charles?"

"I saw his car drive off one morning last summer. He hasn't been back since."

"How do you know he hasn't been back?" King asked gently.

"No rye crusts in the bin."

"No shit," Elliot, said. "Good work, Charlie."

"Charles, please. Before he left—early, around eight in the a.m., there was a line of cement trucks here in the alley."

He pointed to a row of hedges. "I was sleeping back there, first time I'd had a good sleep in a while. They woke me up, those goddamned trucks. Sounded like the Exxon station on the corner was blowing up."

King said, "This is very helpful, Charles. We appreciate your cooperation."

"You want me to finish or not?"

"Yes, of course. Go ahead."

"A little later I saw Stein's car pull out of that door there and drive off down the alley. The goddamn trucks stayed half the day, making racket and pouring cement into the shop's coal chute."

"That's interesting," Elliot said. "Would you care to show us where that chute is, Charles?"

The bum led them to a big wrought iron plate that looked like a sewer cover. King tried to lift it, then saw the lock. "Should I shoot the thing off?"

"Have you lost your mind?" Elliot said. "We'll need a warrant to do anything like that. You go blasting away at that lock and you'll lose your badge before you get used to wearing it. Can you read, Charles?"

"What do you mean, can I read. I have a Masters Degree in English lit."

King could see Elliot strangling a wise crack before it got out of his throat. "Did you happen to notice a company name or any other form of identification on those trucks, anything like that?"

"Yeah, I noticed but I can't remember."

King said, "Do you live around here, Charles?"

"Around here? No, I live *here*."

He pointed toward the hedges. King could make out the corner of a clapboard shack, illegal but what the hell.

"Good. We might need to talk to you again. Can we find you here."

"Unless you're blind. Maybe you could think about buying me a meal."

"We ain't rich," Elliot said. "It'd be cheaper to arrest your ass."

"My partner's just kidding," King said. "I'm good for a meal. If you come up with that name, you can order anything on the menu. In fact, Charles, we could go over there right now."

"Peas and meatloaf today," Elliot said. "It was good. Come on, Charlie, think of the name of those trucks. I'm a tight son of a bitch, but I'll spring for seconds if you're still hungry."

"I'm hungry, and I'd still be hungry, but I told you. I can't remember the name. I can almost see it, just can't remember it."

"Tell you what," King said. "Give us a call if you do. The meal ticket's good until we get another lead."

Elliot handed the bum his card and a quarter. "That's for the phone, buddy. Don't spend it on coffee. I'll be back for it if your memory doesn't improve soon."

Chapter Nineteen

In the days following the Chicago crash, the administration's search for someone to blame for the escalating air safety crisis had coalesced around Frank Warner. Whether or not he should be relieved of his duties at the NTSB had become an open topic of discussion among Washington's powerful and in the national press.

Warner wasn't a political animal, but he believed he had an obligation to the American flying public to fight his dismissal in any way he could. Jackson Penn, a classmate of the President's at law school who knew a lot about politics and little about aviation, had been mentioned in a *Washington Post* editorial as a good choice to succeed Warner. So had Marlin Watson, a DEA investigator who couldn't tell a flap from an aileron.

These frightening prospects convinced Warner that he'd better occupy center stage at the White House meeting to which he had been summoned—a meeting rumored to have as its sole purpose Warner's dismissal.

His only hope, he thought, was to catch the administration's hatchet men off-guard at precisely the moment they were trying to make a media event of his beheading. The meeting, which had just begun, was already forcing him to control his temper. He beamed his rage at the window behind Jeff Galloway, the President's Chief of Staff. Now was the time for self-control; the time for self-defense would come soon enough.

"Anyway," Galloway continued, "what the President, everyone in this room and, I dare say, everyone in the country, is asking right now is why *you*, Mr. Warner, have not been able to tell us what is causing these crashes. In addition to killing a lot of people and wiping out a Ford plant, they have terrified travelers and thrown the ailing airline industry into an even deeper crisis. If they are allowed to continue, we're going to start seeing major damage to our economy. We can't stand idly by while this happens. So what's your problem, Mr. Warner? I want to know what is causing these crashes. Why are you unable to tell us?"

Warner would have preferred to leap across the table and punch Galloway in the face. Instead he looked down at his notes. "Let me make a minor correction to your statement, sir. Thanks to the dedicated work of hundreds of men and women who serve the NTSB in one capacity or another, I *have* been able to tell you the cause of three of the four crashes, and to supply a probable cause for the fourth. If you'll give me a minute to go over the results of our investigative work, I think it might help all of us proceed from a factual rather than an emotional point of view. May I?"

"Go ahead," Galloway said grudgingly. "But it appears you still don't get it."

Warner stood up abruptly. "I get it, Mr. Galloway. I know that you, the President, everyone in this room and everyone in the country want to know what is causing these crashes. Fine. Let's go over the results of my work again. The 767 crash in Atlanta was caused by a defective engine mount. The 757 crash on the Hawaii track appears to have been caused by degradation of the O-rings that keep oil from leaking out of jet engines. Those engines are five thousand feet beneath the Pacific now, so the cause remains probable. The 767 crash in Pittsburgh was caused by four defective engine mounting bolts—bolts which have nothing to do with the engine mount that failed in Atlanta. And the Seven Five crash in Chicago was caused by the failure of a lock on a pressurization valve that sent one of the engines into reverse thrust during take-off.

"We have completed these investigations in record time, and with conclusive results. That's our job at the NTSB. So don't try to make us scapegoats, Galloway. This isn't the right issue for you and your people to play politics with. If we intend to find out why so many crashes are occurring, it's going to take the cooperation of all Federal agencies represented here today—the FBI, the CIA, the FAA, and the NTSB. Leadership has been lacking, I agree. Not my leadership but the leadership needed to coordinate and direct the work of these agencies. And that, Mr. Galloway, means the leadership of your administration."

Warner didn't know if it was standard practice for people to applaud in the Cabinet Room, but they were applauding when he sat down. Galloway cleared his throat to make a rebuttal, but for the first time in anyone's memory he could find no words. Whether this was good or bad, Warner wasn't sure. Galloway was known for dirty tricks and an almost pathological vindictiveness.

FBI Director Bill Daniels took advantage of the lull to speak his mind. "Frank, thanks for putting things in perspective. If we're going to go around apportioning guilt, I'm prepared to take some of the blame. Until that last crash, I simply could not bring myself to believe foul play was involved.

"Now I'm willing to consider the possibility, thanks to the convincing case your man, Simmons, made yesterday. I'm sure Jeff Galloway and the President realize that your skills are invaluable to us right now. You're the best in the world. You're in constant demand from other governments whenever they can't solve a crash of their own. I know this administration isn't foolhardy enough to consider asking the best to resign at a time like this. And just to make sure everyone understands what I'm saying, let me state my position even more clearly: if Warner goes, I make my disagreement with the administration a matter of public debate."

Papers shuffled, glasses of ice water clattered, a throat was cleared, Galloway's.

"Thanks, Bill," Warner said modestly.

Secretary of Commerce Cathy Williamson said, "My agreement with Mr. Daniels is total. If Frank Warner is forced out, I will also go public with my opposition."

Secretary of State Olsen, one of the most skilled negotiators of the postwar period, jumped in to rescue a rapidly deteriorating situation.

"All right, all right," Olsen said. "That's enough. Bill, Cathy, your position is understood. The important thing for us now is that we approach this mess rationally. We will all be losers if we have a palace revolt when we've got a national crisis on our hands."

Warner felt a great surge of relief. He was getting the support he had hoped for, and getting it from some very important members of the administration.

Secretary of State Olsen went on. "If it was Jeff Galloway's assignment today to come here and ask for Mr. Warner's resignation—and I'm going to give him the benefit of the doubt and assume that it was not—then I'm sure, now that he better understands the feelings of some of the top members of the cabinet, that he will work hard to convince the President to change his mind.

"If, on the other hand, it was Mr. Galloway's assignment to set in motion a coordinated investigation, which I hope it was, then I suggest we drop the rancor and get on with our agenda. Will you buy that, Jeff?"

"Yes, of course," Galloway said. "And the record should show that Mr. Warner's attack was uncalled for. We are not interested in scapegoats. We're united in our—"

"I'm pleased you're not interested in creating scapegoats, Jeff," Olsen said, deftly taking control of the meeting. "So let's move on. Who would like to speak next?"

Warner nodded at Hal Larsen. He knew the Boeing CEO had been invited as window dressing, a symbolic presence from the private sector that would add legitimacy to the Warner beheading. Now it was beginning to look as though Galloway had made another mistake. Circumstances had conspired to give Larsen the chance to speak, and judging from what Larsen had told Warner on the phone, he had a lot to say.

Warner nodded at him again, urging him to grasp the moment.

Larsen got the message. "If I may," he said.

"Of course, Mr. Larsen," Olsen said. "In fact, it will be refreshing to hear someone's perspective who is not caught up in the political fray."

Thank God for a few good men, Warner thought. Instead of being a political farce, this morning's meeting had acquired the potential to get an effective investigation off the ground.

Larsen, managing to show none of the discouragement Warner knew he felt, began his presentation with his usual board room authority. "I want to thank all of you for inviting me to this closed session," he said. "I am aware of what the appearances are, Mr. Secretary, Mr. Galloway. As you know, the parts implicated in these crashes were all new parts that had been installed during recent servicing procedures. Our private research has confirmed that the parts were indeed manufactured by Boeing or its suppliers.

"This looks incriminating, I agree. But what you do not know, what nobody knew until I spoke with Warner this morning, is this. The results of independent tests, copies of which I'm going to make available later, show beyond a shadow of doubt that some of these parts were manufactured *years earlier* than their serial numbers would indicate."

There was a chorus of murmurs in the room, punctuated by the staccato of Galloway's pen hammering like a tiny gavel on the table top.

"Go on, please," CIA Director Willis said.

"The tests involve molecular analyses of surface metals and show degrees of harmless but telling corrosion that can date the origin of these parts quite accurately. The tests were conducted by different labs who did not know their work was being duplicated. In one instance, the part in question is at least seven years old, but according to its serial number, it was manufactured in January of 1994."

"Excuse me, Mr. Larsen," FBI Director Daniels said. "But you are saying that you, as an engineer, are convinced these tests are correct."

"Exactly, sir. I hope you'll run tests of your own. I assure you, you'll come up with the same findings."

"What, in your view, does this mean, Mr. Larsen?" FAA Chief Shelton asked.

"Simply this. That the parts that have failed and caused the recent sequence of disasters had been extracted from the production lines *before* they were stamped with serial numbers; that the parts were then modified to make them defective; that the defective parts were then somehow exchanged for good parts and given serial numbers matching those of the parts whose place they took in parts stream."

"Okay, all right," Galloway said. "This is a great-sounding idea that would explain everything. But with all due respect, Mr. Larsen, how the hell is anyone in his right mind going to believe your scenario? The only way it could be true is for someone to have started a massive sabotage operation against us years ago."

Larsen took a sip of water and raised his eyebrows. "That is correct."

CIA Director Willis said, "I think you're grasping for straws there, Mr. Larsen. If parts were modified, and if these were parts lifted from your assembly line several years previously, this means the foundation for the present sabotage—if it is sabotage—was laid a long time ago. But who back in the seventies and eighties had a motive for sabotaging our commercial airline fleet?"

Larsen said, "The Soviets. The KGB. Whenever there's a war, we use those commercial aircraft to ferry our troops to and from the front. They obviously knew of this practice from Vietnam, if not before."

"That's correct," Galloway said. "But the East Bloc no longer exists. Hell, there's not even a Soviet Union. These crashes we're talking about did not begin until 1995. Therefore you have an inconsistency between motive, which you place with the Soviets in the Cold War period, and deed, which I gather from your written statement that you place with the Iraqis in the present."

"Respectfully, sir," Larsen said, "there is an inconsistency only if you permit your thinking to be limited by a static view of the world. If there was a sabotage network in the States aimed at our civil aviation industry, then the individuals responsible for setting it up did not necessarily disappear with the collapse of Communism. If you fear our ex-Cold War enemies might sell nuclear warheads to countries such as Iraq and Iran, why is it far-fetched to think that Iraq might have bought the end product of an old KGB plot to sabotage our commercial fleet?"

The room erupted in whispering and buzzing. It was clear to all those present, Warner included, that Larsen, left in the lurch by official Washington, had been waging an intense private battle to understand the calamity that had befallen his company.

He might not have all the answers, or even be on the right track; but he was at least forging new hypotheses. This was sorely needed. Warner hoped Larsen's example would inspire everyone, himself included, to rise above the assumptions that had shackled their thinking.

* * *

Driving home late that afternoon, listening to NPR on his car radio, Warner reflected with satisfaction on the results of the meeting that had been convened to end his career. Rather than being fired, he had received a vote of confidence.

And he was going to get some badly needed help. Bill Daniels, the director of the FBI, had decided to throw his agency's vast resources into the investigation.

Even the sluggish FAA had come to life. Agency director Jack Shelton had accepted Warner's request to ground all Boeing 767s and 757s operated by U.S. carriers, and Boeing had volunteered to issue Air Worthiness Directives to carriers beyond the authority of the FAA, instructing them to return at Boeing's expense all Boeing and Pratt and Whitney parts ordered on or after the date of the Iraqi break-in.

Not bad for a day's work.

The traffic was horrendous. Stalled, he watched overhead as jets from National Airport climbed and banked steeply to the right. People were still flying; they had to. But he doubted they would ever board an airplane again with the same peace of mind.

A National Public Radio reporter, usually so knowledgeable, was talking nonsense about the NTSB's failure to answer everyone's question of why. It seemed to Warner they wanted him to be some mythical Hollywood hero: air crash detective, cop, spy.

Sorry, but real people had limits.

Irritated, he switched stations just in time to hear the new Delta Airlines commercial. They were being responsible, they were looking after their loyal customers, they were building a new fleet whose acquisitions would be limited to the world's safest jets, the state-of-the-art aircraft of Airbus Industrie. And just to make sure everyone understood that Boeing was out, the commercial went on to describe the orders Delta had just placed for 90 new Airbus 330s and 340s.

Ninety!

Warner knew from Hal Larsen that this was coming. But there was an aspect to Delta's strategy he hadn't grasped. By placing orders rather than options with carriers other than Boeing—orders that would cover the airline's needs for the next decade or more—and by making this fact public, Delta might force its competitors to do the same.

American, Northwest, TWA, U.S. Air and Continental had already cancelled or postponed extensive orders and options with Boeing. Warner had assumed they would come back to the corporation that had served them so well in the past as soon as the problems causing the recent crashes were found and remedied.

But now, given Delta's bold step and the short-range planning mentality of American business, the other U.S. carriers might feel constrained to make similar deals with Airbus. If they held off, Delta could rake them over the coals for being wishy-washy on their commitment to change. It would be like a price war on air fares; one airline would start the insanity, the rest would be forced to follow.

The implications of such a possibility sent a chill down Frank Warner's spine. It would mean that leadership in the manufacture of commercial aircraft would go to the Europeans, an unimaginable scenario just a short time ago. He didn't want to think about the drastic political, economic and *symbolic* consequences of a passing of the torch of this magnitude. It would certainly give credence to all of those critics at home and abroad who saw the decline of America, not the collapse of Communism, as the legacy of the 1980s.

As Warner pulled into his driveway in Silver Spring, the sun was setting in a wreath of pollution. He sat in his car a while, stunned. A thought had just taken possession of him, body, mind and soul.

Could it be that Airbus was behind the crashes? The company certainly had a motive, and the French government hadn't gone to any great lengths lately to hide its contempt for the U.S. There was also a precedent of sorts. French intelligence agents had been caught last year spying on Hughes Aircraft. Could economic warfare have reached such despicable heights?

He knew Jean Duvalier, the director of Airbus. He had never met a more principled man. Airbus involvement wasn't even a remote possibility.

Or was it?

He felt baffled. He simply did not know. The international scene had changed so drastically in the last few years he had lost his sense of the ground rules. The French had been caught spying at Hughes Aircraft. Didn't this say enough about the extremes to which supposedly friendly countries would go?

He experienced a tremor of self-doubt. Maybe Galloway and the NPR reporter had a better case against him than he realized. Maybe he had remained too rigid in his thinking, too unwilling to take a leap into the grotesque. Sure, he'd given Simmons the go-ahead to look for irregularities. But what had he himself done? Nothing. Not a goddamn thing. He had continued to cling fiercely to the belief that his job was to view each air crash as an occurrence in its own right, not part of a larger mosaic of crime. His friend, Hal Larsen, had changed with a changing world. Warner had not; not yet.

*   *   *

He got out and slammed the door of his government Caprice. In his home office, he poured himself a scotch, sat down at his desk and lit a cigar, his first in months. It was time for him to break the shackles of his *Weltanschauung* and reach out. He knew someone in France who might be able to help. He would begin with her.

He had renewed his acquaintance with Sophie Marx several years ago when he spotted her during his noon walk on the Mall. She was besieged by a group of enthusiastic young Washington journalists. He couldn't get close to her so he called out, "Sophie, is that you?"

"Frank! Frank Warner. I was going to look you up at the NTSB tomorrow. I hardly ever make it back to the States. Marriages and funerals, that's pretty much it."

"I hope this visit is the former."

"In fact. My brother, Michael. Never mind it's his seventh. Hope springs eternal. How about dinner this evening? It would delight me to reminisce."

They went to a pub at her suggestion, not some fancy French place he would have hated, and stayed half the night talking about those incredible six weeks in the spring of 1974. That's when the French government had invited Warner to help investigate the crash of a Turkish Airways DC-10 in the Forest of Ermenonville outside of Paris. He'd barely arrived at his hotel when the squabbling, the rivalries and the politics made it evident he wasn't going to be able to do his job. Then *New York Times* bureau chief Sophie Marx, a total stranger who said she had anticipated his troubles, showed up and appointed herself his translator and adviser. She allowed him to play the role she said God had intended him to play, that of the world's most talented air crash investigator.

When he left, Warner had conclusively linked the DC-10 crash, the worst to date in aviation history, to a defective design of the rear cargo door. He had told Sophie he owed her one, a favor as big as any she could dream up, but she had never asked for anything in return. Helping him make air travel safer, she said, was quite enough.

Well, here he was preparing to ask her for another enormous favor. Frank Warner wasn't an ingrate, but as he dialed Paris at one a.m. Central European Time, he felt like one.

He hung up an hour later, discouraged by his failure to make inroads into Sophie's friendly but immutable skepticism. He was preparing for another wave of depression to hit when he heard a car door close. He pulled open the curtain and peered into the autumn twilight.

Claire, suitcase in hand, was walking toward the front door. She had come back, and she looked as lovely as any creature he had ever seen.

Chapter Twenty

"Anyway," Sophie said, "the big break came around ten last night when Father Roget telephoned me at home."

"Father Roget?" Steven said. "He still remembered us?"

"I don't know about you, darling, but he remembered me. I think he rather enjoyed the interview. You know how old people are. Talking about the past lets them relive a time when they had more to look forward to. I hope I don't bore you to death with my reminiscences."

"Are you kidding? You've had the most fascinating life of anyone I know. I dreamed a few nights ago you stole my motorcycle and roared off through town chasing a story. It seemed credible enough."

"You know how to charm a woman, Steven, even an ancient one. While you were having your dream, I was no doubt fumbling through the medicine cabinet for laxatives and sleeping aids."

Steven laughed. His mood was finally improving after Sophie's unannounced five a.m. wake up call. He had wanted to meet with her today: he had his own pressing agenda to discuss. But after last night, seven o'clock would have suited him better.

He had dragged himself out of bed, and Sophie had led him down deserted city streets to the Jardin de Luxembourg. They had been here talking ever since.

It was dawn now, the cloud cover broken and spotty, the rain of the previous night over. Plants and flowers in the opulent park were coming to life, glistening with moisture in the pale morning light.

The scent of freshly baked bread wafted in from somewhere, a deceitful scent, Steven thought, a prelude to the diesel stench of a Paris rush hour.

"So what's this big break?" he asked.

Sophie took his arm at the elbow. They stopped walking. She looked at him earnestly. "I trust you remember the essence of our interview with Father Roget. There were times your mind seemed to be wandering."

"It was, but I remember the important part."

"Which was?"

"What is this, Sophie, an exam? He really zeroed in on how the 'Anglo Saxons' treated De Gaulle and the Free French during the War, on how the history of that humiliation stoked young Michelet's hatred of us Yanks. Did I pass?"

"C minus."

"C minus?"

"Steven, every Frenchman to the right of the Anarchists agrees that the British and Americans pushed the Free French around. It's no surprise they're still bitter. Michelet has made his feelings on the subject clear. In fact he does so in every campaign speech. It isn't even newsworthy."

"It is to me. Shows you how much I know about the guy. The daughter…now that's a different story."

She didn't say anything, didn't laugh or even smile. He had better quit playing buffoon, he thought. She didn't want to joke around; she had something she needed to tell him. If he didn't shut up and listen, he might end up with a D minus for the morning—a morning for which he had great expectations.

"Sorry, Sophie. Maybe I *was* asleep. What was the important part?"

"Our discovery of the little clique of patriots Michelet put together at Saint Claude prep school. If you recall, one of his followers was Albert Haussmann, who is now the richest entrepreneur in France. But there was another boy whom Father Roget referred to as extraordinarily gifted in mathematics. Roget hadn't had him as a student and couldn't remember his name."

"Now Monseigneur has suddenly remembered?"

"That's right. When he called, he said he didn't want us to think he had held the name back intentionally. He swore up and down that he'd been trying to think of it ever since the interview. The instant it popped into his mind, he picked up the phone."

"You don't believe he delayed us? He didn't need to say all those things."

"As I said before, Steven, I think he enjoyed the interview. I think he wants our good will."

"Your good will. So, don't keep me in suspense. Who was this mystery boy?"

"Paul Delors."

"Who the hell is Paul Delors?"

"Presently, Steven, he is the Deputy Director of the SDECE, French Intelligence. I'll know a lot more about him by nightfall."

Steven reflected for a minute. "Okay, I admit this is very fascinating. Of the three fire-breathing patriots who hung out together in prep school, one is now Minister of Industry, one is Deputy Director of the French CIA and the third is the richest man in France.

"I guess it could be a conspiracy that began long ago and is now bearing fruit. But what's the present connection among these three guys, Sophie? Isn't that what counts? And how can you say getting Delors' name is a big break. I mean, it might be, but how can you say for sure before you've done any research on him?"

He thought for a moment. "Or is there something I don't know? Something you haven't told me? Such as, he's a member of Nouvelle France?"

Sophie said, "He's not officially a member, of course, or he would not have been able to maneuver himself into such an important post in the Eighties. But you're right. There is something you don't know. I was going to come down and tell you last night, but it sounded rather like you had a visiter."

Steven grinned. "I did. Father Roget wasn't the only active one last night. My visitor supplied us with an incredible piece of information. So incredible I came up to fill you in the moment she left. But you were on the phone, Sophie. I didn't want to disturb you. Were you still talking to the good father at one o'clock in the morning?"

"Heavens, no, Steven. I had a call from the States."

"An old lover?"

"No, an acquaintance, a friend. A person in the government—and in a bind. It was a sad talk, the sadder the more I think about it."

"Oh, yeah?" Steven wasn't interested but Sophie seemed to be trying to get something off her chest. He might as well encourage her; she'd done the same for him a hundred times. "Why's that? I mean, why sad?"

"Because, Steven, my friend is a good and competent person who is being put under pressure to explain what is causing all of those air crashes in the States. He's unable to do this, so he's started to grasp for straws. This is what I felt compelled to tell him at some length."

"So what does he think's going on? Why did he contact you?"

"He thinks, darling, that Airbus might somehow be involved in Boeing's misfortunes."

"Who's to say they aren't? These people have a real thing about Americans."

"Steven, don't be ridiculous. If a large public concern such as Airbus were sabotaging American planes, there'd be hundreds of leaks. You can be sure I'd be privy to at least some of them. To make a long story interminable, my friend asked me to investigate the situation here in France. He's a good man, as I said. He's done a lot for the safety of air travel. It was painful for me to turn him down. Now, if you don't mind, I'd like to continue with what I brought you here to report."

"Sure," he said, anxious for her to wrap things up so he could present her with **his** discovery.

"Well, Steven, in our business it usually goes something like this. You chase down a lot a leads, you put out a lot of feelers. For a long time, nothing happens. Then, all of a sudden, the work starts to pay off. I've reached that point, darling. It sounds as if you may have, too."

"Yep, I'd say so."

They walked a little further in silence. She seemed to be thinking.

Morning had come. He listened to the first wave of cars and cabs on Boulevard St. Michel. Engines snarling, brakes squealing, horns being warmed up for a long day's use.

He breathed in a lingering whiff of freshly baked bread and prepared himself for the traffic fumes.

Sophie stopped again and looked him in the eye.

"You understand, Steven, that as far as anyone knows, Haussmann is not a member of Nouvelle France, either. But I've had my doubts about that for a long time. After our interview I asked my brother in New York do some checking up for me."

"The one who's the international financial whiz"

"Yes. Uncle Emmanuel has the intellect *and* the connections."

"Uncle? I thought you said 'brother.'"

"I call my brother Uncle Emmanuel—that's another story. Anyway, he has been as upset as I have about the blatant fascist overtones of Nouvelle France. Don't forget, Steven, that we lost six million of our people and most of our family to this same sort of patriotic barbarism.

"In any case, Uncle Emmanuel decided to call in some favors. He seems to have uncovered a financial link between Haussmann and Michelet that dates back more than twenty years. In fact, it looks as if Haussmann has bankrolled Nouvelle France from the start. We might be able to prove it."

"No shit."

"It could be big, very big. But let's return to Delors. Let your mind play games for a moment. He's listed as a member of the Republican Party, the moderate center, and has been ever since he stepped into public life. If this allegiance is genuine, it means he gave up the rabid nationalism of his youth a long time ago."

"Did he?"

"I don't believe so, Steven. I have a suspicion that Delors has played political chameleon for decades. If so, and if he and Haussmann are both in this movement together with Michelet, their prep-school alliance forms the core of a very ugly and dangerous adult political force. Think Pulitzer, Steven."

He whistled and watched her closely.

She seemed more driven, more obsessed than he had ever seen her in the past.

He said, "If you're right, this is amazing."

"Yes it is, darling."

Now it was his turn, and he felt terrific. She had gotten her biggest break, but how big was it, really? She could derive a lot of interesting theories from it, but how in the hell was she going to verify them?

He smiled. He didn't think she could. He, on the other hand, was in a perfect position to find out with total certainty whether she was barking up the right tree. This was no small achievement for a guy his family thought of as a tennis-playing bum.

"Tell me something, Sophie. Did you know that Michelet has been holding Wednesday night political meetings at this place out in the country? He's been having them for as long as Nicole can remember."

She shot him a piercing look, which he recognized as a sign of her fierce ambition to succeed, the tip of a submerged iceberg. His dad and brothers exhibited that same type of fierce ambition all the time, but with them it gave off a bad odor. For some reason, Sophie's ambition didn't stink.

He had a thought that warmed his heart. Maybe his dad and brothers were just assholes. Maybe you didn't have to be like them to succeed in life. He had always assumed you did.

"No, I didn't know that," Sophie said.

"Well, now you do. And according to Nicole, the prick has built his entire movement at these meetings. So here's what I've been thinking. If Haussmann and Delors are in on this, they'd be attending these meetings, wouldn't they?"

"Most likely, yes. But are the meetings still taking place?"

"You bet. Last night was Wednesday. That's why Nicole felt comfortable staying at my place until late. Her father was out in the country. No chance he would show up at home before two in the morning."

"Steven, this is a piece of very fine work on your part. It's exactly what I hired you to do. Do you suppose you could find out—in a subtle way, or course—where the meetings are held?"

"I already did."

"Subtly?"

"As subtle as you can get. We were talking about something else and the subject just came up."

"Out of the blue?"

"Yeah, right."

"That worries me. It sounds almost as though she's holding out a piece of bait to see if you'll bite. I hope you didn't show too much interest."

Steven gave her a friendly tap on the arm. "Hey, relax. You haven't heard the whole story. We need a place to meet outside the city. I didn't see the problem until we got our asses photographed yesterday in some obscure café."

"Not good."

"It wasn't anything, just a kid on a moped. But it woke me up. I guess I didn't realize the extent the gossip columnists had picked up on her."

"You should read more, darling."

"I'm too busy. Anyway, when we came back to my place, I made some suggestions about how to conduct an incognito relationship in the city. It turned out she had her own plan, much better than mine."

"This is yummy, Steven."

"It gets better. Talking about her plan is how the subject of her dad's meetings came up—just something in the context of something else."

"Fortunate."

"No shit. Anyway, Michelet inherited *his* father's country home about fifteen years ago. He kept it up real nice, but only for the meetings. He's never there otherwise, so Nicole wants us to make use of it. Except on Wednesday nights, of course."

"Careful, Steven. There must be caretakers. If they see you, they could betray you to Michelet."

"I don't think so. The caretakers are an old peasant couple. Nicole is very close to them. She spent her vacations with them when the convent school closed. Sounds like her dad didn't know what to do with her."

"He didn't. He will, however, if he catches her with you. You'll have to lay low when you're out there. Believe me, Steven, these old retainers don't bite the hand that feeds them. So take my advice, take a sleeping bag and keep out of sight. Being seen there would be worse than being photographed in Paris."

They had come full circle around the park for the third time. They both stopped simultaneously, as though attuned to each other's thoughts.

Steven said, "Well, it's too late to change plans now. Nicole is driving out there this morning to visit the caretakers. She's going to tell them she has a boy friend she doesn't want her dad to know about. She's sort of announcing my arrival in advance, you know, giving me a nice French introduction. She thought it would be a good idea."

"Steven, they'll know you're not French. Your command of the language is excellent, but you still have a slight American accent. They'll hear it."

"Wrong. They're deaf. Listen, Sophie, Nicole and I are going to meet there this coming Friday. I'll get the lay of the land, see if I can find out where those meetings are held and whether there's a place I can hide and listen. If there is, I'll sneak in on Wednesday. If I get lucky, I might be able to bring home some serious bacon."

Sophie was looking at him now, scrutinizing him, studying him. He couldn't tell whether she was impressed, nervous or angry.

She kicked the gravel like a loitering teenager. She rubbed her hands together, started to form a word, stopped in mid syllable and looked at him some more.

"What's wrong?" he said.

"Wrong? What you're proposing, Steven, is way beyond what I engaged you to do. You could get yourself in a serious mess. You must remember that Delors is near the top of one of the world's most vicious intelligence services. These people don't play games. If they feel threatened, they hit back.

"I want you to forget about eavesdropping on a meeting. In fact, on second thought, I don't want you going out there at all. I'll work on finding you and Nicole another place to meet closer to Paris, a place where you can really relax."

"Know something, Sophie? I haven't seemed to do anything right for a long time. Things are changing now, I can feel them changing. I've reread LeConte's List of Lacking Virtues. I've discovered perseverance, thanks to you. I'm sticking with this one whether it's part of my job or not. I'm going in."

"Steven—"

"Look, Sophie, I refuse to piss away all the work and money you've invested getting me in this position. Until now all I've done is entertained myself and gotten laid. You've done the hard work. So I'm going to do my part, for a change. I don't give a damn how dangerous it is. I'm going in there and I'm going to get the scoop. I'm going to find out what makes Michelet and his band of *nouveaux nazis* tick. Then you and I, we'll sit down and write one hell of a story."

Her silence was stony.

"Come on, Sophie, loosen up. I know you. You're a blood hound. You've got to admit this idea intrigues you."

"Whether it does or not, Steven, I can't sanction it."

"You don't have to. It's my decision."

"We'll talk about this again before Friday."

"Sorry, I won't be around. The club's sending me off to play some exhibition matches, and that's the truth."

"Where?"

"Forget it, Sophie. I'm doing this for me as well as for you. You're not going to change my mind."

Chapter Twenty-One

Michelet paced the study of his Paris home like a wild boar. He reread the letter from Claussen for the hundredth time, then lit the pages one by one and dropped them into the fireplace. He paced some more, trying to gain control of his smoldering rage. Wisps of smoke curled in front of the dour portraits of his ancestors.

This was *unacceptable*.

Delors had assured him this would not happen.

How could it have been *allowed* to happen?

That was the first answer he needed.

How?

It was an unmitigated disaster. Now their plans would have to be revamped from the bottom up, and that was the least of it. If Claussen made any little mistake and got caught, the world would learn what he, Michelet, had done. If this happened, he would not take his place in history as the first great Frenchman to follow De Gaulle. He would not be remembered as the man who had restored honor, prosperity and dignity to his country.

He would go down in history all right, but as an aberration, an embarrassment, a despicable criminal who had made a mockery of his movement's claim that France was the most civilized nation on earth.

Francoise knocked, as he had asked her to do.

"Yes?"

She opened the study door a crack. Her face took on a strange expression. She looked at his cigar. She said, "You have switched brands, monsieur?"

At first he didn't think he had heard right. When he finally understood, he just stared at her.

So many clues, so many tiny things that could go wrong.

Switched brands? The cunning old bitch, he thought. She knew he had been burning papers. That's what he meant about little things going wrong. What if she had opened that abominable letter by mistake? What if she had been paid by the opposition to monitor his personal mail? What would she have done? Did a quarter of a century of service to the household guarantee loyalty?

Obviously not, if history was a guide.

Sacré bleu, he had to calm down before he blew a gasket. He had to distinguish real danger from paranoia.

What if Francoise *had* read the letter? She wouldn't have had any reason to suspect that it was about airplane crashes. Claussen had been very cautious with the wording.

Francoise said in a raspy voice, "Monsieur, your guest has arrived. He is waiting to see you."

"Very well," Michelet grumbled, breaking the strange silence. "Show him in."

"And monsieur?"

"What?"

"I must talk to you about your daughter." She stepped into the room and waved a newspaper. "It's abominable. You must do something about it."

"Don't bother me with personal matters now. Do you understand me, Francoise? Do you **understand me?**"

"Yes, but—"

"Francoise!"

She stared at him for a split second, then put the newspaper down on top of a bookcase and went out.

Michelet walked to the window and turned his back to the door. This was how he wanted to greet the man he had trusted for so many years, the man who had persuaded him of their invulnerability, only to allow Claussen to find out who they were.

The idea had been to sell the whole undercover job as an SDECE assignment. If it hadn't been, Michelet would not have agreed to it. Claussen was never supposed to know who his employers were. That was to have been their ultimate security.

Well, now he knew. The names, the addresses and God knows what else about all three of them!

Delors, whom Michelet could hear coming into the room, had a lot of explaining to do.

A lot.

Which he began to do almost immediately. "We have a problem, Georges. The problem is not Claussen, and it is not our risk of exposure. Though you might not understand this yet, we are in no way compromised by the letter."

"Oh?"

"The reason we are not compromised is that we did not plan to kill Claussen. Now, we will simply take even better care of him. So Claussen's knowing who you are, and who Albert is, is not, per se, a problem."

Michelet spun around, his face twisted in fury. "Excuse me for my stupidity, Paul. What *is* the problem?"

"Albert is the problem. He's refusing to pay. As you know, Claussen is to be paid at our next meeting. I've spoken with him, explained to him there were some logistic delays. He has agreed to accept a forty-eight hour postponement. But if we don't have the money by then, there *will* be a problem.

"Therefore, I suggest that you and I have it out. You don't look pleased. I can understand that. So let's get on with it, then bury our differences. Because, Georges, if we do not, we won't to be able to present a united front to Albert.

"And we must present a united front on Wednesday night. We must convince Albert that the letter changes nothing, which it does not *unless we allow it to.*

"If we fail, if Albert remains blockheaded in his refusal to pay, we shall be forced to go elsewhere for Claussen's fee. You know what that means, Georges. We will have left a footprint in the sand, our first.

"We might get away with it, we might not, but we will be at risk. That must be avoided."

"Really? Sit down."

Michelet ground out his cigar, lit another, paced furiously, then stopped beneath a second portrait of his father.

"How could you have let this happen?" he shouted. "I want to know, Paul. I want an answer NOW."

"I don't know how he found out," Delors said. "He's a master of his trade, as you can deduce from his work in the States. I am perfectly willing to admit he bested me on the secrecy issue.

"The important thing, however, is that his little victory does not damage our position—as long as you and I are successful in convincing Albert."

"You and I!" Michelet boomed. "What do you mean, you and I? You'd better work on convincing me before you speak of you and me in the same breath. You certainly haven't done it yet."

* * *

Frank Warner slept for the first night in weeks. He awoke to the smell of toast and coffee coming from the kitchen.

He got up, showered and went out on the terrace. Claire had set the table for breakfast and squeezed fresh orange juice. He gave her a quick kiss and sat down. He hadn't realized how much he had missed her.

It was a glorious fall day, not hot, not humid. The sky had more blue in it than haze, and several of the big trees in his back yard were showing subtle changes of color.

He watched Claire move with graceful efficiency between the kitchen and the terrace. Toast, smoked salmon, butter—she even remembered the toast. When you grew up in Winnemucca, Nevada, you ate toast, not bagels.

She poured his coffee, sat down, put her elbows on the table and looked into his eyes. "Thanks," she said.

"Thanks?"

"For being you. For not doing some defensive male ego thing because I left."

He smiled. His face felt almost stiff. He realized it had been many days since he had smiled. "My male ego might react more conventionally the next time. I don't blame you for going, but I was jealous as hell."

"There might not be a next time," Claire said. She brushed her blonde hair from her forehead, and held a piece of toast and salmon in front of his lips. He took a bite.

"I haven't changed," he said. "Let's be clear on that. It's crazy around here, and it's going to get worse."

"I know, Frank. It'll be miserable. I'll want to be with you and you'll be far away, totally absorbed in your work."

"Why did you come back, Claire?"

She smiled the sexy, ironic smile he adored. "Why did I come back? Because I made a great discovery on this most recent voyage of the liberated woman."

"Oh? Care to let me in on it?"

"They're all jerks out there, Frank. The choice is, a lot of them or a little of you. I've made my choice."

The phone rang, the emergency phone. "Goddammit, not now," Warner groaned.

"Frank, the world needs you, I need you. I come second. I've accepted that. Go answer your telephone."

*   *   *

It was Tim Simmons. "Frank, we've had another one, right up there with the Atlanta disaster. Osaka, Japan, All Nippon Airways. A Seven Six on Instrument Landing came down a couple of miles short of the runway. It took out a shopping center."

"Jesus. What are they doing flying 767s? Didn't they get the packet of information on the FAA's groundings here? What about the Air Worthiness Directives? Larsen assured me Boeing would fax them out last night."

"They got everything, Frank, but the only foreign carrier to pull its planes off the line was SAS. They've been seeing these crashes differently overseas."

"How can you see a crash differently?" said Warner, his blood pressure rising. "Stop speaking in tongues."

Simmons remained calm. "I'm not talking about technical people, Frank, I'm talking about the flying public abroad. They've been avoiding the U.S. carriers, yes, but not the Boeing aircraft operated by their own domestic airlines.

"I think it's in their minds at some subliminal level that the American carriers are the target of whatever's going on. It was probably put there by those who stood to make windfall profits on international routes if our airlines were shunned.

"That's the only positive aspect of this crash, Frank. At least that false perception abroad will change now. Whoever's been making all the money off it will get rightly stiffed."

"Dammit, Tim, I don't want to ever hear you say anything like that again. There are no positive aspects to an airline disaster. Never. Period. Got it?"

"Sorry, Frank. I was using a metaphor—"

"Got it?"

"Yes."

"Good."

Warner glanced at Claire, who was already clearing the breakfast table. He saw his salmon and toast make its trip back to the kitchen with only one bite missing.

Welcome home, darling, he thought.

"Look, Tim, we can discuss peripheral items later. Give me the barest essentials on the crash. Are you at home?"

"Yes, just getting ready to leave."

"Then come by and come pick me up. We'll drive to National together. I know Nikasuno is going to want us in Osaka as soon as we can get there."

"You're wrong, Frank. I've just spoken with someone in their Air Transport Ministry. The tail broke off, just like it did in Atlanta. They've got the black box and CVR. They're going to send them over with one of our military jets as soon as they run backups of the data so they have something to work with."

"They don't want us at the crash site?"

"Politics, Frank. Perceptions of American incompetence. You know how they feel about the riveting job on the tail of that Japan Air Lines 747 that went down in 'eighty-five."

"For Christ's sake, we were the ones who discovered the cause of that crash. It had slipped right by them."

"But we, meaning we Americans, were also the ones they hold responsible for the faulty riveting job. Look, I don't know the whole story. All I know is, they don't want us over there yet. We can't just show up without an invitation."

"All right. Have they got any ideas on cause?"

"They're convinced the Autopilot is at fault. They think you'll agree when you examine the material."

"They're missing something, Tim, unless this crash is totally unrelated to the others. Bendix manufactures the Autopilot."

"I know, Frank. Bummer, huh?"

"I assume they're wrong about the cause."

"I don't believe so, Frank. I heard some of the CVR tape over the phone. I've talked them into faxing us transcripts of the relevant portions. I think the Autopilot did fail."

"Which gives new life to the theory that we are dealing with random manufacturing defects rather than sabotage. Sloppy American workmanship and quality control. No wonder they don't want us over there."

"It could also be more broadly based sabotage."

"That's hard to believe."

"It's all hard to believe. What do you want me to do now?"

"Jesus," Warner repeated. "You can't win for losing. Set up a communication line with the Japanese Air Transport people working the crash sight. See if you can find someone there who speaks the kind of English it doesn't exhaust you to listen to. Call me back. I'll be at home. If the line's busy, keep trying."

Claire came in with a grave look on her face. He shrugged his shoulders. "Osaka. Two thousand dead, maybe more. It sounds like the world is at war, doesn't it?"

"Do you have to go?"

"Not immediately, but I have to make some confidential calls."

"I understand." She went out, softly closing the door.

It took a half hour to track down FBI Director Bill Daniels. "What about the Atlanta hypothesis, Bill?" Warner said. "Do you have answers yet? Did anyone happen to die around that time who might have been in a position to slip that bad engine mount on to the aircraft?"

"Delta hasn't responded to our inquiries regarding their work force yet. You know how the South is. Some critical person in the chain of command has probably gone fishing. I'll get on them right away."

"What about Pratt and Whitney?"

"We'll be starting a new investigation into the cause of Dave Melchior's death. The state and local authorities seemed pleased to have us aboard, for a change. They're understandably desperate to find something that will exonerate one of Connecticut's largest employers and tax payers. You know, given the cancellations from Europe."

"What cancellations?"

"Engines for the new Airbusses. The European Consortium has decided to switch manufacturers, even though this will result in delays and lawsuits."

"I see. This must be recent."

"Yesterday. I'm told the decision will cripple Connecticut's economy. I don't think I was fully aware of the magnitude of this disaster."

"You still aren't. None of us are. We're going to find out the hard way exactly how important the aircraft industry is to our country's health. I assume you've been briefed on Osaka?"

"Yes, Frank."

"All right. Let me get to the reason for my call. I don't know if the Japanese are correct, and won't for some time, but the component they suspect is the Autopilot, which is manufactured neither by Boeing nor by Pratt and Whitney but by the Bendix Corporation."

"Shit."

"Exactly. Listen, Bill, since you're already into this thing up to your knees, I think it would be a good idea if you extended your investigation to Bendix."

"Meaning?"

"Do what you're trying to do in Atlanta. Look into the deaths occurring among Bendix employees in the last six months. See if you come up with anything suspect."

"We'll get right on it, Frank. This thing has to be solved, and solved fast."

"Amen," Warner said.

Pilot's Dawn

When he hung up, he pulled back the curtain to see if Claire's new red Toyota was still in his driveway.

Incredibly, it was.

✱   ✱   ✱

Officer King, off-duty after a long, thankless day in the patrol car, didn't feel like going directly home. He was tense and irritable. The kids would be screaming, the kitchen of their small apartment would look like it had been bombed, Mary would be yelling at him for not making enough money. He was an easy-going guy most of the time, but tonight he just didn't need it.

He undid the belt of his uniform to give his expanding stomach a little breathing room. So where should he go, what should he do? He could have a few beers somewhere, but he didn't want to get into the habit. Maybe he would just drive around until he felt better.

He was driving through a run-down section of Wallingford when he remembered the bum in the alley. He hadn't thought about him since he and Elliot had talked to him last week. He wondered if old Charles the Third had remembered the name of the cement company he had seen on the mixers that had filled Stein's basement.

Maybe Charles had phoned in, and the Department had given the case to someone else. He might as well find out while he was here in the area.

He called dispatch on his radio, which the Department had been decent enough to install in his private car. "Hi, Elouise, this is King."

"Who?"

"Officer Bill King, one four seven nine, the rookie."

"Oh, yes. What's up, Officer?"

"Well, I'm off duty, on my way home. Just remembered some questioning Sergeant Elliot and I did somewhere around here last week. A man was supposed to call in with the name of a cement company, a guy named Charles. Don't have the last name with me. It relates to the Stein case. I need to know if someone has made the call. If not, I'll pay Charles a visit."

"Just a minute. I'll have to check upstairs."

King parked his '84 Bonneville and waited. The gals upstairs could be slow, especially this time of day. No use having to turn around and drive back, given the price of gas.

He stared out the window at the passing pedestrians. He was in uniform, and everyone seemed to notice. They avoided his eyes, they crossed the street or veered away from his car. Sergeant Elliot was right, King thought: in this neighborhood, everyone was guilty of something. You could probably help the D.A. with his conviction stats by making random arrests from dawn to dusk.

"Officer King?"

"Got something, Elouise?"

"Not what you want to hear. I talked to Betty. Nothing new in that Stein file. I guess your man didn't call in."

"Okay, thanks."

King started his engine and cruised down the alley behind Stein's shop. The grass was a little longer, the windows dirtier, the dandelions healthier. Stein obviously hadn't come back from his extended vacation.

He parked, got out and made his way through the hedges on the other side of the alley.

Charles was seated on a beat-up aluminum lawn chair in front of his clapboard shack. He was either meditating or praying, thought King. Or maybe he was just drunk.

Charles was none of these things. "Good evening, Officer," he said, not bothering to open his eyes. "I would gladly offer you a seat if I had one."

"Thanks, Charles. It's supposed to rain tonight. You gonna be okay in that thing?"

Pilot's Dawn

"Me? I'm always okay. You don't like my house? Why not? I got tar shingles under the clapboard, I got a heater that burns anything from coal to paper, and most of all I got my peace. Bet you can't say the same for yourself."

"Why would you think that, Charles?"

"You married? Got kids?"

"Yep."

"Wife work?"

"No."

"Take bribes?"

"No, of course not."

"Then let me say it again: you got no peace when you go home."

"Well, sometimes that's true," King conceded.

Charles seemed a lot smarter than most of the criminologists from the university that came to lecture at the Department. Maybe he really did have a Masters, King thought.

He said, "I might not have any peace, Charles, but I do have something to eat when I go home. How about you?"

"I do tonight, Officer. They're serving roast beef, mashed potatoes and gravy over at the diner. Free refills on coffee. I was going to call you but your colleague's quarter managed to get away from me. I was hoping you would come by."

"You mean, you remembered the name?"

"Ten seconds after I spent the quarter. Shall we dine?"

King smiled. This was by far his most pleasant encounter of the day. "Roast beef and mashed potatoes sounds pretty good."

Charles, who was in his sixties, maybe older, sprang easily to his feet. "You're all right, Officer, know that? For a man who's got no peace, you're all right."

*   *   *

Driving home after dark, King no longer cared if his kids screamed, his wife yelled or if his apartment was a mess. He had done another good piece of detective work.

He had a talent for something after all, and it was something he enjoyed. When he reported to his supervisor in the morning, he would ask permission to go out by himself and talk to these people at DiStefano Sand and Gravel.

Or with Sergeant Elliot.

That would be okay, too, just as long as they didn't take the investigation away from him.

Chapter Twenty-Two

"Have a seat, monsieur," Isabelle said. She dried her hands on her apron and gestured to the long wooden table in her kitchen. It had been readied for a mid-morning snack of bread, cheeses, sausage and coffee.

Henri, whom Steven had met when he and Nicole first arrived, clumped into the old stone cottage and put down a bowl of fresh grapes. "From the vineyard," he said. "A shame to waste them by eating them prematurely. If permitted, they would become good wine. But what can I do, monsieur? My wife insists, so that's that. Well? Have a seat, won't you?"

"Merci," Steven said. He pulled out a chair, trying not to be too polite or smile too much. He felt ridiculous. During their car trip from Paris, Nicole had drilled him on how a Frenchman of his age and social standing would conduct himself in the presence of his girlfriend's father's caretakers. He was having trouble with his act. He reminded himself of that insufferable tennis pro, Philippe. Besides, he liked these salt-of-the-earth farm people. It was hard for him to pretend he thought of himself as their superior.

Yet, to borrow a line from Henri, what could he do? Nicole had insisted, and he had promised. So he swallowed his urge to chat, suppressed a smile and tried not to pay too much attention to the feast spread out in front of him.

Isabelle poured the coffee and hot milk into big *café au lait* bowls. He started to thank her but didn't. Nicole was watching him like a hawk. She gave him a tiny nod of approval.

"Where are you from, monsieur?" Henri asked. His overalls and shirt were homespun, his hands large and calloused, his skin like leather from a lifetime of outdoor work.

"Paris," Steven said.

Henri read his lips and laughed. "No, no, not where are you from *now*. Everyone is from Paris now. I mean your family—your ancestors."

"The north," Steven mumbled. He buried his mouth in his huge bowl of *café au lait*.

Henri said, "Excuse me, monsieur, I didn't quite get that."

Steven felt a stab of panic. Had Nicole told these peasants where he was from but forgotten to tell him that she had told them? Or *had* she told him? Had *he* forgotten? It wouldn't be the first time.

Nicole came quickly to his rescue. "The North," she said with exaggerated lip movement. "The Province of the North. Steven, you must not forget that Henri and Isabelle do not hear well. You must make more of an effort to talk with your lips."

"Sorry," Steven said. "My family is from the North."

"Ah, *Le Nord*, Henri said. "*Le Nord*."

Steven nodded coolly. This was hell. He took comfort in the thought that he wouldn't have to keep up the front much longer. Nicole had told him Henri and Isabelle didn't have time to sit around all day, that they were in the middle of harvesting their wine grapes. They had a vineyard they cultivated for their own consumption, large because of Henri's gargantuan thirst.

The *vendage*, harvesting the grapes, was a precise operation. You didn't move it a day or two this way or that to make it fit your schedule. When the grapes were ready, which they were, you had to be there or you risked losing your vintage for the entire year. Or so Nicole had claimed.

"Have some of this cheese, monsieur," Isabelle said, pointing with her knife. "It's our very own goat cheese. We made it here on the property."

"Merci," Steven said. Things were going all right, he felt, so he ignored Nicole's warning not to eat like a pig. He took a slice of freshly baked bread and heaped on the cheese.

"That friend of yours is all right, Nicole," Henri blurted out, slapping Steven on the shoulder. "You know how the young people from the city are these days, Isabelle?"

"Yes, they don't eat," she said, reading his lips with ease.

"That's right, they don't eat. They won't touch anything that isn't 'healthy.' What do they think's so unhealthy about food like this? I tell you, there's no sense in what they're doing."

Steven crammed another gigantic bite of bread and goat cheese into his mouth, skewered a sausage and nodded his assent.

"Look at me," Henri said. "I'll be seventy-five next month; my father lived to be ninety-seven. He drank wine, plenty of it, ate butter and cheese, and a hundred grams of *pâté de fois gras* on Sundays. He enjoyed life, a whole century of it—"

Henri was seventy-five? thought Steven, sampling the Camembert. Remarkable. The man didn't look a day over sixty. A couple of years from now he could see himself sitting down with the old codger, opening a bottle of this year's vintage and interviewing him on the secrets of life.

"So here's what I say to you, Nicole," Henri continued in his gruff but warm voice, "You've got yourself a friend who knows the important things. That's good. We should drink to that."

"Not me," Nicole said. "It's too early."

Isabelle waived her husband off but Steven made no attempt to refuse.

Henri poured two glasses of *marc* and shoved one across the table in his direction.

He tipped his glass and nodded at Henri, still careful not to smile. He was feeling better. He hadn't blown it, his instincts hadn't given him away. But he hadn't offended these great country folks, either. As long as he could express his genuine emotions through a display of grateful gluttony, he supposed he could keep up the nastier aspects of his facade.

Steven finished his third sausage and drank another shot of *marc*.

Henri stood and fastened his suspenders. He pointed a thumb at the door. "Isabelle," he said, "to work."

He looked at Steven and Nicole. "Ah, yes, and *mes enfants*, you have a good time today. You remember where the keys to your father's house are, don't you, Nicole?"

"Yes, of course."

"Well, be sure to go over there. Isabelle has prepared you a picnic lunch. She left it in the kitchen refrigerator, no room for it here."

"Thank you, Isabelle," Nicole said.

"It's not much," Isabelle said, stacking the dirty plates. "Oh, by the way, monsieur, I've been meaning to ask you. What do you do for a living?"

This one had been part of the drill.

"Commerce," Steven said. "My father has purchased an American firm, **Plastiques de** New England. Opportunities are good."

"*Bon dieu*. Did I understand him right, Nicole? His father has purchased an American company?"

Nicole smiled. "That's right."

"Well, my dear, I think your fears are not necessary. I am sure Monsieur Michelet will approve of Monsieur LeConte. He is helping France defend Herself against the foreigners. Isn't that what your father wants all of us to do?"

"I'm not sure what he wants," Nicole said. "Perhaps you are right, and father will accept Monsieur LeConte—when the time is right. But the right time is not now. Promise you won't forget, Isabelle."

The old peasant woman held a finger to her lips. She had a twinkle in her eye. Steven couldn't read her. He hoped Nicole knew what she was doing.

* * *

They kissed for a long time in the foyer of the old manor. "Let's do it in grandfather's bedroom," Nicole whispered. "We'll make him roll over in his grave. He deserves it. He was even more rigid and unfeeling than father."

"How about that wine cellar you were telling me about?" Steven said. "I've always had a fantasy of taking you in the wine cellar of some old French country home."

"How about both?" Nicole said.

"I think you've solved our dilemma."

They had just taken a leisurely tour of the manor. Steven had noted the location of three rooms: the library, the dining room and the drawing room. He was certain that the Wednesday night meetings would be held in one of them.

Fortunately, all three rooms were in the forward half of the house. Nicole had said that the wine cellar was in the basement, and he needed an excuse for checking it out. He believed he was moving in the right direction.

"I have *not* solved the dilemma," Nicole said. "At least not entirely. The question remains, where first?"

"I say, the wine cellar. While we're down there we select a good bottle for lunch, then we take Isabelle's picnic basket out to where they're harvesting the grapes. We have a walk, maybe a little nap in the sun, *then* we come back and start your grandfather rolling."

She kissed him again, hotly. "Grandfather's room is closer. Come on." He picked her up, swung her around, and kissed her some more. "Listen, woman, I can't always let you get your way. Where's the wine cellar?"

"Outside and around. But my legs are too weak. I might not even make it to grandfather's room. Steven, know what? You could take me right here. Standing up. You told me it was possible."

He slipped his hand under her light summer dress, ran his fingers around the edge of her panties. She sighed. She wasn't joking. She was ready.

Right here sounded good, but he held himself back. "This is the compromise," he said. "We do it standing in the wine cellar."

"And you carry me the whole way."

"Deal." He slung her over his shoulder and carried her out the door. "Which way?"

"Left, around the side of the house. You'll see it. Do you have the keys?"

"In my pocket."

"Hurry. I'm dying for you. Don't trip."

They both started laughing. He came to a row of hedges that grew alongside the manor. He tried to take a shortcut by hugging the wall. There might have been enough room to slip through if he bent down below the fattest part of the hedges, but with Nicole on his back he couldn't do it.

He wiggled out and took the long way outside the hedges. He hadn't gone far when he came to a brick path and a break in the foliage.

"It's here," Nicole said, still laughing.

At the end of the path, abutting the manor wall, was set of horizontal doors, the kind they put on storm cellars in the States.

"Hang on," he said. "I have to put you down so I can unlock this thing."

He dropped to his knees. She clung to him, pretending she refused to let go. She was young, she was a kid having fun. It wasn't only the sex that excited her but their play as well, the sort of play he imagined she had missed during her entire growing up.

He laid her down on top of the door, which looked rather new and was made of smooth heavy-gauge metal. She stretched out on her back and sighed while he fumbled with the keys, trying to find the right one.

"We could do it here," she whispered. "Look how alone we are, Steven. There's no one within a mile."

"On a metal door?"

"Why not?"

"No. A deal's a deal. Standing up in the wine cellar."

"Then hurry."

"Dammit, I'm trying."

When he found the right key, the lock sprang open. It was an expensive lock, smooth and easy to operate. Nicole wouldn't get off, so he lifted the door a crack with her on it. She squealed and slid a few inches to the side. He let the door close again.

There was something he didn't like. A light in the cellar had come on automatically when he opened the door. This could be a big problem if he tried to sneak in when it was dark. It could alert someone in the house to his presence. He would have to think about how to deal with it.

Yes, think about it. But later.

He got physical and rolled Nicole onto a patch of grass. He scarcely had to pull. The door came up as if it had a will of its own and stayed open, like a garage door. It was a quality door, heavy but counterweighted for easy use. The hinges were smooth and silent. He imagined it was break-in proof for someone who didn't have the key, which wasn't a bad idea where the protection of old vintages was at stake.

He glanced at Nicole. She was watching him intently, lying on her back in the grass. She had stopped laughing, she was as still as the fall day. Had she grown suspicious? No, he didn't believe so. She smiled at him, a trusting smile.

Her dress came up above her legs, whether a consequence of her own doing or their tussling, he didn't know. Her breasts rose and fell with her breathing. God, she was beautiful. For now he would prop the door open and leave the light on. He had a very pleasant job to do, a job he couldn't postpone any longer. He reached over, slid her panties off and stuffed them in his pocket.

"Right here?" she whispered.

"No. Come on." He dragged her to her feet, shifted her behind him and lifted her piggy back. He started down the steep, narrow steps. The stones were worn in the center from two centuries of use. The footing wasn't great. No railing. He was glad he had strong legs.

The basement wasn't at all as he had pictured it. Though the outside walls of the manor were gray and smooth, the low vaulted ceilings and the floor were of red brick. He saw a maze of passageways, but no wine.

"Where's the damn wine cellar?" he whispered.

"To the left up there, toward the front of the house."

"Thanks." He picked up the pace. She kissed his ears, reached down, pulled out his shirt and unbuttoned it, ran her fingers over his chest.

Two more turns and he came to an ancient wood and metal door that looked to have been reinforced. "Give me the keys," whispered Nicole.

He dug them out of his pocket and handed them to her. She was still riding piggy back. He bent his knees and turned sideways so she could insert the key in the lock.

The door opened with a shriek, no new hinges here. No lights came on either. He stepped into the dim rectangle and noticed an immediate change in temperature and humidity. Whoever took care of the cellar—Henri, he imagined—knew what he was doing.

He located the light switch but didn't use it. The basement outside was lighted, it wasn't pitch black. Better a little too dark than a lot too bright.

He backed up to a stack of cases whose top was just below shoulder height. Nicole sat on it. He turned around and faced her, kissing the insides of her thighs while he worked his fly open. Now he was ready, very ready. He put his arms around her waist and slid her down on him.

When he entered her, she gave a sharp little cry and wrapped her legs around his torso.

She started moving in a way that drove him crazy. She was breathless, she wouldn't be long. Neither would he, unless he slowed things down.

"Let's torture ourselves," he said. "This is so good I don't want it to end. Let's make it last, okay? Don't let me come, and I won't let you come."

"I don't know if I can wait," she sighed.

"Yes you can. I'll show you." He held her buttocks tightly so she couldn't move. "Be still for a minute. Then we'll start up slowly…so slowly. We'll pretend we're floating around in sea of eternal pleasure."

"Steven, I love you. I never want to lose you."

"Don't worry," he said, letting her move again. "You're not going to lose me. I love you, too, Nicole."

She closed her eyes and sighed. "Steven, I can't do it. I can't, I—"

"Neither can I. Jesus, Nicole…Jesus Christ."

He let her go, he let himself go. Her cries rang in his ears. He couldn't believe the intensity of his pleasure.

It was good, better than good, spectacular.

When they finished, he felt too weak to hold both of them up any longer. He returned her gently to the top crate where he had first deposited her and, still standing, lay his head in her lap.

She stroked his hair. He could feel her tears falling on the back of his neck.

Things between them were too good, just too goddamn good. How long, he wondered, until it all collapsed?

He clung to her tightly, disturbed by the thought. He knew it would be better to keep his mind clear of such distractions.

As his eyes adjusted to the dim light, he saw that one entire wall was lined with bottles stored individually in little cubby holes and protected by a mesh wire door. The expensive stuff.

Another wall was dedicated to crates and boxes from elite vineyards, like the case of Château d'Yquem Nicole was sitting on. He could make out names of wines he knew, expensive wines, and a lot more names of wines he didn't know.

The third wall was Henri's. His double bottles were housed in wooden crates marked only with the year. One crate was marked 1961.

The wine in there, he thought, was older than Nicole, older than him. But 1961 seemed pretty recent when you were in a house built before the French Revolution.

He hopped up on the stack of cases beside Nicole, put his arm around her and pulled her close. She nestled her head against his chest. While he stroked her hair, he looked up. He could see most everything now. There were heating ducts overhead, modern ducts. Some were part of the climate control system for the wine cellar, but most of them branched off to other destinations.

He knew what he needed to know. The basement was navigable, the manor had an updated heating system. With a little time alone down here, he could devise a way of eavesdropping on the Wednesday night meetings regardless of the rooms in which they were held. If the ducts he was looking at right now went where he hoped they did, he might not even have to leave the wine cellar. They selected their lunch wine, a 1964 LaFite Rothschild, and left the cellar arm in arm.

The lights were still on in the basement, the bright lights that had come on when he opened the cellar door. On their way up the narrow steps, he saw a switch. He reached up and closed the basement door. The lights went out and they were plunged in darkness. He flicked the switch. The lights came back on even though the door remained closed. Good to know what everything did.

"Scare you?" he said.

Nicole laughed. "Terribly." She squeezed his arm. "Could I have my panties, please?"

He drew a momentary blank, then remembered they were in his pocket. He handed them to her and glanced at the inside part of the basement door lock while she stepped into them.

Very good. It was the type of lock with a little knob on the inside, not another keyhole. Easy to operate when you were in a hurry.

Outside again, they walked hand-in-hand toward the back of the manor. "Are you hungry yet?" she asked.

"Ravenous. And thirsty for this. You have that effect on me. Shall we do our picnic?"

"We shall. But not with Henri and Isabelle, all right? Let's be by ourselves. I'm enjoying it too much."

"Fine. So am I. Do you have a place in mind?"

"Of course, Steven. I have already choreographed the rest of our lives, starting this instant. At the south end of the property is a little stream with ponds and lilies. It looks like something Monet would have painted. Maybe he did, who knows? I used to go there when I was a little girl and felt sad. I wonder how it will make me feel when I'm happy."

"We'll find out," said Steven, holding her close.

She said, "I'll run in the kitchen and get the picnic."

He gave her the keys, thinking he mustn't forget to take them back so that he could make imprints in the wax of the little key duplication kit he had brought with him.

He sat on an ancient wrought-iron bench.

The chestnut trees all around him sighed in the breeze. Puffy white clouds scudded across the sky, moving rapidly. For a moment, they dimmed the sun.

Nicole was right. You had to be precise about the harvest of the wine grapes. A storm was coming, he could feel it. It might hit tonight, it might unleash a devastating bombardment of hail. If Henri and Isabelle had waited, they might have lost the fruits of a season's hard work.

Nicole disappeared into the manor, leaving him alone with his thoughts. He had to be precise, too. He had to know when the time was right, then go for his scoop no matter what.

He didn't particularly want to come back here this Wednesday. He knew he had a bad habit of relaxing after each success—and today had been a success. But he had to come back. The time for his harvest was at hand. If he procrastinated, he risked losing everything he and Sophie had set out to do.

Chapter Twenty-Three

Chuckie Stafford watched the last of his uncle's employees drive off down the pot-holed dirt road toward the exit gate.

Not a bad Monday, he thought. Three big jobs completed, two new jobs in the hopper. And one of these was a cash deal it took him about five minutes to set up.

So what was this shit his uncle kept giving him about the cement business being tough? Chuckie this, Chuckie that, Chuckie you don't know nothing, so how d'you expect me to take a vacation?

That had been bullshit, too, just to get him thinking it was a big responsibility to run a piss-ant little operation like this. Just to keep him scared while big shot Uncle Joey DiStefano got a tan on his dick in the Virgin Islands.

He took a Budweiser out of the fridge, opened the twist-off cap and sky-hooked it at the waste basket beside his desk. Bad shot. The cap skittered under some shelves. He could almost hear Joey screaming at him to go get it.

Fuck you, Uncle, Chuckie thought.

He entered the check he had gotten for the day's first job in the computer—$3,249.26, including tax, all nice and legal. He put his copy of the invoice, which was stamped "paid," in the file folder for September.

Now for the fun part, the tax-free part. He took out the roll of bills he had harvested on the second and third jobs and counted them again. Forty-two $100 dollar bills and change, all gravy.

Uncle Joey had the business figured out, he'd give him that. But you didn't have to be a genius to make it work. When Joey got back from the

Bahamas, or wherever the fuck he was, Chuckie would have more cash in the safe than his uncle would have made. That's how he would prove he was Joey's equal in business, not just a dago punk with a WASP name.

In the safe. He'd better put it there now before he started thinking about all the things he could do with it.

He did, grabbed another beer on his way back to the desk and hit the waste basket dead center with his lid shot. He stopped in his tracks when he saw an older model Bonneville drive in through the wire gate.

This was bullshit, the office was closed. Well, maybe, maybe not. Depends on what they wanted. He'd better listen. Sometimes those big cash jobs came in after hours right off the street.

The car stopped out front. He played it cool, went to the john, took a leak and combed his hair. When he returned, a pair of city cops were standing at the door.

City cops, the guys you treated politely, the guys you paid off, the guys you needed if you were going to make money in a small business these days.

Chuckie opened the door. "Officers, good evening. Come in. My uncle, Mr. DiStefano, the owner, is away for a couple of weeks. Anything I can help you with?"

"Maybe," the older one said. He was a pink-faced Irish type with a gut and veins in his nose. Chuckie wondered how a guy like that ever got laid.

"You off duty, officers? How about a beer?"

"Thank you but no," the younger one said. "I'm Officer King, this is Sergeant Elliot. We would like to ask you some questions regarding a job you did in early August."

"Hey, you don't wanna ask me, you wanna ask my uncle. Like I said, he's the one who owns the joint. I wasn't working for him in August anyway."

"Your name, please," Elliot said, as if he hadn't heard.

Chuckie guessed he'd better answer. "Stafford. Charles R. Stafford."

King said, "Mr. Stafford, what's the tatoo there on your arm?"

Chuckie smiled. He pulled the sleeve of his T-shirt all the way up and turned his muscled bicep toward Elliot.

"What is it?" Elliot asked.

"You blind? It's a girl and pony show. Like it?"

"On stage," Elliot said. "On you it looks like shit."

Chuckie shrugged his shoulders. What did these guys know?

King said, "Why, Mr. Stafford, did you tell us you were not working for your Uncle in August when, in fact, you were?"

"Hey, what are you talking about? I said I wasn't working for him so I wasn't. I wasn't even in the state, okay?"

Elliot said, "Where were you, then, hotshot? We'll check it out."

King raised his hand. "Let me handle this, Stan. We know you were working for your uncle in August, Mr. Stafford. People we've spoken with saw you."

"Oh, yeah? So how did they know it was me?"

"Your tatoo was described to us in detail. You must have had your sleeves rolled up on the day we're interested in."

"Hey, just a minute. I—"

"Let me finish, Mr. Stafford. I understand it's no fun having to answer questions, especially at dinner time. Maybe it will help you to know that you and Mr. DiStefano are not the subjects of our investigation. You are not implicated in any wrong-doing."

"But if you continue to lie to us, punk," Elliot said, "that could change real fast."

"Yes, it could, Mr. Stafford."

Chuckie went for another beer and sat on the edge of his desk. He dropped the cap straight down into the basket, no way to miss. "So what d'you wanna know?"

"Let's start again," King said. "Were you working for your uncle in August?"

Pilot's Dawn

"Yeah, every goddamn day except Sundays."

"So you *were* present when your trucks poured hundreds of yards of concrete down the coal chute of a tool and die shop just north of Pacific Street in Wallingford?"

Oh, shit, Chuckie thought. They'd somehow found out about the undeclared forty large in cash. What the fuck was he supposed to say? How could Uncle Joey just fly off to Cancun, or wherever the fuck he was, and leave him to deal with shit like this?

"Mr. Stafford. We're waiting for your answer. You were at the—"

"Yeah, goddammit, I was there. I told my uncle it seemed fishy, pouring some basement full of concrete. But it was all legit. The guy who ordered the job had some city inspector on his ass, said his shop was sinking and they'd condemn it if he didn't get it fixed. Insurance had already paid him for the repair. All he cared about was getting the job done fast. What's the problem, officers? You think someone's down in that hole?"

"We don't know," King said. "We're trying to find out. Do you remember the name of the man who ordered the job?"

"Hey, I pour a lot of cement, got a lot of customers. I don't remember. I swear, that's the truth. I don't fucking remember."

Elliot took an invoice form out of the tray on the desk. "DiStefano Sand and Gravel," he read. "That you?"

"Yeah, that's us."

"Seems to be corporate policy not to remember. If you don't remember the guy's name, look it up in your goddamn records."

"Huh?"

"Look it up in your records. You got a computer there, and I assume you file your paid invoices somewhere. Look it up."

Chuckie took a deep breath and tried to play it cool. If he blew this one, his uncle would never let him live it down.

No, it would be worse than that. His uncle Joey might go to jail. Hell, *he* might go to jail. He'd better start lying with a little more authority.

"Look, officers, my uncle keeps all of the records like that at his house. He'll be home in two weeks. You can ask him then. Or I could call his kids and see if I can get the number where he's at. Maybe he'd let me go looking for what you want."

Elliot didn't seem impressed. He didn't even respond to the offer. Instead, he walked around the desk and slid out the file cabinet drawer beside Chuckie's knee. He found the August folder and started flipping through the invoices stamped "paid." His face lit up.

"Little jobs, eh? I see here you got one for eleven grand in August. Hey, here's another one for sixteen. Little jobs? You're feeding us a crock, buddy. We didn't come here to investigate you but, like I said before, if you don't square with us *right now*, all that's gonna change in a big way."

"I"m telling you the truth. I—"

"Know something, kid? They got a guy here at the local IRS office who loves to bust wops. You a wop? Your uncle a wop? I'd say so. Forget the name, you don't look like no high court Brit to me."

Elliot gave him a shit-faced grin before continuing.

"Maybe you even know this wop buster. His name's Luciano and that ain't for Lucky. He knows all about you people, how you love to pay taxes, things like that. So here's your final bottom line, Staffordini. You tell us about this cement job—and I mean every little detail. You do that and we walk out of here."

"On the other hand," King said, breaking in, "you don't tell us about the cementing job, we take that computer and all of your records with us—we got a search warrant, see?—and we call in Luciano. When your uncle gets back from vacation, the Feds'll be waiting for him at the airport. Not us, the Feds. Think he'd be pleased?"

Chuckie felt like he'd been kicked in the privates. He tried to compose his thoughts, but all he managed was a beer belch.

Jesus Holy Christ, talk about being between a rock and a hard spot. He'd heard of that fucking turncoat, Luciano. It would be like bringing home the Devil to let that guy in here. He had no choice. He had to believe these cops weren't after him; he had to take the chance.

Elliot sneered. "Well, kid, you gonna talk now?"

King held up his hand again. Good cop, bad cop—the oldest trick in the profession, but it worked. "Mr. Stafford," he said politely, "I want to repeat that we did not come here to look into your affairs. If you've got tax problems or relative problems or beat your sister, that is not our concern today. All we want from you is information *on somebody else*. Why would you turn a harmless chat into possible criminal charges for yourself? I guess I just don't understand."

Chuckie slapped the table. "All right, goddammit, all right. I get the point. I'll talk. Under one condition. You don't tell my uncle I told you nothing."

The two policemen looked at each other. The older one nodded.

"All right," King said. "We won't tell him. Hurry up. It's getting late."

"Yeah, okay. It was strange. We get this call, like I said. A guy with an accent, foreign guy. Tells us just what I told you."

"All that stuff about the city inspector and insurance?"

"Yeah, and he wants the job done yesterday. It's a real good paying job, forty, maybe fifty grand. So we go out there at eight o'clock the next morning, right on time. We had to postpone three other jobs to do it. Pissed off a lot of contractors."

"The man's name was Stein, wasn't it?"

"Yeah, now that you mention it. Stein. That's right."

"Continue, please."

"Okay, we're there at eight, a whole line of trucks, and Stein pulls up in his car—"

"What kind of a car? Do you remember?"

"Yeah, corporate memory's getting better. It was one of those big Audis, a big gray Audi. Stein says, okay, this is where I want the concrete. He shows us the coal chute door, unlocks it, we lift it off. Takes all three of us, heavy fucker. It's kind of weird because the chute looks real slick, sort of polished. You know, like no one had ever put no coal down it."

"And?"

"He says, pour it in there, mix it wet so it spreads out and fills the 'second basement.' See, there was this second basement under the first one. It was dug too deep. That's what was causing the shop to sink. That's what the man said.

"Anyway, he paid the bill in cash, plus a tip of a grand or so. Then he drove off, and we never saw him again."

Elliot grunted. "And you just happened to forget about that cash haul?"

"Hey," Chuckie said, "what kind of bullshit is this? That's off limits, ain't it? The deal was, I answer your questions, you don't give me any shit about other stuff." He looked to the good cop for a ruling.

King said, "Sergeant Elliot, I believe Mr. Stafford has a point. We don't care about the payment or what these people did with it. As far as we know, his uncle accounted for it elsewhere in the proper fashion. So Stein drove off in his gray Audi and you never saw him again?"

"That's right."

"And you finished the job."

"On time. Then we locked up the chute cover like he told us to do."

"Thank you, Mr. Stafford," King said. "Oh, one more thing before we leave." He reached into his breast pocket and took out a photograph. "Was this the man in the Audi, the man who paid you? Was this Mr. Stein?"

Chuckie looked at the picture. "This dude? Shit no, no way. The guy who paid us was a rich guy, expensive clothes, looked down on us cause we was pouring cement. You know how they are."

"Can you describe the man you saw?"

Chuckie thought for a minute. The image of the man swam up from the depths, an image you wouldn't forget. "Yeah. Maybe a hundred sixty pounds, five ten, in his fifties. The hair was brown, slicked straight back.

Pilot's Dawn

He was a strange bastard, not real big or nothing, but he had this look in his eyes that said, 'Don't fuck with me.' Not like a thug or nothing. Like a rich guy used to giving orders. Lots of orders. You follow me?"

King nodded. "Would you recognize a picture of him?"

"Guaranteed."

King said, "And you're absolutely positive this man in the photo is *not* the man who drove the Audi and paid you for the job?"

"Hey, this guy here's some working man, like me or you. Look at the clothes, look at the face. The guy who paid us *looked* rich, like a doctor or something. I remember his hands, long fingers. Uncle Joey said he got manicures. He didn't shake hands with me so I didn't feel 'em. Wouldn't shake with me 'cause I wasn't the boss. He was that kind of guy. So who's your picture of?"

"The real Mr. Stein, the owner of the tool and die shop where you poured the cement."

"No shit?"

"That's right, Mr. Stafford. And what you're saying is that you have no idea who the man was who paid you?"

"He said he was Stein. That's who I thought he was. If he wasn't Stein, I got no idea."

King glanced at Elliot. "Well, Stan, we'd better talk to the captain about this. He might want us to start digging."

The cops left a few minutes later. Chuckie watched them drive off, bouncing along the pot-holed road in the old Bonneville like one of his uncle's employees.

It was spooky, goddamn spooky. When they'd poured the cement, he'd made a lot of jokes to his uncle about someone being down in that hole. But they weren't jokes, at least not entirely. Because he'd had this strange feeling someone really was down there.

He wondered if Uncle Joey had known all along.

He wondered if Uncle Joey knew who it was.

But most of all he wondered how those cops were going to dig up an underground bunker of solid concrete.

*   *   *

Michelet walked past the newspaper again. He'd walked past it a dozen times since his housekeeper had left on the book shelf in his study, but he had been too caught up in the storm unleashed by Claussen's letter to bother with it.

Besides, even in the best of times, those sensationalist rags infuriated him. Whales giving birth to human beings, and UFOs full of little green people landing in the gardens of the Elysée Palace. Just touching the paper on which such trash was printed made him feel dirty.

But Nature was calling and he had misplaced *Le Monde*. He had nothing else to take with him to the bathroom. So he grabbed the *Inquisitor* and hurried off down the hall. He vaguely remembered Francoise saying something about his daughter when she'd left the paper.

He saw the photo on page eight when he was about to wad the disgusting thing up and stuff it into the waste paper basket. The page, which bore the headline "The Many Faces of Love," was divided into four rectangles, each a photograph of a couple embracing. Two men; two women; a black man and a white woman; and in the lower right hand corner, in the only normal pairing, his daughter being mauled by a handsome blond man. He couldn't tell whether Nicole was trying to fight the man off or was succumbing passionately to his advance.

The photograph had captured one of their drinks just as it was being spilled. The ice cubes and pale yellow liquid were blurred by motion, like the UFOs on the front page. Probably added in the dark room for effect, he thought. Another example of form without substance, an American disease shoved off like AIDS on the French.

The caption read, "Nicole Michelet, daughter of Minister of Industry Georges Michelet, finds love with unidentified man."

Michelet stormed into Francoise' quarters, still hitching up his trousers. He turned off her TV, held up the *Inquisitor* and shook it like something he was trying to kill.

"Do you know who this man is with Nicole?" he thundered. "Do you?"

She gave him the "I told you so" look he detested. He felt like slapping her in the face.

"Answer me, madame. Do you know who this man is?"

"Yes, monsieur. He is the American tennis pro who replaced Philippe Denis du Pèage last summer at the Roches Fleuries."

"What? **What?** She was seeing an *American* down there and you failed to inform me? I hired you to raise her with proper values. How could you let her associate with trash like that? How could you, madame?"

"I had no proof. I heard rumors about playfulness on the tennis courts, that is true. I reprimanded her sternly and asked reliable friends to keep an eye on her. Perhaps you might say I suspected, monsieur, but that is all. You gave me explicit orders not to trouble you with such matters until I had hard evidence."

Michelet grunted.

"I sympathize with you, monsieur, for this most embarrassing situation. However, I do not think it is fair to hold me totally responsible."

Michelet wasn't listening; he was staring at the photograph. "I've seen this son of a whore somewhere. Dressed the same way, blue jeans, a flowered shirt…no, impossible, where would I see a person like that? What were you saying, madame?"

"That I am not responsible. I waited, monsieur, until I had the evidence, and even then it was no small matter to get your ear. You refused to speak with me on the subject of your daughter, you waited several days to open the newspaper I left you. Therefore, monsieur—"

"That will do," Michelet said. "There is no reason to act in this hysterical fashion. I will set the situation straight. What is the man's name, madame? If he is here legally, it will be easy to track him down. If he is not, I shall find him through Nicole and have him deported. So tell me his name and spare me the rest, if you don't mind."

"His name is Steven LeConte."

From his study, Michelet telephoned a friend at Immigration.

"Ah, yes, Minister, we have records of this individual. He has been in Paris for the past two years. Legally? Yes, I think one can say that. He's been chronically late with his employment papers and residency documents, but otherwise nothing...his address? Of course, Monsieur Minister. Place Maubert, Twelve."

*   *   *

Captain Bullock looked harshly at King. "What does Sergeant Elliot think?"

"Well, he thinks it would be a waste of money, thinks we'll spend millions to get down there and either find Stein or not find Stein, and that it won't make any difference one way or the other."

"And you? How do you see it, King?"

"A crime was committed, possibly a murder. We've checked out all the stories the man claiming to be Stein told the cement boys. They were all bogus. There was no city order requiring structural improvements to Stein's shop. There was no payment made to Stein by Stein's insurer.

"Also, sir, we know that the man who paid for the cement job in person was not Stein. We know that the car this man drove away matches the make and serial number of the car that turned up in New York stripped and abandoned—the car our computers say belonged to Stein.

"So, Captain, it seems clear to me that this man killed Stein. It seems clear that this man is hiding something beneath the cement in that basement—either Stein's body or some other incriminating evidence.

"Now, sir, if I understood my training lectures correctly, it is our duty as police officers to pursue such matters, period. If we drop investigations because of cost, then rich people can avoid justice by placing expensive obstacles such as this concrete bunker in our path."

Captain Bullock gazed out at the downtown. His sad drooping eyes reminded King of a dog he had had as a kid.

"You know, Officer," the captain said, swiveling in his chair to face him, "there's always a trade-off. We have a limited budget in this department. If I allocate a hundred grand to dig up your basement, that's a hundred grand I don't have to pursue rapists, drug dealers and dirt heads who blow away convenience store clerks for fifty bucks.

"So, yes, Officer King, we have an obligation. We have lots of obligations. We can't meet them all because we don't have the money. Your obligation is expensive, and finding out who killed Stein—if, in fact, he is dead—will bring the department no relief. Catching the Renton Rapist, on the other hand, will get about five hundred people—politicians, fathers, husbands, loud-mouthed journalists and shrieking women's activists—*personally* off my ass. Therefore, Officer, the answer to your request that we pursue this particular obligation would logically have to be a resounding NO, wouldn't it?"

"But, sir—"

"Wait a minute, King. I haven't finished. I don't want you to get the wrong idea. I don't want you to think you can come to me in the future with requests like this and have them funded. We can move on this particular obligation because of an FBI directive that came down from Washington the other day."

"I'm afraid I don't quite understand, sir."

"Neither do I, King, but the Feds are looking for something. They gave us a list of criteria to be on the lookout for. Your crime meets three of these. Therefore, it qualifies for federal funding. Believe me, Officer, if it didn't, we couldn't pursue it."

King's heart was soaring. His first investigation, which had begun in a Polish deli, was now being funded by Washington!

"So, Officer," Captain Bullock said, "go dig up that goddamn basement. Spend Washington's money, everyone else does."

"Thank you, sir. Thank you. Does that mean you're putting me in charge?"

"Why not, King? You don't have a reputation to lose."

"Well...well, sir, I suppose that's true. How should I start? I mean, I'm not really all that familiar with—"

"Relax, King. I'll see that you have all the help you need."

* * *

"Where are you calling from?" Steven said. "We've got a lousy connection."

"It's not the connection," Nicole whispered. "I have to talk softly. I'm on the train. There are people around."

"The train? Which train?"

"The TGV to Grenoble. I'll be staying with Aunt Jeanne for a while."

"Who?"

"Aunt Jeanne. You remember, Jules and Luc's mom."

"Nicole, why didn't you tell me you were leaving?"

"Because I didn't know until a couple of hours ago. It wasn't my idea. The photograph that damned kid took of us ended up in the *Inquisitor*."

"*Merde*. Your father saw it?"

"Thanks to Francoise. He's ordered her to accompany me to my aunt's home. She's in the toilet right now."

"Jesus. Did he hurt you?"

"No. If you look at the photo a certain way, you get the impression I'm trying to fight you off. I told father that's what I was doing. I don't know if he believed me. He didn't seem that interested. He just said he wanted me out of Paris for a while."

"How long?"

"Steven, I don't know. All of this just happened."

"Can I call you down there?"

"No! Francoise is staying with me. She'll be watching me like a hawk. I wanted to let you know."

"I'm glad you did. The picture, was it on the front page?"

"Page eight last Friday. I doubt anyone in the government saw it. If they had, you can be sure father would have been a lot more abusive than he was. Steven—"

"Yes?"

"It's a rather nice picture."

"Some consolation. What do you think he'll do?"

"I don't know. Maybe nothing if we lie low for a while. He seems really preoccupied. What about your papers—visa, work permit, all that? You have them, don't you?"

"Sure. I might be late on some renewals."

"You'd better get everything current. I can't imagine he'd confront you personally, but I can see him trying to cause you some bureaucratic headaches."

"Nicole—"

"Yes?"

"I want you to know I'm in this with you all the way. Forget what I said before. If we have to, I'll find enough money for us to live somewhere else."

"Okay," she whispered. "Thanks. Steven, I'd better get off."

"When will I see you again?"

"I don't know. As soon as possible. I'm all right, Steven. Promise me you won't get crazy and try to contact me."

"Okay, if you think that's best."

"I know it's best. Get your papers in order. I love you."

Thomas Kirkwood

"I love you, too. But, Nicole, can't we—"
"Adieu. I have to run."
He started to say something but the line went dead.

Chapter Twenty-Four

No dogs, thought Steven, that was it. He had felt something was unusual about Michelet's country home the first time he was here, but he hadn't been able to put his finger on it. Until now.

No dogs! He couldn't remember visiting a rural farm or estate in France—or anywhere else—that had no dogs, not even an old flop-eared hound sleeping in the barn yard.

Navigating the dense forests, he smiled. Nicole had chosen a good time to get herself sent to Grenoble. He hadn't even had to lie to her about where he would be this Wednesday night. And sneaking in here without a pack of dogs at his throat was a joke.

It was the first week of October, an excellent fall day. In the late afternoon he stopped at the ponds where, the previous Friday, he and Nicole had enjoyed Isabelle's picnic lunch and drunk the best bottle of red wine he'd ever tasted.

His Harley was stashed on the other side of the forest near an old tractor path he had discovered on their after-lunch stroll.

So far, so good.

He took in the surrounding countryside. Smoke rose in two plumes from the small vineyard about a half mile away. His eyes were keen; he could just make out Henri and Isabelle's denim-clad forms as they raked the vine trimmings from the recent harvest into the fires. Unless they had developed superhuman eyesight to compensate for their poor hearing, they would not be able to see him.

No dogs, and the caretakers were hard at work a safe distance away. So what was he waiting for? It was time to move. In a few minutes he could be in the basement, mapping the furnace ducts that would pipe the sweet music of Michelet's political secrets to his ears. The bastard might be looking for him right now, but Steven had beat him to the punch!

He started across the swath of open pasture that separated him from the shrubs and trees of the lawn. The approach to the manor was the part of the break-in he worried about most.

Well, he could stop worrying. No one but Henri and Isabelle came here except on Wednesday nights. It wasn't Wednesday night yet. He wore the tans and greens of the land; he was camouflaged well. What difference did it make if he felt as though a thousand watchful eyes were upon him? They weren't.

Keep moving. There was no trouble here.

The autumn sun blazed down; the vine smoke he had hoped would settle like ground fog rose into the opaque blue sky, sucked upward by some mighty inhalation of Nature. He had never seen the air so clear. Every bush, tree and blade of grass seemed to stand out in perfect relief.

A hundred yards to go. Should he run, or could movement alert old peasant eyes?

Should he get down like an infantry grunt and slither on his stomach the last stretch, or was that being ridiculous?

It was being ridiculous.

Fifty yards to go.

He took a deep breath and held it. Not much farther. He had been watching his step, moving slowly and deliberately in spite of his unsettled thoughts. Now he permitted himself a glance toward the vineyard.

A wave of reassurance swept over him. They had not stopped working! He could still discern their movements as they raked. He was going to make it!

He crouched down and moved ahead. Thirty yards to that first fat grove of trees where he could take cover...twenty yards...fifteen...

Pilot's Dawn

Out of nowhere came a big black bird, some kind of a French crow. He froze in his tracks. This was almost as bad as dogs.

The crow buzzed him like a noisy model airplane, nicking his cap and cawing loudly. He watched it rise and circle, and cursed under his breath.

He took another step forward, hoping the attack was over.

No such luck. The squadron leader returned with a flock of pals. They buzzed him in combat formation, strafing him with war caws.

Now he hit the ground. What else was he supposed to do?

The birds relented for an instant, but he could see they were going around for another pass. He used the respite to take a quick glance at Henri and Isabelle.

Jesus, had they noticed? They were standing perfectly still. They looked like scarecrows, their rakes poised motionless at their sides.

Baby crows, that was the problem. These disgusting birds had a nest somewhere in one of those trees he had been regarding as welcome cover.

Calm down, calm down. All sorts of things could set off a crow alarm. It didn't matter, he had heard birds like this before. They always got excited about nothing. Those shrieks hardly meant someone was trying to break into the Minister of Industry's home.

He forced himself to think clearly. Henri and Isabelle were stone deaf. They had looked in his direction, but so what? There was no way they could have heard the crows and no chance they could have seen him. They were farther away now than they had been when he had started across the meadow.

He lifted himself up on his elbows, craned his neck and looked back at them.

He almost swallowed his tongue. Henri was waving at him. Not only waving but walking toward him!

Shit! The old man must have binoculars.

Stay calm! He had to make a choice, and he couldn't afford to make the wrong one. Should he wait for Henri? Or should he make a dash for the basement and hope the old man decided he was chasing a mirage.

Steven got to his haunches, took an angry swat at the nearest dive bomber and turned his eyes to his destination, the dark space between the wall of the manor and the hedge row.

He had to go for it. He hadn't come this far to get derailed. Besides, he didn't feel like being interviewed by Henri.

He resisted the urge to look back. He would know soon enough if the old guy really had seen him.

Go!

He started for the house, then stopped abruptly. He couldn't believe his eyes. Cars were arriving at the front gate, an entire procession of them.

He fell back on his stomach and crawled to the nearest tree. The crows must have pitied him, for they left him in peace.

While his heart thumped in his chest he watched, mesmerized.

Henri hadn't seen *him*. He'd seen those cars pulling up at the gate. He'd been expecting them. He had waved and started out to meet them.

Steven hammered a fist into the earth. If he'd kept his cool, he would be in the basement. The way it was, he would now have to slip past a contingent of men who not only had good ears and sharp eyes but automatic weapons.

And dogs!

Jesus Christ, four men in business suits were unloading a pair of German shepherds from the back of an unmarked van!

Who were these guys? Did Michelet have a personal security force?

Probably not. As a Minister, he would enjoy state protection if he requested it. These were some sort of security agents.

A fifth man jumped out of the dog van and confirmed Steven's fears. He was wearing a black wind breaker with the initials of the French Anti-Terrorist Police stenciled in bright yellow on the back.

Pilot's Dawn

Jesus, just what he needed. First crows, then a whole company of gung-ho cops. He was down love-five in the final set. He had to take chances.

The men did not have the key to the gate. Technically they were still locked out.

Should he make his break *before* Henri arrived to let them in?

And if he made it, should he head for the manor or retreat for the woods?

He looked back over the open meadow he had crossed. No cover, bright sunlight, the possibility of a renewed crow attack. Strike that one from his short list of options.

If he moved in the other direction, toward the house and the hedges, he would at least enjoy the cover of several tree trunks. He would be exposed for only a couple of seconds, but he would be very close to these men, and moving right at them.

What about the dogs? Would they be let inside the gate? If so, it didn't matter which way he moved. They would be on him in a micro-second. Waiting did not seem like a wise idea.

His conclusion: he had to go now, he had to go into the teeth of the storm.

As he was getting to his haunches, a four-door sedan pulled up out front. The heads of the waiting men turned. This was someone important.

The car blocked his view of the dogs, which meant it blocked their view of him. It wasn't going to get any better than this.

He shut off his mind and bolted forward, staying low. To hell with the tree trunks, he was going for broke.

He stumbled at the corner of the house and dove into the dark space between the wall and the hedges. His breathing sounded like a rasp in his ears. Nothing he could do about it, so he just let it rip.

He didn't hesitate. He fought his way forward. It was tough going. The hedges grew closer to the wall than he remembered.

He came to the horizontal basement door and flung himself down next to the lock, trying desperately to quiet his breathing.

Work fast! They were obviously planning to search the place for tonight's meeting. Once the dogs got through the gate, he was hound feed.

He took out the keys he had had made from the imprints in his wax kit. He couldn't remember which one went to the outside door, which to the wine cellar. No time to think. He would have to try them both.

He heard the dogs barking, heard greetings meant for Henri.

He slid the first key in the lock. It jammed, he couldn't get it out.

Jesus Christ Almighty, could anything else go wrong?

It sure as hell could, he thought, as the key finally popped out. What if neither of the goddamned things fit? What if he had made imprints of the wrong keys? What if the guy on the Left Bank who had sold him the kit had ripped him off?

What if? What if?

You could drive yourself crazy with questions.

The second key slid into the lock. It turned easily. He lifted the door.

The lights inside the basement came on automatically. He was glad for the blazing sun.

He rolled through the opening, touched his feet to the ancient stone steps and let the door down on top of him.

The lights went off. A welcome darkness engulfed him.

No time to celebrate. He didn't know if he had been spotted. He didn't know if they would search the basement.

He took out his tiny flashlight, locked the door and went looking for a place to hide.

The basement was huge. He might be able to find a spot, he thought, maybe inside the furnace. It wasn't winter yet. The heat wouldn't be turned on. He could crawl into the air return and be invisible.

Invisible, maybe. But if those goddamn dogs came down here, it wouldn't do him any good. They would sniff him out wherever he was.

He wandered through the vaulted passageways in the dim light. Before he found the furnace, he noticed a little vent near the top of the foundation. He tilted its metal louvers slightly upward. He could see the main gate. It hadn't been opened yet.

The entourage was still milling around. A man in civilian dress was directing traffic, getting all the cars parked in an orderly line across the street.

Michelet must be a suspicious bastard, Steven thought, a man who wouldn't even let his own security people park on his property. What did he think they might smuggle in? A spy from another party? A journalist?

He had to smile. If they didn't catch him and hang him from the crow tree out back, he might just spend an enjoyable evening.

When Henri finally unlocked the gate, a man with a clipboard was the first to step inside. He chatted with Henri briefly, then signaled to the others. They entered one at a time, the man with the clipboard checking off something when each man passed by him.

He was counting!

Michelet must have wanted to make sure everyone who went in also came out! This guy was not suspicious; he was paranoid.

The dogs and their handlers were waved through last.

Steven heard footsteps overhead fanning out in all directions.

Time to go.

In a far corner of the basement, he found two furnaces, one modern, the other ancient and defunct. They didn't seem to offer a place to hide, but on the wall behind them was a rotting wooden door that looked more promising.

He was about to head for it when the basement lights came on. They were here! He began to move slowly toward his goal. He could see his shadow creeping along the cobwebbed brick wall.

He didn't know how many men had entered the basement or if the dogs were with them. But they had definitely come: he could hear their footsteps.

He hadn't expected this. The basement transmitted sound like an echo chamber. His heart was thumping loudly again. He was too late. He couldn't open the door without risking a noise that would give away his presence.

He moved silently toward a pool of darkness beyond the next vaulted archway. This was hardly adequate cover, but at least he wouldn't stand out like a neon sign.

He held his breath and listened.

Heavy footsteps on old stone, visions of the Gestapo. But the voices were not German. They weren't even ill-tempered. He must not have been seen!

From what he could hear, he concluded there were only two men. He was trying to figure out why they hadn't brought the dogs when one of the men asked, "Why didn't you bring the dogs?"

The other man said, "Because our future President showed up two minutes ago. Gandoff was trampling his herb garden trying to run down a crow. When Guillaume ordered him to stop, he took a big shit in the geraniums. Thatcher got the idea it was okay and squatted. You know how Michelet feels about dogs. He ordered them off his property."

"I don't understand why he doesn't like dogs. Foreigners, yes, but dogs?"

The footsteps changed directions.

"He might not like dogs, but he likes wine. How about you, Gaston? Do you like wine?"

"Do the thighs of a woman in heat cry to be parted?"

They both laughed.

"You been down here before?"

"Can't say that I have."

"Well, Michelet's got one of the best wine cellars in France. You're going to see it shortly."

Pilot's Dawn

"You got the key?"

"Yes. The old man gave it to me along with a list of what to bring up for tonight's dinner. Said it's getting hard for him to go up and down those stairs."

The voices grew weaker, the men were moving away.

Steven stayed where he was. Maybe they would take the wine and leave. They didn't seem overly serious about the search, and he didn't want to risk changing their attitude with an inadvertent sound.

He heard the wine cellar door squeak open, heard it shut some time later, heard the men's admiring comments as they headed in the direction of the stairs.

They were going! It was a miracle!

The basement door clanked shut and the lights went out.

Steven felt a smile creasing his face—a big, involuntary smile. If Michelet went to this much trouble to make sure no one listened in on his Wednesday night meetings, you got the idea his secrets were worth listening to. The prospect of delivering them to Sophie thrilled him in a new and wonderful way. She had had faith in him. She had invested a lot of money in him; now she was going to get a healthy return.

But he shouldn't celebrate yet. A lot remained on the agenda. First, he needed to find out which heating ducts went to the rooms in which the meeting would be held. Since these guys upstairs were probably most concerned about electronic surveillance, he reasoned that a lot of them would end up searching the meeting place.

He'd be able to hear them overhead and determine where they congregated. He would know exactly which ducts to cut. Nice of the French Anti-Terrorist cops to provide such help.

Then there was the problem of getting out. Did these agents stay for the meetings or leave? If they stayed, did they conduct another search afterwards. God, he hoped not.

He couldn't worry about that now. There was a logic to the footsteps overhead. They were all converging on one room. He followed the noise and ended up at the wine cellar door.

Convenient, he thought, opening it.

Inside the footsteps were even louder. They went in circles, or criss-crossed. He could hear furniture being moved, and muffled voices.

He climbed up on to the stack of Château d'Yquem cases, the same stack on which he had put Nicole down. He followed a trio of silver heating ducts with his flashlight, the ducts he had selected during his previous visit as probable conduits to the library, the drawing room and the dining room. Which went where, he couldn't say. They all bent into the ceiling a foot to his right.

He took out his pocket knife and sunk the blade into the first duct. It was made of some new insulation material that contained no metal. Quickly and silently, he cut out three sides of a small rectangle. Using the fourth side as a hinge, he bent the rectangle into an open flap.

Nothing.

He cut the same kind of flap in the second duct.

Again, nothing.

The third duct was a charm. The voices above instantly became less muffled. Here and there, he could catch a word.

He climbed down, fetched another crate, used it to make his stand higher. He hoisted himself back up and put his ear to the hole in the duct.

He could hear; God, how he could hear!

Chapter Twenty-Five

Warner's telephone rang at 4:00 a.m. Claire sat up in bed and groped for the reading lamp. "Oh, Frank, not another one."

He took her hand so she didn't turn on the light and picked up the receiver.

"One moment," he said, and hit the Hold button. "Claire, it's all right. It's not the emergency line. Go back to sleep. I'll take it next door."

"Thank God," she murmured. "Thank God."

Warner tugged on his robe and hurried to the phone in the guest bedroom. "Yes?"

"Frank, it's me, Simmons. Daniels called me about ten minutes ago. He wants us to fly to Seattle this morning. Wants us there as close to eight o'clock as possible, Pacific Time. Can you be at National in an hour?"

"If you pick me up."

"No problem."

"Do we have our break, Tim?"

"I don't know, can't say. The cops out there claim they've found a bunch of aircraft parts buried in concrete. Maybe they're not even aircraft parts. Maybe they are, but have nothing to do with our problem. But the FBI isn't taking any chances. Daniels wants the guys who know their stuff to assess the situation immediately. I guess that's us, chief."

"He must be hopeful."

"He didn't sound it."

"No?"

"No, Frank. He sounded worried Larsen would use the situation to publicize his firm's innocence. He feels that such a move could finish Boeing off if this thing turns out to be a hoax or some kind of dumb error."

"He doesn't know Hal Larsen."

"I agree, chief. But I think he's right about one thing. I think the NTSB should be first to check it out."

"All right. One more question. Did Daniels mention anything from the other investigations?"

"As a matter of fact, he did. Around the time of the Atlanta crash, Delta's head mechanic at the engine rebuild facility was killed in a car wreck. Seems unrelated. As for Pratt and Whitney, they've exhumed Melchior and are conducting another autopsy. No results yet."

"Bendix?"

"They've found something there, too. A stocker in the parts department drowned the night Melchior supposedly suffered his heart attack, rammed his boat into a pier. Blood alcohol level, point one seven. Also seems unrelated. But it's not unrelated, is it, Frank?"

"I don't know. Come get me. We'll talk about it during the flight."

Warner hung up. He showered, shaved, dressed, wrote Claire a note and kissed her good-bye without waking her.

His cool weather bag stood packed and ready beside the front door. He picked it up and walked outside to wait for Simmons.

In spite of the season and early hour, the air was warm and humid, like summer. It was very dark, but Warner could make out a faint glow of dawn along the eastern horizon.

"Pilot's dawn," he'd called it when he had flown for the Air Force. Pilots saw that subtle first lifting of night more often than anyone else. You saw it in Winnemucca, too, when you got up while it was still black as a witch'es cave to go hunting. He had always considered a pilot's dawn something special, though he had no idea why.

Pilot's Dawn

He imagined what the world looked like right now on the other side of the Atlantic. It would be mid-morning. Men and women in Germany, Britain and France would be hiring on by the thousands to meet the avalanche of new orders received by Airbus.

In Seattle, by contrast, it was still night. When morning came, unemployment lines would swell down city blocks and around corners. Later, the heirs of the men and women who had built the Flying Fortress would be returning home in droves with nothing to do but watch afternoon TV and wonder what had happened to their careers. America's best and brightest would be idle at a time when their country desperately needed them.

* * *

At 9:20 a.m., Pacific Time, the government car pulled into the alley behind Stein's Tool and Die.

"Here's where it's happening," the driver said.

Simmons and Warner got out. While Simmons did his athletic stretches, Warner groaned and looked around. He felt stiff, tired, and old.

It seemed like any construction site—dump trucks, a huge backhoe belching diesel fumes, the nerve-jangling chatter of air hammers, laborers in open shirts barking the national blend of profanity and expert opinion.

A big cop with a pleasant face walked over from the excavation site and extended his hand. "I'm Officer King. I take it you are Mr. Warner of the NTSB?"

"Yes, that's right, Officer. And this is my associate, Mr. Simmons."

King led them to the back of Stein's building, where workmen had torn down a wall to make room for the backhoe. The bricks that had been removed were stacked on palettes in the overgrown yard. A thick steel beam had been placed across the top of the hole to keep the second story from caving in.

"Have a good look," King said. "There was a basement below the regular basement. That's why the hole is so deep. The second basement had been poured full of concrete, but the top basement was still just a basement. We were already eight feet down when we started digging."

"Impressive," Warner said, peering thoughtfully into the hole. He counted a dozen men working in the concrete cavern. Some were using air hammers to crack areas circled with a ring of red paint. Others, dressed in khaki, probed the rubble-strewn floor with sonar devices.

"Archaeologists," King shouted over the noise. "Those guys in khaki are archaeologists. They're mapping where it's safe to go down another two feet. When the instruments beep, it means there's metal below, probably aircraft parts. We're being very careful not to damage anything."

"Good," Warner said. "Tell me something, Officer, where did you find archaeologists who would dig up a basement?"

King laughed. "Captain Bullock sent them over here. Look at those guys. They'll dig up anything."

"Well, let's get down to business. All we know is that the FBI thinks you've found something we should look at."

"That's right, I'd say we have," King said. "Let me start from the beginning. I mean, how we made this discovery and—"

"If you don't mind, Officer King, I'd first like to look at the items you suspect are Boeing aircraft parts. If they are, we will certainly want to go over the details leading up to their discovery. If they are not—well, we can save each other a lot of unnecessary talk."

King had the face of a dejected school boy. He was obviously excited about telling his story. But he soon perked up and smiled. "Sure, Mr. Warner, let's have a look at them. They're right over here in the police van."

Warner started brusquely toward the van, with Simmons at his side. King followed, chattering away. "Gentlemen, slow down, I have to unlock it anyway. You must be hungry. I'm going to let you in on the best-kept secret in this part of town. Believe it or not, there's a good diner across the street. I already checked the special for today. Chicken and dumplings. They start serving at eleven. We could talk over lunch."

Warner waited until they had arrived at the van to respond. "Thank you, Officer King. If we're still here, we'll do that. Now, why don't we take a look?"

King unlocked the van. The parts were in the carpeted cargo area. They had been laid out on an archeological template showing where in the basement they had been found, and at what depth.

Numbered stickers on the parts and corresponding numbers and outlines on the template meant that the parts could be picked up and examined without risk of forgetting where they belonged.

Warner nodded at Simmons, who winked.

The parts were slightly discolored. Clumps of cement still clung doggedly to the metal in spots, and there were fresh dings from the tools used to dig them out. Evidently the sonar wasn't infallible.

Warner picked up a mounting bolt and studied it carefully. Someone had worked the metal with a wire brush to get the cement off. The surface was badly scratched, but the serial number was on its cap, and it was legible.

He was about to show it to Simmons when his assistant turned to him with a larger and more complicated part.

"Recognize it, Frank?" Simmons asked.

Warner peered around King's jowly face, then reached over and took the part. "I would say offhand that we are looking at a right aft engine mount for a Boeing 767 Extended Range 300."

"Can you make out the serial number?"

"Yes. Also the parts number."

"You're sure it's the right mount?" Simmons asked.

"Positive."

Simmons frowned. "And it was the left aft mount that failed in Atlanta, wasn't it?"

"Left, yes."

"Interesting," Simmons said. "Do you suppose there's a defective part bearing this same serial number on someone's parts shelf. Or installed in an aircraft? Or is this a defective part?"

"Hard to say. Larsen should be able to tell us."

"He should. Looks like we might finally be getting somewhere, doesn't it, Frank?"

"Yes, and it's about time."

Chapter Twenty-Six

Heavy footsteps overhead put an end to Steven's siesta. He glanced at his watch, which glowed brightly in the dark wine cellar. 8:03 p.m.

Michelet had arrived several hours ago, just in time to save his ass by chasing off the secret service dogs. There had only been goings since then. Now, at last, it sounded as if someone had come. Time to consult the vent at the front of the basement.

He scrambled out from behind the stack of crates where he had been resting, used his flashlight to illuminate the ancient hinges and gave them a second precautionary shot from his miniature spray can of WD-40.

He waited a few seconds for the lubricant to do its job, then pushed open the door and started through the maze of dank, vaulted passageways.

He made a wrong turn, backtracked, resisted the temptation to use his flashlight. Feeling his way along the cool brick walls, he quickly recovered his bearings. In the murky distance he soon saw his polar star, the louvered vent trimmed in bright light from outdoors. He hurried to it and began twisting it open a little at a time.

As the louvers separated, the cool evening breeze touched his clammy skin. A cat mewed on the other side of the foundation. His heart began to thump.

He could hear voices outside now, and car doors opening.

Someone *had* come! Another inch or so of rotation and he would be able to see who it was. He hesitated; the air on his skin and the light coming through the vent made him feel dangerously exposed.

The cat swished by, turned around, rubbed up against Steven's only view of the secret world of Georges Michelet. Steven hissed under his breath. The cat leaped away.

He heard a car door close, then another. The voices of the men outside moved closer, mingling with the sounds of the country night.

Either he took his chances and looked now, he thought, or he would be a blind man eavesdropping on strangers for the rest of his stay.

He stepped out of the light and opened the vent all the way. He made a quick assessment of the danger of being seen and, deciding it was small, put his face near the louvers.

He wanted to shout for joy. The three men Sophie believed to be conspirators in Nouvelle France were walking toward him on their way to the house. Michelet was in the middle, looking burlier and more anxious than Steven remembered him.

To Michelet's right was Paul Delors, whom he recognized from a photo Sophie had slipped under his door. He wasn't the kind of man who would stand out in a crowd. Just an ordinary middle-aged guy in horn-rimmed glasses and a conservative blue suit.

Not so the man on Michelet's left. He had a face known round the world. The face belonged to the man reputed to be the richest entrepreneur in Europe.

In person, Steven thought, Albert Haussmann emanated even more animal vitality than he did on TV. Tonight, this compact, elegant package of bald-headed energy didn't look happy.

In fact, none of the three looked happy.

That's what pissed him off most about the French, he thought. They never knew how good they had it. These guys were about to sit down to an unbelievable feast whose aromas had been working their way into the basement for hours, driving him mad. They had it all—power, money, any pleasure the human race could dream up. Yet they looked as sour and irritable as a bunch of Parisian waiters in August.

Just hang on a little while, boys, he thought, and I'll give you a reason for your ill humor.

Trouser legs swished by within a few feet of him as the three men, silent now, climbed the front steps and went inside. Steven surveyed the lawn and circular drive in front of the manor.

Michelet had closed and locked the gate. There were no cops left behind, no secret service men and no drivers. Two cars were parked inside the gate, a Mercedes 600 SL and a 4-door Citroën. No trouble guessing which belonged to whom. More importantly, it told him Delors and Haussmann had driven themselves to the meeting. Getting out of here after he had dined on their conversation would be a piece of cake.

He shut the vent and followed the footsteps. He had a map of the house layout in his mind and expected the men to head straight for the dining room. Instead, they turned in the direction of the library. He hurried to the wine cellar and quietly shut the door. They were above him now, pacing, shouting, arguing.

Another break. They seemed to be holding their meeting before dinner. He might be home earlier than he thought!

Careful not to make a sound, he climbed on to the stack of Château d'Yquem cases, bent back the small flap he had cut in the heating duct and put his ear to the opening.

The voices were clear, distinct from one another, filled with purpose. He began trying to assign them each a face. He needn't have bothered. His subjects were using names.

Paul Delors was the steady voice of reason, the calm collected voice urging an objective assessment of a situation "that is only a problem if we—meaning you, Albert—allow it to become one."

Georges Michelet was the gruff, impatient voice demanding "a clear decision—will you or won't you?—before we leave this room."

And Albert Haussmann was the voice of cynical outrage—the mocking, cutting, mellifluous and fiercely intelligent voice.

But what in the hell were they arguing so heatedly about? Steven had missed the first few words, not to mention the things that had been said during the trek from the cars to the library.

He listen intently. He needed to find his place in this cataract of words.

Haussmann was saying, "I want, I *demand*, to know *exactly* how this happened. Here, look at these. They came in the mail today. Regular mail. The goddamned post! Photographs of the three of us right here in front of this very house taken by Claussen or someone who works for him. This is worse than that abominable letter."

Delors said coolly, "Albert, if you don't calm down and listen to reason, you are going to jeopardize everyone's cover, including your own. Is that what you want?"

"Excuse me, Paul, but I was assured in unequivocal terms that this supposedly manageable ex-spy of yours would never know who we were. That, if you recall, was *the* condition for my involvement. Now that condition has been violated. Nevertheless, you still want me to hand the man two hundred fifty million dollars."

"Albert, please just—"

"My answer, Paul, is no. This whole thing was a bad idea. It was a bad idea because it included someone we did not know and could not trust, someone who was not French and did not share our devotion to our country. I'm not getting in any deeper. You and Georges will have to find the money elsewhere. I have committed no crime as yet. Given the circumstances, I don't intend to."

"Committed no crime!" Michelet thundered. "How could you say something that preposterous? Without your agreement to foot the bill, Paul and I could not have commissioned a single crash, let alone twelve. Besides, Albert, answer me this. Which of us has already profited most from Boeing's misfortunes? Let me answer for you. I've seen the latest statistics at the Ministry. The industries of the Haussmann Group that supply Airbus have made a killing—or stand to make one in the near future. You were in a lot worse trouble than you let on. We've bailed you out and now, suddenly, you don't want to honor your part of the bargain. That's unacceptable, Albert. Unacceptable. So I suggest you hold your tongue and listen to Paul."

Steven's head was spinning. Had he heard right? Michelet saying he could not have commissioned crashes without Haussmann's agreement to pay? Talk of a 250 million dollar bill to some ex-spy named Claussen coming due, some ex-spy who wasn't supposed to know who these guys were but had found out? Mention of Boeing as the loser, Airbus as the winner?

Jesus! It was clear as day. These were the pricks bringing down those U.S. airliners! He shuddered. You wouldn't catch him again with that big American grin on his face, not Steven LeConte. The days of his blissful innocence were over. The truth would see to that, the hideous truth. Nicole's dad was not only a murderer. He was the biggest criminal since Adolf Hitler!

He turned on his flashlight and took his note pad out of his pack. He would write everything down, just in case. Names, dates, relationships, the whys and wheres, whens and hows, whatever he and Sophie would need to nail these bastards to the wall.

He felt dizzy. He reminded himself to breathe. The men were still arguing, spilling more and more information with every word.

Operation 26…Volkov…an East-Bloc plot to cripple American aviation in case of a land war in Europe!

Now, in the wake of the Cold War, had come the great economic war. Steven had always thought this so-called war was between the U.S. and Japan. According to these guys it was between the United States and Europe. And the decisive battle was being fought right now. It was the battle between Boeing and Airbus for international market share, a battle that would decide where hundreds of billions of dollars went over the next 20 years, a battle that would decide who won and who lost the war—or at least who won the next French presidential election. It was in their view a battle so important it justified using the weapons of military conflict. Operation 26 was alive and well in the New World Order. No wonder things hadn't gotten any better since the East Bloc collapsed!

From what Steven could tell, Airbus didn't know where it was getting all the help. Airbus was not involved in this unspeakably dirty action. In fact no one was involved except the three men in Michelet's library and a spy named Walter Claussen.

And, as of now, one American whose lacking virtues had put him in the right place at the right time.

Hold on, this was incredible. Claussen was supposed to report here night after tomorrow for his payment and further instructions. The next meeting was on Friday!

The sons of a bitches didn't know it now, thought Steven, but they were going to have some unexpected company.

* * *

Shortly after eleven o'clock, Haussmann finally agreed that his reaction to their uncloaking by Claussen had been exaggerated.

Yes, he said, he could understand how a man like that would want to establish a balance of power with his employers; yes, he could understand how Claussen would want to be protected against elimination, especially since Haussmann himself had once brought up elimination as an option; and, yes, he would pay the bill as planned, even though he still found Claussen's fee, which the spy based on the replacement value of the Boeing aircraft he destroyed, outrageous, to say the least.

The three conspirators made their peace, exchanged some mumbo jumbo about the glory of France and went off to dinner. Steven folded the tab in the heating duct back into place, climbed limply down from the stack of wine crates and gathered up his things.

He crouched on the worn stone steps beneath the basement exit until he was sure that everyone had moved to the other side of the house,

Pilot's Dawn

then pushed open the metal door. The basement lights came on automatically, illuminating the hedges outside, and a crescent of lawn.

He wasn't frightened. He knew he wouldn't be caught. This was his night, he could feel it the way he felt the tide of a big tennis match when it shifted irrevocably in his direction.

Climbing out, he closed the door and locked up. He started back across the broad expanse of yard, his path lit by the harvest moon. The crows were asleep, the breeze had died, the smoke of the smoldering vine fires rose vertically in the pale, milky night.

He paused at the lily pond to catch his breath, then slipped into the forest, following the path by which he had come. His bike was where he had left it, just off the tractor road hidden in the tangled undergrowth. It started on the first try. He emptied his head of thoughts and concentrated on what he was doing. He drove home more cautiously than usual. Who was he to risk a high-speed accident tonight? Fate had entrusted him with the safe delivery of a valuable package—himself—and he intended to get the job done.

✶ ✶ ✶

It was almost 3:00 a.m. when he buzzed at Sophie's door. He had expected a long wait but she opened at once. She was wearing dark slacks and a flowered blouse which, if he wasn't mistaken, was the outfit she had worn the day she proposed that he go south in search of a story. She gave him a big hug, then held him away by the shoulders and looked him over.

"It's me," he said. "Did I wake you up?"

She laughed her husky laugh. "No, darling, you kept me up. I've been worried sick. I want to hear everything. Come in and sit down. I'll get you a drink."

"Thanks, Sophie. Just water." Steven flopped on the sofa and started digging through his pack for his notebook. "You don't know how good it is to be here," he murmured.

She took a few steps toward the kitchen, then turned around and stared at him. "Steven, are you all right? You're acting rather strange."

"Yes, I'm all right. Other than having been deprived of my sanity, I'm fine. Sophie—"

"What is it, darling?"

"Go on. Get me some Perrier. I'm parched and I'll be talking for a long time. And not about what you think."

When he began to pore over his scribblings, the enormity of what he had stumbled on to erased everything else from his awareness. He didn't hear Sophie sit down across from him, didn't hear her setting out plates and silverware, didn't even realize she had left the kitchen until she tapped a spoon on the coffee table.

"Sorry," he said, jerking his head up.

She showed him a bottle of wine. "Barolo, darling, nineteen fifty-nine. A gift from an Italian admirer. I've been keeping it for just the right occasion. Shall I open it?"

"Thanks, Sophie, but not now. I've got some serious stuff to report, and we've got to make some serious decisions about what to do. We'd better stick to mineral water."

"Well, Steven, if it's so important we must pass on a fifty-nine Barolo, I suppose you'd better tell me what's happening."

"Michelet…Michelet is behind those Boeing crashes! I'm not kidding, Sophie. He and his buddies are paying a shitload of money for some ex-KGB spy to sabotage the planes! That guy who called you from the States was sniffing in the right direction."

She put the wine bottle down and stared at him. "Steven, I know you've got a lot on your mind, but that can't be. You've misunderstood something, bless your heart."

"It can't be, Sophie, that's right. I agree. I couldn't agree more. It can't be—but it is."

"I'm sorry, Steven, but you're mistaken. I've spoken with people in Washington who are close to this whole mess. It's not public knowledge yet, but there's a growing body of evidence that Iraq is the responsible party. The evidence is so compelling the United States is gearing up for military action. That's off the record, of course."

Steven opened the Perrier and poured them both a glass. "The growing evidence is bullshit. It was planted so people would come to the wrong conclusion."

"Steven"

"I don't want to argue. Can't you suspend your doubts for a while and just listen?"

"I'm sorry, darling, it's those pesky journalistic instincts of mine. I don't mean to be a difficult audience. Go ahead."

"Okay. I sneaked into Michelet's place as planned. I had a feeling I might get lucky when a bunch of cops and secret service agents showed up for a search."

"Steven, they could have caught you."

"They almost did. Michelet saved me, can you believe that? He got pissed at the dogs for taking a crap in his flower bed and ordered them off his property. The cops left a little while later but Michelet stayed.

"So there I was, down in the wine cellar with nothing to do but wait. Around eight o'clock, your boys from Saint Claude showed up."

"Haussmann and Delors?"

"That's right, Haussmann and Delors."

"But you didn't actually see them?"

"Wrong, Sophie. I watched them arrive. There's a little vent at the front of the basement. When I heard movement upstairs, I went for a look. Michelet met them outside and they all headed straight to the library."

"You're sure it was them?"

"Positive. They were having a crisis meeting for reasons I'll get to. My listening post was almost directly beneath them. When I put my ear to a little hole I'd cut in the heating duct, I might as well have been in the library smoking a cigar with them. If you still think I didn't identify them correctly, listen to this. They used names: Albert, Paul, Georges and, on occasion, last names too. It would have been impossible to misunderstand anything."

"Impossible? Steven, I'm sorry but I'm having a hard time with this."

"Look, if I was someone else, I'd be having a pretty hard time believing it, too. Christ, I had a hard time believing it while I was listening to it. But, Sophie, it's true. I heard it all first-hand, every word of it."

"Then go ahead, and tell me the rest. I'll try to do as you asked and suspend my doubts."

"It will get easier. Guaranteed. But there's something else you should know before I start. Michelet might be looking for *me*. That photo I told you about, the one a kid shot of me and Nicole kissing in a café. It was in last Friday's *Inquisitor*, page eight."

"You knew?"

"Monique showed me. I was hoping no one of importance would see it. I didn't want to distract you."

"Well, it didn't work out that way. Nicole's housekeeper not only saw it but showed it to her father. Because of it, Nicole's a prisoner with her aunt in Grenoble and Michelet knows who I am. Not just how I look but who I am. By name, Sophie."

"Don't worry about it, Steven. You can stay with me. We'll see if he comes for you, but I doubt he will—at least not right away. If what you've told me is true, he'll be too involved in his own crimes to worry about the ethnic purity of his daughter's male friends. And as for your work, having her out of town will be a big help. She actually couldn't have picked a better time to get herself sent away. Now, darling, let's get on with your account."

*   *   *

By the time morning rush hour came, Sophie was a believer, though not the enthusiastic believer he had expected.

"I don't know about you," Steven said, "but I could use a few gallons of coffee."

Sophie nodded. She looked pale and shaken. He could see her 70 years, usually so well hidden by her exuberance, inscribed in the folds and creases of her face.

"That sounds good, Steven. I'll call the baker and have him send us up some bread and croissants."

She reached for the receiver. He took it from her and put it back in the cradle. "Why don't we eat the hors d'oeuvres we didn't touch last night. I feel like something with substance."

"All right, darling. I'll put the coffee on."

He walked with her to the stove, his arm around her shoulders. "You're worried about me, aren't you?"

She gave him a hard, no-nonsense look. "You bet."

"Well, I guess I'd rather have you a worried believer than a happy skeptic."

"Steven, I don't know what to say. I think you're going to have to drop this thing entirely. You've had a run of beginner's luck, but the chances of it continuing are zero. This is no game. You're dealing with professional killers. It's not any place for a journalist to be."

"No place to be, but I'm there. That's one fact we can't rewrite."

She put water in a kettle and set it on the stove, shaking her head while she worked.

"Steven, let me put the situation in perspective for you. I would like you to imagine that you are approached by a man who is in good shape and athletically gifted but has never held a tennis racket in his life. This man challenges you to a match. Do you think there's any way he could beat you?"

"Maybe—if he shot me."

"This isn't a joking matter."

"I know, Sophie. But you made a lousy analogy. I'm not going to challenge these guys at their game. Being an amateur might be the winning card. I don't know the tricks of the trade. Christ, *I* don't know what I'm going to do next. How the hell could they?"

"Steven—"

"Just a minute, please. I want you to understand one thing. I'm going to pursue this, period. After what I heard last night, there's nothing that could stop me. So let me use an analogy to put my position in perspective for you. Let's say, Sophie Marx, that you had discovered the death camps before anyone else knew of their existence.

"Let's say your knowledge, if handled properly, could have brought you early recognition for being the great journalist you are and, more importantly, could have saved a lot of lives and a lot of human suffering. Are you going to tell me you would have been able to pack up and remain silent for the rest of your life because you faced some hypothetical danger?"

She poured boiling water over the freshly ground beans. "An especially bad analogy," she said. "If I had discovered the death camps, it would have been my discovery. This is different. I sent you in there, Steven. I persuaded you *against your better judgment* to seduce Georges Michelet's daughter. I did this so I could learn more about the man. Do you hear all the I's? There are more. I could not handle it if anything happened to you. I simply couldn't take it."

She wasn't her usual efficient self in the kitchen. Steven thought he detected tears in her eyes. He felt badly for her. The joy of breaking their big story had evaporated. It was as if they had gone off joyously fly fishing for trout and had hooked a shark they didn't know what to do with.

But he wasn't going to cut the line, and he didn't believe she would either, once she had recovered from her shock and gotten past her fears. This was, after all, the Mother of all Stories, the big one she had been chasing her entire professional life.

He took cups from the cupboard and heated milk in one of her battered copper pans. He told her to go sit by the window, that he would finish up.

When he brought her a perfect *café au lait*, she looked at him adoringly.

"Feeling better?" he asked.

She smiled and squeezed his arm. "Yes. And I suppose we had better not waste any more time. We've only got two days and a night. Sit down. Let's get busy. We need to discuss how we're going to proceed."

He felt himself smiling, though he had vowed never to smile again. "I knew you'd come around, Sophie."

"Of course you knew, darling. You know me a little too well. I'm going to do the best I can not to worry about you. If we put our heads together, perhaps we can devise a strategy so brilliant it's both safe and effective."

He hugged her for a long time. He had his soul mate back. "I'm sure we can. So what do you think? Should we involve the police?"

She raised her eyebrows. "The police? With what evidence?"

"What do you mean, 'What evidence?' What have I just spent half the night giving you?"

She drained her cup. Her energy was coming back now, he could feel its force.

She said, "You've spent half the night giving me a detailed account of what you heard. Unfortunately, Steven, just because it's true doesn't mean its evidence. You and I know what's going on, but who's going to believe us? Have you thought of that?"

"I...Jesus, no. You're saying, when it comes down to my word against theirs—"

"Precisely. In the white corner you have a charming young American who's stupfing Michelet's daughter. In the black corner you have three powerful French public figures who will corroborate each other's every syllable. I doubt the *Inquisitor* would listen to you."

"Thanks. I should have taken a goddamn tape recorder."

"How could you have known?"

"I could have been better prepared."

"You did just fine, Steven. Look what you've brought home. I will not permit you to transform your triumph into a miserable rite of Protestant self-abasement. Drop the guilt."

"I can't. What I've brought home is useless. You just said so."

"Useless as evidence, I said. Which is why we have to think in larger terms than our little brains are accustomed."

"Think, Sophie! Your brain's bigger than mine. What about the man who thought it was Airbus? Didn't you say he was in the government? Does he have any clout?"

"That's a good question, Steven. He's been taking a lot of heat lately. I don't know if people are still listening to him. I'll certainly find out."

"So, who is he? Can you tell me?"

She reflected for a moment. "Yes, of course. He's the man I hope you've been reading about in the newspapers, the poor bastard entrusted with solving these crashes."

"You mean that NTSB guy the administration was trying to get rid of?"

"Yes, precisely. Frank Warner."

"And you know him?"

"I do. We met here in Paris after that horrible DC-10 crash in 'seventy-four. I helped him get along with the French. He wasn't a big fan of journalists, but I think he considered me an exception. We became friends and we've remained friends."

"What are we waiting for? Let's call him."

Sophie looked at her nails. "I don't have his unlisted numbers, Steven. He tried to give them to me, and I stupidly refused. I wanted to underscore how little I thought of his Airbus hypothesis." She sighed. "We all make mistakes, darling, though this isn't one I'll soon forget. We'll just have to wait until the NTSB opens—and hope Warner's not out in the field somewhere."

"Well, that's a start. What about here in France? Isn't the CIA active? The sabotage of U.S. planes should be right up their alley. They should jump on our information."

Sophie shook her head. "Sometimes I think 'should' has become the most common word in our vocabulary. Yes, darling, they should indeed be interested. But you mustn't forget you're talking about bureaucrats. Their hands are tied until they get the go-ahead from Langley. And Langley's hands are tied until they get the green light from the White House. To tell you the truth, Steven, I don't see that happening. France is an ally, and Michelet is a member of the French government."

"France isn't an ally if they're bringing down our planes, and Michelet is an asshole."

"Yes, but remember. We have no evidence. If our government were to authorize the secret service to spy on Michelet, it would be like the French authorizing their intelligence people to spy on one of our cabinet members—in the United States. I promise you that no American president in control of his faculties would risk a monumental international scandal without hard evidence. That's just the way things are, Steven."

"Jesus, this is frustrating."

"Yes, it certainly is."

"Okay, I've got an idea. I think this is one you'll like."

"Let's hear it."

"We know Claussen is coming to Michelet's to collect for the crashes Friday night. We know the others will be there. If one of the CIA people working in France went with me—you know, off the record—and hid in the wine cellar, he could make recordings of everything with all that bugging equipment those guys use. Then we'd not only have our evidence; we'd have a believer inside the establishment. And you wouldn't worry as much about me. What do you think?"

She stood and paced in a counter-clockwise direction around the kitchen, a sign that her thoughts had shifted into high gear. "That would be ideal, Steven—if we could find an agent willing to put his career on the line. I don't mean to sound negative, but I doubt we'll find anyone willing to take that risk."

"For Christ's sake, risk-taking is what they're paid for."

"When it's bureaucratically sanctioned. You can't have spooks running around carrying out private agendas. That's what Delors is doing. But there is something I can try. I knew the old CIA capo for France, a gentleman by the name of Devon Fairchild. When we were teenagers, our parents vacationed at neighboring beach houses in New Jersey. He had a suffocating crush on me, and though that side of our relationship never amounted to much, we became good friends. When he took on the French assignment, we often shared information. Very confidentially, mind you."

"So where is this guy now?"

"Dead. But his son, William, whom I also know, is at the embassy now. He's CIA, followed in the footsteps of the old man. I'll pay him a visit. Perhaps I can put the memory of his father to use."

"Excellent, Sophie. What about Walter Claussen? He lives in East Germany now. Delors referred to that fact a couple of times. Where did he live when he was putting together Operation Twenty-Six? In the States? Seems to me he would have had to."

"Probably, Steven, but probably not under the name of Walter Claussen. I'll check it out, though. We've got some pretty good computer search capabilities with the new software the press is using these days, and I have other contacts I can try. That should keep us busy for this morning, don't you think?"

He stood and tapped her on the arm. "Sophie, we're going to pull it off. I have this very strong feeling we're going to get the breaks we need. Don't you?"

When she looked at him, he was surprised that her exuberance of the last hour had vanished. In its place was the same sadness he had noticed earlier, a deep mournful sadness that seemed to pull her down into herself.

He didn't ask her what was wrong, but he no longer believed it was her fear for his life. It was something else, something bigger, a sadness that came, he thought, from a life devoted to discovery of the truth.

She had discovered the truth again and again. The truth was supposed to be good and beautiful. But all too often, staring up at her when she peeled away the layers of deception, was the face of human cruelty.

He didn't like that face either, but he didn't feel at all discouraged. In fact, he felt energized. Okay, maybe he wasn't going to change human nature. But he was going to put a few mean bastards out of commission. For now, that seemed like enough.

Chapter Twenty-Seven

It was a cool cloudy morning in Paris. While Steven caught up on sleep, Sophie took the Métro to the American embassy.

William Fairchild, whom she had cajoled on the phone into giving her an appointment, ushered her into his office. He buzzed for coffee and gestured for Sophie to have a seat in the straight-back chair across from his desk.

"Well, Ms. Marx?"

"Well, William, nice to see you. It's been a long time."

"My father's funeral, if I'm not mistaken."

"That's right. You have a good memory. You know, William, I'm not exaggerating when I say Devon Fairchild was one of the finest men I've ever known."

"That may be, Ms. Marx, but if you came here expecting special treatment because you and dad were friends, I must disappoint you."

Not a good beginning. She remained silent while the secretary brought American-style coffee in styrofoam cups. Fairchild fished through heaps of creamer and sugar packets, poured in a few and stirred the tan liquid with a plastic stick.

She said, "I quite understand your misgivings about seeing me, William. But I assure you this isn't what you think it is. In the course of my work, I've stumbled onto an ugly piece of information. The sabotage of our airliners is being orchestrated in France."

"Oh, really? Care to be a bit more specific?"

"William, I'm going to forgive you your initial skepticism but I hope it doesn't blind you permanently. Some months ago, a group of prominent

Frenchmen reached an agreement with an ex-Soviet spy. Their objective was to bring down a number of Boeing planes."

"Now, now, Ms. Marx. Why would they want to do a thing like that?" He put his feet up on his desk and started to fiddle with his pipe.

"To benefit Airbus and the French economy."

"Well, Ms. Marx, it's an exciting scenario. I'm sure it will play well in the media. But I must disappoint you. We have solved the mystery of those crashes. All that remains is to decide on an appropriate response. The French are not involved."

Sophie gave an exasperated sigh. "Iraq has been set up by the conspirators to look like the villain. You haven't swallowed that rotten piece of bait, have you?"

Fairchild lit his pipe and gazed out the window. "Ms. Marx, in my line of work, unlike in yours, it is customary to present evidence. Real evidence. Hard evidence. You haven't. When and if you are able to do so, I will have someone look into your allegations."

"Thank you, William. You will have your evidence tomorrow night when you or one of your agents accompanies my colleague to a meeting of the conspirators. I promise your efforts will yield the sort of proof you need. These men's identities will shock you as they did me. One is a member of the governing coalition."

"Is that so? I'm afraid, Ms. Marx, that I must disappoint you again. We don't go around spying on the politicians of our allies. To do something like that, I'd have to submit a request to Langley. It would have to be approved at the highest levels or government.

"Furthermore, a request to assign an agent to this…caper would have to include proof that we were following more than an outsider's hunch. Hearsay won't do, Ms. Marx. I would need a detailed summary of how you came to this information in the first place. My account would have to include at a very minimum such things as the name of your colleague, the names of the suspects, the address of the meeting and so on. This is even more the case here, Ms. Marx, because your dramatic scenario strikes me as highly unlikely."

"History, William, is a compilation of highly unlikely events. Don't let history pass you by."

"I need more information. Names, places…"

"Sorry, William, you'll have to wait until tomorrow night. What I tell you now is merely hearsay, and you've left no doubt as to how you feel about hearsay."

"Langley would—"

"Forget Langley. There's not time to consult Langley. You'll have to act on your own."

"Sorry."

"I'm going to leave you my telephone number, William. As I said, the agent who accompanies my colleague could be you. And, William, you won't get caught. You'll do your snooping from a basement that has already been prepared, secured and tested for battle. Your superiors don't have to know what you're doing—until you submit your incriminating tape."

"Is that it, Ms. Marx?"

"That's it."

"Then I guess we're finished."

They both stood. Their eyes locked in fierce mental combat.

Sophie was angry. Being polite hadn't gotten her to first base with this obtuse bastard. It was time to try the bludgeon.

She said, "I'd hate to be in your shoes, William. Imagine how you'll feel when the rest of the world learns that you sat on your duff stirring coffee with a plastic stick while amateurs did your job for you."

"Ms. Marx, I resent—"

"Resent it all you want, William. In the meantime I suggest you try growing a set of balls. I don't want to hear about rules and regulations. A man can still act like a man from time to time. I have evidence of this. Your father did, which is why Eisenhower died a natural death. My present colleague does, which is why I am in a position to keep you, the Agency and the country from committing a drastic error. So call me if you feel a new weight rattling around in those Brooks Brothers trousers. Now, William, if you'll excuse me, I've got to run. Things are happening—everywhere but here."

She left her card and stormed out, not bothering to look around.

*   *   *

Back in her office after the failed meeting at the embassy, Sophie glanced at her watch. Eleven a.m., still only five a.m. in Washington. It was too early to call Frank Warner at his office, and she hadn't been able to con the operator or anyone else into giving her his unlisted numbers at home. It had not been a good morning. She hoped she wasn't losing her touch. Well, no time to worry about that now.

She booted her computer, sent Monique out for pastries and began a search for information on Walter Claussen.

There were seven Walter Claussens in the U.S. data base. Of these, three had immigrated from Germany after the war, four had been born in America. She limited her search to obituaries to see who was still around.

The *Kansas City Star* of October 23, 1980, reported the death of Walter F. Claussen of Kansas City, Kansas, who had spent his career in agricultural fertilizers.

Walter H. Claussen of Dubuque, Iowa, the *Register* reported, had died after a long struggle with lung cancer on June 12, 1987. His survivors were suing a pesticide manufacturer.

And Walter J. Claussen of Schnectady, N.Y., had passed away on Christmas Eve, 1989, in the home in which he had lived since coming to the States in 1947.

The other Walter Claussens, those born in this country, were too young to be the man they were looking for.

Sophie sat back in her chair and sighed. There were a lot of combinations of initials to search, perhaps as many as a hundred. And search them she would. She only wished she wasn't so tired.

In the anteroom, she could hear the first salvos of a verbal artillery duel. She went out and surprised Steven and Monique, who were battling over a plump chocolate pastry Monique had brought back from the *pâtisserie*.

Sophie claimed the prize for herself, then sent Monique, who was in an even worse mood than usual, out for more.

"You look terrific, darling," Sophie told Steven when they were alone. "Feeling okay?"

"Not bad, just hungry. Why don't you fire that bitch?"

"Now, now, not everyone can be as charming as Nicole. Come in here. We'll share this monument to sugar and cholesterol and your friend will never know."

"Friend, my ass. I'd like to set her up with Michelet."

"A pleasant thought. Did you drop by your place?"

"Yep. Showered and dressed in there. No sign of trouble."

"That's good."

Steven followed her into her sanctum sanctorum.

He wiped his mouth and stared wide-eyed at the computer screen. "Hey, there he is! Walter J. Claussen! How did you find him?"

She sat on her piano bench, the seat she used when she was at the computer. "Unfortunately, Steven, the name you are looking at belongs to a person of no relevance to us. Either the software missed our man, which is improbable, or his official first name is not Walter. Of course, the most likely possibility is that he went by another name altogether while he was in the States."

Steven leaned close to the screen, careful not to disturb the faxes that curled like bleached tropical leaves around the monitor. "Did you look for Mrs. Claussen?"

"No, I did not."

"Well, we should give it a try while you're doing the obituary search. He married an American woman. I heard Haussmann ask if she could present a danger. Delors said, 'No, because she's dead, died just before he moved back to Germany.'"

"You didn't tell me that, Steven."

"I didn't?"

"Don't worry about it. No harm done. You've had a thing or two on your mind. Think hard. Did Delors mentioned the woman by name?"

"Just Claussen's wife."

"All right. We'll check for a dead Mrs. Claussen who stands out for any reason. Maybe we'll get lucky—*if* he called himself Claussen and *if* she took his name."

She started the search.

"What can I do?" Steven asked.

"I think I heard Monique come in. You can hone your already impressive skills by persuading her to prepare us some coffee. If that fails, dispose of her in any way you wish and make the coffee yourself. I had the most dreadful brew at the embassy."

"You've been to the embassy already? Jesus, Sophie, I thought you'd gone back to bed."

"I might as well have. I'll tell you about that fiasco later."

He just stood there staring at her.

"Steven—"

"Yes?"

"I know you're tired too, but if you don't bring me coffee soon, my brain will to fall into an eternal slumber."

When he went out, Sophie broadened her obituary search to include all persons by the name of Claussen. Then she narrowed the search to the years 1989-1991.

Inge Claussen, Ute Claussen, Käte Claussen…Germans, Germans. The wife was supposed to be American. Alice, Jane, Pam, where were all those nice middle-American names she had never been able to escape—until now?

Well, thought Sophie, maybe this phantom wife did not have a middle-American name. Maybe Claussen married a German-American. She was going to have to read a hundred obituaries in search of a clue.

The computer worked tirelessly while the decibel level of the battle in the anteroom swelled to a crescendo, then gradually began to abate.

Sophie's eyes burned with fatigue as she scoured the list of deceased female Claussens.

Number 37 caught her attention.

Her name was Rose Claussen.

Did she want to read the obituaries on Rose Claussen (Y/N)?

Damn right she did. The name had a promising cross-cultural ring to it.

Steven came back into the room just as the text from the *Denver Post* obituary, dated October 17, 1990, appeared on the screen. Sophie could feel him behind her looking for a place to put down the pastries and coffee. She shoved the remaining mass of papers off the piano bench. He deposited the tray and read over her shoulder.

"Holy shit!" he exclaimed as they reached the end. "This time you've done it! '…survived by her husband, a respected aerospace consultant!' That's got to be him, doesn't it?"

"It doesn't have to be, but it could be." Sophie fed the computer fresh commands; Steven fed her coffee and pastries while she worked.

"What are you doing?" he asked when she stopped chewing and sipping for a moment.

"I am looking for a description of the automobile accident in which she died. Maybe the husband is mentioned by name. Come sit beside me. You need to preserve your energy for tomorrow."

"Thanks."

He was starting to relax when he felt her body tense. "What do you make of this, Steven? 'Rose Claussen is thought to have died instantly when the car her husband was driving careened out of control and struck a bridge abutment on I-25 just south of the mousetrap. Hans-Walter Claussen emerged from the accident shaken but unhurt. He was released from University Medical Center this morning. The couple's 1985 Mercedes was equipped with a driver's side air bag, which the police credit with saving Claussen's life.'"

Steven whistled. "Hans-Walter Claussen. I'll be damned. He killed her before he went home, didn't he? He just aimed that big Kraut panzer with a driver's side air bag at a bridge abutment and said, 'Aufwiedersehen, honey?'"

"But is he our man? Let me run the new name."

"Good idea."

*   *   *

The search took a long time. Steven had started to daydream. Sophie clapped her hands and he jumped. "I believe we do in fact have our man. Look at that, would you! Page ten of the *Seattle Times*, November, 1991."

She watched his mind come back from wherever it had traveled and read the article over again with him:

METALTECH TO SHUT DOWN

Metaltech, the respected aerospace consulting firm, announced today that it will close its doors upon the retirement next month of its founder and general partner, Hans-Walter Claussen.

Claussen, who emigrated to the United States from Bremen in Western German in 1963 and became a U.S. citizen in 1965, worked as a private consultant in the aerospace industry for 25 years. His firm, which was largely a one-man operation, pioneered modern methods for stress-testing the alloys used in aircraft construction.

"That's him!" Steven said after he had gone through the text several times. "That's gotta be him. It says here 'West Germany' but he would never say he came from the East. What now, Sophie?"

"Hang on a second." It was 12:20 p.m., getting on lunch time, but still only 6:20 a.m. in Washington. Sophie called the NTSB and got a recording.

"Well?" Steven asked.

"We have another two hours and forty minutes before a real person answers. That's a lot of time."

"It sure is. I guess there's nothing we can do while America wakes up. I think I'll take a nap."

"No!" Sophie said sternly. "Absolutely not. We're flying to Bonn. There are hourly flights from Charles De Gaulle."

"Bonn! That's in Germany."

"So it is. But, Steven, we need to know more about Claussen. If everything were to go our way, a quick visit to his home after he's been locked up could yield some very interesting material. We'd have to beat the police to the punch. Do you understand what I'm getting at?"

"Yes, but not why we're going to Germany. Why do we need to go to Germany to find out where Claussen lives? Can't we do that on the phone?"

"Perhaps we could. But there are other things I want as well, things I must be there in person to receive."

"Do you know someone?"

"Yes, darling. A man named Zell, a top official in Customs and Immigration.

"A Kraut?"

"Not a 'Kraut,' Steven. A German and a fine man. This is not as rare a combination as you seem to think. Andreas Zell spent the war organizing resistance to Hitler. He lost his family, his left hand and his youth, and saved the lives of thousands of Jews in the process. He ended up in Sachsenhausen, might as well have been one of us."

"Don't speak German with him. I won't understand a word."

"It won't matter, Steven. You won't be with us."

"What?"

"While I badger Andreas, I want you to check into the Residenz Hotel. We'll call Mr. Warner from there."

"But…Germany?"

"Steven, it's not even an hour away by air. The more we can tell Warner about Claussen, the better. If you had been with William Fairchild this morning, you would understand."

"Who the fuck's William Fairchild?"

"Excuse me, Steven, but we have to hurry. Run down and flag a cab, would you, please? I'll call Air France."

"Make sure it's an Airbus," he said on his way out.

Chapter Twenty-Eight

Sophie swept into the Bonn hotel room just as Steven awoke from his nap. A little rest made a lot of difference in the way he felt.

She pulled a photograph from her briefcase and tossed it in his direction. "There's your Hans-Walter Claussen."

He sat up and stared at it. "Not a face you'd forget," he said.

"No, it isn't. Here, I'll trade you."

She took the picture and handed him a photocopied document.

"A real-estate map?" he asked.

"A plat. Number three, a ninety-acre tract. Claussen bought it when he came back to Germany. It's in the East, the former German Democratic Republic. Makes sense, doesn't it?"

"Yeah, it sure as hell does. How did you get what's-his-name to give you this stuff?"

"A professional secret. Look here." She used her finger to trace the curve of a river running through the top right corner of the plat. "That's the Augraben."

"The *what*?"

"The Augraben River, Steven. I know of it because downstream a few kilometers is a famous old estate. Bismarck is rumored to have spent weeks there planning his attack on France."

"No shit. Maybe the soil produces belligerent assholes."

"It could be the water. Claussen's land used to be a small state-run farm. No telling what he does there now."

"We're going to find out, aren't we, Sophie?"

"Yes, as soon as it's safe. We'll have to be quick on the draw to beat the authorities."

"We'll beat them. This is our story."

"I like your attitude, Steven. Let me show you exactly where the place is located."

Sophie reached into her briefcase again and took out a map of Germany. She unfolded it across the coffee table. Using her pen as a pointer, she tapped Bonn, then moved eastward until she came to Berlin. "If you go due north from here, up past Neubrandenburg, you'll come to the village of Altenhagen. See it?"

"Hold on a second. Okay, I see it."

She tapped some more, then drew a little star. "The farm is here, in this space between the village and the river. Now excuse me for a moment, darling. I'm going to wash up before we make our call."

She left the room. He studied the spot and committed the ugly sounding syllables of the nearby towns to memory.

It felt good to know where the son of bitch lived.

* * *

Warner poured himself another cup of black coffee, his fourth that morning, then went back to perusing the endless list of parts taken from Stein's basement. From time to time, he glanced at the enormous cement-caked stamping press he had ordered brought to his office. It had been excavated from the basement, next to Stein's body.

Nearby had lain the only aircraft parts in the entire depot bearing serial numbers. These were the parts the archaeologists had dug up first, the parts he and Simmons had driven over to Boeing. They were in Washington now, with Officer King's full knowledge, on order of the FBI. The much larger stash of parts—623 items, to be exact—bore no numbers and had been stored in bins along the walls.

This was clearly a big-time operation, and the possibility that there might be other storage depots elsewhere in the United States weighed heavily on Warner's mind.

He needed to make sense of all this; and do it quickly. He would review the facts from the beginning again. This time he hoped he could draw some conclusions.

First, not every part in the depot belonged to a Boeing aircraft. In fact, all of the American manufacturers that had built commercial airliners in the last three decades were represented: McDonnell Douglas and its predecessor, Douglas; Lockheed; General Dynamics.

Since the latter two companies hadn't built airliners for many years, and since some of the parts belonged to dinosaurs as old as the Boeing 707, this meant that the parts depot had existed for a long time.

More importantly, it meant that the initial target of the sabotage operation had not been limited to Boeing aircraft but had encompassed the entire long-distance commercial fleet of the United States.

Second, the unnumbered parts, or at least the 74 that had been tested to date, were defective. The numbered parts, on the other hand, were not defective. In addition, three of the numbered parts bore serial numbers matching those of the defective parts involved in the recent crashes.

Knowing this much, it was obvious that "good" parts had been removed from the parts stream and replaced by matching "bad" parts from the depot. The stamping press, whose ingenious plates had survived intact, had been used to create perfect counterfeit serial numbers. Since only defective parts destined for Boeing aircraft had been slipped into the parts stream, it seemed clear that the Boeing Company had been singled out as the target of the sabotage.

Hal Larsen had argued at the meeting in the Oval Office that Iraq might have bought a Soviet sabotage capacity that had existed for years. This, it seemed to Warner, was at least theoretically possible. But if Iraq had acquired such a vast arsenal to avenge its humiliation on the battle field, why would Iraq have limited its operation to just two newer models of Boeing aircraft? Why would it have omitted the Boeing 747, the Lockheed Tri-Star, the MD-11 and the DC-10—all capable of carrying at least as many passengers as the 757 or 767? And why would Iraq have targeted only a few aircraft if it had the capacity to destroy many more with almost no additional effort?

The answer, it seemed to Warner, could only be that Iraq was not the perpetrator. This was not an indiscriminate strike at the US; it was a campaign to discredit Boeing.

Tim Simmons came in and tossed his jacket over the stamping press. "Chief, sorry to disturb you."

"You don't look sorry. Is it Galloway again?"

"Almost as bad. We can't get rid of this journalist who claims to be a friend of yours and promises you will want to speak with her once we give you her name. She's been calling back every ten seconds. It's beginning to grate on everyone's nerves. I told her our policy on dealing with the press, but that didn't stop her. She just keeps calling back, tying up our lines. What should I tell her?"

"Why don't you first tell *me* what her name is?"

"Her name? Marx, I think she said."

Warner sprang to his feet. "Marx? Sophie Marx from Paris? And you've been giving her the brush-off?"

"Right, chief. That's policy, isn't it?"

Warner tried to control his frustration. It **was** policy for unsolicited press calls. Sophie had convinced him she wouldn't be calling, so he hadn't notified his staff of a possible exception. This whole thing was his fault. "Look, Simmons, whatever you do, get me that lady back on the line. I don't care if you have to have a tracer put on the call. Find her number and put me in touch with her. Is that clear Simmons? Is that CLEAR?"

"Sure, chief, I just—"

"Get moving. On the double."

On his way out, Simmons collided with a secretary on her way in.

"Sorry, Gwyn," he muttered.

"It's okay, Mr. Simmons. Mr. Warner."

"What?"

"It's that lady from Europe again. Tim said he was going to ask you how to deal with her."

"I'll tell you how to deal with her," Warner said. "Put her through."

"What, sir? I promise you this isn't someone you want to talk to. She's—"

"Ms. Skidmore, did you hear me or did I speak too softly? I said, **put her through.**"

Warner sat back and waited for the phone to ring. He tried to calm himself. God how he hoped she had come up with something. He was invited to a White House meeting after lunch. He knew Galloway and the other hotheads would be pushing for an immediate military strike against Iraq. His chances of stopping them were nil unless Sophie had come across something he could use.

The call came through a few seconds later. "Yes? This is Frank Warner."

"Good morning, Frank," Sophie said in a husky, confident voice. "I'm sorry I had to be so obnoxious to your staff to get through."

"Forget it. I hadn't told them you might call because I had no reason to believe you would. What's up?"

"A lot. I gather from my sources there's a real conviction in Washington that Iraq is the culprit."

"Yes, that's right, even though Iraq is not involved."

"I know that now, Frank. I hope you'll forgive me for my obtuseness earlier."

"Sophie, what's going on? Do you know something?"

"Do I ever. Not by design, mind you. The French are behind this débâcle. Not Airbus but a group of nationalists. Iraq has been set up to appear guilty."

Warner closed his burning eyes. "Jesus, I hope you have the proof."

Pilot's Dawn

"Unfortunately it's not yet bankable. I've already been to see William Fairchild, the top CIA man in France. He treated me as though I had an advanced case of Alzheimer's. The problem is this. My associate stumbled onto the story by chance. He wasn't prepared to make tapes when he found himself listening to this ugly piece of news."

Warner was squeezing the receiver so hard his fingers turned white. "Where was he? When did this happen?"

"Last night in Fontainebleau, Frank. He sneaked into a wine cellar below the room in which a meeting was taking place. He cut a hole in the heating duct and listened. He was hoping to come up with leads for an unrelated story. It took him about two words to realize he was listening to the men who had hit Boeing."

"Jesus Christ. And you're sure this associate is reliable?"

"Entirely. And you'll be pleased to know that you won't have to rely on my feeble account for long. There's going to be another meeting in the same room tomorrow night. The French are working with a former KGB agent, a man who had developed the capability to sabotage American aircraft during his thirty year tenure in the States. He's the one who did the actual dirty work. He'll be at the meeting to collect for the crashes he's caused. Frank, he's going to receive a quarter of a billion dollars in cash."

"Holy Christ. And you say this meeting is going to take place tomorrow night?"

"Tomorrow night, eight o'clock Paris time."

"So what you need is some sort of credible documentation of the proceedings?"

"I'm glad somebody understands. I would say I need a spy, Frank, a person with high-tech listening devices, a professional whose findings will be taken seriously in Washington."

"I'm sure I can get someone over there to help you. I'm meeting with the crisis leaders in a couple of hours. CIA Chief Willis will be present. I'll make sure you get your man. In fact, Sophie, I'll guarantee it. I don't know how to thank you. You can't imagine what this is going to do for me personally and for our country."

"Don't thank me. I said No to you, Frank. It's blind luck I have anything to report."

"That's all irrelevant now. All that matters is that we don't let these sons of bitches get away. I'd like to hear more. Do you have time?"

"Yes, but I want you to use discretion with what I give you. In other words, don't tell the CIA anything they don't absolutely need to know. They might try to bypass me and go it alone if they think they have enough information."

"What's wrong with that?"

"Everything, Frank, and I think you know it. They would blow the entire operation. I've seen enough of their covert operations to know this. My associate knows the ropes. He can get an agent in, which the CIA can't—not on such short notice. I want you to have the person who'll be working with us report to me."

"They'll balk."

"I'll make it easy on you. I'll only give you my address."

"Okay, we'll try. Could you get on with your account now?"

"Yes, Frank, but first I'd like to ask you a question."

"Shoot."

"Has anyone over there visually laid eyes on a man who could be considered a suspect."

Warner thought for a second. Hadn't King, the young cop, told him something about the guy who poured the cement saying he'd dealt personally with Stein? Yes, that was it. But when King had shown him a picture of Stein, he'd said it was someone else. Someone who was not Stein but had claimed to be Stein, someone who had ordered, supervised and paid for the cement job.

He said, "I don't know if you'd officially call him a suspect, but yes. Why?"

"Because I have a picture of the man who set up the sabotage operation in the States. I'm going to transmit it to you when we finish talking.

Pilot's Dawn

His name is Hans-Walter Claussen. He's an East German who emigrated to the U.S. in 1960. His papers showed him to be a resident of the West German city of Bremen, but I've done some checking in Bonn and that was not the case. Anyway, he left the States in 1991 and bought a farm in what was formerly the DDR. He must have reached this ghastly agreement with the French after his return to Europe."

"By all means, transmit the photo. I'll run it by the people in Seattle. If it's the man they saw, then we've finally made it to first base."

"We're a lot farther along than that, Frank, but I know you don't want to get your hopes up. This must sound too good to be true."

"But it *is* true, isn't it, Sophie? You have no doubts about that, do you?"

"None, whatsoever, Frank. You won't either once I've filled you in."

* * *

King looked at himself in the mirror. Very copy and proud, a little too much fat bulging out around the collar but he'd take it off as soon as Elliot's doughnuts weren't part of the daily routine. In the bedroom he strapped on his pistol and leaned down to kiss his wife. He hoped his breath didn't still smell of beer from last night's celebration of his hundred buck a month raise.

The phone rang. He answered it the only place he could, in the kitchen of their tiny apartment. "Officer King here."

"Officer, good morning, this is Frank Warner in Washington. I'm glad I caught you."

"Mr. Warner! How are you?"

"Fine, Officer. There's something urgent I need you to do for me."

"I'll be glad to, Mr. Warner. What is it?"

"I've transmitted a photograph to you, care of Captain Bullock at the Seattle Headquarters. I want you to go by and pick it up."

"A photograph?"

"Yes. I need you to run it over to the cement contractor who took payment from the man he thought was Stein. I need to know if the man in the picture is the person he dealt with. You've got to hurry, Officer King. I don't want to be overly dramatic, but the future of this country's commercial aircraft industry might be riding on how quickly you get back to me with an answer. I'm going to leave you my emergency telephone number. You can reach me anywhere at any time. I hope you'll do just that within the next hour. Is it a realistic possibility, Officer?"

"Maybe, Mr. Warner, if you could call the Captain and have someone who is already at Headquarters drive the picture over to DiStefano Sand and Gravel. That would save me a good forty-five minutes, but I'm afraid I don't have the clout with those people to ask for special favors."

"All right, Officer, head for DiStefano's. I'll make sure the photo is there to meet you. And call me the instant you have an identification—positive or negative."

"Right, sir. I'll do it."

Warner gave him the emergency number and hung up. King went out and quietly locked the front door.

His Pontiac started on the second try and he drove off shaking his head. No doubt about it. He was a born investigator. But he didn't understand what Mr. Warner meant when he said the future of America's commercial aircraft industry might depend on how fast he got back with Chuckie Stafford's answer.

Oh, well, you didn't have to understand everything to do your job.

King put his detachable light on the roof and turned on his siren. The confirmation that the photo was on its way to meet him crackled over his radio a few minutes later.

Chapter Twenty-Nine

A White House staffer ushered Warner into the Cabinet Room at two p.m., the exact hour Galloway had told him to be there. Galloway had given him the impression the meeting would not begin until his arrival, but Warner could see that the participants had been at it for some time.

He had been tricked. It was written all over Galloway's welcoming smirk. He tried to control his temper. He had a job to do. He couldn't let himself be distracted by this hyena. He stepped further into the room, nodding at the Chairman of the Joint Chiefs, General Salinski, who stood with a pointer in front of a map of the Middle East.

"Hello, Frank," Galloway said in a voice as glib and confident as that of a motivational speaker. "It would have been thoughtful of you to let us know you were going to be late. We needed your input a couple of hours ago."

Warner took his seat without uttering a word. What could he say? This was his fault. He should have called around and checked the time that other members of the administration had been told, as any politically savvy administrator in his position would have done. He had been in this town long enough to know that personal vendettas and dirty tricks superseded the national interest more often than you wanted to believe. He roasted Galloway with a quick stare, then took in the rest of the room.

The players had changed dramatically from the last meeting on the air safety crisis. The two members of the administration who had spoken out in Warner's defense, FBI Director Daniels and Secretary of Commerce Williamson, were absent. So was Hal Larsen, who had made the first credible case for Iraqi involvement but had recently expressed doubts.

In their stead were the military and foreign policy people: Chairman of the Joint Chiefs of Staff, Salinski; Admiral Chalmers; the hawkish Chairman of the Senate Armed Services Committee, Sam Narr, his House counterpart, Secretary of Defense Wes Allison, and a gaggle of experts from State. The only holdovers of note other than Galloway were CIA Director Willis, Secretary of State Olsen and FAA Chief Jack Shelton, an obsequious lap dog of the airline industry.

At today's policy meeting, the usual bickering and infighting were conspicuously absent. The air was heavy with righteous indignation and unflinching purpose.

Typical, thought Warner, trying to read the expression on Ed Willis' face. The one time these guys got their act together and agreed to move in the same direction, it was the *wrong* direction. He had his work cut out for him getting them to abandon their present mind set.

"Don't let me disturb you," Warner said, knowing he would have to disturb them in some drastic fashion later. "Go ahead, General Salinski. I apologize for the interruption."

"No need to apologize, Frank. But it's too bad you missed the President. He didn't know much about military matters when he was first elected. You should have heard him today."

Warner lowered his head. Things were worse than he realized. By excluding him from the meeting until now, Galloway had deprived him of the chance to influence the proceedings. Opinions that were perhaps still divided a few hours ago had now crystallized around the destruction of Iraq. If he was going to stop this dangerous juggernaut, he would have to do it soon.

Salinski thundered on about the country's military options. Warner tuned him out but it didn't help. He was unable to think clearly. The call he'd gotten from Sergeant King after lunch kept running through his head like a broken record.

It was all so mind-boggling, so incredible: "Hey, Mr. Warner, looks like we've got something here. The guy at DiStefano Sand and Gravel, the guy named Chuckie Stafford, positively identified your photo. Even better, sir, the owner was back from vacation. He also identified the man in your picture. That's the individual who paid them for the cement job at Stein's Tool and Die—"

Salinski wrapped up his presentation and asked for questions. Warner decided he should jump in as soon as the general sat down. But he still had no plan of attack, no idea how he was going to make the men in this room understand that the conspirators could only be nailed by knowing more about Claussen and his recent contacts. And that was only part of what he had to get across. He had to make them see the horrible consequences of punishing the wrong party. The country would end up looking ridiculously inept, the guilty would walk and, worst of all, the United States might remain vulnerable to future attacks on its airliners.

That should be enough to deter them if they remained open to the truth.

Should be. But when the politicians were desperate to appease an irate public, when the military brass were searching for a way to become heroes again, the truth could be a low priority. Still, he had to try.

The drone of the meeting intensified around him like a growing swarm of bees. Arguments broke out during the questioning session. They were not arguments over whether to hit Iraq but how and when the attack should take place.

This was a war council working itself into a bellicose frenzy. Secretary of State Jerry Olsen, the man who had taken control of the last meeting, tried valiantly to interject a word of restraint. He was shouted down. Things were not looking good.

Galloway hit the table with his gavel. "All right, that will do. We've outlined the situation. We've heard the options. I'll brief the President on what was said after his departure. I know he'll make the right decisions. This meeting is adjourned."

Warner sprang to his feet. "Just a minute, Galloway. You're about to steer the country in the wrong direction. I have new and conclusive evidence that Iraq is not to blame."

"Mr. Warner, didn't you hear me? This meeting is adjourned!"

"Look, Galloway, if you want to bomb Iraq, go bomb Iraq. But don't try to justify it with the present air safety crisis. There is no connection between the crashes and any Middle Eastern nation. I know who is responsible. While you were in here trying to influence the President, I was out gathering information. Does anyone in this room care to hear the truth?"

"Be quiet, Mr. Warner. We've had to suffer your incompetence long enough. The evidence is in and, believe me, it's conclusive. I don't know who you're trying to protect with your eleventh hour histrionics, but this administration cannot and will not tolerate any more diddling. The public won't stand for it. I won't stand for it. And the President won't stand for it. Good day."

"Mr. Hopkins!" Warner shouted at the White House aide who had been taking notes of the meeting. "Don't stop! Write my remarks into the record. I was intentionally told the wrong time for this meeting by Mr. Galloway. He knew from Hal Larsen that there were holes in the existing evidence, and that I would challenge it. Iraq is not to blame. I know who is. I want the President to be informed that I know. Would you kindly get that on paper."

"Don't write a word, Hopkins," Galloway seethed. "And delete anything you have written from the point I adjourned this meeting onward. What is said after adjournment does not constitute part of today's session."

Galloway put an arm around General Salinski's shoulder and led him into the corridor to make sure Warner didn't approach him. The others left too, avoiding Warner as if he had some dread disease.

Pilot's Dawn

Warner caught up with CIA Director Willis in an anteroom and blocked his exit. "All right, Ed, let me have a word with you."

"Sure, Frank, but not here. I'll be available around ten this evening."

"You're available right now. You're not going anywhere until you've heard me out."

Willis tried to keep walking. Warner glanced around to see if anyone was watching, then grabbed him by the arm and viciously jerked him down into a chair. "I need an agent in Paris tomorrow night. Your man, William Fairchild, has been notified of the situation. He or one of his people could fit the bill. He cites the need for approval from the top. You're the top, Ed. I want you to get on the wire and get your Paris contingent moving."

Willis rubbed his elbow. "What the hell's gotten into you, Frank? I spoke with William Fairchild this morning. I know about that crackpot journalist who came to see him. I hope she's not the source of your information. Because if she is, Frank, all I can say is that this crisis has put you under more stress than any of us realized."

Warner had to take a deep breath to calm himself. "Look, I have new evidence from Seattle which I'll gladly share with you. What the journalist told your man in Paris is correct. Those who commissioned these atrocities are French, not Iraqi. They are going to meet tomorrow night in a house outside of Paris. I have access to a listening post. With proper nighttime equipment, we can also shoot photos."

"I'm sorry, Frank, but I've heard the entire ludicrous—"

"Just a minute. I haven't finished. You're going to hear it again. A large sum of money is to be paid to the ex-Soviet agent hired to bring down the planes. If you will work with me, we can record this transaction. We can solve a terrible crime and return our civil aviation industry to health.

"If I'm wrong, Ed, what's the downside? There isn't one. It will take some time to organize a military action. The proponents of the Iraqi hypothesis will not be delayed. However, Ed, if you are wrong—"

Willis stood abruptly. "All right. I get the point. Now tell me something, Frank. Are any of these Frenchmen whom you believe, for reasons I can't fathom, to have commissioned these crashes, per chance in public life?"

"Yes. You know that from Fairchild."

"Then what I have to say to you is this: I cannot authorize the Agency to do what you're asking. We do not have the authority to conduct operations against friendly governments. However, if you believe this strongly you're on to something, why don't you go over there yourself? Put your own career on the line, not someone else's. If you bring back hard evidence of the sort I can use, I guarantee you'll have the Agency behind you."

Warner reflected for a moment. They weren't leaving him much choice. "Suppose I were to do just that. Would you be willing to furnish me with cameras and listening devices?"

"Frank, come to your senses. We already know who the culprit is. You're not going to find anything over there. Most likely, you're going to get caught. In that case, I must be in a position to shrug my shoulders and claim I had no idea you were in France. If you're schlepping around a bunch of our equipment, that would be difficult to do, wouldn't it?"

Warner almost took a swing at him. "Fuck you, Ed. If you're representative of our intelligence community, it's no wonder the Soviets had thirty years to perfect Operation Twenty-Six. Get out of here before I lose my temper."

Warner lingered for a few minutes, trying to remember if anything in the NTSB charter gave him the authority to exercise what had become his last option. Literally speaking, the answer was no. But in a broader sense, the answer was yes. This wasn't the normal situation for which bureaucratic rules were written. Whatever the book said, his responsibility to the millions of men and women who boarded commercial aircraft every day was more important. A court of law or governmental disciplinary body might disagree. He didn't care. He had to go.

*   *   *

Simmons paced nervously around the office, waiting for the promised call from his boss. He had accompanied Warner to the White House for the meeting. During the drive, Warner had brought him up to date on the contents of the call from Sophie Marx and the positive identification of Claussen's photo by the cement people in Seattle.

What a relief! Trying to make sense of the puzzle created by these crashes had driven him crazy. Now it was clear they hadn't been dealing with an ordinary succession of crashes but with the work of a brilliant sabotage operation. No wonder they had not been quick with answers. In fact, if it weren't for some damned good luck in Seattle and the coincidental discovery by the woman in Paris, they still wouldn't have a clue.

He only hoped they hadn't come upon the solution to the puzzle too late. He hoped that Warner had been able to convince them this wasn't just another false lead. There had been so many. He sat in his swivel chair, put his feet up on his desk and stretched. Yes, Frank Warner would somehow have managed to get the job done.

The telephone rang at last. "Tim, it's me."

"Chief! Did they see the light?"

"No. It was an unmitigated disaster. I'll be on Air France, Flight 23 to Paris, departing Dulles at six forty. I want you to meet me there with my cool weather bag and the best listening and recording device you can come up with. See if Schultz is still in the lab. If so, have him issue you the camera with the infrared lens we acquired last spring. And Tim, get yourself a police escort. Tell them we have an emergency abroad. I want you at the airport in an hour."

"It's rush hour, chief. I—"

"Just be there."

Warner hung up and Simmons burst into action. He grabbed his assistant, Gwyn, who was on her way out, and marched her back into the office. "Get me a driver and a police escort to Dulles. This is an emergency. Emergency, Warner's orders, don't take any guff. I'll be waiting down below in five minutes. I want them out front with motors running."

He rushed to the lab, where Schultz was putting on his coat. "Emergency, Bob, get me the infrared camera."

The old man moved like he had been hit with a cow prodder. Everyone in this building knew what emergency meant and how to respond to it. Never mind that he had taken certain liberties with the usual definition.

Listening device…listening device. While he waited on the lab foreman to return with the camera, his eyes settled on a black box from one of the crashes. Perfect, he could disassemble the shell and take out the guts during the drive to the airport. Hook that little CVR to an independent power supply and you'd have a recorder as good as any.

He started to scavenge. Tools, simple tools, a battery pack, something to carry the whole mess in.

By the time Schultz returned, he was ready. He swung back by the office to pick up Warner's cold weather bag, then took the six floors of stairs down to ground level at a full sprint. No missed aerobics today.

He stepped into the murky evening rush hour just as his car and police escort pulled up.

Part III

Chapter Thirty

"Are you alive?" Sophie asked, pulling off her coat.

It was early Friday morning. Steven was still sprawled out on the divan in her office where he had spent the night. He sat up and stretched. It was good to see a friendly face after six hours alone with the demons of his imagination. "I'm alive, but I'll feel a hell of a lot better when we have those guys on tape."

"We all will, darling." She tossed an overnight bag in his direction. He snared it in mid air.

"What's this?"

"Clothes, *articles de toilette*. I dropped by your flat on my way downstairs. I thought you'd enjoy getting clean before you got dirty."

"Thanks, Sophie, but you shouldn't have done that. There's no use taking risks when we're this close. I was going to go out and buy some stuff when the stores opened."

"It was safe. I didn't sleep a wink all night. You know how that old marble staircase of ours echoes. If you had had visitors, I would have known."

"Well…thanks. Did you check my answering machine while you were there?"

"Of course, darling. There were no calls. Nicole must be convinced her father has bugged your line."

"Yeah. So am I. I'm worried about her, Sophie. It doesn't seem to me her dad would let her off with just a week or two of lounging around at her aunt's. He probably has something horrible planned."

"Perhaps, but he has a lot on his mind. By the time he gets around to you and Nicole, he'll be in prison."

"If I don't blow it tonight."

"You won't. You're going to have plenty of help. Warner will make sure they don't send us a slouch. I've seen him in action. That's the way he is."

"I hope you're right." Steven walked to the window, groaning and stretching. A steady rain had begun to fall after their return from Bonn, and it was still coming down. Place Vendôme looked cold and forbidding in the sodden gray dawn.

The earth around Michelet's country home would be muddy by now, he thought. If he left a thick trail of footprints on the cellar steps, he was a dead man. One more thing to worry about.

"Where's that bitch, Monique?" he grumbled. "I could use a cup of coffee."

"I gave her the day off, Steven. Go get a shower in the john across the hall. I'll have coffee and croissants waiting when you come back."

* * *

He washed in the cramped stall, shaved, dressed in the khaki trousers and olive sweater Sophie had brought him. The sense of unreality that had plagued him during the night returned. In less than five hours he would be on the road to Fontainebleau.

When he opened the door to Sophie's office, a man was sitting with her in the foyer looking at photographs. Steven felt like slapping himself. Things were happening! This was no dream. He could forget about his first worry. The agent was here!

"Come in, Steven," Sophie said. "I've been bringing our guest up to date."

The man was older, probably in his fifties. He wore a pin-stripped gray suit that made him look better armed for battle in business than espionage. He stood and looked directly at Steven. He was an agent all right. Forget the suit, his eyes told the story. They were bloodshot, intense, piercing. This was someone you didn't want to piss off.

"I'm Frank Warner," the man said, offering his hand.

Steven took it. "Warner? Isn't that the name of our friend at the NTSB?"

"Same name, same person. You've done a great job. I don't think we would ever have put the pieces together without you and Sophie."

"Beginner's luck on my part," Steven said. "Sophie must have smelled this story without realizing it. She sent me in. I was just dozing on top of a crate of wine when they started to talk. So, Mr. Warner, when's our agent going to show up?"

"I'm afraid you're looking at him," Warner said. "There were problems. Let's just say it was easier to come myself."

Steven shook his head. "I can't believe this. You had to fly here from Washington because the CIA thinks we're full of shit?"

"That's an accurate assessment."

Sophie said, "It's the William Fairchild phenomenon on a much more disheartening scale. No wonder Operation Twenty-Six got past them."

"No wonder," Warner murmured.

"Well, Jesus, thanks for coming," Steven said, trying to hide his disappointment. Now he had a new worry. He had been counting on the agent to be armed and ready to defend him if they got into a tight spot.

Sophie patted the chair beside her. "Come sit down, Steven. You two get acquainted. Frank finished off the coffee, but I'm making another pot. I'll be right back."

She got up and disappeared into Monique's tiny kitchen alcove, then stuck her head out the door. "And do me a favor, *messieurs*. Use first names. I can't bear the thought of you two gorgeous men trapped together for hours in a dark wine cellar 'Mr. LeConte-ing' and 'Mr. Warnering' each other into terminal numbness."

Sophie withdrew into the nook. Warner said, "She's a pretty unique woman, isn't she?"

Steven smiled. "Unique, magnificent, you name it. Before I met her, I thought a person had to choose between being successful or being human. I was wrong. Sophie's both."

Warner laughed drily. "She certainly is that. I could have used her in Washington."

"Do you ever read her stuff?"

"Not often enough," Warner said. "That's going to change."

Sophie returned a few minutes later with a fresh pot of coffee and a tray of hot croissants. She seemed different, more focussed, more determined. Steven recognized the transformation. He'd seen it before, in the Jardin du Luxembourg.

She said, "We need to organize these next hours. Suggestions on how we begin?"

"Damned right," Steven said. "Let's begin by talking about guns. Remember how relieved you were when Frank told you he was sending us an agent?"

"Where are you going with this, Steven?"

"I think you know. You were relieved because that agent was going to be armed. Well, the agent isn't here and we're not armed. I don't know about you, Frank, but I'd feel better if we were."

"Steven," Sophie said, "if you armed yourselves, you would only increase the risk of a tragedy. I'm sure Frank doesn't know any more about guns than you do."

"I'm from Nevada, lady," Warner said. "I grew up popping gophers from my stroller. I agree with your colleague."

"I still think it's a mistake," Sophie said.

"Let me tell you something," Warner went on. "I've seen the results of the crimes these men have committed. I've seen them up close. I've watched the charred, mutilated bodies of children being carried out of wreckages. I've pushed through the crowds of hysterical mourners at airports, all screaming for an explanation of why it had to happen. I've grappled with my own feelings of guilt for not being able to stop the carnage. I'm a bureaucrat by profession, but I'm also a man. These men have become my personal enemies. I'm going after them, and I'm not going to put myself in a position where I can't defend myself. If Steven hadn't brought up the subject of guns, I would have."

"Therefore, Sophie," Steven said, "we are asking you to visit your old friend, Chabrol."

"Steven—"

"Don't be doctrinaire. This is war. You don't send men into battle without arms."

Warner said, "Steven is right, Sophie. If you have a contact, help us out. It will allow us concentrate on other aspects of our preparation."

She looked at her hands.

"Come on, Sophie," Steven said. "I know what you're thinking but you didn't get me into this. You don't have to feel like you've taken an innocent boy turned him into a violent gun slinger. It's not like that. What happened just happened. We're here and we've got to move ahead. We don't have a choice. We're taking a risk tonight, and if we get caught we've got to be in a position to fight back. So please, Sophie, save us some trouble and some time. You can write about your moral misgivings when the job is done."

Sophie stood and made a single counter-clockwise tour of the foyer. When she came back, Steven could see she had been wrestling with herself.

She said, "You know, I hate the idea of combatting violence with violence. But in this instance I grudgingly admit you've got a point. It would be unfair of me to stand on the sidelines and ask you to go into that basement defenseless. Now, Frank, you are probably wondering who Chabrol is."

"I was going to ask."

Sophie sat down and sighed. "I did a piece on the illicit arms trade in Europe a couple of years ago. Chabrol is a long story, and I'm still not sure I did the right thing. Let's just say I feared for my life and printed more selectively as a result. In other words, I did the man and his associates a favor. He knows it. I think he would be willing to return the favor. In fact, I'm sure he would."

"That would be helpful," Warner said. "Very helpful."

"All right. You've convinced me. I'll do it."

"Brava, Sophie!"

"Let's hope so. Steven, go out and buy the things the two of you will need to sneak into Michelet's place in this weather. In the meantime, I'll do what I would never have thought any person or situation could induce me to do. I'll get your guns."

"We appreciate it," Warner said.

"All right, subject closed. Frank, you mentioned you had some prep work to do on your listening equipment. You can do that here while we're away. Anything else?"

"Food," Steven said.

Sophie said, "I'll take care of that, too. Now, what about transportation? Did you rent a car, Frank?"

"A Peugeot 305."

"Will that get you where you need to go, Steven?"

"No way. We'll have four of five miles of overgrown tractor path to cover, very secluded, very rough. It doesn't look like it's been used for decades. It narrows down to a couple feet where new trees have grown. There are holes all over the place you have to avoid. There were stretches I had to get off and walk even before this rain. We'll have to take my Harley."

"That's all right," Warner said. "The point is to get there." He glanced at his watch. "When do we need to leave?"

"Noon," Steven said. "I'd like to be in the basement before the search starts, not during."

Sophie said, "What about the possibility of arriving *after* the search? Have you thought of that, Steven? The way you described it, they came, rummaged around and left. Why be there when they are?"

"I've thought about it, Sophie. There's a reason we need to arrive early. Michelet comes during the search because he's a suspicious bastard. Doesn't even trust his own searchers. When they take off, he stays. If we wait to sneak in, it means we'll have to cross his lawn with him on the premises sniffing in all directions.

"There are these crows that go crazy when you pass their tree. The servants are deaf but Michelet isn't. Besides, when you open the door to the cellar, lights come on automatically. If it's dark outside, which it might be by six o'clock on a ugly day like today, the lights can be seen from the kitchen and that entire side of the house. Michelet *and* the deaf servants could be tipped off.

"So I think it's better to go early. They don't really search the basement thoroughly—at least they didn't on Wednesday. The dogs stayed up in the yard, and when the security people came down, all they could think about was Michelet's wine cellar."

Warner said, "I don't like this aspect of your planning. The basement wasn't searched the last time. So what? The dogs stayed upstairs the last time. So what? These are hardly guarantees it will be the same this time. We have to be prepared for all contingencies before we take off. Otherwise we stand a good chance of crashing."

"Yeah, all right," Steven said. "I was just feeling lucky, I guess, because I usually am. But I get your meaning, Frank. I just don't see how we are going to come out on top if trained dogs come into the cellar. It seems to me our choice is to take a risk or lose everything."

"There are ways to deal with trained dogs," Warner said. "If you had grown up where I did, you'd know a few tricks."

"Yeah?" This guy, thought Steven, was sounding more like an agent all the time.

Pilot's Dawn

"Another thing. I'd like us to stay together while Sophie runs her errands. It'll only take me minutes to check out the listening equipment. I have some purchases to make after that, and I'm going to need your help getting around the city. I speak German but not French. We better get moving. Do we meet here?"

Sophie was already putting on her coat. She said, "My flat is near my contact and I can shop for your food in the square out front. It's also on your way out of town. Steven has a key if you two finish up first. Why don't we meet there?"

"I'm not going near the place," Steven said. "Michelet might have his castration force staked out by now."

Warner said, "I'll go up alone. You can wait for me around the corner, Steven."

"Until then," Sophie said.

She started for the door. Steven tried to read her expression but her face was a mask. He thought she might be having second thoughts about the guns. He could understand why, given what she had seen in her lifetime.

He hoped she didn't change her mind. Warner's talk about being prepared for all contingencies had made him more nervous than he already was. Going in there without a gun would be like showing up for Wimbledon without a racket.

Chapter Thirty-One

The Harley roared through the rain toward Fontainebleau, bearing two men, a dozen rats and an arsenal of Heckler and Koch automatic pistols. Warner, the passenger, wasn't as miserable as he had expected to be. The boots and weather-proof paramilitary outfit he had bought in Paris kept him warm, the motorcycle helmet shielded him like a hunter's blind from the dense pulse of life around him.

He was tired, sure. He hadn't slept for the past two nights. But he was accustomed to fatigue. And just being out of Washington after his most recent experience was exhilarating. A fine thought reached him through the cloud of anxiety over his renegade mission: maybe he was far enough beyond the politicians' grasp to actually get something done.

South of Paris, Steven turned off the *autoroute* in favor of a winding two-lane. There was no traffic. Pine forests stretched to the horizon, their gentle summits lost in the overcast. Stone farmhouses clustered around lonely crossroads. An ancient church steeple rose in the distance.

Europe, he would never understand it. Why did this womb of art, science and religion produce so much madness? Wasn't Hitler enough for one century? Being here always made him want to go home—not to Washington but to Nevada.

They turned on to a smaller road, paved but badly potholed, and bounced over a railroad crossing. Not many miles later, the asphalt deteriorated into muddy gravel.

Steven drove slowly, watching the trees to his left. He must have seen whatever he was looking for, because he suddenly guided the big bike off the road, over a board spanning a roily irrigation ditch and into a gap in the foliage. He gave Warner the thumbs up sign.

Warner strained to see through his rain-streaked glare shield. This was it, he guessed, the tractor path they were looking for.

A hundred yards into the dripping woods, they had to get off and walk the bike around an enormous puddle. After several minutes of good progress, they encountered mud thick as mortar. Steven stopped the bike. "We'd better stop here," he said. "We're only about a half mile from where I parked before."

"Wise idea," Warner said. "Let's screw on the silencers. I'll give you a quick shooting lesson."

Steven tapped him on the shoulder. "I don't need a shooting lesson, Frank. I didn't want to say anymore about guns in front of Sophie."

"You're comfortable with a nine millimeter automatic?"

"Used it in my firearms course. I play a lot of tennis so my hand-eye's pretty good."

"Well, that's a relief. We'd better split this baggage up. Mind carrying the rats?"

"Hey, no problem. Rats don't bother me. Those boys might be the defenders of my manhood."

Warner was too tense to laugh. He checked to make sure he had everything: the binoculars, the modified CVR, the tennis shoes and infrared camera. He helped Steven secure the Heckler and Koch in his breast holster without getting it wet, and slid the silencer into Steven's pocket. He thumped him on the chest.

At times, Warner found his partner boastful and annoying. But there could be no doubt about his physical condition. He felt like a granite wall.

Warner strapped his own pistol in place while Steven talked to the rats he was fishing one by one out of the Harley's luggage carriers. He placed them carefully in the fold-up wire cage they had bought at the pet shop.

One rat got away and darted for cover. Steven snared it with a grab so quick it startled Warner. The hand-eye remark was hardly an exaggeration. Maybe this kid wasn't a boaster after all; maybe he just struck you that way because he was so handsome and disdainful of convention.

No assumptions, Frank. The truth would reveal itself in the course of their work.

They walked in silence through the forest, encapsulated by the foliage and the rain. Warner was drawn to Steven in spite of his doubts. That special camaraderie men feel when they fight a war together had begun to forge an emotional bond. This was good. If he was going to believe in himself and his mission, Warner needed to believe in the other half of his team.

"Look a little to your left through those trees," Steven said when the forest thinned.

Warner pulled up beside him. "You mean the house?"

"Yeah, that's Michelet's place. The servants' cottage is just to the left, half hidden behind it. Can you pick up any indication of life with your field glasses?"

Warner carefully surveyed the area. "Smoke. A few wisps."

"Where's it coming from?"

"The servants' cottage."

"Nothing from the manor?"

"Nothing."

"We're in luck, Frank. It means they haven't moved over to the main house yet."

"How does that follow? You said the heating system had been converted to natural gas, which means they have gas in the kitchen. A gas furnace and a gas oven don't smoke."

"They have a gas oven in the kitchen, that's true. Nicole showed it to me when we took our house tour. But these peasants have strong traditions. They still use the wood-burning oven from the last century, think it cooks better. Nicole says her father agrees with them. It smokes,

Pilot's Dawn

Frank. I've got another piece of hard information for you. There is a gas furnace, but Michelet likes to use the fireplaces when it's below sixty degrees and he's entertaining. It's one of his trademarks. It's about fifty now. I guarantee there's no one in the house. Let's fly."

"All right, go."

They emerged from the woods, skirted the lily ponds, crossed the meadow. At the edge of the manicured lawn, they paused to take stock of the situation. No sign of life, not even a crow.

They made a dash for the house and waited in the space between the hedges and the wall to catch their breath.

So far so good. Steven had been right about the smoke.

When they reached the cellar door they exchanged their muddy boots for the clean sneakers they carried in their packs. Steven opened the lock.

"Okay," he said, "when I pull this thing up, the lights come on. We want to get down in the hole and get the door shut on top of us as fast as we can. Ready?"

"Ready," Warner whispered.

Steven gave a tug. The heavy metal plate swung open without a sound.

Light hit Warner in the face, irritating light. He ignored it and slipped into the opening. Steven came behind him. When he closed the door, they were plunged into welcome darkness. Steven pulled out his flashlight and locked up.

"Well, we're here," he said.

"Good work. Give me a rat, would you?"

"Coming up. I hope you know what you're doing."

"I do. Hurry."

"Here's a beauty," Steven said. "Gray and fat with a hairless possum tail."

Warner took hold of the hideous creature. Its eyes glowed red in the beam of the flashlight. As they made their way down the old stone stairs, Warner occasionally touched it to the walls.

Steven said, "These are Nazi dogs, man, German shepherds with a lot of training. I don't think this is going to work."

Warner stopped at the bottom of the stairs. "Then you weren't listening when I told you about my method of hunting coyotes when I was a kid. The dogs *are* going to smell us and that is not going to be a problem." Warner glanced at the lighted dial of his watch. It was three o'clock. "Let's get this done. We can talk about the merits of the plan later. Where's the door by the furnace you were talking about?"

"Follow me. I'm glad you're confident."

They started through the labyrinthine basement. Warner kept one step behind Steven, who navigated the dim vaulted passageways with the cage of rats in one hand, a flashlight in the other. He couldn't blame the kid for being skeptical. But Warner knew dogs from a childhood of hunting and a career of sifting through crash wreckage for everything from bodies to drugs. And he knew their masters even better. They were human beings, and human beings had an instinctual urge to make assumptions based upon the first thing they saw.

So he wasn't really counting on his ruse to trick the dogs; he was counting on that instinctual urge of humans, that critical weakness he found without exception in the trainees who came to work for him. It was too much to explain to his partner at a time like this.

They circled the new furnace and passed by the great shadowy carcass of its coal-burning predecessor. Warner kept his rat busy, touching it here to the floor, there to a pipe or wall. Probably wasn't necessary, he thought, but it couldn't hurt.

The beam of Steven's flashlight scoured a pitted concrete wall and stopped on a rotting wooden door a hunchback couldn't have gone through without stooping. "This is it, Frank."

Pilot's Dawn

Warner lifted the wooden lock bar and pushed on the door with his foot. It groaned and creaked as it swung open. "Give me some light in there," he said.

Steven crouched and directed the beam through the opening.

Warner stuck his head in. There were pipes, old and new, cobwebs, and a hard earth floor rising at a sharp angle until it leveled off two feet from the ceiling. The rear quarter of the manor had been built without a proper basement. It was perfect. "Pass the cage, please."

"What's in there?"

"A crawl space. Made to order." Warner tossed his rat into the darkness, then let all but two of the others go. He shut the door and lowered the bar. He took the next to the last rat out of the cage and placed it at his feet. He smiled as it scampered off toward the furnace.

"Keeping one for company?" Steven asked.

"That's right."

"Do we hit the wine cellar now?"

"First the vent. Wherever you go from now until the search is over, take a circuitous route. No direct lines from point A to point B."

"Got it."

They had been walking for less than a minute when Warner heard footsteps overhead. He stopped in his tracks.

"It's the servants," Steven whispered. "Michelet sounds like a black Angus."

"Where's the vent? That needs to be confirmed."

"A to B?"

"We've been weaving around long enough. Pick up the pace."

Steven twisted open the louvers. Warner peered nervously into the gray afternoon. Rain, fog, no cars, not a soul in sight. The footsteps echoed somewhere in the distance. He heard scraps of a gruff male voice.

"That's Henri," Steven said. "He's in the kitchen with his wife, cooking. These men you're about to meet are gluttons. If they weren't knocking down planes, you'd get the idea their goal was to eat themselves to death."

"All right. You've done your research well. Let's set up."

"A to B?"

"No, circuitous."

They walked the maze again. Steven stopped in front of a more attractive door, old but well maintained. Its heavy wood face was polished to a sheen and reinforced with hand-crafted ironwork. He fished out his keys, unlocked the door and reached around the jamb to turn on the light switch. "After you, *monsieur.*"

Warner stepped inside and suppressed his desire to whistle. Hundreds of crates and boxes lined the walls, stacked three to four high and three to four deep, separated by a few strategically placed aisles.

A segment of one wall was set aside for special vintages. Here the bottles were not in crates but nestled horizontally in individual wooden cubby holes. A wire mesh gate with heavy locks protected the treasure. The cubby holes were labeled. Warner didn't know much about wine, but he couldn't help notice vintages dating back to the war.

He didn't look up; the eye wasn't naturally drawn that way. Steven had to direct his attention to the ceiling.

The network of overhead heating ducts was complex. A dozen large-diameter pipes ran parallel to the center of the ceiling, then branched off in different groupings and at different angles. Amid the taping and elbow joints Warner, professional investigator, didn't notice the small rectangular flaps Steven had cut in three of the ducts.

He nodded his approval when Steven pointed them out, showing how the flaps could be pulled out for listening, then folded back in position to disguise their presence. "Excellent," he whispered. "Now I'd like to prepare a hiding place behind the crates."

"We're going to be in here? This is the first place they'll look."

"Not if they bring the dogs," Warner said. "Give me a hand." He picked up a crate stenciled Château LaFite Rothschild 1964 and passed it to Steven.

"Hey, Frank, hang on a second. We've got LaFites from 'fifty eight to 'sixty four in this row, the younger Lafites in the next row, and God knows what behind those. Maybe you think Frogs aren't organized, but when it comes to wine cellars, they're like Swiss accountants. If we're really going to do this thing, why don't we make the bunker over there on that wall? Those are Henri's wines. They're all the same."

"Whose?"

"Henri. The servant. That way we won't have to worry about getting things out of order."

"That's a good thought, Steven. We'll be sure to keep track of what goes where and put everything back in the right place. But I want to camp out behind the expensive stuff."

"A matter of taste?"

"Of practicality," Warner said. "If you were in charge of the dogs, where would you be most worried they might jump?"

Steven grinned broadly. "I think I'm catching on to this rat game."

* * *

"I didn't know you liked Nintendo," Jules said. "I wish you'd told me last summer. Me and Luc brought the whole system down to Nice."

Nicole locked the door to her cousin's room. "Go ahead and play. I'll watch."

"Watch? You said you wanted to play."

"I was kidding. I don't know how."

"Hey, no problem. I'll teach you. If Luc can learn, you know it's easy."

She grabbed his arm. "Jules, listen, I need you to help me. I brought you here to talk, not to play games. Francoise just told me father's coming to Grenoble late tonight. I've decided to run away."

"What?"

"Turn on the Nintendo. Make it loud. I don't want Francoise to know we're talking if she comes up here."

"Okay, all right. Run away? Why?"

Nicole waited to speak until Mario started his nerve-jangling trek across the screen. "Can you keep your mouth shut?"

"If that's what you want."

"It is."

Mario eluded several obstacles with perfectly timed jumps. Everything on the screen seemed to be out to destroy him. Nicole could sympathize. She said, "This is just between you and me, is that understood, Jules?"

"I said I'd keep quiet. What's wrong?"

"Steven, that's what. The tennis instructor from last summer. Why the bizarre look? You remember him, don't you?"

"Sure I remember him. You were doing it, weren't you?"

"Jules!"

"Well?"

"Yes, we were doing it. We still are."

"I thought he'd gone back to the States."

"So did father and Francoise. Then we got photographed in a café. We turned up in one of those disgusting tabloids Francoise reads."

"*Merde.*"

"*Merde* is right. She showed it to father. That's why I'm in Grenoble. Some sort of pre-punishment. Only I'm not supposed to tell anyone."

"You mean all that stuff you gave mother about spending more time with the family was a lie?"

"Not exactly. I would like to spend more time with you. But this particular visit was ordered by father. It's his notion of house arrest. He's holding me here with Francoise as jailer until he decides what to do with me. I know it's going to be awful."

"Excuse me, Nicole, but your father is a real prick. Even my parents think so."

"Yes he is, Jules."

"So what are you going to do when you run away? Head for the States?"

Mario got hit by something and fell into a pit, accompanied by a video-game death knell and silence.

"Don't let the noises stop," Nicole said. "I'm going to go somewhere that isn't France, but I'm not sure where yet. I know father. He'll try to have Steven deported or arrested—or worse. We've got to get out of his reach. Steven promised he would take me away if things got bad. They're bad, Jules. There's nothing to be gained by waiting."

"It doesn't sound like it."

"Then let's make a plan. I've checked the train schedule. There's a TGV to Paris at ten o'clock. I want to be on it, Jules. Will you help me?"

"Sure, no problem. Luc and I go out at night all the time. We've got this rope around the radiator we toss out the window." He made a fist and showed her his muscled arm. "That's where I got these, climbing back up that rope. I'll put another rope in your room. You go to bed early. I'll get sick after dinner. Then I'll meet you down below with the moped. It'll be simple."

She hugged him again.

"Now listen," he said, "we've got a twenty minute ride to the station. You can buy your ticket on the train and pay the fine if you have to. Do you have money?"

"Yes, thanks."

"Good, I won't have to get into mother's purse. Try to be out by nine thirty. And don't worry about Francoise. She didn't come upstairs last night until eleven. If she peeks in on you, I'll be asleep in your bed wearing your slinky nightgown."

He tugged on his long hair, which was the color of hers. "She's half blind. She'll never know the difference."

"You're a saint, Jules."

"I'm a juvenile delinquent. You don't need a saint tonight."

"Teach me how to play Nintendo, cousin," Nicole said, feeling frightened and exhilarated. "It looks like a fun game."

*   *   *

Steven had begun to worry that the meeting might not come off in the proper fashion. He had been holding vigil at the vent for the last hour and a half. Night was coming on fast, fog swirled around the yellow lights on the gate.

The temperature was dropping, too. Every time a puff of air came in through the louvers, he felt another degree or two of wind chill. Bad travel weather—and getting worse.

Impossible to say where the three conspirators would be coming from. Michelet and Delors had probably not left Paris. But what about Haussmann? He might have flown to an obscure country in Latin America or Asia to get the money. This fog could delay him for hours, especially if all of Europe was socked in.

And God knew where Claussen was, where he had to come from.

If the man with the money *or* the man scheduled to receive it couldn't get here, the meeting might turn out to be a *grande bouffe* rather than a source of what Sophie and Frank called conclusive evidence.

What if Michelet and Delors sat around all night talking about pussy and Cuban cigars? Frank might decide his partner had been hearing voices the other night, the kind lunatics hear.

Well, at least someone was coming to dinner. He had heard Henri build fires in the library and dining room, and the smells that had begun to work their way down into the basement were even more aromatic than they had been on Wednesday night. He could say one thing about these bastards: they didn't let crime spoil their appetites.

He was ready to go give Warner an update when he heard the purr of an engine muffled by the fog. He waited until a Citroën stopped at the gate. Delors, who had driven himself, flashed his lights several times.

Footsteps boomed overhead in response. Henri walked out the front door waving his arms, his peasant pant legs brushing within a few feet of Steven's eyes. By the time the hobbling old servant made it to the gate, the rest of the convoy had arrived.

Mesmerized, Steven watched a replay of the Wednesday night search.

The man with the clipboard took up his post by the entrance. The van with the dogs parked in the same spot, and anti-terrorist agents began pouring out the back. The German shepherds, Gandoff and Thatcher, appeared just as Steven was beginning to think they hadn't returned. Military cops and radio technicians swarmed down from other vehicles lined up across the road.

A palpable energy was building out there as the men organized to conduct the sweep. Someone shouted at Henri to unlock the gate. He shook his finger as if to say, Not yet.

Steven had seen enough to know what was coming next. He shot eight photos with the NTSB camera, catching a good one of Delors in hot conversation with the clipboard man, then retreated to the wine cellar. "They're here," he whispered.

"Good," Warner said. "I was beginning to wonder. How do you feel?"

"Scared shitless. Michelet still hasn't come. Michelet is the one who ran the dogs off before. You were right. I shouldn't have assumed he'd be here."

"We've done what we could. Let's get into position."

Steven locked the wine cellar door from the inside and studied the wall of crates in front of their bunker. If they had put anything back in the wrong order, he couldn't tell. "You first," he said. Warner squirmed up on the cases that were stacked solidly, avoiding those in the second row that they had stacked to fall if subjected to excessive kneeing—or pawing. He reached the far wall and slid into the gap in the final row of crates where they had left their backpacks, the weird looking recorder, and the cage holding the last rat.

Steven turned off the light and went to join him. In the cavern, they staggered the crates to either side of them inward, buttressing them against each other at the top. Warner checked the rat passage to make sure rodent number 12 could squeeze his plump body through.

None too soon. The trample of footsteps echoed above them in the library; the search for listening devices had begun.

Steven and Warner were squeezed together in the tiny space, breathing and sweating as one. There was a clang in the distance. A narrow band of light appeared under the wine cellar door. The searchers were in the basement. They were coming.

Steven tried not to breathe.

Jackboots on old stone, gruff voices and beer hall laughter.

But no dogs!

Or at least no barking.

The noises gradually faded as the search moved away from the wine cellar. Steven was about to whisper something to Warner when the sound of a key in the lock caused his heart to leap. The wine cellar door opened, the lights came on.

Jesus, it was Henri! Thank God. The old man was talking to himself, mumbling about manners and city folk. The smell of perspiration, garlic and alcohol reached them as he opened the wire mesh gate to the special wines.

Henri mumbled more loudly than most people speak, calling off the names of wines he was looking for. Clos de Vougeout, 'seventy three, Château Brieuc, 'sixty one, Bâtard Montrachet, 'eighty eight…

Glass on glass, the ring ever so delicate, as he stacked the bottles in his carrying basket.

More grumbling, more searching. Everything seemed normal, no indication Henri had noticed their presence.

Then came the exhilarating sound of the wire mesh gate being closed and locked.

Footsteps stopped directly in front of them. Silence, as if the old man had ceased to breathe. Then came a grating sound on the floor as crates were shimmied gently across the concrete.

Steven felt Warner tense.

"Château Lafite Rothshild, 'sixty four," Henri mumbled. "Why doesn't the fool put the rest of these in their proper place before he ruins them?"

It was nothing. He wanted to tell Frank. Henri was not looking for them. He was trying to get to the bottles in one of the crates in the second row, a crate Steven remembered well.

They were safe. There was nothing at all unusual in the way they had reconstructed that row. The irregularities didn't begin until row three. It would take Henri a little more moving, that's all, and he would be out of here. Then they could relax and wait for the real show to begin.

Henri got what he wanted after a lot more grumbling, cursing and searching. He started to leave. Steven exhaled and gulped air. He had been holding his breath even though Henri couldn't hear. It seemed more natural that way.

The old servant had had time to get to the door by now. Why didn't the light go out? Why didn't the door close? Why didn't he leave? What the hell was keeping him?

The answer came like a cruel blow. The search was coming to the wine cellar after all, rumbling through the great labyrinth of the basement.

Everyone in the search party, which Steven guessed consisted of a half dozen men, sounded agitated. They came closer, and their words were suddenly comprehensible.

Steven was glad Frank didn't understand French. Maybe he could stay cool and save the day.

"There could be someone down here," one of the men announced. "Thatcher don't chase rodents and small animals. She learned in school not to chase rats. Gandoff, that's another story. He's thick-headed. Not Thatcher. She sat at the crawl space door and refused to move. We opened up. Gandoff took off like an Exocet. Thatcher took one step inside and backed out. Nothing in there but rats. Could've been put there."

Henri said, "Talk louder. I'm deaf. I didn't hear a word you said."

Someone else said, "Talk with your lips, Guillaume. You could set off dynamite next to his head and he wouldn't hear it."

A malevolent hiss cut through the room as the man repeated his suspicions with exaggerated enunciation. Steven shut his eyes though he couldn't see anything with them open. The dogs were here, he could hear them now, whimpering softly. They must have been trained not to bark. The ones that didn't bark were the ones that bit. They were going to get bitten.

He felt his hand moving to his breast holster. Warner stopped him. Warner didn't know what was going on. He couldn't understand French.

"Get those dogs away from the wine!" Henri bellowed. "Sure we have rats down here. Winter's coming and we have rats. They don't hurt anything. But if you let those dogs rummage around, they'll destroy a million francs of wine. Take them upstairs. You know what monsieur thinks of them. Go on. Get out."

"Sorry, old man. We gotta do our job."

Steven pictured Henri blocking the doorway. He was old but not someone you bowled over easily. "What?" he shouted.

More hissing as the man enunciated.

"Nonsense!" roared Henri. "You saw that lock up there."

"Maybe it's you, old man. Maybe it's you, I said. How do we know *you* haven't been paid off by socialists or the unions to let someone sneak in here. Move over or I'll have to move you."

Scuffling, pushing, cursing. Steven's heart pounded as if it would explode.

The dogs burst into the wine cellar. Their whimpering locked on the bunker like canine radar. Steven went for his gun again. This time

Warner didn't stop him. Warner was digging for the rat. He pushed it into the tunnel they had made for it and gave it a poke.

All hell broke loose on the outer perimeter of crates. Paws scraped wildly, heading for the bunker. Voices, loud raw voices, shouted contradictory orders.

And then came the crash, the ugly, sweet crash of a crate of priceless wine tumbling into a crevice, pushing other crates to the side and splintering against the floor.

Steven waited, his automatic pistol trembling in his grasp, while the agents restrained the dogs. There was a long silence before the man who hissed finally spoke. "I'll be damned," he said. "In all these years, I've never seen her chase rats. What's wrong with you, Thatcher? Sorry, old man. We'd like to help you clean up but we're on a tight schedule. Let us know what's broken. The government will replace it."

"Do yourself in the ass," Henri growled. "Get out of here before you break anything else.

The contingent left, the tension gone from the voices, some of the men laughing.

Steven listened to the fading tatters of their conversation. Someone said, "Last time Gandoff took a shit in his geraniums. This time Thatcher trashes his wine cellar. I say we leave the dogs in the van from now on. This guy is going to be President of France some day. Why risk pissing him off?"

And then there was only grumbling, intimate grumbling nearby, grumbling that reached their ears on fumes of sweat and garlic. Henri worked for a long time. When he left, when the lights went out and the door slammed shut, Steven gave Warner a hug around the neck.

Chapter Thirty-Two

Midnight came and went without a sign of the others. Warner had been holding vigil at the vent for hours, staring out into the fog like a pilot on instrument landing, his camera ready. He cursed the foul weather for stranding him in the eye of the storm. They should have been on their way back to Paris by now, the condemning evidence safely captured on film and tape. Instead they were in a holding pattern, waiting for a break that seemed less and less likely to occur.

His back was killing him. An anxious, bone-weary fatigue had replaced the nervous energy generated by the search. It wouldn't be a bad idea, he thought, to get some rest.

He sat on the concrete floor with his back against the wall and closed his eyes. He was a light sleeper. The first sound of a car engine would jolt him into wakefulness, so he knew he could doze without risking a missed photo opportunity.

He had drifted off when approaching footsteps ended his rest. "It's me," Steven whispered, sitting on the floor beside him. "Our luck seems to be holding. Michelet and Haussmann will be on their way shortly."

"How do you know?"

"A telephone call. Delors took it in the library. Michelet was at Orly waiting. Haussmann's plane just landed."

"In this weather?"

"It's raining. The fog has lifted. How long since you looked out?"

Warner glanced at his watch. "Twenty minutes. That's welcome news."

"It sure is. Listen, I brought you something to eat and the dregs of the coffee. This will probably be your last chance to fuel up."

Pilot's Dawn

The coffee was cold, the pâté had made the baguette soggy. They tasted great. "Thanks," Warner said. "How long from Orly to here by car?"

"About three quarters of an hour. Now the bad news."

Warner stood and peeked out the vent. The yellow light on the gate post, which had been softened by the fog, now shone brightly. "What is it, Steven?"

"The house must have gotten cold in spite of the fires in the fireplaces. The furnace has started to kick on. When the goddamn thing's running, I can't hear anything through the duct but a big whoosh of air. If we don't figure something out, your tape will sound like a jet taking off."

Warner said, "We'll figure something out."

"I was thinking," Steven said. "Maybe we could disconnect the wires that come into the furnace from the thermostat. That'll keep it from coming on."

"That's a good start, but we can't leave the heat off for too long. Someone might come down here to see what the problem is."

"All true. But if we don't shut the thing up, we might as well leave now."

"Don't jump to conclusions. Let's say I camp out beside the furnace where I can activate the thermostat manually. All I would need would be a signal from your listening post in the wine cellar whenever the conversation turns irrelevant. I'd let the furnace run for a few minutes, then turn it off and wait for you to signal me again."

"So how am I going to do that?"

"I was considering the light switch in the wine cellar. If we loosen all the bulbs in the basement except the one near the furnace, we'll have our system up and running in no time."

"I don't get it. If I turn on the switch in the wine cellar, the wine cellar light comes on, not the basement lights."

"That's because I haven't worked on it yet. I don't know if you've noticed, but the wiring down here is all external. It's no big deal to tie that switch into the other circuit."

"If you say so."

"I do. Let's get on it. You loosen the light bulbs, I'll work on the switch. Don't miss any. We don't want the entire basement lighting up every time you signal me. All we want is a quick flash from the bulb by the furnace. It won't be noticeable if anyone happens to be strolling by outside."

"Hey, Frank—"

"What?"

"If you can really do this it's a brilliant idea, right up there with the rats."

"Thank you," Warner said. "I can do it."

Warner returned to his vigil shortly after one o'clock in the morning, confident the jerry-rigged system they had just finished testing would not let them down. The rain had moved off toward Germany, the sky was trying to clear. The moon appeared briefly through ragged heaps of cloud. A condensation trail from a high-flying jet cut across its face. Warner doubted it was a Boeing. He used the minutes until the men's expected arrival to review in his mind the photographs Sophie had shown him.

He was conjuring up an image of Haussmann when the sounds of a car drifted in across the dark countryside.

As the car drew near, he thought he heard a second car off in the distance. He listened carefully. There could be no doubt about it. Two cars were approaching the manor from opposite directions.

Minutes later a gray Mercedes sedan, coming from Warner's left, pulled up to the front gate. Footsteps cracked above as someone walked to the entrance to greet the new arrival. Before the car's doors opened, headlights appeared at the crest of the hill to Warner's right.

Pilot's Dawn

Pantlegs momentarily obscured his view as the man who had been inside the house stepped into the night. A hand out the window of the car at the gate motioned him back inside. The man retreated to the foyer directly above Warner's head.

The Mercedes window closed, the car backed up without lights and stopped a few yards down the road. Headlights from the second car swept across wet forests and muddy fields, coming close enough to the vent to induce Warner to duck from view. He waited until he heard the car's engine drop to idle, then looked out again.

The second car was also a Mercedes sedan, burgundy in color and a few years older than the first. The driver's door opened, a man whose face was lost in the shadows got out and stood staring at the parked car. He was of average build and height, dressed in a nondescript gray overcoat. His hair, which was combed straight back, shone in the yellow light from the gate post.

Warner held off taking the first photograph: he was sure this was Claussen, but there was nothing visible by which the man could be conclusively identified.

The seconds passed, nothing happened. Then the headlights of the first car came on. A large man in a dark business suit stepped out of the driver's side and stood motionless, staring at the other man.

It seemed a strange face-off until Warner remembered what Sophie had told him. Michelet and Claussen were never supposed to meet. Claussen was never supposed to know who his boss was. But Claussen knew and he was here. That explained a lot.

Michelet reached back into his car and said something to the other man. The iron gate with the spikes on top opened. Michelet pointed to Claussen, then to the gate.

As Claussen walked to his car, Michelet waved in the direction of the house. Delors must have been watching. He stepped out the front entrance again, accompanied by an old man.

Claussen drove through the gate. Henri walked out to meet the car and guided it to a parking spot that faced the wall surrounding the manor. Michelet wasted no time pulling up behind him, blocking any unwanted departure.

Engines died, doors opened. The moon flickered through ragged fast-moving clouds as three men got out into the night.

While Claussen initiated a handshake with Michelet, the third man—short, compact and energetic—walked briskly to the rear of Michelet's car and took out a leather valise. Henri offered to carry it, but Haussmann waved him off with a jovial backhand. He was in a damn good mood, thought Warner, for someone about to part with a quarter of a billion dollars.

The three men walked toward the house in silence. Delors came down the steps and strode out to the gravel driveway to meet them. He shook hands with each, using their first names.

Then, suddenly, all four conspirators were facing him, coming toward him, coming closer with each step. It would have been easy to take out all four of them with his automatic pistol. He hoped he would not regret having passed up the opportunity.

He focussed his camera and took three photographs. When the men reached the stone walkway, he put his camera down. The shutter made a tiny clicking sound, the gravel no longer crunched underfoot and the night was utterly still.

The clouds opened, the moonlight poured through the vent. He had seen enough. He melted back into the darkness and waited for the trample of footsteps to cross the foyer. Then he went to alert his partner that their hour had struck.

   ✴   ✴   ✴

Steven hadn't returned until three in the morning last time, thought Sophie. This was why she had sworn not to let herself get nervous a second before 3:01.

So much for mastery of the emotions. It was barely one a.m. and already her mind had taken on a will of its own, spinning out one tragic fantasy after another: Warner assassinated and stuffed down a country well; Steven castrated with a dull rusty knife and buried—howling, bleeding and alive. The visions kept on growing more hideous, more vivid and more realistic.

She opened the bottle of Armagnac she had been saving for her heroes' arrival. She had to do something. At this rate she would be in a nut house before they came home.

If they came home.

It was the guns, she *knew* it was the guns. When you slipped as silent as dust, as defenseless as lambs, into the lair of evil men, they did not detect you. Their world view failed to include a category for people who were kind, gentle and good, yet able to muster levels of courage greater than their own.

But once you strapped on their weapons and resorted to their tactics, you were singing their song, playing their game by their rules. When that happened, you appeared on their unconscious radar scopes no matter how meticulous your planning.

She had made a big mistake procuring those automatic pistols.

She took a sip of Armagnac and walked to the window. Clouds charged across the moon. Bach was on the CD player. She suddenly wished she had chosen Débussy.

This was silly, she thought, trying to get hold of herself. She was being self-indulgent and not a little ridiculous. Steven and Warner would have managed to get their own guns without her help. Their minds had been made up. Therefore she had not been the one who had determined the style of their mission. Her help in procuring the weapons had done nothing but undermine her own arguments, which they weren't going to listen to anyway.

At least she had remained true to her beliefs in one respect. When Chabrol had offered to arm **her** and teach her how to take care of herself properly in this hostile, violent, high-tech world, she had told him to take a hike.

To hell with it, she couldn't handle Bach anymore. She made herself walk to the CD player. While she was trying to locate the Débussy disc, she heard footsteps running up the marble staircase.

She gasped. A pulse of terror shot through her breast. She had a flashback to Chabrol, a smile on his smooth, fine-featured face as he imitated her using the gun he wanted her to have. A little silver thing, so elegant, so simple. Bang, bang, the job was done, the Algerian gorilla who had come to brutalize her fell to the floor, dead; and Sophie Marx lived on to write another fine piece about the immorality of the arms trade.

She had laughed, yes she had laughed. Chabrol was a charming, exotic young man with brass balls and the features of a movie star. But she had not been close to taking him up on his offer. Now, as she crept in stockinged feet toward the door, her heart pounding like an air hammer, she almost wished she had…

The footsteps stopped. She opened her door a tiny crack and heard a voice sweet as bird song calling Steven's name.

She stepped out on the cold marble, leaned over the railing and peered down at the source of the song. In front of Steven's door stood Nicole Michelet, disheveled but radiant, begging him to be there and wake up and let her in.

Sophie had a sudden powerful urge to be with this young girl. Another woman was what she needed right now—not a firearm but a woman who would spill her own fears and understand Sophie's, who would speak the same language and ache with the same emotions.

"Nicole, is that you?" she called down.

Pilot's Dawn

The girl looked up, baffled. "Who are you, madame?"

"A neighbor, dear. Don't worry. Steven asked me to be on the lookout for you. He had a feeling you might drop by tonight, and he wanted to make sure he didn't miss you. He asked me to let you in if you arrived while he was away. He also asked me to bring you up to date on a few things. Let me get my keys. I'll be right down. And don't worry. He'll be home soon."

Sophie went back inside her flat, wondering what had caused her to unleash a gusher of spontaneous lies. The answers came to her as she gathered up her purse and the Armagnac: she had lied because she hadn't wanted Nicole to leave; she had lied because on this horrible night she wanted company...

And there was something else. Ever since she had gotten Steven involved in his terrible dilemma, she had longed for the opportunity to get him out of it in a way that would leave his relationship with this lovely girl intact. If she succeeded in doing that—and if Steven and Warner made it back safe and sound—tonight might turn out quite differently from the way she had imagined it.

* * *

This was beautiful, beautiful, thought Steven. They were doing it all in the dining room where his duct connection was as good as the one to the library.

They were saying the most incriminating things, talking about the number of crashes commissioned, Operation 26, the consequences that the discovery of the parts in Seattle would have, and how none of it would matter after the United States vented its fury on Iraq.

It would, Claussen said, be like a mighty orgasm which would leave the country lying in a blind satisfied stupor for months.

Haussmann laughed. Yes, yes, that's how America was, long stupors interrupted by short paroxysms of insight and action.

Oh, God, the things they were saying...and the things they were not saying each time Henri or Isabelle came out to serve them. Then the conversation turned to wine and sauces, meats and herbs, nothing of interest to crash investigators. That was when he hit the light switch. The wine cellar remained dark, but the furnace came on with a whoosh. It was perfect, utterly perfect! As soon as he had their discussion of payment on tape, he would have documented their entire plot in a way that nailed them to the wall. He and Warner could pack their bags and beat a fast retreat to warmer climes.

The whooshing of the furnace stopped. He pressed his ear to the duct, sharing the opening with the microphone. Haussmann was speaking. He was sniffing around the subject of the money. It wouldn't be long now.

Chapter Thirty-Three

The hand on Henri's shoulder while he was preparing to fire the *crème brulée* made him jump and knock his wine glass off the table. He spun around and gave Isabelle a piece of his mind for startling him.

He immediately felt bad for his outburst. This had been a long evening for both of them, not knowing if dinner would happen and having to get it ready in record time when it did. At this late hour—and at their age!

He apologized profusely for his harsh words; she apologized for startling him. Isabelle didn't seem upset, for which he was grateful. She dutifully cleaned up the broken glass and spilled wine, then poured him a fresh goblet. "Henri, may I say something now?" she asked.

"Yes, but quickly. The oven's just right."

"Monsieur would like you to bring up his father's cognac from 1913."

"The cognac he wasn't going to drink before the new century?"

"I only know what he told me, Henri."

"Well, I can't fetch it until I have finished preparing the dessert."

"That's another thing, Henri. The guests do not want dessert. Monsieur has asked us to return to our quarters for the night as soon as you have brought the cognac. And he wants it right away."

"How can they pass up a proper *crème brulée* after a meal like that?"

"I don't know, Henri, but you'd better hurry. Monsieur had that impatient look on his face."

"Very well. They were otherwise pleased with the dinner, you think?"

"Of course, *chéri*."

"No *crême brulée*," he grumbled as he picked up his heavy metal flashlight. He'd made a habit of taking it with him to the cellar ever since a power outage had caught him down there and thoroughly disoriented him. He had felt like he was in a tomb. At one point he actually believed he had died. It was an experience he did not want to repeat until the real angel of death came for him.

The night was cold. His breath steamed in the light from the kitchen windows as he circled the house. Fog still lay in the low areas, but most of the clouds had broken up and scudded off to the east. The stars had come out to join the moon. Wouldn't be long until winter, he thought, wouldn't be long until the rains fell as snow. A good thing he had his grapes safely fermenting in their old oak casks.

He leaned down and unlocked the horizontal door, then gave it a slight tug. It came up without complaint, silently, obligingly. A good door, he thought—but for some reason the basement lights did not come on when he opened it.

No problem, he would turn them on manually. He located the switch he had installed near the entrance, put there to keep the lights burning in winter when he shut the door behind him. He flicked the switch up. No lights. He flicked it back down. Still no lights.

This was very odd. During the power outage, the electricity to the entire house was off. But tonight he could still see light from inside the manor slanting across the top of the steps.

Well, what difference did it make? It would be the circuit breaker, which he could reset in the morning. For now he had his flashlight and his orders to bring up a specific bottle of cognac whose location he knew very well. He'd best get that taken care of and call it a night, especially if Isabelle had correctly read monsieur's mood.

He closed the door against the cold, descended the steps and hobbled down the familiar basement passageways. Ninety feet later he came around a corner and nearly bumped into the open wine cellar door. He stopped in his tracks, extinguished his flashlight and held his breath.

Pilot's Dawn

This was much stranger than lights that did not work. He had been the last person down here. Delors didn't have the keys, and Michelet had not shown up until dinner time. He always locked the door of the wine cellar when he left. It was second nature, like taking off his boots at bed time.

Still he had been pretty agitated by those wild dogs and their idiot trainers. The crate they knocked down broke several bottles of irreplaceable wine, an ugly occurrence for which monsieur might take *him* to task. He wasn't young anymore, either. There were times when his memory failed him. This was probably one of them.

He was about to turn his flashlight back on when he thought he saw something in the wine cellar, a movement in the darkness, scarcely detectable but real. He was probably seeing things, but instinct told him to cautious. What if those idiot dogs and their trainers were right? What if there had been more than just rats down here? The hair on the back of his neck stood on end. He'd better find out. It was his job as guardian of the wine.

He moved forward with small steps, trying not to scrap his boots. His eyes were slowly adjusting to the darkness.

This was strange, too. There were no lights on anywhere, but for some reason it did not seem as dark down here as it had seemed the night of the power outage.

It was not as dark! In the penumbra of the wine cellar, he could make out the neatly arranged crates and the wire mesh gate. He soon spotted the source of the light. It was a tiny dial that resembled the lighted face of a stereo, sitting on top of a stack of crates. His first thought was that it might be a timing device for a terrorist bomb.

Then he saw legs to either side of it. He looked up, feeling short of breath. On the crates stood the ghostly figure of a man. A big man. His back faced the door, his head was resting against a heating duct. He was an eavesdropper, it didn't take an educated man to figure that out. The thing with the glowing dial was some kind of tape recorder.

He was probably a journalist, thought Henri. Or someone hired by political opponents to listen in on monsieur's secrets. No one dangerous, not like a wine thief. Nevertheless, he owed monsieur this man's head on a platter, tape recorder and all.

Henri tightened his grip on the heavy flashlight. He could deal the intruder a powerful blow, but not while he was up so high. Should he grab one of his legs and try to pull him off the crates? No, he would have to think of something better than that. The man looked strong. If they got into a free for all, he would probably escape. Besides, he was perched on top of the Lafite from the late fifties. Monsieur might prefer having his political discussions recorded to losing a bottle of that nectar.

Then a good thing happened. The man climbed carefully down from the crates and got himself into a position on the floor where he could be knocked silly. Henri knew he wasn't going anywhere; he had left the recording machine where it was. No, he was fishing around in his backpack for something. He pulled out what looked like a pack of batteries and began to open it, still on his knees, still facing downwind.

Henri approached silently, raised his flashlight and delivered a crushing blow to the man's head. The man flopped on his stomach and lay motionless. Henri raised his flashlight again but decided he'd better stop. He'd read in the newspaper about some guy who thought he had a right to kill an intruder and had ended up in jail for doing it.

He turned on his flashlight to get a look at the man's wounds. Nothing. He had wrecked the bulb. What did he expect? The thing wasn't meant to be a club.

He made his way over to the wall and turned on the wine cellar light. It remained dark but the furnace came on. He felt its hot breath blowing through holes the intruder had evidently cut in the ducts.

Henri checked on his victim. The man was breathing evenly. This was good. He wasn't dead, just out cold.

He took the recording machine down from the crates, pulling on a wire until a miniature microphone jumped out of one of the ducts. The dial still glowed. He held it near the unconscious man's face—and felt as if he was going to have a stroke.

Jesus, Holy Madonna, in the name of the Father, why was the world so complicated? This man was Nicole's boyfriend, soon to be her fiancé, soon to be family! Had she already told her father about him? Had monsieur accepted this man and entrusted him with the task of recording tonight's conversations?

Or was this young man a scoundrel deceiving the whole Michelet clan?

What was he going to do? What he always did, he supposed: ask for Isabelle's advice.

The man Nicole called Steven groaned and stirred. Time to go, Henri thought, it was definitely time to go. He put the recording machine under his arm and hobbled down the dark passageways to the exit.

Isabelle was waiting for him at the entrance to the kitchen. Her concern turned to curiosity when she saw the strange looking apparatus he was carrying; and the blood on his flashlight.

*   *   *

"So you just up and ran away?" Sophie asked.

"I had some help," Nicole said. "I have a teenage cousin who can be a nuisance. But he was great tonight. He got me to the station on time and he's now wearing my nightgown and sleeping in my bed, just in case anyone checks on me. By the time they figure out I'm gone, Steven and I should be out of France."

"You really love him, don't you?"

Nicole averted her eyes and blushed. "Yes, I do. I hope he loves me as much."

"He does. I can promise you that."

"Does he talk about me a lot?"

Sophie nodded. She felt restless. She knew she had to begin her monologue at some point if she was going to say what she wanted to say before Steven returned. But it wasn't easy. They had been chatting amiably for almost a half hour. Nicole had warmed up to her somewhat but they were still basically strangers.

The right moment to broach topics so personal and painful did not seem as if it would come of its own accord. Sophie decided she'd better dive in and trust that Nicole could handle it.

"He talks about you incessantly, dear," she said. "He loves you more than you can imagine. But there is something about Steven you should know. I have entrusted myself with the task of telling you."

Nicole sat up straight, her beautiful face drawn with tension. "What is it?"

"This is very difficult for me. What I'm going to say doesn't just involve Steven. It involves your father, it involves me. I want you to try to keep one thing firmly in mind as I make these revelations. Steven loves you with all his heart. You must not doubt his loyalty. He is totally committed to you. If you're going to be angry with anyone, that person should not be him. It should be me. Or your father."

"What in the world are you talking about?"

Sophie poured them both a snifter of Armagnac. Nicole watched her intently, too curious, or too worried, to drink.

"First, Nicole, you owe your original meeting with Steven to me and my machinations. My name did not seem to ring a bell when I mentioned it earlier. You've got a lot on your mind, but you're an informed and well-read person. I suspect you've heard that same name on many occasions."

"Sophie Marx, the journalist?" Nicole said.

"That's the dirty word. Journalist."

"You're her?"

"Yes. Nicole, I think you'd better drink your Armagnac. You see, I hired Steven to befriend you. I was trying to gain information about your father."

"What?" She was stunned.

"Please, Nicole. I beg you to keep an open mind and listen to me. I'm not proud of what I did, but when you've heard me out, I think you'll agree it wasn't such a bad thing."

"The tennis club? All that was a lie?"

"I arranged for him to get the job, yes."

Nicole started to tremble, tears of rage welling in her eyes. "You mean his coming on to me, all of that was *theater*? You paid him to get me in bed? You paid him? And all along I was saying to myself, he's so different from these arrogant French boys, so interested in me as a person and not just my body, so kind—"

"Nicole, please. He fell in love with you before anything intimate happened. He called me from Nice and told me he was quitting the assignment, that he simply couldn't reconcile his feelings for you with what I was asking of him. Do you know what it meant for him to give up that assignment? Nicole, he wants to be a journalist. I had given him a start the likes of which few young hopefuls ever receive. I was paying him a lavish expense account at a time when he was very broke. And still, he chose you over all of that. It's the truth, Nicole, the absolute truth."

"Then he quit with this nonsense of spying on my father?"

"No, not exactly. He tried to quit. I was shameless. I was ruthless. I was manipulative. I needed him to get my story, so I gave him more money. I ridiculed and cajoled him. I convinced him your father had plans for you that would ruin your life."

"He did. He does. But that's beside the point. Steven had no right to deceive me. No right whatsoever. It is a denial of trust and honesty and everything else that love demands."

"It's not that cut-and-dried, Nicole. He fell in love with you, he fell in love with the dream of helping me do a great story on a man I considered dangerous to the future of his country and the world. Steven was in a dilemma from which he did not know how to escape. He was trying to get out, though. Trying to find the courage to confess to you. He put it off for the second time when you mentioned your father's Wednesday night political meetings."

"Oh, my God, he's taken such advantage of me. Is that where he was when he said he was playing a tournament in Dijon? After I had introduced him to the caretakers and given him a tour of the house? I trusted him. I trusted him with my life. This...this is disgusting."

"Nicole"

"I can't talk anymore. I have to go. I can't take this at a time when everyone but me is trying to run my life. Perhaps my father is right. Perhaps I am naive and need to be protected from the scoundrels of this world."

"I understand why you are upset, Nicole. But before you leave, I would like to tell you what Steven overheard at your father's country home."

She was already on her feet. She did not answer.

"If you're looking for scoundrels, Nicole, leave Steven out of this. Your father has a monopoly on the title. He and a group of his cronies are sabotaging Boeing airplanes. He is responsible for the deaths of thousands of innocent men, women and children. He has done this horrible thing for political gain. He thinks that if he turns the economy around while he's Minister of Industry, he will be elected President of France. That, my dear, is what the man who truly loves you learned while he was eavesdropping on your father's Wednesday night meetings."

"It can't be," Nicole said. "How can I believe something like that? I know father isn't a kind man, but a saboteur of passenger jets? No, that's hardly possible. He hasn't a heart, but he's not evil. He's not, is he, Madame Marx?"

Sophie knew she had almost lost Nicole, but now she could feel her coming back. She said, "Steven is at the manor right now with a member of the United States government. They have photographic equipment and listening devices. They will be here shortly. You can decide then whether or not these allegations are true."

"No…they cannot be true. I assure you, they cannot be."

"Nicole—"

"What?"

"This was a very dangerous thing for Steven to attempt. Your father's group is making payment to an ex-KGB agent tonight for his role in the crashes. This man, whose name is Walter Claussen, is to receive one and a half **billion** francs. You can imagine the type of security Steven and his colleague are up against. It's possible they won't make it back at all. Please stay here and wait with me. I beg you. If things go badly we're going to need each other."

Nicole began to tremble again. Tears streamed down her ravaged face. "I…I don't know what to do or whom to believe. I'm…so tired."

Sophie took her gently by the arm. "Why don't you lie down and have a rest. There'll be a lot to talk about when he returns."

"What if he doesn't return? What if—"

"Shhh. Rest now."

Nicole did not resist when Sophie led her to Steven's bedroom. She lay down and curled up, clutching a pillow. Sophie tiptoed out and closed the door. She had done what she set out to do. Whether it had been a good idea or not, she wasn't sure.

Chapter Thirty-Four

Warner received the light signal, the first in a long time. He held the pocket knife across the control box terminals, and the furnace roared to life.

But the light, for some reason, did not go out. Had Steven gotten careless? Or sleepy? This was entirely unacceptable. He reattached the thermostat wires, fearing it could grow noticeably colder upstairs if he did not and, seething with irritation over his partner's slothfulness, headed for the wine cellar.

Groaning met him as he approached the door. Steven was on his knees, blood trickling down the side of his head, his hands groping aimlessly for support.

Warner grabbed him with both arms and hauled him to his feet. "Jesus Christ, what happened?"

"I...don't—"

"Where's the CVR?"

Steven seemed confused. He pointed to the crates where he had been standing. It was not there. He tried to sit back down, but Warner wouldn't let him.

"Steven...Steven! What happened? Try to remember."

"I don't...know. I just woke up down there."

"Try to remember!"

"I feel sick."

"Steven, do you know where you are?"

"Huh?"

"We've got to go. Now. We've got to run."

"The CVR? Did you…find it?"

"Steven, someone has been here. They've knocked you out and taken the recorder. Come on. Get tough. If we don't get out of here, we're finished."

Warner slung the dazed man's arm over his shoulder and half dragged, half carried him to the steps. "Can you walk on your own now?" he asked, puffing like a locomotive.

"I…I think so."

"Then move. We've got to get out of here."

Steven started up the stairs, fell, took a few steps on all fours, then got to his feet. His head seemed to be clearing. He pushed open the door and hit the lawn running.

Jesus Christ, he was in shape, thought Warner, following. He took a quick glance through the kitchen window as they raced away from the house. Henri! It had been Henri who had come into the basement! He was holding up the CVR, making some sort of animated presentation to his wife. This meant they had just been discovered in the last few minutes. Judging from Henri's behavior, the men in the dining room had not yet been told.

Now was the critical time, thought Warner. Now was when they had to give it everything they had.

He caught up to Steven, who was keeping a fast steady pace. "You okay?"

"I'm all right, Frank. Still dazed but all right. Jesus, what happened?"

"Henri must have come down for wine while you were listening. He's in the kitchen with the CVR right now. Don't talk. Save your strength. We have to cover some ground."

They passed under the trees where the crows had once mounted a noisy attack and reached the edge of the meadow that led to the lily ponds. The forest glistened in the moonlight. It seemed far, far away. Patches of ground fog clung to ditches and indentations in the terrain. Cover if and when they needed it. Not much but some.

Warner's lungs were on fire. His legs felt as though they had turned to jelly. He could hear himself hacking and rasping as his feet pounded the wet grass.

"It's my fault," Steven said. "I lost the tapes. They were perfect. They were everything we needed and more. How could it happen? How did I fuck up?"

"Christ, quit blaming yourself. It was nobody's fault. Let's work on getting out of here before they get organized."

Steven started to say something, then fell silent and picked up the pace. He had recovered from the blow to the head; he wasn't hurt. Warner tried to keep up, but his 53 years were more than a match for his will power. Better to concentrate on not spraining an ankle, he thought, than on doing the impossible.

They circled the lily ponds, took the path to the forest and came to the irrigation ditch that formed the boundary of Michelet's estate. It was covered with a thick blanket of fog rising several feet above the ground.

Once they crossed it, Warner knew they couldn't be seen from the manor, not even with the best infrared field glasses Delors and the SDECE could muster. He stopped and lifted his binoculars; he felt it was worth the small delay to try to get an idea of how much time they had until hell on earth broke loose.

He could see through the kitchen windows, which were the only windows without drapes. He focussed while Steven helped him steady his arms.

Isabelle was guarding the CVR, which sat on the counter like a piece of smoked meat. Henri was gone, no doubt making his report in the dining room.

Warner believed they would have time enough to get to the bike. Whether they could to ride it to safety depended on the response these bastards mounted.

Pilot's Dawn

He didn't want to underestimate them. There was a member of the government present who could pull all sorts of strings. His right-hand man was the deputy director of French intelligence, who could mobilize his own substantial forces. And there was Claussen, a spy who had fooled the CIA for 30 years. If ever they needed a little luck, now was the time.

* * *

Michelet banged on the table when Henri entered the dining room unannounced. "What do you think you're doing? Where's the cognac?"

"Monsieur, Isabelle and I must talk to you in the kitchen at once."

"What did he say?" Haussmann said.

"No idea," said Delors. "He was mumbling."

Claussen lit a cigarette. "He said he and Isabelle would like to talk to Minister Michelet in the kitchen. At once."

"Please excuse yourself," Michelet bellowed, shaking a fist at his servant. "I asked that you bring the cognac and return to your quarters. As yet you have done neither. At least have the decency to GO HOME. We will fetch the cognac ourselves. Now, go."

"But, monsieur, it is about the cognac and the other items in your wine cellar that I must speak to you. It could be, monsieur, that someone has made an unauthorized entry into the basement. It could be that a wine thief was present."

"Well, did he steal anything? Did you check the inventory?"

"I could not check the inventory, monsieur. The lights failed to come on. The intruder left a device behind I want to show you. Perhaps it will give you an idea who this person is."

Claussen said, "Minister, go see what he has found. It won't take more than a few minutes."

"Very well. Let's go, Henri." He followed his servant into the kitchen. When he saw the odd looking device with the lighted dial, he immediately locked the door to the dining room. No use upsetting his colleagues until he had an idea what was going on.

"Henri, what happened? Whisper."

"Yes, monsieur. I might have done something very wrong. I do not know. But someone in the cellar has been listening in on your conversations."

Michelet grabbed him by the lapels. "Get to the point. To the point, understand? Skip the rest. Tell me what happened when you went for the cognac."

"First, monsieur, first you must tell me whether you gave your permission to Nicole's boyfriend to go into the cellar and record the conversations you are conducting tonight."

"Have you lost your mind? What are you talking about? Nicole doesn't have a boyfriend."

"Oh, yes, monsieur. That fine young man from the province of the North by the name of LeConte—a blond Frenchman whose father has purchased an American company."

"Steven LeConte?"

"Yes, monsieur. That is how Nicole introduced him to me."

"**What**? He was here? She brought him here?"

"Yes, monsieur. And it was this same LeConte I surprised in the wine cellar tonight with this very recording machine you see here. I hit him over the head with my flashlight and took it from him. I brought it instead of the cognac."

Michelet shoved Isabelle aside and grabbed the device. "Both of you, go home. Now! Understand?"

"Did I do the right thing, monsieur? I was only trying—"

"Go home!" shouted Michelet. "Go home! I'll do the rest. Is he down there now?"

"I don't know, monsieur. He was knocked out when I left."

"Go home. I'll have a look for myself."

"Take another flashlight, monsieur. You will need it."

"Well, don't just stand there. Get me one. Get me a pistol, too. Do you still keep your pistol in the kitchen?"

"Yes, monsieur."

Michelet stuck the old six shooter into his belt and rushed out the back door. He took a deep breath and started toward the basement, trying to keep his rage from blinding him. On his way down, he tripped on the worn stone steps and almost lost his grip on the flashlight.

He approached the wine cellar gingerly, the pistol drawn and cocked. Too late. Blood was still on the floor but LeConte was gone. There was a blood trail he hadn't noticed. He followed it and ended up back at the basement entrance.

The son of bitch had escaped. He was going to have to report the news to the others, as unpleasant as this might be.

He stopped in the kitchen to catch his breath, then returned to the dining room. He felt dizzy. He didn't know if the thick blue haze all around him was caused by cigar smoke or his own fuzzy perception.

"Gentlemen," Michelet announced, holding up the odd looking contraption from the kitchen, "it seems we have been the object of a mean-spirited practical joke. My daughter, hoping to injure and embarrass me, has taken an American boyfriend. It would appear she has smuggled him into the wine cellar tonight in an attempt to get some negative material on me.

"Well, if he's managed to hear anything, he's certainly gotten his material. But we have the recorder, and the tape is still in it. I think it's safe to conclude that the American has no proof. What he'll do with his information—if he in fact heard anything—is another matter. He lives in Paris, Place Maubert Twelve. I had become aware of his involvement with my daughter a few days ago and had procured his address from the Immigration Services. Unfortunately, I had not yet had time to intervene."

Murmuring and whispering filled the room. A frantic, furious, incredulous expression contorted Haussmann's face. Delors tried to calm him while Claussen stared into space, smoking a cigarette.

"Listen," Michelet said, "Calm down, all of you. This is something we can deal with. It is not our first crisis, but it will be our last. My daughter is in Grenoble with her aunt. I'll determine exactly how much she knows. Believe me, gentlemen, if she knows anything, I shall willingly turn her over to Paul and the SDECE."

He stared at the table, reflecting, the way he did at well-rehearsed political speeches. He kept his eyes down longer than usual: he did not want to see how his colleagues were judging him in the wake of his horrible blunder.

He said, "As for this boyfriend, this Steven LeConte, we need to find and eliminate him. He of course has no proof of anything. The proof, if it exists at all, is in that recording device. I assure you, he is not a credible person. If he told what he has possibly heard tonight, no one would believe him. Nonetheless, we do not need rumors circulating at this stage of the game. Let me ask you, Herr Claussen, how you suggest we proceed."

No answer. Michelet looked up but Claussen was no longer there. "Where did he go?" Michelet thundered. "Did he take the money?"

"No, Georges," Delors said. "The money is here. He went to inspect the basement."

"I was already there."

"We know, Georges. He wanted to see it himself. He is better trained than you in evaluating such situations."

"Then we shall wait for his return."

"Yes, we shall."

Claussen came in a few minutes later and sat beside Michelet. "The heating ducts were cut. I listened to you. 'My daughter is in Grenoble with her aunt…' This person knows what was discussed tonight. Let there be no doubt about it.

"Nor do I agree that he is not a credible person. The device on your table is a piece of aviation equipment. It is called a CVR or cockpit voice recorder. Mr. LeConte has ties to the aviation industry or he would not be using such a device.

"Furthermore, it is not just any CVR. It is the recorder from the Pittsburgh crash of a Boeing 767—a crash you commissioned.

"Yes, Minister Michelet, he must be found and eliminated at once. We have no time to waste. Therefore, this is how we shall proceed. Paul, you set up a code red manhunt using crack units of the secret services and the anti-terrorist police. I would suggest sealing off an area twenty kilometers in diameter with its center here.

"Get on the phone now, Paul. Every second lost exponentially increases our risk of disaster. Minister, have yourself taken by helicopter to Grenoble. Keep your daughter in your custody until I have time to interview her. Monsieur Haussmann, please put your suitcase in my trunk and move Minister Michelet's car. I am ready to depart."

"Wait," growled Haussmann. "Wait just a minute. Payment upon successful completion of the job. That was the deal, wasn't it?"

"Don't argue with me, Monsieur Haussmann. It would not only be tasteless but quite unhealthy for our collaboration. My part of the job, the part for which you hired me, has been carried out flawlessly. I am not willing to pay the price for your leader's blunder. Minister Michelet made a serious mistake, as I'm sure he would be the first to admit. However, his mistake can still be corrected—if you don't upset the amicable working relationship among us."

"I'm not paying you until—"

"Pay him," Delors said. "He is right. We also need his help. You haven't lost any money, Albert. You're probably a net winner already. Don't get greedy."

"Pay him," Michelet said, tossing Haussmann his keys. "And move my car. We don't have time to squabble."

"Where are you going, Mr. Claussen?" Haussmann said cynically. "I would think a quarter billion dollars at least buys me the right to ask you that?"

"I intend to visit Place Maubert, Twelve."

"That's foolish," Michelet said. "He will have learned from my daughter by now that I know who he is. He won't go back there."

"I quite agree," Claussen said coolly. "Which means he won't have removed such things as address books. Leave this part of the clean-up to me. I assure you, gentlemen, that when the sun rises, Steven LeConte will not be alive to watch it."

∗   ∗   ∗

They made their way through the woods, staying out of the dense underbrush and taking the high road wherever they had the chance. Speed now, stealth later, that had been Warner's idea. Once the search began, they would have to depend on any cover they could find.

Their route took them into a depression in the forest floor. The ground fog was as thick as mustard gas, the undergrowth tugged like barbed wire at their boots. Their pace slowed. Steven used the opportunity to talk. "I've got this studio on Rue Monge," he said, "a sublet of a sublet. I was supposed to register it with the cops but I never did. I was thinking I should go there if we make it to Paris. I'll drop you off somewhere along the way. You can take a cab to your car, then drive to that Air Force base in Germany like you were planning."

"You should come with me, Steven. Staying in France serves no purpose other than getting you killed."

"I can't just walk out on Nicole. The studio will be safe for a while. I'll figure something out."

"Don't be suicidal. You told me Nicole doesn't know anything. Nothing will happen to her. You have to take care of yourself."

"I said I can't leave her, okay?"

They came up out of the fog. The moon was bright; almost too bright. They started jogging again, and did not speak.

∗   ∗   ∗

When they found the motorcycle, the first wave of helicopters was already rumbling across the forested hills of Fontainebleau.

"Give me a hand," Steven said as he leaned over and grabbed the handlebars. "Let's get this heavy mother rolling."

Warner helped. Steven jumped on and hit the starter. Warner climbed onto the rear. "Hold on tight," Steven shouted. "I'm not stopping for anything."

"Go!"

Steven gave gas. He resisted the temptation to turn on the headlight. Helicopters were coming. He didn't want to give them any greater advantage than they already had.

The huge puddle they had walked around earlier spanned the trail ahead, its surface rippling in the moonlight. Warner's arms closed around him. The man was reading his thoughts.

Steven hit the throttle instead of the brakes. The bike fish-tailed in the mud, then accelerated powerfully. He leaned forward over the bars and slammed into the water at 70 miles an hour. The rear of the bike started to hydroplane, but they reached the other side before he lost control.

They roared through the trees until they came to the end of the path, then turned on to the potholed gravel road. They were making good time until a shaft of light descended from the sky and swept across the road several hundred yards ahead.

Steven slowed and looked up. It was an ugly scene. Helicopters circled everywhere, searching forests and fields with bright lights.

Ahead, on the gentle rise he was about to climb, a blazing halo appeared. It started coming directly at him down the road.

No time to think, no time to worry about his passenger. He let up on the throttle, stared to his right at a row of passing oaks and turned the wheel when he saw an opening.

The bike hit on the other side of the ditch, plowed forward in deep mud and fell on its side. Pain shot up his leg as he bent around to see where Warner was. The circle of light charged past them, still on the road. He could see men inside the glass front of the helicopter.

Too close.

He lay and waited for the sound of the chopper to fade. The bird was still flying away from him, he could see it, but for some reason the engine sounds seemed to be growing louder.

Through a gap in the foliage, he caught a terrifying glimpse of another chopper. Its twin searchlights skimmed above the trees as it approached from the other direction, scouring both sides of the road.

He heard Warner whisper nearby. He threw his jacket over the Harley's chrome and dove under a bush.

The lights closed in, turning, probing, burning like a scythes of fire. The chopper stopped overhead. The forest around them lit up bright as day.

Steven held his breath for what seemed an eternity. At last the chopper moved on. A break! A miracle! They hadn't been seen! Fresh resolve pushed him to his knees. The fight wasn't over yet. Not by a long shot. He gritted his teeth and rolled over to check on Warner.

"You all right?" he whispered.

"Banged up but all right," Warner said. "How about you?"

"The same."

"That was good driving, Steven."

"Thanks. Let's get out of here."

"Just a minute. Look how they're changing their helicopter formations. Take in the scope of their entire action. What do you see?"

"Airborne assholes," Steven said. "Let's go."

"Listen to me. They're setting up a perimeter, putting a road block on every donkey path that leads out of here. We'll have to try to slip by them on foot. They've got us in a noose."

"Forget it," Steven said. "Those dogs and about ten thousand of their pals will be back. I've had enough of them for one day."

"We don't have a choice."

"You're wrong."

Steven pulled Warner to his feet and righted the motorcycle by himself. "Hold on tighter this time."

"I jumped," Warner said, helping him drag the Harley across the ditch and back onto the road. "I'd like you to tell me what you're going to do."

"No. Get on." Steven hit the throttle as soon as Warner's arms locked around him.

Warner was right. They were setting up roadblocks. A mile ahead, a helicopter landed on the road. Another remained in the air, hovering directly above. Another break. The noise around the roadblock would be deafening. They were unlikely to see the bike if he didn't use his light, and they wouldn't hear it if their ears were filled with the clatter of their own choppers.

They came out of a long S curve. Moonlight shone on the tracks that crossed the road half a mile ahead. Steven reached around, poked Warner and pointed. Warner must have understood, because he poked him back.

The bars were up, no trains coming just now. It was a double track, a main line, concrete ties and electric lines overhead.

Which side did the trains run on? Or did they run on one side in particular?

How the hell should he know? He eased the bike between the first set of rails and accelerated. The vibrations caused by the ties were horrendous, almost enough to knock them off the bike, but when they reached a certain speed, the ride grew more tolerable.

He was beginning to get comfortable when another blinding light on this night of lights swept around a curve and bore down on them. He heard Warner's yell above the roar of the Harley. He couldn't respond, no time, but he knew they were all right. Just before the train exploded out of the darkness, it had lit up the rails in front of it, those on the right a little more brightly than those on the left. So let it come. Don't look at it and get blinded but let it come. It wasn't on their track.

Steven ducked down to handle-bar level, anticipating violent turbulence. Good idea. The air pushed ahead of the freight hit him like a wall of water. Deafening sounds exploded in his ears. The bike seemed to lift off the ties for an instant, the vibration of the ride replaced by the crescendo of sonic fury beside them.

And then it passed as quickly as it had come. The night was calm, the bike settled into its roadbed rhythm.

Glowing signals, green, red. Lights beside the tracks, lights on the pylons for the overhead lines, light from the moon sculpting the tracks into gently curving rivers. They were making progress, making time.

Another headlight, another train. This one was more difficult to read, coming straight at them over the crest of a hill instead of rounding a bend. It seemed to be coming faster, too.

Steven slowed the bike. The vibrations increased until it was hard to hang on. He stared into the blinding light, but could not see which track the train was on.

Warner banged on his back with a fist. He was trying to tell him something. Steven took off his helmet flung it away.

He felt Warner's breath lashing his ear, hot in the cold wind. His words had the ferocity of a shout, but the noise reduced their volume to a whisper.

He thought he heard, "Wrong track! Wrong track!"

No time for clarification, he would take Warner's word for it. He was doing 80, Frog trains did 200. He could see a crossing ahead, the bars down and red signals pulsing. He would have a 20 foot stretch of road where the asphalt was built up to the level of the rails, 20 feet to make a perfect maneuver and change tracks without dumping the bike.

But could he get to the crossing ahead of the train?

He didn't know.

Pilot's Dawn

He buried the throttle, lowered his head and engaged the oncoming behemoth in a race to the crossing. No big difference whether you were doing 120 or standing still if you hit a train head-on.

He got there first, only by yards but what the hell, swerved to the right and landed between the parallel set of tracks.

It was an express. When it had passed, he felt Warner's hand squeezing his ear lobe. "We're outside the search perimeter. Get the fuck off this line."

Steven smiled to himself. He reached around and patted the side of Warner's helmet.

They rounded a bend. There was a crossing 300 yards ahead, and the gates were up.

Steven took the exit fast to avoid the horrible vibrations of slowing down while driving on the ties. Warner whacked him on the shoulder as he turned the Harley onto a deserted secondary road and headed for Paris.

"It's guys like you who win wars," Warner shouted. "Nothing but fuck-ups in peace time, but you're the ones who win the fucking wars."

"This is war," Steven screamed back. "Count your blessings."

Chapter Thirty-Five

For Sophie it was a moment of relief when, shortly after 3:00 a.m., a soft knock sounded at Steven's door.

She glanced toward the room in which Nicole had fallen fast asleep, wondering if she should wake her.

No, she decided, she would let her catch up on her rest. She knew this was selfish, but she couldn't help it: she wanted Steven and Warner to herself for a little while first.

She left the Mozart piano concerto she had dug out of Steven's otherwise deplorable music collection on, picked up her snifter and hurried to the door.

All the things she should have thought and done but had not hit her in one terrifying moment when she opened and found herself standing face to face with a stranger. He made no attempt to push his way into the apartment, but when she tried to shut the door he blocked it with his foot.

"What do you want?" she said. "Get out of here before I call the police. If it's a phone you need, there's one just across the square."

The man smiled, thinly, arrogantly. His eyes seemed to bore into her soul, intelligent eyes, cruel eyes. She recognized Hans-Walter Claussen from the Bonn photograph. She also recognized him from her nightmares: he was the Face of Evil that had haunted her since the Holocaust.

She hoped she hadn't let on that she recognized him, though she feared she had. She said, "Look, I want you to leave. I'm not going to ask you again. I'm going to count to three, and then I'm going to scream so loud half the Paris police force will be here in seconds."

His smile remained unchanged, as if it were frozen on his taut perversely handsome face. "This *is* an unexpected pleasure. Madame Sophie Marx, the world-famous journalist, a professional whose keen analyses I have admired for years. One cannot help but wonder how you became associated with a nobody like Steven LeConte."

"Who are you?" she said harshly, trying to hide her fear with a firm steady voice. If you've come for Steven LeConte, I am not associated with him. He is out of town until tomorrow. We are acquaintances. He looks after my flat when I'm away and I return the favor."

The man didn't seem interested in what she was saying. He pushed his way inside and locked the door. "You know who I am, don't you, Madame Marx?"

Sophie backed up, uncertain what to do. "No, of course I don't."

"I asked you a question," he said, snarling through his smile. "When I ask you a question, I want a truthful answer. You know who I am, don't you?"

"What kind of nonsense is this? I told you I did not know who you were."

"The civilized approach you seem to favor in your writings is not working, is it, Madame Marx? I suppose we'll have to try something else."

She gasped when she saw the long slender blade. "One cry out of you, Madame Marx, and you will force me to do what is otherwise unnecessary. You see, I do not have to kill you. I do not particularly wish to kill you. I would rather trade your life for some other type of service, say editorial input on my memoirs. I guarantee it would be the most interesting assignment you have ever had, a fitting way to cap a brilliant career. But, as they say, let's make no bones about it. If you do not wish to live, that is not a problem either. The choice, Madame Marx, is yours. Now, who am I and what do you know about me?"

She stumbled back toward the sofa, fighting to keep up some meager semblance of composure. She sat and poured more Armagnac into her snifter. He sat across from her in Steven's favorite armchair, knife drawn and pale blue eyes unwavering.

In that moment Sophie knew she had no way out. She was going to die. But something else flashed in her awareness, a dazzling revelation that gave her the strength to resist despair. Steven and Warner had escaped! Otherwise, Claussen would not be trying to extract information; he would simply have opened the door and killed her. Steven and Warner were on the lam. She couldn't help herself but maybe she *could* help them. If she succeeded, her last deception would be her best.

Claussen said, "I'm on a tight schedule, Madame Marx. Forgive me if I insist that we keep our conversation brief. You are going to begin by telling me what you know about me."

Sophie let the tears flow. She shuddered violently. "How? How can I? I don't know you."

Claussen was beginning to lose his patience. "Of course not, Madame Marx. That is why you—the best investigative journalist in Europe, a woman wielding a talent that has brought down Willi Brandt and Giulio Andreotti—just happen to be sitting in the apartment of the man who has cracked the Airbus affair, a man whose only credentials would seem to reside in his shorts. I'm sorry, but to believe your tale one would have to be very naive. I am not prone to naiveté, Madame Marx. I am going to give you one final chance to talk. What do you know about me?"

She started to say something, then stopped. Claussen leaped to his feet, jumped over the coffee table with cat-like agility and sat beside her on the sofa. He wagged his knife back and forth.

She cowered, the move had startled her. She didn't believe he would do anything yet, but she was wrong. He touched the knife to her throat. He had cut her! She felt the hot blood trickling down her neck.

She gasped and tried to writhe away. He grabbed her hair and twisted her head backwards. "Now Madame? Now do you wish to say anything?"

"Okay, let me go."

"Talk first."

"You worked for the KGB," she choked.

He smacked her head against the wall and released her. "More. Quickly."

"You directed Operation Twenty-Six for decades. You never had the opportunity to test it."

"Never? **Never?**" He grabbed her hair again and showed her the stiletto. "I want to know more about myself."

"You…you are testing it now by sabotaging American jetliners for the French. You are being paid for this work."

He smiled and let her go. "And now, Madame, comes the prize-winning question. How much am I being paid. No, let me be more specific. How much am I being paid *tonight*?"

"I…no idea."

"I said, how much?"

"Two hundred fifty million dollars."

"Well what do you know? You guessed right. You hit the jackpot." Claussen smiled. "Now, Madame Marx, you are going to tell me where Steven LeConte is."

"He was supposed to play a—"

"You're dealing with this poorly, Madame Marx. You're still not getting the picture. I have offered you the chance to live. You know where LeConte is or where he is planning to go, just as you knew the details of my own life. He will die, that's not one of the variables we must deal with. Holding back information to save him will accomplish nothing. However, it will make my task of dealing with him a trifle easier, and for that I am willing to let you live out your natural life—in utter silence about the things we have discussed tonight, of course."

The moment she had dreaded for 70 years was near. She was about to leave this life she loved but did not understand, this life she wished desperately to cling to in spite of its cruelties and imperfections. Her tears were real, her words were sincere.

She said, "Mr. Claussen, I do not want to die."

He pushed her down on to the floor, shoved her on her back and straddled her. He tapped the stiletto on her chin. "How strong is your desire to live, Madame Marx? Strong enough to tell me the whereabouts of Steven LeConte?"

"I...I can't."

"Very well. So be it." He ran the stiletto across her neck again, so gently she felt little. But as before, the sensation of hot blood on her skin told her she had been cut. She touched her fingers to the wound, and closed her eyes when she saw them.

"A surface cut," he said. "Don't be squeamish. We'll try your heart next. It's a quite awful, I'm told, to feel the blade violate that reputed source of love and emotion."

He poised the tip above her left breast and drove it an inch into her flesh before withdrawing it. The pain this time was excruciating. She knew it had to be now, she had to tell him what she planned to tell him or she was going to lose consciousness.

"Stop," she pleaded. "Stop, I beg you."

"You're prepared to tell me?"

She gave a reluctant nod.

"Then talk. Where is he?"

"Grenoble. He's going for Nicole. She's with her aunt."

"Thank you, Madame Marx. I'm sorry I can't honor my part of the bargain."

She tried to get up but the blade caught her in the throat and ran her through. She wheezed, flailed and choked on her own blood. But the agony was brief. Soon, a profound peacefulness enveloped her.

She watched Claussen, feeling as if they were both underwater, while he cleaned the knife on her blouse. He stood and started for the door.

She died not knowing if he got there.

Pilot's Dawn

She died believing the door was the exit to the hallway, not the entrance to Steven's bedroom.

*   *   *

If this kid had taken up combat flying, thought Warner, he could have shot down the entire French air force in an afternoon. He hoped he never had to ride on a motorcycle with him again, but he wasn't complaining for now.

As they hurtled toward Paris on dark secondary roads, there were signs everywhere of a great movement of military force into the zone of the manhunt. More helicopters streamed south out of the capital. Huge, low-flying prop planes shook the earth as they passed overhead, transporting what Warner knew were paratroopers. Troop convoys rumbled in the opposite direction down main roads, some passing within a few blocks of their route.

Steven throttled back as they entered the Red Belt, the ring of factories and drab tenements around Paris. He merged with the sporadic traffic, driving anonymously.

They made a 20 mile semi-circle to avoid coming in on a bee-line from the south, crossing the city limits from the north at the Porte de Clignancourt. The white dome of Sacré Coeur rose majestically above an endless sea of rooftops.

The two men hadn't spoken since Warner had given Steven the remaining helmet to hide his blond hair. Presently Steven motioned him to lean in close. "You're wondering why we came all this way"?

"I'm beginning to trust you judgment."

Steven said, "There's some all-night action around Montmartre and Pigalle. Mostly Americans and Germans who think they can get laid. They're easy prey for the crooks and cabbies. We need them both."

"What's your idea?"

"I know where the gypsies hang out. I'll park the bike in harm's way. They'll have it in the back of a trailer in minutes. They'll change the serial number, the paint, everything. It'll be in Romania before anyone here lays eyes on it."

"Cabs?"

"They swarm around Pigalle. You'll see."

"Sounds good."

"Then I guess that's about it. I'm going to let you off up ahead. Walk toward the white church. When you come to a main street, you'll find a cab to take you to your car."

"Steven, I'm going to drive by your studio in case you change your mind. What's your street number on Rue Monge?"

"Forget it, Frank. Things didn't work out. You've got your agenda and I've got mine. Maybe you can open some eyes with your photographs."

"Steven—"

He stopped the bike. "Here's where you get off. Good-bye, Frank."

Warner climbed down. What else was there to say? He couldn't get through to him, couldn't talk reason. It was a lost cause, and it was too goddamn bad. He watched the mud-caked Harley disappear into a small alley. He didn't expect ever to see Steven LeConte again.

Warner discarded his ripped, filthy jacket, straightened his shirt collar and went in search of a cab. There was a healthy contingent of rabble around Place Pigalle, the sort of folks he usually avoided. Tonight he was glad to see them. He sank into their midst and made his way to the Boulevard de Clichy. When he flagged a taxi, the driver didn't bat an eye at his appearance.

*   *   *

Nicole awoke to the sound of people talking. She recognized Sophie's voice and hoped to hear Steven's. Instead she heard a man with a slight German accent threatening Sophie. Her heart began to pound. This could not be happening. She had to keep her wits about her. God, what a way to wake up! What should she do? What *could* she do?

Was there a telephone in the bedroom? She reached over to turn on the bedside light but decided against it. The intruder did not know she was here. Better to keep it that way for now.

No telephone. She remembered now that it was in the kitchen.

She was growing frantic. She would have to find help down in the square. That was it. Help below. She tiptoed to the balcony, opened the French doors and went out, careful not to make a sound.

The square was deserted. It was later than she realized.

She left the balcony doors open and hurried back to the bed. She straightened the quilt and pillows, and put on her sneakers. She could hear the voices again.

Oh, God, this was horrible. A lot seemed to have happened in a short time, none of it good. He was hurting her, and Sophie was making strange noises. Sophie pleaded with him to stop what he was doing. It was heart-rending. It was awful.

"Are you prepared to tell me?" the man said.

A pause.

He said, "Then talk. Where is he?"

"Grenoble," Sophie choked. "He's going for Nicole. She's with her aunt."

The lights went off in Nicole's head. Sophie was trying to save her and Steven!

God, he wasn't really going to kill Sophie, was he?

The man's words dashed her hopes. He said, "I'm sorry but I can't honor my part of the bargain."

A struggle ensued, not very intense. She heard Sophie choking and wheezing.

Nicole began to faint.

No! She must get hold of herself. Sophie was being killed. She must help her!

She started toward the door, not knowing what she would do. Then she heard sounds that made her realize it was too late. She knew those sounds. She had been in the room when her mother died. Some things you never forgot.

The man was whistling quietly. Joints creaked as he got to his feet. Oh, God, he was going to search the apartment!

Footsteps came toward the bedroom, footsteps on parquet that echoed like bombshells in her head. Still fighting to stay quiet, she ran on tip toes to the balcony, went out and shut the doors behind her. She spun to the side, staying close to the building so he wouldn't see her if he looked out. She heard the bedroom door opening. The room lights came on, illuminating the balcony and stripping her of the protection of night.

She could hear him rummaging around inside now, yanking open drawers. Would he come out here?

She heard people. She looked down on the square. Several noisy teenagers were strolling by, shoving each other and laughing. A big help they would be.

She felt paralyzed. The footsteps were coming again. She could not cower in the shadows until he found her. She had to do something.

There was only one place to go. She climbed out on the narrow ledge and started moving as fast as she could toward the corner of the building.

Her foot hit a piece of lose stucco. She slipped, gasped, but managed to hold on.

She reached the corner, found a foothold and began turning it just as the intruder stepped outside. Her foot came off the ledge, the foot she had already slung around the corner of the building. She bit her lip and tottered. More stucco rained down.

One of the teenagers let out a booming laugh. The man looked to his right first, toward the kids. Where he looked next, Nicole did not know.

She was out of sight around the corner, legs shaking and heart trying to bump her off the wall.

*   *   *

The cabby was French. He spoke English he said he had learned in Trinidad. "Hey, wake up, buddy. Place Maubert right here. You say you want out here?"

Warner opened his eyes as they drove slowly down one of the boulevards flanking the deserted square. This was the right spot, though it didn't resemble Place Maubert during the busy morning, when he had come to Sophie's flat for the guns. About the only thing the same was the sign above the Métro station.

His car was parked on a side street. He'd written down the name, but couldn't recall it. He was about to tell the cabby to let him out here when he glimpsed a lone man walking through the shadows on the far side of the square. The man wore an informal coat like the one Claussen had worn when he arrived at Michelet's. His hair was combed straight back, and he carried himself with the same confident insouciance. Could it be?

"Pull in that alley," said Warner. "Hurry."

"The sir wakes up like a watch dog. Will do, sir."

The cab turned off the square and stopped. Warner didn't have change. He paid the cabby three times the amount on his meter and got out dragging his pack.

"Don't drive back through the square, understand? Understand? Drive off slowly. Get going."

"Will not drive there, sir."

Warner raced to Place Maubert. Too late. The man was gone. He heard an engine starting, heard a car pulling away. And then the night was calm.

He let out a deep breath he hadn't realized he was holding. That was that. He would never know if the man was who he appeared to be or a figment of Warner's fevered imagination; never know what he would have done if it had been Claussen.

He was turning around to go when the clatter of debris raining down a wall distracted him. He noticed light in the third story flat of Sophie's apartment building. Steven's flat, if he wasn't mistaken.

He felt an intense burst of annoyance. Could that careless bugger have gone up there? If so he really was trying to get himself killed. What should he do? His irritation level was climbing toward the red line when he heard the clatter of debris again. It seemed to come from near Steven's balcony.

He stared at the dark walls and windows to either side. He spotted a shadowy figure on a narrow ledge, making its way toward the light. He approached cautiously, remaining across the street, alert for new arrivals in the square.

When the figure came within a few feet of the wrought-iron balcony rail, he could see that it was a girl. She seemed to be intent on sneaking into Steven's flat. She slipped, almost fell, managed to grab hold of the rail. When she hoisted herself on to the balcony, the light from the door momentarily illuminated her face. He recognized Nicole Michelet from the photographs Sophie Marx had shown him that morning.

He bolted for the apartment door. It was locked. He hit the button beside the name LeConte and waited for a voice to answer him through the tiny speaker. No response, so he began to talk to the microphone. "Nicole, I am a friend of Steven's. Do you understand English? You must let me in. It's important for Steven. Let me in!"

Nothing. "Nicole, listen to me. Danger! You must get out of there. You will be harmed. Now, please, let me in!"

Finally there came a click as the heavy door unlocked. Warner ran up the loud marble staircase to the third floor. Steven's door was unlocked. He didn't wait for an invitation to go inside.

Pilot's Dawn

He stopped in his tracks when he saw the body sprawled in a pool of blood. Nicole cowered against the wall in terror. He bent over Sophie and felt for a pulse in her throat. No good. She was dead.

"Claussen," he murmured as he walked to Nicole. "He was here. You're lucky to be alive."

She was too shaken to speak or to move. He put an arm around her. "Come, Nicole, we must go. Steven is waiting."

"Steven…Steven…he is okay?"

"Yes. He's in his studio on Rue Monge. Do you know where it is?"

"Yes."

"Do you have a key?"

"No."

"Come."

"But we cannot…we cannot leave her here like this. We must call someone."

"It's too dangerous. Nicole, you must come with me now, very calmly, as if nothing has happened."

Warner turned out the lights and extended his arm. "Come."

* * *

Steven showered and dressed in the few things he kept at his Rue Monge studio, a sanctum he told Sophie would someday produce great things. Well, at least it was producing a place to hide. He had just begun to brainstorm on his options for the near future when the buzzer from the street entrance sounded. It sent a shock through his gut. He grabbed his pistol from the table and paced.

Who the hell was it? Only a few friends knew he worked here. He hadn't registered with the police, so he didn't see how Michelet and his buddies could have found the place yet. And if they had, they wouldn't have bothered to buzz. One of the SDECE guys would have picked the lock down below, and they would have come bursting in like a pack of mad dogs.

Which meant it was probably Warner. He must have telephoned Sophie and gotten the address.

Well, he appreciated Warner's concern. But this was going too far. Warner would try to convince him to escape, which was a waste of everyone's time. Warner needed to get the hell out of France before someone figured out he was here; and Steven needed to work on a plan for getting in touch with Nicole. Two agendas, as he had said on the bike.

He went to the window and peeked through the shutters. It was Warner, all right. He could see his rental Peugeot parked near the corner. The odd thing was, he could also see Warner sitting behind the wheel. So who had buzzed?

He craned his sore neck for a better view of the sidewalk down below. When he saw Nicole, his heart skipped a beat. He ran down the stairs and opened. She fell into his arms, weeping, trembling and too upset to tell him what had happened. He held her close and stroked her hair and didn't push her to talk. There would be time. For now he was just grateful and hugely relieved they were together again.

Warner knocked a few minutes later. The three of them went upstairs to Steven's tiny studio. Steven was ready to talk now, to find out what had happened, but Warner wouldn't let him. He said, "Sit down. We have to tell you something and it isn't good. When I got to Place Maubert to pick up my car, a man who resembled Claussen was crossing the square. He disappeared before I could be sure it was him. Then I saw Nicole climbing onto your balcony. I went to your apartment. Claussen had been there. Sophie was dead."

"It was my fault," Nicole cried. "I came to see you, Steven. I ran away from Grenoble and came to see you. I decided we should do what you said and go live somewhere else. She heard me at your door. She came down to keep me company."

Steven couldn't breathe. He sat at the table, dumbstruck.

"Sophie's dead?" he whispered numbly.

"Yes," Warner said. "I'm sorry. She was a great lady."

"Nicole—"

"Yes, Steven."

"Nicole...you were there?"

She nodded between sobs.

"How did you escape?"

Steven realized he was speaking English to her for the first time. He didn't feel like switching to French.

Nicole struggled to regain her composure. "I went out on the...how do you say, Mr. Warner?"

"Ledge."

"Yes. I was in your room, Steven. I was taking a rest. When I woke up, the man was out there with Sophie. I wanted to call but there was no telephone in the bedroom. I went out on the balcony to find help, but there was no one in the square. I should have done something. I was a coward. I was...afraid."

"You did the right thing," Warner said. "If you had gone into the living room, he would have killed you, too."

Steven was incredulous. He said, "Didn't he come looking for you?"

"Yes. That's when I went out on the ledge. That terrible man, he came into your room. Then he came out on the balcony. He almost saw me but I got around the corner of the building first."

Steven slapped the table. He was crying and he didn't care. "Okay, Nicole," he blurted out, "this is it, now you're going to hear it all. About me, about your father, about us. I haven't been able to tell you. I might not be able to tell you tomorrow. Right now I can tell you."

Nicole stood beside him. She put an arm around his head and stroked his hair. "Steven, it's okay. Sophie told me everything. She told me how you and I met. She told me about the terrible things my father has done. Steven, she tried to save our lives. I heard her tell the man after he had done all sorts of horrible things to her that she would tell him the truth. You know what she told him?"

Steven was too choked up to answer. He shook his head.

"She told him you were going to Grenoble. She told him I was with my aunt. But I was in the bedroom, Steven, and she knew you weren't going to Grenoble because she was waiting for you to come home."

Steven just shook his head.

"It's okay," Nicole said. "It's okay what you did, Steven. It's a good thing someone checked up on my father. If the other part is true, I don't care anymore that you deceived me."

"The other part?" he whispered.

"That you love me."

"Nicole, it's true. I'm going to spend the rest of my life proving to you that it's true."

Nicole leaned over and hugged him. They wept together. He couldn't believe it. Sophie had not only sent Claussen on a wild goose chase; she had given him one last very special gift. She had solved his dilemma for him. It was too much for any one person to do. He was devastated. She was the light of his life. He could not accept that she was gone.

Warner said, "Steven, I don't mean to be insensitive, but the rest of your life isn't going to be long enough to crow about if we don't get out of France. There's nothing holding you here now. Both of you, come with me."

Steven stood up and walked in a daze to the window. The pain he felt just kept getting worse. Then, deep down where it hurt, he felt the stirrings of a new emotion being born, a white-hot rage like nothing he had ever felt. What did Warner have in mind for him *after* they got out of France? Steven wasn't going to get involved in maybe propositions and half-ass scenarios. He wasn't going to allow this one to be turned over to the William Fairchilds of the world. He would go back to the States when he had proof, the sort of proof that would insure that Claussen and the others went down.

Pilot's Dawn

He said, "I'm not going back to the States with you, Frank. I want you to know that."

"Then what the hell are you going to do? Hole up here until they find you?"

"No. I'm going to finish the job we started and I fucked up. The evidence we need might be in Claussen's house. I'm going to have a look."

"You don't know where Claussen lives."

"I do."

"How is that possible?"

"Sophie. She made a lot of things possible."

"Where *does* he live?"

"In a farmhouse in the eastern part of Germany. Here's what you can do for me. You can give us a ride to the Air Force base in Germany and get Nicole some sort of protection there. I'll do the rest. I'll get you your evidence."

Warner said, "Steven, I've got a lot riding on this one, too. I think our chances will be better if we work as a team. Now, grab every map of Europe you've got in this place and let's get out of here."

Chapter Thirty-Six

Warner's rental car wasn't a station wagon, but you could fold the rear seat forward. This extended the luggage compartment from the backs of the front seats all the way through the trunk to the end of the car.

Steven and Nicole were able to lie down and stretch out. With blankets and maps from Steven's studio, and well-arranged articles of clothing from Warner's cold weather bag, they could cover themselves and hide from view whenever Warner came to an *autoroute* toll booth.

Driving out of Paris, they had debated whether to take the *autoroute*, the high-speed expressway, or less traveled but slower country roads. They had decided it made sense to go for broke, to try to get across the Belgian border, scarcely two hours away, before the manhunt was made public and extended to the rest of France.

They were near Valenciennes, the last French town before the border, when the 6:00 a.m. news forced a change of plans.

"Frank, this is bad," Steven said. "Get off the road. I mean *off* the road. Down that embankment. Forget the border. They're looking for this car."

Warner pulled onto the shoulder and turned off his headlights. The morning was chilly, perhaps 40 degrees. It was still dark, but the metallic gray arc of dawn glowed to the east.

"Drive on down there," Steven said. "You can make it."

"When these trucks pass," Warner said.

The news droned on in French. Warner hated not being able to understand it. But there were a few words that rang loud and clear through the sonorous cascade of meaningless sounds, words such as Marx, LeConte and Nicole Michelet.

The Belgian border was just five miles ahead. Five miles, he thought, could be a long way.

The news report ended, replaced by irritating European rock. Warner checked his rear view mirror. No one coming. He eased the Peugeot down the steep embankment and bumped onto the service road. He came to an intersection and opted for an unmarked two-lane.

"Steven, what did they say?"

"Everything we don't need to hear. The police are looking for me. They think I stabbed Sophie and kidnapped Nicole. Can you believe it? They also say I might be in a rental Peugeot, the model and color of this one. They gave a license number. I assume it's ours. How the hell could they know that, Frank?"

"I don't know. Claussen must have recognized the CVR as a part from one of the Boeing crashes and taken if from there."

"But how?"

"Steven, it's pointless to speculate. It doesn't change our situation. All that matters is that we're in serious trouble. I think you should know that, Nicole. I'm not just talking about me and Steven. These are desperate men, your father included. If we are taken into custody, they'll find a way to justify getting rid of all three of us. As I said, we're in serious trouble."

"I know," Nicole answered. "I don't want to think about it, Mr. Warner, but I know what you say is true."

She was, Warner thought, showing a lot of composure after what she had been just experienced.

"It gets worse," Steven said. "They described me and Nicole. The police apologize for delays at airports, toll booths, ferries and border crossings. And they're involving Interpol. They'll be looking for us all over Europe."

"Shit."

"Amen. Listen, Frank, here's another question for you. If they announced Nicole's name, why aren't they mentioning you?"

"Because they don't want to alert our government. I will fall into the Sophie Marx category if we're caught."

"Meaning?"

"You killed me for the car."

"Terrific. Let's not get caught."

"Good idea."

Headlights were coming toward them, bouncing eerily through the early morning mist. The tree-lined road was narrow and the approaching vehicle large. Warner turned off on a dirt tractor path to let the aging fertilizer truck clatter past. He was about to continue his aimless drive when spotted something that jolted his mind into high gear. He pointed into the mist. "See it?"

"What?" Steven said.

"Just look."

"The wind sock?"

"That's right. Where there's a sock, there's usually a plane."

"You know how to fly?"

"Yes."

"Well, why not?" Steven said. "I don't see any other way out of here."

Warner slammed the Peugeot into reverse, bumped back onto the two-lane and turned up another dirt road that ran in the general direction they wanted to go.

* * *

The air sock was attached to a sawed-off telephone pole at the end of a narrow grass strip. Warner got out and walked the field. There were signs of landings, depressions in the soft earth, but none looked recent.

Steven came up beside him. "Well? Where's the plane?"

"Either in that old barn with the tanks out front or somewhere else for the winter. Shall we have a look?"

The entrance was secured with a fat padlock. Warner pried one side of the rickety wooden door open and shined his flashlight through the crack. There was an old yellow bi-plane inside, the prettiest thing he had seen since Claire came home.

"Go get your maps out of the car," he told Steven. "I'll need to do some plotting before we take off. And bring your gun. Screw on the silencer and shoot the lock off. Carefully."

"There's really a plane in there?"

"There really is. A Boeing Stearman, if I'm not mistaken."

"A Boeing, huh? Holy Christ, Warner, when I first met you I was worried you were like my father. It turns out you're crazier than all of us."

"I probably *was* like your father. Hurry."

While Steven trotted back to the car, Warner looked over the three red tanks just outside the barn door. They were mounted high off the ground on wooden stilts that were laced together like railroad trestles. He climbed the first ladder, pulled down the hose from the number one tank and sniffed it. Some kind of pesticide, forget that one.

He climbed another ladder, very rickety, and felt around for the hose to the second tank. Nothing, it had been removed. He looked at the tank more closely and saw that the bottom had rusted out.

The third tank had the word "Essence" scrawled across it in black letters. The ladder looked sturdier than the last.

The hose was in good shape. He took a sniff. Aviation fuel. There were no dials or gauges to indicate the level of the liquid inside. He climbed on top of the tank, unscrewed the cap and shined his light down the filler hole.

The strangest things, he thought, could look beautiful in the right circumstances. Such as a battered yellow crop duster; or the reflection of liquid in a dark hole.

He glanced across the field at Steven, who had the maps in his back pocket and was holding his automatic pistol carelessly while he leaned in the window to say something to Nicole. She raised her head, and he kissed her.

"Get your ass over here," Warner shouted. "When we're in the air, you can nuzzle all you want."

Steven flipped him the bird without turning around. He kissed Nicole again, then made up for lost time with a sprint across the field. "Stay up there, Warner," he said. "No telling where this thing'll go."

Warner, safety advocate for the nation, was still trying to scramble down from the tank, picturing the ricochet hitting 500 gallons of aviation fuel and sending him up in a fireball, when he was greeted by the dull report of a silenced automatic pistol.

"Goddammit," he mumbled. He was used to being around people who shared his values; or pretended to.

By the time he got to the bottom of the ladder, Steven had already opened one side of the creaking double door and stood staring at the old yellow bird.

Warner picked up the lock, which lay in the wet grass with a neat round hole through its center. The kid could shoot. The kid could do a lot of things. Inspiring confidence wasn't one of them.

"Jesus Christ, Frank, is this thing gonna fly?"

"You bet she's gonna fly, Steven. The old Stearman's still in use all over the world. She might not meet FAA regulations, but if the truth be known, not much does these days."

"So, how old's this crate?"

"I'd say, about sixty years. But look at this. It's been retrofitted with a Pratt and Whitney R 985 engine. That means four hundred fifty horses and not too much oil consumption. We'll fly out to one of those deserted islands off the Dutch coast, put her down and cover her before they get any kind of a search organized, then fly our final leg in the dark."

"This thing looks like a museum piece."

"Let's immortalize her. Give me a hand."

Steven motioned for Nicole, but here Warner drew the line. He said, "I want her to stay with the car and keep watch. We're going to be concentrating on getting this airplane ready. We need her to do something useful."

"I thought maybe she could be useful here. You know, load the old barge up, things like that."

"Not yet."

Warner met Nicole halfway across the strip and had a word with her. He spoke gently. Here was a young girl being hunted down by her own father. Even in her fear, confusion and sadness, she was pleasant to look at, pleasant to talk to. She graciously accepted his explanation of why she needed to stay with the car. He liked her. It hurt him deeply to know that she would probably come to harm before this day was over.

Warner found Steven going through tools on a greasy workbench. "By the way, Frank," he said, "how much fuel did you find?"

"Plenty, a lot more than the aircraft will hold. I'd like to convert those pesticide tanks under the wings into supplementary fuel tanks."

"You think we can make it to Claussen's without refueling?"

"Easily. We've got less than a thousand kilometers to cover and prevailing winds at our tail. We'll need some oil, but that's it. We'll take a few liters with us and top up when we land on the island. Come here. You get started flushing those tanks. I'll rig a fuel delivery system."

* * *

Nicole put on Steven's other baseball cap, the one he wasn't wearing. She got out and sat on the trunk of the Peugeot. Every once in a while she glanced at the barn. The door was open. She could see Steven and Warner working on the airplane. She had no idea what they were doing, but whatever it was gave her reason to hope they might somehow escape her father's noose.

To the east the sun was rising, transforming the cold gray mist along the horizon into a blanket of orange and pink. She tried to concentrate on the gentle undulations of the hills near Belgian border; tried to find some semblance of inner peace.

But she found none. She was grappling with the realization that her father had been involved in Sophie's murder and the deaths of thousands of innocent people.

She did not begin to feel better until she saw Steven and Warner pushing the old yellow bi-plane out of the barn and into the first light of the sun. They rolled it next to the row of tanks. Steven climbed a ladder and passed Warner a hose.

When the fueling was completed, Steven climbed into the cockpit.

Warner took hold of the propeller and heaved.

Nothing.

He did it again and again. On the sixth or seventh try, she saw smoke belch from the engine. Several tries later the engine coughed and sputtered to life.

Steven climbed down and shook Warner's hand. She was smiling and waving at them when an unshaven man with a scythe stepped out of the woods. The man stopped in front of her, staring with small suspicious eyes.

"What's going on over there at Bonier's hangar," he growled. "You know those guys?"

"Yes, I do. I am with them." She was frightened, but this time she was determined not to fold in the face of danger. She looked him over as if *he* were the intruder.

"Well, what in the hell are they doing?" the man snapped.

"Do you work for Monsieur Bonier?" Nicole asked.

"No, I don't work for him. I look after his property when he is in Paris."

"Oh, I see. Then he must certainly have told you about the service on his crop duster."

"What?"

"Monsieur Bonier engaged Churchill Aviation, an English firm that specializes in aging planes, to take over the maintenance and service."

"What are you talking about?"

"I'm surprised you don't know. Monsieur Bonier is adamant that the repairs be done right this time. His airplane might have to be flown to England if it can't be fixed here. He has of course given his permission."

"Oh, really?" The man scowled, then turned and disappeared into the forest as swiftly as he had come.

Nicole drove to the barn and reported the incident.

"He'll be back," Warner said from the wing. "Let's pick up the pace. You two start transferring things we need from the car to the plane—maps, blankets, four liters of oil, the minimum. Weight is a problem. I'm going to drain some fuel. When you finish, pull the car into the barn and drape the lock over the hasp. Let's move!"

∗ ∗ ∗

After his surprise encounter with Sophie Marx, Claussen drove toward Grenoble. It took him less than an hour on the car phone, arm-twisting former members of his Cold War network in Washington and the airline industry, to reach the conclusion that Frank Warner was the source of the CVR. Warner's involvement, together with the knowledge Sophie had managed to acquire, meant that his adversaries were more numerous, and in higher positions, than he had initially believed.

When a call to Delors produced the shocking news that Nicole Michelet was no longer at her aunt's, Claussen decided the hour had struck to end his association with his partners and slip off to his second home in Bolivia.

He faced only one obstacle: French Intelligence, should they divine his traitorous intentions before he made it out of Europe. For this reason, he knew he must scrupulously disguise what he was doing.

To feign his continued active participation in defense of the conspiracy, he fed Delors his information on Sophie Marx's murder and on Warner's arrival in France. To emphasize the intensity of his commitment, he came up with a brilliant scenario even Haussmann seemed to like: the French police would attribute the murder of the journalist and the "kidnaping" of Mademoiselle Michelet to Steven LeConte, an American drifter.

Claussen was certain they would use Warner's rental car when they made their break. They wouldn't get far with the entire European law enforcement apparatus looking for them. They would soon be arrested and taken into custody, either in France or in another Common Market country. Once that happened, Delors and the SDECE would know how to deal with them, how to make things look "right."

"And you, Walter?" Delors asked. "What are your intentions?"

Claussen was approaching the *autoroute* intersection at Beaune. Instead of continuing south toward Grenoble, he turned east on A36 and headed for Switzerland. "I shall continue to supplement the work of your forces. Quietly, of course. This LeConte character seems to be a careless type. His address book reads like a road map to his circle of acquaintances in Europe. If he and the others should somehow manage to slip through your net, which I doubt is possible, rest assured they won't slip through mine."

Delors said, "We can still pull this off, can't we, Walter?"

"Absolutely. Judging from what I've been able to learn in the States, no one suspects the real reason Warner is here. He told his staff at the NTSB he was in need of a brief vacation. I'm sure that's what he's told everyone else."

Claussen chuckled and pushed his foot a little deeper into the accelerator. "Who could blame him, Paul? He has been rather busy since May."

"What about Sophie Marx? She can't have been working on this alone?"

"On the contrary. The reason she was using a bum like LeConte was to keep every aspect of her story under wraps. Now she's taken it to the grave with her. Don't worry. LeConte will be soon to follow."

"I still feel uneasy. I want you to keep searching for anyone else who might know or suspect—and take the appropriate action."

"Of course I will, Paul. Remember. Disclosure would hurt me as badly as you. Now, let me tell you something that will help you relax. The United States is planning to devastate Iraq in the early hours of Monday. Once they've killed a few hundred thousand civilians with the entire Arab world looking on, they'll be our best allies in making sure the truth is never known.

"Now, Paul, go to work. Turn your dogs loose. Have every border crossing sealed. Have every airport, railroad station and ferry dock watched. Have every road patrolled. Alert Interpol and don't neglect to actively involve your citizenry. Get descriptions out of the fugitives and their car. Saturate the air waves with bulletins and photographs. Depict this as a truly revolting crime perpetrated by an American derelict, the type of person who poses a danger to everything decent—everything French. If you do that you'll have very little to worry about."

"Perhaps, Walter. I must say one more thing before we end this conversation. I'm still a little stunned by the incompetence of Michelet. His daughter was an obvious Achilles heel. Neither Albert nor I can fathom how he let it come to this."

"Nor can I, Paul. But first things first. We'll have time to deal with him later."

"Good night, Walter."

"Good night, Paul. Good luck."

Claussen deactivated his cellular phone. He crossed the Swiss border at Basel and stopped for gas and food. He looked at the sky while the attendant was filling up the large Mercedes tank. High pressure had moved in behind the cold front. He could feel it in the dry crisp air, and see it in the stars blinking hard and cold as diamonds. The day would break clear, the driving would remain good, while he attended to money and automobile business in Switzerland.

He forced himself to eat, as he always did during periods of peak stress, then got back in his car, selected a classical station and proceeded toward Zurich.

As the night wore on and the driving became monotonous, he let himself fantasize about the future. Sometime tomorrow night he would pick up his memoirs and the boxes of records from old KGB and Stasi files, all of which he kept at his home near Altenhagen. He would then travel as Reinhart Schmidt from Berlin to La Paz, taking a backwards route over Asia in case they were on the look-out for him in the West.

Once he reached Bolivia, the good life would begin. He had set up a second identity in an elegant suburb outside of La Paz at the beginning of Operation 26, a safety valve in case he ever had to flee. He owned a villa, kept a small permanent staff, and had close friends in the government, police and military he had treated well over the years. He activated his second identity and touched base with his second home every few months. He had been doing this for the last thirty years. Cautious and intelligent men did not get caught. It was the fools, like Michelet.

Claussen, or rather Reinhart Schmidt, was known, simply, as a man on the go. Now he would be seen as retiring at last.

Retiring not to shrivel and die but to complete his memoirs in a German prose unequaled since Nietzsche—and to watch his revelations shock the world while the CIA blundered to new heights trying to find out where he was.

A fitting retirement, one which he deserved, one for which he had planned his entire adult life.

Dawn came, and with it scattered clouds and reports of a vile murder in France. He was bored. He switched off the car radio and reached over to the passenger seat for the piece of fake parchment he had gathered up with the rest LeConte's papers. Holding it to the windshield, he read it with the perfect amount of backlight.

"LeConte's List of Lacking Virtues." He laughed. Didn't that say it all? America with its pathetic failings wrapped up in one underachieving young man. If Sophie Marx had not become infatuated with this loser, she might be alive today.

The light faded, a cold rain slapped the windshield and fog swirled across the highway. The front must have stalled, Claussen thought, lighting another cigarette.

The front, but not his plans. A minor delay on account of the weather was of no importance. In a few days, Reinhart Schmidt would be enjoying the sun on his Bolivian flagstone terrace.

Chapter Thirty-Seven

One leather flying hat, one pair of goggles and two mildewed sheepskin jackets were the extent of the wardrobe the pilot kept in the barn. Better than nothing, thought Warner, but it left a lot to be desired.

The Stearman had two cockpits, one behind the other, with seats as hard as bicycle leather. The passenger, Nicole, would have to travel more like luggage than human cargo, lying across the skeleton of wooden spars in the hollow section of fuselage between Steven's seat and the tail. Heat and windows she wouldn't have, so Warner showed her how to make a cocoon with clothes and blankets.

He pointed out the control cables running to the stabilizer, impressing on her the need to keep them free of any obstruction—hair, feet, blankets. He asked if she was claustrophobic, and was glad she said no.

Following his instructions, Nicole entered her cabin head-first so that she would be facing forward and would have the use of her legs to brace herself against the back of Steven's seat in an emergency landing. Her head was in the narrowest part of the tail, surrounded by ancient creaking pulleys and cables.

Warner and Steven put on every piece of warm clothing they had before squeezing into the flying jackets, which were as large as they were odorous. Warner wore the hat and goggles, Steven donned the motorcycle helmet. They climbed up on the wing and slid into their seats.

Although primitive, the plane's instruments were adequate for flying in poor conditions. Warner was glad to see an artificial horizon and a vertical speed indicator. He would need them for the second leg of their journey if the night turned stormy.

Pilot's Dawn

He entrusted Steven with the field glasses and infrared camera. His partner was going to have to function as night co-pilot, a prospect Warner tried not to think too much about.

Shortly after nine a.m. Warner revved up the loud 7-cylinder engine. He taxied to the end of the strip, studied the sock and pushed the throttle forward. They bumped along the sodden earth, sinking into muddy troughs that slowed their acceleration. The northwest wind hit them at an angle, the morning sun blazed behind them, the engine sounded like a giant lawn mower with a defective bearing.

Warner knew after a short roll that they were too heavy. He was about to abort the take-off and jettison more fuel when he saw the farmer with the scythe run onto the muddy strip, gesticulating wildly with his free hand.

What was safety? Turning around? Hell no. The crate would have to fly.

They were almost halfway down the strip now. The throttle was buried, the engine was howling like a tortured beast, the airspeed indicator read 40 kilometers an hour. Warner felt as though a fast dog could have caught them and chewed up their tires.

He glanced at the trees looming ahead. The huge oaks towered at least 100 feet too high. He spotted a gap in the forest to his left. It was his only hope. Working skillfully with pedals and rudder, he transformed their take-off roll from a straight line into a sweeping curve.

When he hauled back on the stick at the last possible moment, they were traveling at 85 kilometers an hour, the slowest take-off he had ever attempted.

The old Stearman struggled into the air, fell back and lifted off again.

The gap was a dirt road. Their wing tips nearly brushed the trees to either side as the plane fought, shuddering and creaking, for every foot of altitude. When they reached a house at the end of the road, they were so low that Warner had to fly between the twin chimneys.

Behind the house was a lawn, a meadow and a long plowed field. Things were looking better. He lashed the old crate up to 90 feet—and had to dive like a bird of prey when he spotted high tension wires glinting across his path.

They brushed the ground but had more airspeed now. Warner coaxed his craft up to 120 feet and held her there, dodging the higher trees.

Keeping low was the secret, so low radar could not detect them.

He crossed a heavily forested stretch of the French-Belgian border and wove a northward course, avoiding the population centers of Tournai and Gent.

A lovely patchwork of farmland and forest passed beneath their wings as they approached the English Channel. As soon as they were over water, Warner descended to 50 feet. Steven slapped him on the back and yelled the good news to Nicole.

Warner allowed himself a sigh of relief. They had done the impossible. They had broken out of a noose made up of hundreds of thousands of police and military people. Warner throttled back to save fuel and oil, and shed another 20 feet of altitude.

Two hours later, as a brisk tail wind pushed them from the west, he spotted the first of the sandy islands running along the Dutch coast. Some were large, with posh bathing resorts and ferry service from the mainland. But others were small and uninviting, desolate islands whose beaches were littered with flotsam.

Warner chose his island carefully, cris-crossing above it until he was certain they would be alone and measuring the only stretch of unbroken beach to make sure it was long enough for a landing and take-off. He feathered the prop seconds after they touched down and barked orders at Steven while they were still rolling.

"We're going to rest, but *not* until we have this aircraft totally camouflaged. As soon as I park, I want both you and Nicole to start dragging scrub brush over here. We'll cover the plane first, then hide under the wings. I want a thorough job. Yellow stands out like a beacon to anyone looking down from the air."

Warner got no response. He twisted around and looked behind him. Steven was asleep, his motor-cycle-helmet between his knees.

Warner poked him. "Wake up, buddy, and wake up Nicole. We've got work to do, lots of it."

"No problem, chief." Steven was alert by the time the plane came to a stop. He jumped down easily from the wing and held out his hand for Nicole. Minutes later the two of them were rolling and shoving the first load of scrub from the sandy earth above the beach toward the plane.

✳   ✳   ✳

When Warner awoke, night had fallen. He pushed his way out of the canopy of brush covering the plane. It was a lot darker than he had anticipated. A thick overcast hung over the water, blocking the light from the moon and stars he had counted on for take-off. The tide was out, the wind had died, the sea was quiet. He felt as though he was at the end of the earth.

He roused Steven and Nicole, instructed them to start clearing the brush off the plane, and walked toward the surf. The tide had deposited a line of debris in the wet sand. Using his flashlight for a brief search, he found two bottles and shook the water out of them. Back at the Stearman, he felt around the underside of the engine until he located the fuel inspection drain cock.

After filling the bottles with aviation fuel, he planted them in the sand a safe distance away from Steven and Nicole, who were hauling off armfuls of brush without regard for where they stepped.

"I'm going to top up the oil," Warner said. "You two keep up the fast pace. We'll be ready to go in a few minutes."

Steven stopped in his tracks. "A few minutes? How the hell can we take off in this blackness, Frank? Can you see anything?"

"Not yet, but you and Nicole are going to build me a big-city runway."

"How?"

"First things first."

When the brush had been cleared away, Warner directed Steven to heave on the prop. The engine roared to life on the third try. Warner let it idle and climbed down. "Come with me, you two," he said, feeling his way to the bottles of aviation fuel. He handed them each one.

"I drained a little fuel from the engine. Listen carefully. The beach runs in a straight line for about a thousand feet. I want you and Nicole to gather up a bunch of twigs from that brush heap you pulled off the plane. I want you to walk down the beach parallel to each other, about fifty feet apart, using the surf as your guide. Make a wood pile every hundred feet or so. Just a few sticks, understand, nothing massive. We don't want this looking like Kennedy Airport an hour after we take off. Douse each pile with some fuel from your bottle. Don't light it, just douse it."

Warner handed them each a book of matches he had picked up in the White House conference room. "When you get to the end of the beach, you'll damn well know it," he said. "There's a deep inlet. You would have gotten a bird's eye view of it, Steven, if you hadn't slept through the landing. "I was awake. What are you talking about?"

Warner ignored him. "Stop when you get there, put a match to your final wood pile, then turn around and head back. You should have enough light from that first little blaze to see where you're going. Once you start back, I want you to hurry—but make sure each pile will stay lit before you move on. The wood should burn long enough to get us airborne. Do you understand, Nicole?"

"Yes, Frank."

"Then let's go."

Warner slid into the cockpit and put the radial engine through its warm-up paces, listening for irregularities. There were none.

Minutes later, a flicker of light caught his eye. A thousand feet down the beach, two tiny flames were burning, marking the spot at which he would have to lift his wheels out of the sand.

Steven and Nicole had made torches. He couldn't see what they had used, but it seemed like a much better idea than relying on his wimpy paper matches.

They came toward him rapidly, like runners bearing an urgent message, stopping briefly to put fire to each little pile of fuel-soaked wood. When they clambered into the plane, Warner had his runway—a little wavy in spots, but more than adequate.

He pushed the throttle forward. The engine howled, the old Stearman rolled slowly at first, shaking and groaning. But the sand was harder and smoother than the mud of Bonier's field. By the time they reached the ninth pair of flickering piles, they were airborne.

Warner glanced in the direction of the island as they banked steeply over the sea. He saw nothing but blackness. The propeller backwash and swirling sand must have blown out each little flame as they passed it. The lighted runway had lived exactly as long as it was needed, he thought, and not a second more.

Warner leveled off at 60 feet, skimming the bottom of the sagging overcast, an eye on the altimeter, an eye on the artificial horizon. As midnight approached he spotted a row of lights ahead softened by the fog. They were nearing the coast of Denmark.

The one-hour flight over the Danish peninsula was the segment of the flight he considered most dangerous. They would be crossing a densely populated area with TV towers, smoke stacks, high-voltage lines and tall buildings. If the moon didn't break through so that he could dodge potential obstacles, he would have no choice but to climb to 300 feet. At that altitude, he would show up on the radar screens of one of the Europe's most vigilant air defense systems. Not a reassuring prospect.

He glanced back at Steven, whose head in his motorcycle helmet hung at a limp 45 degree angle. The co-pilot was sleeping again. Probably a good thing, thought Warner. He might well be in for a strenuous workout later, if they had to find Claussen's abode in a soup of fog and clouds.

The clouds opened as they overflew the coastline. They passed low over a sandy marsh, glowing eerily in the moonlight. Warner did a visual estimate of his altitude, and found that it was within ten feet of the reading on the venerable old altimeter. No need to change settings.

The engine was running well, the temp and oil pressure holding steady. The aircraft had been maintained a lot better than he had anticipated. If the moon would only stay out, he thought, he could keep on flying low and forget about radar.

It was not meant to be. The overcast thickened again, and a cold rain began to fall. His visibility, which hadn't been great before, dropped to zero. He pulled back on the stick and tried to look at the bright side.

At 300 feet they might pick him up on radar. In fact, he was almost certain they would. But picking him up and finding him were two different things. If he increased his air speed, he could make it across Denmark in less than 45 minutes. Once he came out over the Baltic, he could dive to 50 feet again and disappear from their screens forever...

Turbulence increased, causing the old bi-plane to groan like a ship about to break up. Rain splattered on Warner's goggles and ran under his collar. The air grew colder, the muscles of his arms and back grew stiffer.

He kept a flashlight trained on the instruments, whose illumination had picked a fine time to die. His feet were busy with the rudder pedals, holding her level and trimmed though he sometimes felt as if he were banking or flying in loops. Thank God for the artificial horizon.

His airspeed indicator remained at a 155 kilometers an hour, and he knew he had a pretty stiff tail wind. This gave him an ETA in Claussen's

Pilot's Dawn

neighborhood of roughly 2:45 a.m. Good timing, he thought, if he could see anything. The world would be asleep.

He turned around to look at Steven, who was still asleep, his head now tilted to the other side. He consulted his watch. In his mind's eye, he heard the screech of jets sent up to intercept him. He heard the clatter of canon, and felt the Stearman's wooden frame explode in a hail of gunfire. But the night remained wet and calm, and the flight proceeded without incident.

Half an hour later he whacked Steven on the helmet. "Wake up, first officer. We should be over the Baltic by now. We're going down for a look."

"Okay, good," Steven said groggily.

"Two hundred feet," Warner called back. "Get the infrared camera lens trained on what's below. Let me know as soon as you see something other than clouds."

"Okay."

"One hundred fifty feet. One hundred feet. Anything?"

"Soup. Thick as before," Steven shouted.

"Seventy-five feet...sixty...fifty."

"Soup."

Warner turned around and glanced at Steven, who had taken off his helmet and seemed to be using the camera correctly. He decided to descend a little more.

"Forty feet. Thirty five." He licked his lips. The rain was mixed with the salty taste of sea spray.

"It's gotta be close," Warner shouted. "Ten more feet and we go back up."

"Hey, hold it!" Steven screamed. "Ocean below. There she is. Big waves, mean looking mothers. Can't you see it?"

Warner shook his head No, then turned around. "Okay, we'll hold her right here. My plotting says we should intersect the main shipping lane to Rostock somewhere around here. I'm going to try to pick the lighted buoys. Use the infrared. What do you see if you look up ahead?"

"Water, waves, clouds skimming right above your wings."

"All right, you're my eyes. Don't let me run into anything."

"Got it."

Ten minutes later, Steven yelled. "Climb! Left!"

They just missed a freighter's mast, but soon after leveling off, they both spotted the buoys of the shipping lane.

"Good work!" Warner screamed. "Put the camera away. I can see them fine."

During the next hour, the fog thinned and the rain pushed inland. The moon, that same bright harvest moon that had looked down on them the previous night, broke through the overcast, this time to stay.

Still over water, they flew north of Rostock, a rusty port that had once been the center of East German shipbuilding. From Rostock, they continued east along the white sand beaches of the Baltic. At the deserted resort of Graal-Müritz, Warner turned inland. He overflew a broad stretch of heather, crossed an egg-shaped tidal basin and came to the estuary of the Recknitz River. Following his flight plan, he headed due south.

At 2:15 a.m. his path over the sparsely populated marshes, dunes and heather of northern Mecklenburg intersected with the Augraben River. The moon and stars were out now, and patches of ground fog gave off an ghostly phosphorescent glow. He had not anticipated such an easy approach.

He turned to Steven, who gave him the thumbs up sign. Nicole stuck her foot up behind Steven's seat in response to his inquiry about her condition. His crew and cargo seemed to be thriving; he turned all thoughts to locating the farmhouse and putting the plane down in a field neither too close nor too far from their goal.

Twenty minutes later he spotted an ironwork bridge spanning the river. He climbed to 1,000 feet so he could get his bearings. The straight untraveled road that crossed the bridge from the northwest ran to the dark village of Altenhagen. He knew it well from the map. It was the first landmark of his final approach.

He circled back upriver, climbing to 2000 feet, then feathered his prop and began retracing his path in a slow glide. Five miles south of the first bridge was a second bridge. The road across it forked just west of the river. One fork ran to the horizon. The other disappeared into a grove of pines and surfaced again not far from a sprawling stucco farmstead. He pointed, then held his hand back to Steven. From the force of the shake he got in return, he knew his co-pilot was looking at the same thing.

Warner floated silently over the house and massive barn at 800 feet. There was no sign of human presence, but he could make out what looked like a gaggle of large, restless geese patrolling the barnyard.

They passed over a pine forest, its trees precisely stagger-cut. Beyond the forest, an oblong meadow stretched alongside the river.

There was no use restarting the engine, he thought. The old crate glided as well as it flew, and sounds on this crystal night would carry like a gunshots.

"Tell Nicole to brace for landing," he called back. "We're going to overfly the meadow and circle back. We'll be on the ground in a minute."

He heard Steven's command, heard the wind whistling through holes in the canvas, heard a nighthawk objecting to the intrusion into its territory. He floated over the meadow. It was perfect, long and level. A good pilot, he thought, could have put down a 727 here. He made a steep descending turn and headed back toward the farmhouse.

Fifty feet. God, he'd flown halfway across Europe at this altitude. He was ready to touch solid ground.

The moon slid behind a cloud, the field went dark. He didn't care, this one he could do by feel. The moon came out when he was near touchdown and dropping smoothly as a bird. No turbulence, no wind, just the even sound of air rushing across the wings.

A blur of heather and meadow grass came up to meet them. Almost there.

He touched down, braked gently, hurtled through a dense wall of ground fog and burst into the clear, starry night. They were going to make it. By God, they were going to make it.

They weren't rolling much faster than a slow bicycle when he saw the deep narrow ditch. Warner hit the brakes hard. The plane skidded slightly to the right.

Too late. They stopped with an abrupt jolt. Steven's head banged into Warner's back like a bowling ball. Warner's harness restrained him so powerfully it squeezed the wind from his lungs. For a moment he sat gulping for air.

"Let's move," Warner whispered when he had his breath back. He climbed with difficulty onto the wing and tried to straighten up. He was frozen in the shape of a question mark. He had never in his life been so stiff.

Steven wrenched his seat forward and started talking to Nicole in French.

"Let's move," Warner repeated, still trying to straighten his legs. "We're within a half mile of where we need to go."

"She's hurt," Steven said.

"What?"

"Hurt. Broken ankle. Jesus Christ, Frank, I think I can feel the crack in the bone."

"Shit."

"It's all right," Nicole sobbed. "I'll be all right. I'll wait here for you."

Warner and Steven both took off their jackets and passed them back to her. Steven spoke in French again.

Pilot's Dawn

Warner was about to intervene and ask him to hurry, but Steven jumped down before he could say anything, then held up his hand to assist him. "Come on, old man, I'm ready."

Warner took the offer of help. He had his own ankles to worry about. "Bad luck," he said as his feet hit in the soft earth. "I hope she's all right."

"Yeah, me too. Will the plane fly when we get back?"

"We'll have to drag the landing gear out of the ditch but that should be all. We were lucky the prop didn't break."

"Okay, Frank. Nice flying. I didn't see the ditch either. Let's get this job done and get the fuck out of here. I'd rather be in Connecticut."

They started across the pasture. Warner, who had been proud of his stamina during the long flight, felt like he had been hit by a train. Every joint seemed locked in the position it had held for the last few hours, every muscle felt as if it had atrophied beyond hope of resurrection.

Steven waited for him several times, then grabbed his arm. They entered the forest. The trail took them near the river. Its tiny whirlpools swept silently by, like living creatures washed in moonlight.

Warner was uneasy. He had the feeling the river was watching him, listening.

Chapter Thirty-Eight

They hadn't taken more than a few steps toward the house when the geese came toward them in a cackling mob. Steven kicked them out of his path, but this only intensified their attack. "Goddammit," he whispered. "What are these things? Watch geese?"

"I think they're hungry," Warner said. "Open the barn. Maybe they'll go in there."

Steven removed the bar and swung the door open. A huge steel tank loomed in the entryway, mounted on a brick base. There were cables above it that looked like part of a primitive pulley system. Through an opening in the brick base he could make out an enormous gas burner, its pilot light a flickering blue flame. A long chute came out the side of the tank and emptied into a conveyor trough. The trough ran to some kind of a large old press.

Nothing high-tech here. He couldn't see any further into the barn without turning on his flashlight, and his batteries were getting low. The important things would be in the house.

The geese had rushed past him and were pecking violently at large sacks stacked along the walls. Pellets the size of marbles rained down through rips in the paper.

"Dog food," Warner said. "This is an old dog food plant from the communist days. He must feed this stuff to his geese. Look at them go."

Steven nudged Warner outside and closed the door on the ravenous birds. "Irritating fuckers," he said. "That's a good place for them."

They walked to the farmhouse, which was about 50 yards away. Steven said, "You think there's a burglar alarm system, Frank?"

"We'll find out."

Warner examined the back door. "A dead bolt. Go ahead and break the window."

"With what?"

"The butt of your pistol. Hold the safety on."

"Frank, my gun's with Nicole. You didn't think I was going to leave her unprotected out there with a broken ankle, did you? Would have you done that to your wife?"

"I don't have a wife, I have a girlfriend," Warner whispered, wrestling the Heckler and Koch from his breast holster. "Yes, I would have left her out there. What do you think's going to get her? Werewolves."

"Hey, Warner, this is Germany. Ever read about this place? Skinheads, Nazis, what the hell do I know? Look who lives right here. Break the window."

Warner did, precisely, thoroughly and without much noise. He cleared the remaining glass from the frame. No alarm sounded, and nothing in the house stirred. The place was deserted.

Warner pushed his pistol back into its holster. "Give me a boost, will you?"

Steven made a step with his hands and hoisted Warner up on the window sill. He waited for him to drop inside and followed. With the weakening beam of his flashlight, he probed in all directions.

White stucco walls, beautifully finished doors, a kitchen with a black hooded stove and no modern appliances, a stairway. He was about to go upstairs when Warner said, "Let's finish looking down here. There's a hallway we haven't checked."

"I'll go up, you stay down."

"No. We're staying together."

"Whatever you say, boss."

★ ★ ★

Nicole's ankle throbbed. She tried to rest, but the stillness before dawn had an unnerving quality. It had seemed so quiet when Steven and Warner trudged off. Now, gradually, the night began to fill with tiny sounds. A mole in the grass, a branch cracking under its own weight, a night bird crying from a distant perch. And the river, that was the worst, the river lapping softly, persistently, as if it were trying to find and devour her. Her mind conjured up dark water and swirling moss. She saw a school of eels writhing inside a hollow submerged log. She saw her father standing on the grassy bank, his blank eyes on a drowning child.

She was becoming frightened. She peeked out through a hole in the canvas fuselage, hoping to put the sounds in perspective, to free her mind by returning them to their proper places in the night.

Lights flickered through scrawny pines, far, far away. She listened. She heard the sound of a distant car. The sound gave her comfort. It drove off the primal visions and replaced them with images of cities and people, of daytime and health.

The car had been traveling in a direction that brought it no closer to her. She was about to stop watching it and try again to rest when it slowed and turned. The hum of its engine became the lapping of the river, soft, persistent, searching.

She held her breath and waited for the car to pass. It was still a couple of miles away. It was just a car. It did not have to have Claussen's farmhouse as its destination. That was just her fear, she told herself, and it was once again creating monsters out of nothing.

Then the car's lights went out. She listened. It was still coming, more slowly now, so quietly she could hear the night bird cry, and the river lap and the mole rustling the meadow grass.

She knew then that it was Claussen. The night had been trying to tell her something. She had listened and failed to understand.

Part of her terror remained; part of it turned into purpose. She felt enormous strength surging inside her pain-racked body. She knew she needed to work fast. Practical considerations were what mattered now. If she didn't get there in time, it would be the same as not getting there at all.

She struggled out of her cocoon in the plane's tail, dragging her useless ankle and Steven's pack behind her. She stepped on the lower wing with her good foot and heaved the pack down beside her. She dug for the pistol, found it and shoved it into her belt.

The moon shone brightly. She could see where she needed to go. But how was she to get there? She put a little weight on her ankle. The pain was like a tooth being drilled without anesthetic. Take a moment...take a moment. You must devise some sort of support.

What was that roll she had moved to get more comfortable in the plane? She climbed back inside, suppressing a cry when her ankle hit the seat back. She felt around in the dim light until she found it. Patching canvas, the same stuff the plane's skeleton was covered with.

She heard the car engine stop. She needed to hurry, she knew she needed to hurry. She felt as if she were stuck in mud, as if her most trivial actions took an eternity.

On the wing again, she tore through Steven's pack in search of a knife. Wet clothes, remains of provisions...Did the plane have a tool kit aboard?

She found it under Warner's seat.

Moonlight, thank God for the light. She rummaged through the old tools, some of which she didn't recognize. The search finally paid off. The knife had a wooden handle and a small rusty crescent blade. It felt sharp enough to do the job.

Time passing. Everything took time.

The width of the roll seemed right, about ten inches, but the material was very stiff. She held onto the end of canvass and threw the roll overboard, then hauled a yard of the material into the cockpit. It didn't cut easily, she needed two hands to stretch and hold it, another hand to cut it. She used her teeth as a third hand and started sawing. As she worked, she struggled to maintain her composure against rising waves of panic. Why was everything taking so long?

Her shoe was already off. She raised the leg of her jeans and wrapped her ankle as tightly as she could, then pulled the pant leg over the bandage to keep it from unraveling. It wasn't a cast, it wasn't perfect, but it was the best she could do. She had to go.

She slid on her stomach off the backside of the wing, landed on her good foot and started to walk. The pain was excruciating. Several steps and she couldn't bear it any longer. She tried to hop on her good foot. She tripped on a clump of meadow grass and landed face-down.

She crawled the last 30 yards to the forest, breathing so hard her lungs felt like fire. Her ankle had stopped throbbing when she came to the dirt path that led through the forest. She would try to walk again, but first she had to rest for a few seconds.

The river lapped at the bank beside her. She could judge the speed of the current by the little whirlpools floating past in the moonlight. If she hadn't been traveling upstream, she would have been tempted to swim.

She got to her feet and tried to walk. The first time she put her bad foot down, pain rocketed through her like a lightning bolt. She thought of Steven and Warner being surprised and murdered just because she could not tolerate pain. She had given up too easily, she decided. She picked up a stout branch and used it as a cane. She hopped two steps and put her bad foot down again. The same pain shot up her leg, but it was noticeably less than it had been. Or had she gotten used to it? She gritted her teeth and took a normal step. The same pain but less intense. Her ankle was going numb!

God had finally heard her cry for help. She could move, she could walk, she could fly! They might have to chop off her foot because of what she was doing to it, but she didn't care. It was not far now, she knew it wasn't far.

✶   ✶   ✶

Pilot's Dawn

In a large airy first floor room with a chair and sofa but no windows, Warner and Steven found Claussen's roll top desk. Warner opened it.

Hundreds of handwritten pages were piled in neat stacks. He selected one of the pages and began to read. Steven looked over his shoulder.

German! It might as well have been Greek. No use hanging around.

He went to work checking out the rest of the room. The walls were white here, too, and there were none of the watercolors he had seen in the corridor. The sound system looked expensive. At least the guy enjoyed music.

Steven peeked in on his collection of discs: all German, all classical. Sophie, he thought, would have approved of his taste. How people so different could like the same music was something he would never understand.

Sophie. The pain that accompanied the tiniest thought of her doubled him over. He felt his fury rising, as it had done again and again since he had learned of her murder. This was the lair of the man who had killed his number one soul mate. Those pages in the desk might prove the role Claussen had played in bringing down the jets. They had come here to find just such proof. Yet the victory already seemed weak, pale and incomplete. He wanted Claussen. He wanted to ring the bastard's neck with his own hands. He wanted to watch the scum bag suffer.

Pumped up with fresh ire, Steven opened a closet. There was a row of five or six boxes inside that had been stacked along the wall. They were numbered and labeled in German.

He opened one of the boxes. It was filled with official-looking documents. The alphabet was Cyrillic, the symbol at the top of each page the Hammer and Sickle.

"What's in there?" Warner called from the desk, where he had not moved since he began to read.

"Documents, man. Could be KGB records on Operation Two-Six. You read Russian, Frank?"

"No. Are the boxes numbered?"

"Yeah, numbered and labeled. What are you finding?"

"Memoirs, the man's memoirs. I think he's using your material over there for research. He's got piles of notes referring to documents in this box or that."

"Those are his memoirs? That stuff in long hand? He's not using a computer?"

"Evidently not. Maybe he thinks writing by hand separates him from the dim-witted masses."

"Maybe he doesn't have a copy."

"He's arrogant enough to make that sort of mistake. Whatever, Steven, this is a find of unprecedented proportions. From what I have seen, I would say you and Nicole could make a fortune selling it to a publisher."

"You're in for half the proceeds," Steven said.

"No, not me. As a member of the government, I would be bound to turn it over to the authorities. I'm sure you agree *that* would be a shame, given the grand job the government has done in solving this case."

"Goddamn right, I agree."

"I'll ask you to loan me copies of the documents I need to prove my case in Washington. The documents are yours. Remember, without you and Sophie I would still be at first base. I owe you a lot."

"You don't owe me anything, Frank. We wouldn't be here if you hadn't come to France."

Steven walked over to the desk and took another look at the stacks of pages. The handwriting was small, tight and fastidious. Notes in the same hand filled the desk's many cubby holes. Warner was right, this was something big. It was time to load it up and hit the road.

"You're a genius, Frank," he said. "Let's start hauling this stuff back to the plane right now. Three trips should do it."

"Patience, Steven. We went to a lot of trouble getting here. Let's make sure we don't leave until we have everything we can use."

*   *   *

Pilot's Dawn

Claussen, driving a BMW 750 registered in the name of Peter Weiss of Bern, Switzerland, thought he glimpsed a faint light in the windows on the east side of his farmhouse as he approached on the country road from Altenhagen. When he came within a mile of the entry gate, he turned off his headlights and slowed to a crawl. He parked on the side of the road and completed the final segment of his journey on foot.

He knew someone had been on his property when he saw that the geese were missing. He circled around behind the farmhouse, where he noticed the broken window.

His first thought was that he had underestimated Delors. The bastard had divined his intentions and sent an SDECE commando unit to intercept him.

He rejected that theory forthwith. The SDECE was sloppy, yes, but not even Cuban intelligence would announce its presence in such a glaring fashion.

His second thought was that Bauernsachs' greed had gotten the best of him. The farmer who used the dog food plant had sold his geese, and now he was trying to make their disappearance look like part of a burglary.

Bauernsachs would pay dearly if he were the perpetrator, but Claussen's loss would be nil. The last thing a common thief would take would be documents and memoirs. Bauernsachs was shrewd enough to know this. He wouldn't bother to touch them. He would go for the stereo system.

The same would apply, of course, if an actual burglary was in progress. If this turned out to be the case, Claussen would simply let the scoundrels go. He had not come for his earthly possessions—at least not those he could replace with money.

He stuck his head through the broken window and listened. He heard voices that brought a smile to his lips. All of his theories were wrong. The intruders were speaking English, American English.

He had to restrain himself not to laugh out loud. It was hard to believe they had really come to him.

The poor pathetic bastards! All of Europe to hide in and they had chosen the one spot from which they could never escape.

Americans! He almost felt sorry for them. They were shallow enough to believe the naive optimism of their national myths. They thought they could do anything, and do it better than anyone else. This belief had made them easy prey for Operation 26. It would make them easy prey now.

He silently unlocked the dead bolt and slipped inside. This little encounter was going to be enjoyable, a nice feather in his cap before his departure for Bolivia.

* * *

Warner was about to say something when his mouth froze in a horrible grimace. Steven thought he was having a coronary until he saw Warner's hand go for his pistol. The collision between the emerging gun and a foot in a hard leather shoe took place before he had the chance to look around. Warner's pistol landed on the hardwood floor and clattered under the sofa.

"Greetings, gentlemen," Claussen said, retreating to the doorway. He drew his stiletto. "I must confess. It flatters me that you consider my work so important. However, it also irritates me when mediocre men take the liberty of meddling in my affairs."

Steven backed up to the wall and began to move slowly toward Claussen. His heart was pounding but his mind was clear. Sophie's killer had come back. Sophie's killer was going to make his day.

"Come a little closer," Claussen said calmly. "Well, come on, LeConte. What are you waiting for? It's between you and me, no? Look at your partner. He's exhausted and out of shape. He has chosen to sit this round out."

"Fuck you," Warner said. Steven watched him begin approaching Claussen along the opposite wall.

Pilot's Dawn

This was the right move. Claussen had a knife, but to kill a strong healthy man with a knife you had to do a lot of jumping, parrying and thrusting. It took a long time even if the man was not armed. Warner would be coming from one side, Steven from the other. Claussen would have to choose whom to strike first. When he did that, the free man would have a clear shot at his rear—a kick to the thigh, a kick to the kidney, a chop to the neck when he started to falter...

Steven said, "Let's see your fancy stuff, cockroach. Or do you only use it against old women?" Claussen looked Steven in the eye, then used the diversion to catch Warner off-guard with a lightning fast kick to the chin. He smiled now, and shook the knife at Steven.

Warner tottered and slumped in a heap against the wall. Claussen, his blue eyes still boring into Steven, delivered a vicious back kick to Warner's temple.

"Twenty minutes," Claussen said. "He'll be out for twenty minutes, give or take a few seconds. It's one-on-one now, a fair fight. A sixty-year-old man with a knife, a big muscled kid with his fists. Have you got a plan or are you like your country, big and dumb? Well, LeConte, you'd better do something. I'm getting bored."

Steven's eyes flashed to Warner, who was out cold. He tried to locate Warner's gun but couldn't see it. And he couldn't dive for it, either, not without getting a blade in the back. The sofa under which it had slid was of heavy oak and very low to the floor. Forget the gun. It was out of play.

He faced Claussen directly, knowing he must keep his eyes on him every second. His best bet, it seemed, was to draw out the fight and hope this son of a bitch got tired or made a mistake. Claussen took a step toward him. "Put out your hand, LeConte. Let's see the color of your blood. It's going to happen sooner or later. You're not a procrastinator by any chance?"

Steven tried to block out the words. He circled in front of the roll top desk, reached behind him while keeping his eyes on Claussen, picked up a smooth granite paper weight and faked a throw at Claussen's head.

Claussen ducked and lunged at the same time. Steven spun out of his way. He held up the paper weight. "Pretty clumsy, asshole. You Europeans should play more baseball."

Claussen kicked at the weight in Steven's hand, using the same move that had sent Warner crashing to the floor.

Steven was feeling good. He saw the shoe coming like a weak serve. He stepped easily to the side. He had the impression he could have caught Claussen's leg, upended him and ripped it from its socket.

But if he had missed...if he had missed, he would have left himself wide open. The fight would have ended then and there with a stiletto through the liver. It was better to be patient and feel out Claussen's weaknesses before taking any big risks.

Yes, but hard to do in the heat of battle.

"You know," Claussen said, coming closer and holding the knife loosely, as if to tempt a kick. "I wouldn't want to put you down. You're a decent combatant, better than I would have guessed. Not many survive this long. But the outcome is not in doubt. Have you ever seen a bull fight, Mr. LeConte?"

Steven kept his eyes glued to Claussen's. His heart pounded in his ears. He needed to do something. But what? The bastard handled his knife like one of those gypsies in the circus.

"Well," Claussen said, "since your fear has turned you into a mute, I'll answer for you. You've seen many bull fights, perhaps in Spain, perhaps only on television or in the movies. You've seen them, so you know what I'm talking about."

Claussen smiled and backed closer to Warner. Steven stepped forward, keeping the distance between them the same. If Claussen turned to stab Frank, Steven was going to kick him in the tailbone so hard every disk in his spine would explode.

Claussen didn't oblige him. It was as if he had eyes in the back of his head. While looking straight at Steven, he delivered a blind heel to Warner's chin. "Add ten minutes to your friend's nap," he said.

Pilot's Dawn

From his peripheral vision Steven saw Warner flop like a sack of grain. He was unconscious when Claussen kicked him, and he was unconscious now.

Steven felt his control over his temper starting to slip away. He was going to say something about Germans liking to kick the guy who was down and then feeling really tough, but he stopped himself. He knew Claussen wanted him to get mad, to lose his temper, to throw judgment to the wind. He wasn't going to oblige him. For once in his life, he was going to control his emotions. He rubbed the granite paper weight.

Claussen charged him without warning, knife horizontal. It was a feint. He stopped just out of range and smiled. He said, "In these dramatic confrontations about which we were speaking, Mr. LeConte, in these blood-stirring contests between brawn and brain, brute force and subtle mastery, who always wins? The bull fighter, of course. I shall grant you that if the bull is particularly strong or adept, the killing may take a little longer. But this only helps to make the contest more interesting. I am in no hurry. How about you, Mr. LeConte?"

Claussen lunged but he had telegraphed his move with his eyes. Steven knew it was another feint. He held his ground and unleashed the paper weight. It hit Claussen in the forehead. Blood gushed down over his eyes.

Now!

Steven stepped forward and sent a straight left crashing into Claussen's mouth.

In the same instant, he felt an ugly sensation in his other forearm. The bastard had taken his punch and somehow managed to cut him.

It was a scratch, he told himself, just a scratch. He refused to look at it, concentrating his attention instead on Claussen's face.

The man's lower lip was split, and blood still poured from the gash in his forehead. But in the center of that grotesque face was his smile, as condescending as ever.

"Well, LeConte, that was it. You, the bull, committed the fatal blunder. They all do. Now, now, you should not feel badly. It was a courageous effort, even though it was not informed by any measurable degree of intelligence."

Claussen kicked the paper weight under the oak sofa, where it hit the pistol with a pinging noise. "You might not believe your wound is serious, but if you were in a position to inspect it, you would see that an artery has been severed. With each beat of your heart, you are pumping away your strength. You don't know enough to know the name of the artery which you so foolishly exposed to my blade, do you, Mr. LeConte? Ignorant, like your country."

The guy was bluffing, thought Steven.

Or was he? The hot pulsing of blood inside his sleeve made him unsure.

Claussen smiled—a different, softer smile.

Steven felt a surge of panic he hoped Claussen hadn't seen. What if he did grow weaker? What were his options? He couldn't think of any.

"So we wait," Claussen said. He ran his arm across the wound on his forehead. The bleeding had almost stopped. He wasn't hurt.

Steven felt the first tell-tale waves of nausea and dizziness sweeping over him. He needed to do something, and fast. But what? He now knew the deadly accuracy of that blade. Any turn away from Claussen, any attempt to upend a desk or slide a sofa, and he would be dead.

He fought to keep his mind and eyes clear, to keep his belief in his ability to prevail alive.

"I read your List of Lacking Virtues," Claussen said in a mocking voice. "Your surrogate mother was a perceptive woman. How shocking, your lack of perseverance. To be fair with you, Mr. LeConte, you have made some improvements in that area or you would not be here now. I commend you while we wait for you to grow just a little weaker.

"Your penchant for procrastination is another matter entirely. It is very bad, this particular flaw. Bad because it prevented you from dealing

Pilot's Dawn

with item number nine on your list, your carelessness in matters large and small.

"Here too, LeConte, you are a remarkable mirror image of your country. The costs of such carelessness, to you personally and to an America in decline, are incalculable. Let us say that they are terminal."

He laughed like a man who was enjoying himself. The thought of losing to him nauseated Steven more than his spilled blood.

Claussen's back was to the door. Steven moved around until his rear brushed up against the roll top desk. He was looking at Claussen, but he thought he glimpsed a shadow on the white stucco wall in corridor.

A goose, maybe. Claussen could have left the door open when he entered. This might offer a distraction, some sort of a chance for him to strike. He couldn't quite form an image of what that chance would look like, but he had a strong feeling it would be his last.

In the meantime, it was critical to keep Claussen's attention focused squarely on him.

For wont of anything better to do, he took a deep breath and groped around on the paper-strewn surface of the desk behind him. He brushed the pages of Claussen's memoirs carelessly about as his hand probed for something, anything, he might be able to use.

Near the edge of the desk, his hand bumped into an object that warmed his heart. He grasped it and slowly brought it around in front of him. It was a cigarette lighter, a gold lighter.

He could see Claussen changing the grip on his stiletto. He wasn't sure what this meant, but he thought it could be the sign he was hoping for, a very good sign.

He flicked the lighter on. He adjusted the tiny, precise knob until the flame burned an inch high. He feigned a weakness, as if his legs had buckled. Claussen remained frozen in his stance. He was no longer smiling.

Could Warner possibly be right? Could this man be so arrogant he had not bothered to make copies of his memoirs? Did he really believe he was immune to the sort of fate that would strike a mere mortal? It was beginning to look that way.

Now it was Steven who smiled. "No copies, eh? Maybe we have more in common than you realize. Maybe you caught something while you were in the States."

Claussen's face became an angry sneer.

The shadow in the hallway appeared again, then vanished. This time there could be no doubt. Something was definitely out there.

One of Steven's knees started to tremble. He locked it, got it under control. But Claussen had noticed he wasn't faking. His expression changed from anger to psychopathic delight.

Steven grabbed a page off the desk and lit it. He tossed it toward Claussen. It fluttered, burning, to the floor. Claussen stamped out the flames. "I have twenty copies," he said. "Save your energy. You're going to need it."

"Yeah, you've got twenty copies all right. Where are they? With those lawyers of yours who are going to release the details of your conspiracy when you get killed? It must have surprised you when your French buddies swallowed that bluff. They believed you would entrust lawyers with proof that you're nothing but a little Himmler clone! They actually believed something that preposterous. Americans, sure. They would have believed it because they believe anything. But the French?"

Steven glanced back through the door into the hallway. He gave a start. Nicole was sitting on the floor, her shoes off and her ankle bound in yellow canvas. With both hands, she was raising the automatic pistol he had left in his pack.

Don't let him look around, Steven thought. Offer him your throat, do what you must, but do not let him look around. He said, "Well, Wally, let's burn the rest of these. You keep your office a little too cold, and since you've got copies—"

Claussen was coming now, coming in earnest. "You are not only dumb, my friend. You are naive."

A tremulous voice rose from the heap against the wall, a voice that grew stronger with each syllable. The voice spoke in English, American English.

"He's naive," choked Warner, "but he's lucky."

Steven dove to the side. Claussen spun around to finish off Warner. When he saw the girl training the pistol on him, his jaw dropped open.

"Shoot!" Steven screamed. "You can't miss."

He and Claussen saw it at the same time. She had mistaken the mode selector for safety.

Claussen dove at her with his stiletto. Steven dove at the same time, bringing Claussen down with a shoestring tackle from behind.

Claussen, on the floor, coiled and spun like a snake, slashing at Steven with the razor sharp blade. When Steven ducked out of the stiletto's deadly path, Claussen went after Nicole. Steven caught him before he could sink the blade into her and jerked him backwards. He crashed a fist into Claussen's thigh, narrowly avoided the slashing knife, and caught hold of Claussen's foot. He viciously twisted his shoe, hoping to snap his tibia.

The shoe came off.

Nicole sat there trembling. She pushed the mode selector into the other position, but the gun still refused to shoot.

Claussen was still ferocious, still dangerous. The stiletto seemed to come at Steven out of nowhere while he sat on the floor with Claussen's shoe in both hands. He saw it in time. He thrust the shoe in the path of the knife. The blade sliced through the leather upper.

Warner clapped his hands. "Nicole! The gun! Throw me the gun."

Steven got Claussen by the foot again. Claussen took another vicious swipe at him, then yanked free, raised the knife and lunged toward Nicole.

Nicole gave the gun a toss, screamed and covered her breasts with her arms.

Steven couldn't get there in time so he flung the shoe. An ace. It glanced off Claussen's hand, deflecting the deadly thrust of the blade into the door frame.

Nicole slid away while Claussen yanked the knife out of the wood. He started to go after her again but the click of a safety stopped him in his tracks.

Warner was still sitting on the floor, still groggy, the gun unsteady in his hand. His bloodshot eyes narrowed. The pistol began to settle down.

"Wait," Claussen said, "we need to talk."

"Talk," Warner scowled. "You're dreaming." His stare was fierce, stony and unrelenting. He squeezed the trigger and put a bullet through the bridge of Claussen's nose.

Claussen landed beside Steven. The stiletto clattered from his grasp. Steven thrust his good arm beneath the sofa and came up with the other pistol.

He didn't need it. Claussen was dead.

"I used to hunt chuckers when I was kid," Warner mumbled. "I knew there was a reason for it."

"What are chuckers?" Nicole sobbed.

"Little birds," Warner said. "They run up the mountainside and fly down. You don't get many shots. When you do, you don't miss. My God, girl, what ever possessed you to drag yourself all this way?"

"Lights," Nicole said, taking a deep breath. "Automobile lights. I knew it was him."

Steven sat down beside her and hugged her. "Frank," he said, "we'd better take a look at my arm. I think the son of a bitch cut an artery."

*   *   *

It was still dark when Bauernsachs left the slaughterhouse in Altenhagen in his horse-drawn wagon. He carried a load of swine innards from the night shift so warm he could see them steaming beneath the streetlights on the town square.

This was capitalism, he thought, crossing the bridge over the Augraben and guiding his team on to the fork in the road that led to Herr Claussen's property. Back in the old days the East German state paid him a set wage to transport the discarded entrails and heads to the dog food plant. They paid Kaltenburg the same amount to bring the grain swept up from the floor of the chafing facility. And they paid old Gerhardt, who ran the machinery, the same amount to keep it going. No one was happy, no one made any money, and the dog food lay around for months until it went bad because the state couldn't figure out how to get it picked up and taken to the state-owned shops.

How things had changed! Bauernsachs now had a contract with the slaughterhouse to dispose of the remains. He collected a fee for his service. He offered the chafing facility the same fee for the dreck they swept up off the floor. They thought he was a fool and laughed about him behind his back, but what did he care? He was getting rich.

When he turned into the barnyard, Bauernsachs felt his heart soar. The geese had run away! This was a happy day. Feeding the birds was costing him too much, and not feeding them when Claussen was away made him feel uneasy.

Bauernsachs stopped in front of the barn and tied up his team. He blew out the lanterns on his wagon to save paraffin. Now he was a capitalist. He had an incentive for cutting costs.

He lifted the bar and swung open the barn door. The gang of geese came at him. He beat the feathery mayhem away with a stick and cursed when he noticed that they had pecked through the bags of dog food waiting to be shipped.

It wasn't such a happy day after all.

When the geese were outside and he could concentrate, he lit the gas burner under the giant cooking tank and started the heating unit on the ceramic pellet press. He checked the conveyor belt to make sure it was working properly, then swung the boom out over the tank in his wagon. He secured the hooks dangling from the cables to the steel eyes around the rim of his tank.

Working the controls, Bauernsachs carefully lifted his load above the cooking tank and dumped it in. When his transport tank was back in place on his rig, he pushed the green button to start the counter-rotating blades at the bottom of the cooking tank. He climbed the ladder on the side of the tank to peer in and make sure the blades were churning the gook.

They were. This was essential. In a free market economy, you couldn't have recognizable chunks of swine snout showing up in your product.

He closed the barn door securely, waved his stick at the geese and drove toward the chafing facility. He would return in a couple of hours with the grain, which he would add to the guts.

Then, when the mixture was perfectly blended, he would send it down the conveyor belt to the pellet press. With some help from his son at the bagging end, he might be able to make up a full load before the transport company from the West came for the shipment.

* * *

"Steven," Warner asked, "are you strong enough to walk to the window? I want you to see something."

"I'm feeling better. You did a good job wrapping the arm."

"Well, shall we try it?"

"Where's Nicole?"

"Already there. I carried her. Give me your good arm."

From the dark kitchen, they watched the man who had arrived in a horse-drawn wagon conduct his bizarre routine.

When he left, Warner lingered a moment to enjoy the delicate first light of morning that glowed to the east.

"Pilot's dawn," he said. "It's going to be a nice day. Now listen, both of you. I've been cleaning upstairs. There's no more blood, no fingerprints, no signs of struggle. His car is just down the road. I'm going to load your boxes into it and drive us to the American base in Berlin. The important, the essential, thing for all of us to remember is that *Claussen was not here*. We came, we found the papers, we left. Understand?"

Steven wasn't listening. He was thinking about something else. "The car!" he said. "Jesus, Frank, have you looked inside yet?"

"Yes."

"Was there a suitcase?"

"Not the one you're hoping for, Steven. It wasn't the same car he drove to France. My guess is that he visited his banks and then switched vehicles."

"Not the same car? No money? Shit."

"It's all right, Steven. He had enough money on his person to get us to Berlin and the boxes to the States. You don't need the other money. You've got the memoirs, you've got the KGB files. Even if you don't write a word, you'll be a wealthy man."

"But two hundred fifty million dollars—"

"Steven, please."

"All right, all right. I don't need it. Those Swiss bankers are the ones who need it. Now what about Claussen's car? You say we should act like he wasn't here. I understand that. But if he wasn't here, what the hell are we doing with his car? How do we get rid of it? How do we destroy the link to the truth?"

"The car, Steven, is registered in the name of a Doctor Peter Weiss of Bern. I guarantee that Dr. Weiss knows nothing about this car. I guarantee it's not traceable to Claussen. It's the automotive equivalent of a throw away gun."

"A spy car?"

"Yes. Satisfied?"

"I...yeah, sure. So what's our agenda for the day?"

"I take you and Nicole to the base for emergency treatment. During the drive, we'll devise a creative story about how we got mugged. Anyway, while you're being put back together, I'll go to the DHL office in Berlin and ship your boxes home. I'll then park Dr. Weiss's car downtown and return to the base on public transit. They're not looking for me, remember?"

"That's right," Nicole said. "They're looking for your rental car but not you."

"Exactly. So both of you sit here and relax. I've made some coffee. Have a cup. I'll come for you when we're ready to leave."

* * *

Steven was gazing blankly at the blue light of the gas burner in the barn. Warner materialized in the distance, accompanied by a swarm of geese. He was carrying Claussen's naked corpse over his shoulder. The wiry little bastard with the hole between his eyes looked evil even in death.

He called Nicole, and together they watched Warner climb the ladder up to the tank of simmering entrails and heave Claussen in. He would be dog food by noon.

Steven wanted to put into words the visceral satisfaction he felt. He was stopped by the sudden memory of Sophie—brilliant, outrageous, wonderful Sophie—proposing that he go south to charm the pants off some lousy politician's daughter.

He was with that daughter now, and he pulled her close to him for comfort. She wiped his tears away with soft fingers smelling of Guerlain and gun oil.

Chapter Thirty-Nine

Michelet stayed in his bedroom to listen to the first edition of the Monday morning news. When it contained no mention of a U.S. military action against Iraq, he knew the time had come to have a stern word with Delors.

He dressed and started toward the library, which the three men had been using as their command and control center since the Friday night débâcle. He changed his mind before he got there and headed for the kitchen. A formal reproach was something that needed more thought and preparation. He would have breakfast and jot down a few words before the confrontation.

Henri and Isabelle, whom he had ordered to be fully awake and ready to serve at 5:00 a.m., were nowhere to be seen. There was no fire in the stove, no coffee brewing and no bread baked. This was an outrage, one which would not go unpunished.

He tried to make his own coffee but realized he did not know how to use the coffee maker. He started to eat the cold cuts left over from the night before, but found he had little taste for them. Suddenly he had a premonition that his partners had abandoned him.

Furious, he stormed into the library. It was as cold and dark as the kitchen. He turned on the lights. There was an old dueling pistol on the desk which he recognized as his own. In a corner of the ornate frame of his father's portrait was a neatly folded note. He grabbed it and unfolded it. He recognized Delors' handwriting as he read:

Thomas Kirkwood

Dear Georges,

Claussen has apparently taken off with the money. Our police and military units have been unsuccessful in stopping Warner and LeConte. We have no knowledge as to the whereabouts of your daughter, but we remain shocked and disappointed that you did not foresee and act upon the security threat she posed for this operation.

We discussed the possibility of including you in our plans for relocation. We decided, based on your fatal error, that your judgment in hiding might be no better than it was in freedom. A final word, Georges. Members of the governing coalition have been tipped off about the relationship between Nouvelle France, the Haussmann Group and the SDECE. This was not our doing. An investigation has been scheduled. It will begin with your arrest today at noon.

We ask you, in penance for the blunder which has cost us all so dearly, to do the right thing. Destroy this communication and take the only honorable way out for yourself. Otherwise, Georges, you will live the rest of your life as an embarrassment to your country.

A deep chill gripped Michelet as he tossed the note aside. The furnace came on, catching the note in an updraft from the heating register near his feet.

Michelet stared at the register for a moment. He did not feel the heat. He would never feel the heat. That register was an icy crevasse through which his most private words had traveled to the wine cellar and out into the world.

Pilot's Dawn

He was not going to be the next De Gaulle. He would not even be allowed to retire from politics and live out his life in peace. Delors and Haussmann, his betrayers, mocked him by calling suicide the only *honorable* way out. It was the only way out.

He picked up the dueling pistol and sat in the overstuffed armchair beneath his father's portrait. His fury was spent, his frustration gone. His political dreams had evaporated, and he had no others. Devoid of emotion, he cocked the hammer.

He sat there for a long time, pointing the gun at his heart, then at his temple, then putting the barrel in his mouth. He could not bring himself to pull the trigger until many hours later, when he saw the government cars arriving outside his gate.

✻   ✻   ✻

Claire brought another bowl of cheese crackers out to the glassed-in patio. Steven had always hated those things, but for some reason he couldn't stop eating them tonight.

Warner stuck his head through the sliding glass door. "I'll be there in a minute," he announced.

Steven counted the days he had known Frank Warner. Friday to Wednesday, less than a week. He wondered what it would be like to know him for a year. Intense, he thought. Not unpleasant, just intense.

Claire said, "Nicole, how's your ankle?"

Nicole smiled. "Oh, just fine. The doctor you sent me to was a magician. Look at this tiny cast. In France they would have put me in something the size of a coal bucket."

Steven leaned over to the stool on which she had propped her ankle, kissed her shin and signed the cast "Baron Richelieu."

"He was a cardinal, Steven," Nicole said, laughing. "Don't you Americans know anything?"

"We have a few lacking virtues." He held up his right arm and touched the bandage. "I wish you could see this. Frank's doctor friend at the base must have been drunk when he stitched me."

Claire laughed. "You shouldn't go around getting yourself cut up."

Warner strode in, wearing a sweater. The side of his face was still swollen, the bruises still black and blue.

He bent down and kissed Claire and Nicole.

"I have news," he said. "Most of it good, some bad."

Nicole smiled at him. Steven could see that she liked him a lot. "Well? What is it, Frank?"

"Airbus is letting carriers who placed orders with them during the crisis cancel if they wish."

"That's very civil of them," Claire said.

"They're decent people. It's an ethical company. I would not have expected less. And the boxes from Berlin are here. There was no problem with customs."

"That's very good news," Steven said. "Very good."

"Indeed it is. And there's something else you'll be happy to learn. You are no longer charged with Sophie's murder or Nicole's kidnaping. I know you don't want to miss Sophie's funeral. It's being held Friday afternoon in Paris. I have the address written down upstairs."

Steven shook his head. The idea of Paris without Sophie was unimaginable.

"Nicole," Warner went on, "there is another service Friday. Your father is being buried in a private ceremony at your home in Fontainebleau. I'm told only the servants, your aunt, uncle and cousins, and a justice of the peace will be present. They want you to come."

"Then I shall be there," Nicole said. "Thank you for telling me this so gently, Frank."

Steven said, "By the way, where are you getting your reams of good information?"

"The Embassy in Paris has decided to be helpful, for a change. I spoke with a fawning little shit named William Fairchild."

"This can't make up for what he did."

"No, it can't. When I get a chance, I'll be speaking my mind on the subject to the president."

Steven said, "I'd like to write your script. Listen, Nicole, while we're over there, why don't we buy that poor bastard, Bonier, a new crop duster?"

"That would be very nice."

"Well, Frank? Are you good for an advance on the Claussen papers?"

"No, but I'll see if I can find some discretionary funds in the safety board's budget. The government will pay for this one."

"Great."

"What's the bad news, honey?" Claire asked.

Warner sighed and took a sip of his scotch. "The bad news is that the blockheads on Capitol Hill still don't want to accept what happened."

"How is that possible?" Nicole said. "The proof is so clear."

"This is Washington," Claire explained. "If it's obvious, it requires endless debate."

"I'm afraid it's not that simple," Warner said. "There are powerful interests that have a stake in the money-making and hero-producing aspects of another war with Iraq. We're on hold but not out of the woods. I'm still searching for a way to put an end to this dangerous nonsense. And now, let's bring this meeting to a close. I've made us dinner reservations at a place I think you'll like."

"American?" Nicole said.

Warner winked at her. "American. Can you handle it?"

"Sure, Frank. You two have made an adventuress of me."

*　　　　　*　　　　　*

Steven drove in the rain to Fontainebleau, still profoundly moved by Sophie's funeral. He wasn't her only admirer. It seemed as though half of the important people in the world had been there.

He took the back roads, stopping at the rural crossing where he had driven up on the tracks. A freight thundered past at 100 m.p.h. He really was lucky, he thought. He was alive and he had Nicole. He was also going to write a book that would pay tribute to Sophie's final coup as a journalist. The only question was when he would get it started.

Henri came out in the circular driveway with an umbrella to meet him. He had expected the ghosts of the conspirators to meet him here, too, but the first memory that came to him was of making love to Nicole in the wine cellar amid the fabulous array of cases and bottles.

This was a good sign. He had vowed never to live in France, not even part time, but he already felt himself relenting. "Where are the cousins?" he asked the old man, enunciating clearly.

"Gone home," Henri said. "They didn't want to stick around. Come. Nicole is waiting for you inside."

She was dressed in a long skirt and sweater when she came down the stairs. She was so beautiful all he wanted to do was stand and look at her.

It was hard to believe he had seen her for the first time in July, down on the coast in a fancy restaurant with her father. It seemed like they had known each other forever.

Let them say what they would, he thought, about a guy being able to settle down and find happiness with any number of women. That was a crock. He didn't know much, but he knew that for sure.

"Hello, Steven" she said. "Come on in the kitchen. Henri and Isabelle are anxious to return to the cottage after that depressing ceremony, but I've got a little something to give them first. You must act as my witness."

"Are you all right?" Steven said. "I mean, did you get upset at the funeral or anything?"

"Upset? About not having a father? Steven, I have never had a father. I cried my heart out for years because I did not have a father. I didn't lose anything I hadn't already lost. Yes, of course I got upset. It was a funeral."

He kissed her. "So did I. Sophie was my best friend."

"I wish I had known her better, Steven. She saved your life."

"And got the two of us together."

"Yes. Come, now, or I'll start crying again."

Nicole had covered the butcher block table in the kitchen with a lace cloth and put out four champagne glasses. The dim red coals in the wood-burning stove gave off a dry and fragrant heat. Henri and Isabelle approached the table, smiling at Steven as if to say they were sorry for Henri's excesses with his flashlight.

Nicole came last, carrying a rare bottle of Moët she had taken from the refrigerator. She handed it to Steven. He assumed he was supposed to open and pour, so he did.

"Don't drink," Nicole said. "I wish to propose a toast first. As you know, the will of my father has been opened and I am heiress to this land. I don't know exactly where I'm going to be—Paris, Grenoble or the States. I do know I won't be here. Isabelle, for as long as you live, I wish you to have this property. We'll have the best lawyers draw up the papers. You can do whatever you wish with it—except sell it. When you pass on, it reverts to me."

Isabelle had tears in her eyes. "Thank you, dear. That is a lovely gift."

"What about Henri?" Steven said.

Nicole smiled a charming smile. "There's one exclusion to Isabelle's lease. It's the wine cellar. Henri *cannot* sell it but he can drink as much of it as he wants. Fair?"

"Fair," Steven said, marveling at Nicole's wonderful ability to bring lightness and joy to all sorts of tough situations.

"Now that we've got that behind us," she said, "let's seal our agreement with a toast."

Henri had turned around to fish something out of his battered satchel on the floor. He raised his hand without looking up. "Not yet,

Nicole. I have a little something for Steven. I would like to include it in our toast."

Steven frowned. This was one of the strangest things he had ever seen. How could Henri have read Nicole's lips? He hadn't even been looking in her direction.

"Excuse me," he said. "Henri was bending down when you spoke, Nicole. He couldn't see your lips. What's going on?"

Henri stood up, smiling. He held a gift-wrapped package in his calloused hands. "Good for you, Monsieur LeConte. You are observant. It is a virtue."

"You mean you *can* hear? You mean all of that deaf stuff was fake?"

Henri laughed. "That's right, my son, though I'm starting to think the time for a hearing aid is near."

"Holy Madonna!"

"Steven, your language!"

"But this is incredible! What about you, Isabelle? Can you hear, too?"

"No, Monsieur LeConte. Just Henri."

Steven was flabbergasted. "Why didn't you tell me, Nicole?"

"Because I did not know. I found out today when they put my father in the ground. It's really quite a beautiful story. Henri, would you mind telling it again?"

"For you, I'll tell it a hundred times. More than twenty years ago, I overheard a conversation. This was not a pleasant conversation. It was about Monsieur financing his political party with illegal money.

"Now you must understand, Steven. Isabelle and I had nowhere to go, no family, no training. On top of that, Isabelle had her disability. We were totally dependent on Monsieur's good will.

"The more I thought about it, the more frightened I became that I might overhear something again, or that Monsieur might think I had overheard something, and that we might be driven from this land because of it.

"So I decided to lose my hearing, too. I had to learn to read Isabelle's lips, so I made it a gradual process, growing a little harder of hearing every month. By the time Nicole's mother died, I was stone deaf."

"Then you knew about the airplanes?"

"Oh, no, Monsieur LeConte. When I became deaf, I was still careful not to overhear anything. It was better that way. It let us live our simple lives in peace. More important, it let us look after Nicole during the summers when she did not attend the convent school. We did not know about the airplanes. But we suspected evil things were going on, especially after all that panic about you in the wine cellar."

"Extraordinary," Steven said. "This is extraordinary."

"Yes," Henri said. "So it is. Now I would like you to open your gift. I hope it is something you can still use."

Steven unwrapped the package, preparing to make a display of gratitude. He didn't recognize the strange-looking reel inside. "What is it?" he whispered to Nicole in English.

"I don't know," she whispered back. "Ask Henri."

Steven held the reel up to the light. "It is…what in the world is it, Henri?"

The old man's face darkened. "You don't know?"

"No, I—"

"It's what was inside that device you had in the wine cellar. Monsieur took it out. But something distracted him and it ended up lying on the table. I picked it up to keep for him when I was clearing the dishes. Later they were looking for it. I was in the kitchen, listening. Before I could go out there as a deaf man and learn what was going on, they decided the German had taken it, the man they called Walter."

"You mean this is the tape from the recorder?"

"Yes, Steven."

"Henri, I didn't know what it looked like. I'd never seen it before. See, it's not a normal tape. You couldn't have given me a better present. Nicole, Frank is going to be as happy as I am!"

"Henri, that's wonderful," Nicole said, smiling sweetly.

Steven took the grizzled old man in his sore arms and gave him a bear hug all of the garlic and wine fumes in the world couldn't have discouraged. "You will someday star in an article I'm going to write."

He walked over and hugged Isabelle, kissing her French style on both cheeks. "Thank you, too" he said. "I thank you with all my heart for protecting Nicole those summers I wasn't here. I always wondered how she could have turned out so perfect with a father like Georges Michelet. Now I know. Thank you."

*   *   *

Warner sat on the edge of his bed and lit the candle. "You should have seen their eyes in the Oval Office today when Simmons played the tape and passed around the photographs. I don't want to sound vindictive, but it was gratifying in the extreme."

"Oh, Frank, I'm so happy this mess is over."

"You're happy?" He climbed into bed and turned off the lamp. In the rose glow of the candle, Claire looked 19 years old. "I've been a very negligent lover," he said.

"Only because you've been away. Remember what I said about quality versus quantity? I also happen to love you. Believe me, Frank, that counts for something.

His hands slid beneath her nightgown. The trips, the night meetings, the intrusions of every sort. How, he wondered, could he do this to her any longer? How could he do it to himself?

The telephone rang, the emergency phone.

"Goddammit," he growled. "For once I'm not here. I am not here."

"Frank—"

"What?"

"Answer it. It's all right. I'm not going away."

Pilot's Dawn

He started to get out of bed and take it in the other room. She held his arm.

"Warner," he said. "Give me the details."

"Good evening, Frank. I hope I'm not calling too late. This is the president. Your assistant gave me your number."

"Mr. President! No, of course it's not too late. How can I help you?"

Claire put her head beside his and he tilted the receiver so she could hear.

"First, let me commend you once more on the incomparable job you did beating the odds. That's leadership, Frank. It's what we need in this administration, and its what we haven't been getting. I've reviewed the behavior of all members of my staff and administration. I thought you'd be happy to know that I've given Chief of Staff Galloway his walking papers. Heads are going to roll at the CIA, you can count on that. I'm going to act on your advice. I'm firing Willis tomorrow, and I've asked for a list of the agency people in Paris who shunned Mrs. Marx. We're even thinking about criminal action here, Frank. That kind of blindness simply cannot be tolerated."

"Those are good decisions, Mr. President."

"I'm also proposing several honors for those who helped you. We can talk more about this later. The real reason I'm calling is that I would like you to take over the FAA. A desk job, Frank, but one with plenty of responsibility. Things are going to change, I assure you. You'll have to give up your travels, but you'll have the opportunity to play a major role in shaping the future of air travel in this country."

"That's an honor, Mr. President, one I wouldn't want to accept without serious thought."

"Of course, Frank. Think until tomorrow morning. I want you to come to the White House for breakfast. Oh, yes, one last thing. After this chat, your emergency calls are being rerouted to your assistant's number. Simmons and I both feel you need a rest. Enjoy it, Frank. I'll see you at nine."

That meant about seven undisturbed hours right here, thought Warner, seven hours he wasn't going to waste on sleep. He lay back on the bed and pulled Claire down on top of him.

Boulder, Colorado
18 months later

Epilogue

Warner didn't like weddings any better than politics, but turning down the LeContes' invitation would have been unthinkable.

It was a fine October day along the front range of the Rockies. The sky was deep blue, the wind calm and the air so exquisitely inviting he hated to go inside.

The outdoor wedding ceremony had been simple and mercifully brief. The reception at the LeContes' home was even more relaxed. The only guests were Steven's parents and brothers, Nicole's aunt, uncle and cousins, Sophie Marx's brother and a few of the newly weds' local friends, people dressed in everything from tuxes to running shorts.

Nicole, with Claire's help, had prepared the hors d'oeuvres. Henri and Isabelle, along with their regrets, had sent a shipment of excellent champagne, wine and cognac.

Warner drifted off by himself. He couldn't speak French, so that ruled out any conversation with Nicole's relatives. He didn't particularly care for the Boulder guests, fine intelligent people that they were. Their contrived eccentricities just rubbed a man from Winnemucca the wrong way.

Well, he thought, he shouldn't complain. He didn't have to deal with the types he had expected—the celebrities, writers, journalists, publishers and politicians. The gritty best-seller Steven had written didn't seem to have gone to his head. This was a pretty down home affair.

Warner went outside to shoot hoops with Nicole's cousins and almost managed to enjoy himself. Later, some delicacy of Nicole's he couldn't pronounce in hand, he strolled across the combination of meadow and horse pasture Steven called the lawn. The home was in a beautiful location, high on the plains about eight miles east of Boulder. There was a good view of the city, nestled in a bowl at the base of the foothills, and a spectacular view of the towering peaks of the Continental Divide beyond. This was where the Great Plains met the Rockies. If you looked one way, you were in Kansas; if you looked the other way, it was Jackson Hole.

Warner had seen enough of the mountains. He turned toward Kansas. At the far end of the meadow was a horse barn. He didn't have anything better to do, so he decided to check it out.

The door was unlocked. When he swung it open a gaggle of at least 40 huge geese rushed out at him. He was trying to coax the cankerous birds back into the barn when he saw something he didn't like. Two yellow ultralights, the most dangerous of all flying machines, loomed in the dusty shadows. What the hell were they doing here?

"Exploring?" Steven asked, walking up behind him. The geese that had remained outside followed him into the barn.

Warner turned around, shaking his head. "My God, Steven, what in the world are these things?"

"I'll show you later. First we need to talk business."

"On your wedding day?"

"On my wedding day. That's why Uncle Emmanuel is here."

"Uncle Emmanuel?"

"Michael. Sophie's brother."

Steven gestured to a gravel road. When they were out of sight of the house, Warner said, "Okay, spill the beans. What's this all about?"

"Claussen's money," Steven said. "I couldn't let it go."

"Jesus," Warner said, disgusted. "Are you still looking for the lost treasure? Why don't you concentrate on your next book? Your first one was terrific."

"I'm not looking for the lost treasure," Steven said. "I've found it. And it's not two hundred fifty million, either. It's three billion. The bastard must have been doing jobs on the side for a long time."

"Slow down," Warner said. "Just slow down. How did *you* find the money?"

"Well, actually, it was Uncle Emmanuel, working with some strange lists of numbers I found in with the KGB documents. Christ, I don't know how he did it, but he's tracked down over thirty of Claussen's numbered accounts. We can remove the money without anyone knowing. *That* is what I wanted to talk to you about."

Warner gazed off at the distant peaks, their whiteness dimming as the sun slid down their backside. "Steven, this is a bad idea. I don't like it. Besides, you don't need the money."

"You do, Frank. Maybe not you personally, but the FAA. I've been reading about what Congress has done to your budget. Would a three billion dollar contribution help?"

"Steven, you can't go around making huge contributions like that. Everyone notices."

"Oh, come on, Frank. Politicians and administrators steal ten times that amount every year and never get noticed."

"We're talking about the government. You can smuggle it out but you can't smuggle it in. Don't ask me why."

"Frank, listen, you've got to be more creative. Here's three billion dollars being offered to the cause of aviation safety, the cause to which you've devoted your entire professional life. And it couldn't come from a more appropriate source—the man who did more than anyone in history to make air travel unsafe. You've got to find a way to take it."

"Okay, all right, I get the point. God knows the money would help. I'll think about it, Steven."

"Seriously?"

"Yes."

"Good. Now let's go back and join the party."

On the way, Warner stopped at the barn. "You distracted me with all this business. I want to know about the geese. And the ultralights."

"Watch geese, Frank. I let them out at night. Just because Claussen was sick and evil doesn't mean all of his ideas were bad."

"Watch geese. I see. What do you feed them? Dog food?"

"You got it. They don't seem to be as aggressive as our man's birds were. I've been trying to remember the name of that dog food we saw the guy with the horse cart making over there. You wouldn't happen to recall it, would you?"

"You're crazy," Warner said.

"Moi? Wait till you see this."

He opened the barn door, affectionately parted his geese as they stormed toward the exit and started both ultralight engines. He taxied one craft out onto the meadow, left it idling and went back for the other one.

Warner watched, unsure if he was experiencing amazement or horror.

Steven stayed in the second ultralight. "You coming, chief?" he shouted.

"Look, Steven, you know I love to fly. But as director of the FAA, I—"

"Cut the bullshit, Frank. The FAA hasn't regulated these things yet. You're a country boy, you love freedom and you're within your rights. Let's go for it."

Warner stalled. "When did you learn to fly?"

"The time I watched you for half the night on the way to Claussen's farmhouse."

"You were asleep."

"I was watching over your shoulder. Nicole's actually better at it then I am. She learned the right way, lessons and all. Hop in. This is something special. You'll love it."

The peaks glowed rose and alabaster in the distance, the air was cool and calm. A more perfect dusk for flying he had never seen.

Warner reluctantly climbed aboard and buckled his harness. Steven LeConte was a bad influence on him.

He taxied to the end of the meadow. When Steven gave full throttle, he followed. They were airborne before Warner had time to reconsider. When he looked down, Jules and Luc were leaning against one of Steven's Harleys, waving from the side of the road.

They flew south, over a brown and green patchwork of farmland. Night was rising over Kansas, where a giant amber moon hung on the horizon. They flew higher and looped back toward town. The peaks at this altitude still burned in the golden fire of the sun.

In the middle of this meeting of day and night, of plains and mountains, was the town, its lights beginning to twinkle.

Flight, thought Warner. He had seen it produce every human horror imaginable. He didn't know why he still loved it, but he did.

He was lost in reflection about how to sneak Claussen's three billion into his agency's budget when Steven veered from formation and did some kind of a self-taught roll.

Warner stared in shock when he saw what he had not seen until now: the geese were following them in a wedge, 40 strong. In the air, he thought, they were a lot more beautiful than on the ground.

When they flew over the meadow in preparation for landing, he saw yet another beautiful thing. Nicole and Claire stood in the dying light of that incomparable evening, arms around each other, waving happily.

They landed. The geese touched down behind them and followed them as they taxied into the barn. "They just started doing it," Steven said. "They were young when we got them. While we were learning to taxi, they learned to follow. What do you think?"

Warner shook his hand. "I think you're a fortunate guy, Steven."

"What about lucky?"

"That, too. I'm not given to New Age male embraces or big emotional outpourings but I'm glad we met."

"It's mutual," Steven said.

They walked over to where the women were standing. Warner kissed Claire on her incredulous smile. Steven hugged Nicole and swayed slowly back and forth with her.

For a long time the four of them stood in silence, watching the peaks relinquish the last embers of the day.

About the Author

Thomas Kirkwood is author of five novels. His prophetic The Quiet Assassin was a Book-of-the-Month Club selection, a Signet paperback, Brilliance Corporation audio book and a best seller in the United States and abroad. It was one of the few books, factual or fictitious, to presage the collapse of the East Bloc.

Kirkwood holds a doctorate in comparative politics from the University of Colorado, Boulder. He is the recipient of a Fulbright-DAAD scholarship and a Lilly Foundation Grant. After many years in France, Germany and Italy, Kirkwood now makes his home with his wife and two daughters in Denver, Colorado. He is presently at work on a novel about the German resistance during World War II.

Printed in the United States
2962